MURDER
IN
TUSCANY

A POSIE PARKER MYSTERY

L. B. HATHAWAY

WHITEHAVEN

WHITEHAVEN MAN PRESS

London

First published in Great Britain in 2021 by
Whitehaven Man Press, London

A CIP catalogue record for this book is
available from the British Library.

ISBN (e-book:) 978-1-913531-10-2
ISBN (paperback:) 978-1-913531-11-9

For my parents

Also by L.B. Hathaway

The Posie Parker Mystery Series

1. Murder Offstage

2. The Tomb of the Honey Bee

3. Murder at Maypole Manor

4. The Vanishing of Dr Winter

5. Murder of a Movie Star

(The stand-alone novella, A Christmas Case)

6. Murder in Venice

7. The Saltwater Murder

8. Murder on the White Cliffs

9. Marriage is Murder?

10. Murder in the London Lights

11. Murder in Tuscany

December, 1924 –
March, 1925
(Central London)

Prologue

Posie Parker, London's premier female detective, found herself running away on Christmas Eve.

Only as far as her office, mind, but running nonetheless.

This was odd, because things should have been perfect.

Posie was newly married and her husband, Richard Lovelace, Chief Commissioner of Scotland Yard, had just moved into her specially-renovated flat at the top of Museum Chambers in Bloomsbury, opposite the British Museum.

He'd moved in with his sweet little daughter Phyllis, and his Housekeeper, Masha.

There was another daughter too; a beautiful blonde baby, Katie. An orphan, she'd been adopted by Richard and Posie at birth, but despite being more than six months old, she was still small and sickly and remained in the expert care of Great Ormond Street Hospital.

Besides this one absence, they were virtually a ready-made family. Ready to spend a wonderful Christmas together. That was the *plan*, anyhow.

But Posie was finding things tiring. Because she was pregnant, only four months along, but feeling every day of it like an eternity.

The holiday week had started on Monday in a suffocating blur of London smog and rain, with a couple of carol concerts thrown in for good measure, and a visit to see baby Katie. Everything was ready for the festivities to begin at Museum Chambers.

There were sugar-paper garlands hung about the flat, and a huge Christmas tree. A splendid side of beef – with all the trimmings – had already arrived from Harrods Food Hall, which Posie felt sick at the sight of. But *that* was nothing unusual: she felt sick most of the time, in fact.

Wretched.

And dear darling Richard, always so manly and commanding, wasn't making any of it any better.

He was fussing over Posie, and she was starting to feel slowly suffocated. She'd tried parking him in an armchair on several occasions, with her copy of the latest Agatha Christie, *The Man in the Brown Suit*, but he just didn't sit down for very long.

It was exasperating.

Today, Tuesday, was Christmas Eve and Richard, mid-morning, had taken Phyllis off on an impromptu last-minute shopping trip to Covent Garden. And Posie had grabbed up her carpet bag and fled.

So here she was, plodding up the familiar steep staircase with its awful old blue carpet to the second floor of the building on Grape Street, where her Detective Agency was housed.

Out on the landing, in the dim grey light, pausing outside the glass-stencilled door to the office, she was surprised to hear voices inside. The place was supposed to be empty. It was Christmas, after all.

Intrigued, softly pushing open the door, Posie almost fell over the outstretched legs of Len Irving, her business partner.

He was lying face-down on the carpet of the waiting room, with Sidney, the teenage office boy, hovering eagerly nearby.

The fire was blazing in the hearth and the entire floor was covered in the photographs which were Len's stock-in-trade. There were at least a hundred photographs here, all numbered with small orange stickers. Len was calling out numbers for Sidney, and the lad was busy gathering up the chosen photographs and taping them into a smart black scrapbook-type book which rested on a nearby desk.

Alarmed, both Len and Sidney turned as Posie stepped into the room, their faces relaxing immediately.

'Oh! It's just you, Miss.'

'That's right, Sidney. *Just* me. I thought you'd be with your mother today? We agreed you could have the whole week off for Christmas, didn't we?'

Sidney grinned. 'We ain't got a nice roarin' fire like this over in Leytonstone, Miss. Nor as much excitement!'

'Excitement?'

'Yeah. Mr Irving got a message to me yesterday evenin' that he'd had a tip-off: he needed some help and would I like to join him? I weren't gonna say no, was I? He's goin' to train me up! We picked up these little beauties early this mornin' from the darkroom on the Strand and now here we are.'

Posie put down her carpet bag and inspected some of the images on the floor.

They showed a man in black tie on some fancy stone steps, knocking at a shiny-painted door. Arms reaching out for him, and the door closing.

Then there was another group of photographs, obviously taken through a window this time, at close range.

These photographs were tense, stolen moments. *Private* moments. An embrace. Hands everywhere. The same man in black tie, in his fifties perhaps, with an immaculate handlebar moustache. Together with a girl in her early twenties wearing a feather boa, and not much else. Expanses of delicate flesh. The girl had very distinctive eyes, like a cat's, with black feline darts of eyeliner.

Posie's face burned in a way which was nothing to do with the fire in the room.

Len laughed at Posie.

'Oh, Po, don't come the old prim buttoned-up governess with me! You and I both know what goes on in the world. This one's a cracker and no mistake. Simon Deverine of all people! At The Pink House in Soho! The prize rotter. Cavorting, and with such a lovely wife at home. She apparently suspected something was afoot, hired lawyers, and she was blimmin' well right! She'll be able to divorce him now. I always thought he was a bit "Holier Than Thou". But he's just a regular man, after all. And best of all, last night's little jolly was *very* well paid. Sid here will get a nice little Christmas bonus out of it, too. Can't be bad, can it?'

Posie bit her lip. Truth be told, she'd never found Len's contribution to the business very salubrious.

Len was a 'shadower', the best in London. He worked for divorce lawyers, trailing around after an agreed 'target'; usually attempting to catch the 'target' in the business of committing adultery. Len's photographs, often riskily obtained, were usually vital to a case. The nails in the coffin on a marriage. The last straw.

A truth laid bare.

'Deverine. Yes, quite. Er, congratulations.'

She sunk down in Prudence – the secretary's – empty chair, feeling a surge of thankful relief at being off her feet. She watched as Len and Sidney continued to work, the images on the floor steadily reducing in number.

Posie's thoughts idly turned to the identity of the man whose photographs were on the floor.

Deverine.

Simon Deverine was a popular and famous Member of Parliament. His seat was somewhere in the Home Counties, although he lived for the most part in London. He'd been very senior in the Royal Air Force during the Great War, and he carried the easy glamour and the danger of those days with him still. But these achievements alone hadn't made him notorious. Two other things had done that.

The first was his non-inherited wealth: a colossal fortune obtained in risky ventures, mainly overseas. A fortune made after the Great War had finished. A fortune which had propelled Deverine into the top echelons of society and onto the boards of charitable foundations everywhere.

His second source of notoriety was his wife, Lady Nella Harewood. The girl was half his age, a golden-haired beauty who came from an ancient but distinctly impoverished noble family; direct cousins of the British Royal Family. A girl about whom little had been known before the marriage. But since her nuptials with Deverine, a couple of years back, Nella Harewood had become quite 'the thing'; she was very photogenic, and was frequently in the newspapers, usually in a flimsy party dress, and, tantalisingly, usually looking downright miserable.

There had been one image in particular earlier in the year which seemed to have stuck in the public's mind; of Nella at some summer party, looking glum and clutching at her bloodied nose. Insinuations of bad behaviour and violence on Deverine's part had abounded, tarnishing the man's name.

To get a divorce on English soil – still highly scandalous – you either had to wait for five years and live apart, or prove adultery and be done with the thing instantly.

Well: Nella Harewood now had all the proof she liked.

Posie looked at Len, standing with his hands on his hips, doing a last professional reckoning.

'Are *you* going to get home for Christmas Eve afternoon, Len?'

He shook his head decisively. 'Nah, not if I can help it. Aggie's got her parents over. Besides, you know how it is; this is my busiest time of year. I've at least another four targets on my list to trail. Even tomorrow – Christmas Day – can you believe it? Lucky for me I've got Sidney here to help out.'

Posie was glad the business was going well for Len. By

contrast, Christmas was always her quietest time of year. She'd enjoyed a jaunty, unexpected little case a week or so back, involving a very famous and glamorous American, but that was unusual at this time of year, and besides, that bit of sparkle was now long gone.

For a second she felt sad. Len caught her gaze.

'Put the kettle on, Sid, will you? Cuppas all round. Rustle up some biscuits too, eh, lad?'

While Sidney trotted off obediently to the kitchen, Len pulled up a chair. He pretended to flick casually through the day's newspaper.

The Times was full of the story about the hero-climber Neville Coleman. The much-celebrated man was fast becoming the stuff of legend, and his hugely-publicised attempt to climb the as-yet-unconquered North Face of the Eiger Mountain in Switzerland had filled the newspapers now for weeks, but not in a good way.

He'd started the climb in the third week of November and had disappeared within days. He had been missing for more than one month now.

The day's news was all about yet another rescue mission.

Len shook his head dismally. 'This doesn't look good for old Coleman, does it? How many rescue missions can they send up? Poor fella. He must be brown bread by now. Not what you want for Christmas, is it, a story like this over yer plum puddin'? And look, there's more drama of a depressin' kind, further on inside, should you want it.'

He flipped *The Times* around and pointed at a small headline: 'MURDERER DIAMOND KING'S WIFE NOW MISSING – YET MORE BLOOD ON THE HANDS OF THE OUTLAW LEIGH O'CREASE?'

Two photographs were included, one of a stunning-looking girl with short, bobbed black hair and dark, sultry eyes, obviously stepping out of a nightclub, huge pearls wrapped around her neck in several creamy rings. The other photograph, beside it, was older and from an archive:

two young men, both in light safari costume, their faces shadowy against a strong sun, giving thumbs-up signs to the camera.

Posie yawned, not caring much. 'What's all *that* about?'

'Don't you remember, Po? Back in the autumn, September, I think? Colossal story. Two great pals – both Irish toffs – Leigh O'Crease and his pal Padraig Kennedy, had been out in Africa workin' on some mines, diamond mines I think, for years. Lucky blighters even missed the Great War! Fellas are rich as Croesus now. Anyway, Padraig fell in love with this little dazzler. The *real* diamond in the piece.'

Len pointed at the dark girl. 'Only, she just happened to be his pal Leigh's wife. Her name is Áine. I think you say "Orn-yah", if I'm not mistaken.' He said the name slowly, carefully, looking childishly pleased at his delivery.

'Well, anyway, the posh lads fell out over her, big time. So much so that they arranged an old-fashioned duel. Back in London, on Hampstead Heath. Both men owned houses on the Heath, and they figured the outcome of the duel would be upheld properly by the London Courts.'

Posie recalled the story suddenly. 'Oh! Yes, that's right! The friend – Padraig – he was killed outright, wasn't he? And Leigh was declared a murderer?'

'Yep.' Len nodded, relishing the grimness of the tale. 'Leigh did a runner, and Padraig's father, Lord this-and-that, put a reward up for Leigh's capture. Like somethin' out of the Wild West, innit?' He laughed. 'And while Leigh hasn't been seen since, the lovely Áine has been livin' the high-life in London, based at the house in Hampstead. But she's also now disappeared. Vanished into thin air.'

'They think Leigh has murdered her?'

'Stands to reason, don't it? She doesn't want her husband back after he killed her lover Padraig, so Leigh has decided if he can't have her, *no-one* can.'

Posie rolled her eyes. 'Sounds a bit far-fetched. Even

for *you*, Len. People are *allowed* to disappear, aren't they? Maybe Áine O'Crease has simply got fed up of London and gone back to Africa? Perhaps she misses the climate? The lifestyle? *I'd* get out of these wretched London pea-soupers if I could. Or else she's met yet another man? She sounds quite the vamp.'

Len threw the newspaper on the floor with a laugh. 'I admit, both those options are mentioned by the journalist here. You're pretty good, Posie Parker! But what is it, Po? You don't seem quite yerself. Not got the festive spirit, somehow. Feeling queasy? You look green, come to think of it.'

'Thanks. And yes: that's about the size of it. I feel dreadful.'

Len blew out his cheeks. He and his snip-faced wife, Aggie, had two children, with a third very much on the way, and he counted himself as something of an expert in these matters.

'When's the bubba due? May, isn't it?'

'That's right. Ages off.'

Len grinned suddenly. 'Ginger. That's what Aggie swears by. Ginger in the tea, ginger in her porridge, ginger lozenges. Try it, what've yer got to lose? Maybe it'll be better next time round, eh, Po?'

'There won't be a "next time around". Mark my words.'

'Ha! Just you wait…'

Sidney – with the teas and the day's early lunchtime post – returned, and shortly afterwards the men went back to work, leaving Posie still sitting at the secretary's desk, sipping at strong tea, with a range of brochures fanned out in front of her.

Travel brochures, to be exact. They'd come in the post. She'd tripped along to Cox and Kings' Travel Bureau in Covent Garden the week before, and had asked them to order a nice range of brochures featuring sun-drenched holidays.

A touch of the exotic.

Posie sighed. She and Richard had spoken of a honeymoon. Of course they had. But that had been *before* the wedding. Since then, with the busyness of the move, and then with Christmas approaching, and Posie feeling so horribly sick all the time, it simply hadn't been high on anyone's list of priorities.

Richard would probably raise one eyebrow incredulously at her if she passed him one of these beautifully-enticing travel catalogues to study. Or else, laugh.

Besides, he'd be right: how on earth could Posie even think of travelling, feeling like *this*?

She pulled her other post towards her unenthusiastically.

A couple of circulars and glitter-encrusted Christmas cards caught the eye. And then, last but not least, there was a cream-coloured envelope from Italy, marked with a heavy black border.

Frowning, Posie ripped it open. A black-edged card fell out, written in an Italian which she didn't understand. And there was also a short accompanying scruffy note, written in a familiar spiky hand on blue paper.

It was dated a week back.

Posie,

Jacinta here. Lovely wedding you had on the 6th, thanks awfully.

Richard is such a darling. Lucky you.

I got back here to San Gimignano just fine. But very sad news awaited.

I enclose the death notice. Giulia, Lorenzo's wife, died very suddenly a couple of days before my arrival here, on the 12th December.

I know you liked Lorenzo and Giulia, and I thought you should know. Apparently, it was a kind of winter flu which got her, although we all know she was a delicate creature at the best of times.

11

Maybe you can send Lorenzo a note? I think he's devastated.
Yours,
Jacinta
P.S. Patsy says hello! Woof, woof!

Posie bit at her lip, her eyes glazed and unseeing as Len and Sidney started tidying up the office.

Giulia Rosario.

Giulia. Lorenzo's wife.

Posie closed her eyes.

She conjured up an image of Lorenzo Rosario first: the proud, black-haired, sullenly beautiful local bad-boy-done-good of San Gimignano, whom half the town's women were in love with.

Posie had spent a wonderful holiday there in August, staying with Jacinta, in the unfussy little English Guesthouse she ran, in a popular square. On the same square lived Lorenzo and Giulia, a couple in their thirties who lived in a flat above their smart, busy, modern Gelateria which was busy all day long, serving tourists and locals alike.

Giulia. So pretty and funny and slightly eccentric with her masses of coloured jewels and silk scarves trailing behind her as she moved. Delicate, yes, but a woman whose strength of character and fortitude shone through every day. What a terrible waste. Giulia had been young, only in her early thirties.

I think he's devastated…

Well, yes. He would be. *Should* be. Lorenzo had always seemed utterly smitten with his wife.

Adoring, even.

Posie picked up a piece of paper and started to write to Lorenzo.

But as she did so, working in the usual platitudes and things you *should* write, she was aware of a sense of unease stealing over her.

Of something being 'off'.

But what it was escaped her, at least for now.

* * * *

The year 1925 was ushered in on a tide of a continuingly horrible winter, followed by a discouraging early spring.

The ever-optimistic crocuses in Lincoln's Inn Fields blossomed in a riot of purple and yellow, but it was painful to walk past them, shivering and tiny against the dark, squelchy earth and the never-ending rain.

But the time passing helped Posie.

Perhaps the ginger, too.

The sickness went. Literally from one day to the next, and Posie walked the rainy London streets again with her usual high spirits, despite feeling the size of a beached sea-lion.

A few cases trickled through the Detective Agency, but Posie wasn't actively seeking new work. Len and Sidney were frantically busy, out most of the time, or else hunched up in Len's room sorting out photographs. Boys from law firms were arriving at all hours, dropping off new instructions, furtively carrying away the black scrapbooks, heavy with the weight of a destructive power which could change a man's – or a woman's – life forever.

One such man was the MP, Simon Deverine, whose star was now firmly in the descent.

Some of Len's juicier photographs of him had been splashed all over the tawdrier newspapers just after Christmas, accompanied by racy headlines.

A divorce had been granted very quickly on the grounds of his adultery. Socially, Simon Deverine was ruined. A *persona non grata*. He had stepped down as an MP, and resigned from his place on the boards of several charities.

There were also a few photographs in the newspapers of a foot-loose and fancy-free Lady Nella, who had apparently found the publicity of the divorce way too much, and had embarked on a trip to the South of France to escape from the cameras, and, no doubt, from the endless London rain.

Posie found it all pretty depressing.

Other news was depressing too – Neville Coleman, the climber, had now properly been given up for dead, the searches which had been made for him drawing a blank.

As March began, the newspapers reported that Coleman had been declared dead for legal purposes. A black flag flew at half-mast for him at the Royal Geographical Society Headquarters in South Kensington.

One early March morning, enveloped in a black mackintosh which could have held two of her former selves, Posie trudged through the waiting room of the office, when Prudence, the Secretary, called out to her.

'Post, Miss! Not much, if I'm honest. I'll deal with the bills, but there's *this*.' Prudence had bobbed over to Posie's side, making a concerted effort not to rub up again the wet rubber of the black raincoat.

She proffered an envelope.

It was cream with a silver edging. Expensive-looking. Foreign-looking, even if you hadn't taken into account the lashings of Italian stamps.

Posie frowned, taking it swiftly. 'This looks like a…'

'A Wedding Invitation, Miss?' Prudence was getting married in the summer, her own nuptials to the newly-promoted Inspector Rainbird of New Scotland Yard having been much delayed by an injury he had sustained in the line of duty back in November.

Not thwarted, the delay had caused Prudence to ramp up the scale of her own wedding, and she had become one of the best-informed women in London about wedding paraphernalia. In fact, Wedding Invitations were a recent speciality of hers, with her own due to be sent out any day now.

'Look at that paper! The quality!' Prudence's stocky mauve-clad figure was almost barring Posie's way. 'Would you mind if I have a look at the *actual* invite itself, Miss?'

'Later,' snapped Posie, rather uncharitably perhaps, and went into her own office, closing the door smartly behind her.

She looked briefly out of the window; the view was of the grey office-backs and a smidgen of smudgy sky, but today it was greyer than ever. Grubby town pigeons were roosting miserably all along her windowsill, clustered together doggedly.

Soaked. Grey on grey.

Struggling out of the thick black raincoat, letting it fall on the floor, she simultaneously ripped open the special envelope, curious.

Posie pulled out a cream card from the envelope. It was deckle-edged, printed in silver. Beautiful.

'Oh! *Goodness me!*'

Excitement and anticipation rose in her as she read the card.

'Golly, this *is* a surprise!'

And without quite knowing how, she'd seated herself at her desk chair, and was placing a call through to New Scotland Yard. And while she waited for the connection, she pulled out the great wodge of travel brochures from Cox and Kings' which she'd stored since Christmas, under her desk.

Posie selected the brochure for Italy. She leafed through the pages until she found the section marked 'TUSCANY'.

'Connecting you to the Chief Commissioner of New Scotland Yard, right now. Hold the line, please.'

'Mnnn.'

She found the page. Towers rising, a walled town surrounded by green undulating hills. A pearl of an ochre-coloured medieval fantasy, trapped in time.

Blue skies, terracotta earth. The City of Fine Towers.
San Gimignano.

Not grey on grey. No rain and black raincoats. No sad wet pigeons.

Posie was scanning the flimsy folded enclosure about train times; connections for the Dover ferry with the 'Golden Arrow' service and the Orient Express.

'Darling? Posie?'

Richard Lovelace's voice cut in quickly, although to be honest Posie had almost forgotten she'd placed the call. Her husband sounded worried.

'I say! Posie?'

'Mnnn?'

'*You* called me, Posie. You don't normally, not at work. Is everything fine with you? With Phyllis? Baby Katie? *Our* baby?'

'Oh, everything is perfect.' She smoothed out the luxurious card. 'Do you remember Jacinta Glaysayer? Came to our wedding? I stayed with her at her Guesthouse in Italy last year?'

A slight pause. 'Er, yes. Yes, of course I do.'

'She's getting married. In San Gimignano. It's all very sudden. Out of the blue, even. It's in two weeks' time, on the 20th March. She's marrying an ice-cream shop owner. Lorenzo Rosario.'

A longer pause this time and a slight clearing of Richard's throat. 'How quaint. Is this good news, Posie?'

'Oh, yes,' Posie said, smiling with certainty to herself. 'For us, anyhow. You see, we've received an invite, and we're going to go. We'll attend the wedding.'

'Darling? You can't be serious! What about the...'

'What about *what*? I'm absolutely fine, and so is the baby. It's not due for at least another two months! And if you don't come with me, I'll bally well travel alone. Just a short trip, I promise. We'll be home again inside one week. We'll travel in comfort; the Orient Express both ways. It will be fine.'

The pause which followed was definitive in its length and meaning, but it ended with a resigned sigh.

'Oh, very well, darling. It might be good for you to get out of London, I suppose – a change of air, these wretched smogs – although I wasn't thinking *quite* so far afield. I'll book some leave. It will do us both good. Some sun. Rest.'

And as Posie stood at her window half an hour later, having quickly booked the trains over the telephone, she saw the rain was coming down ever heavier.

Hopefully there would be sun where they were going.

But '*rest*'?

Somehow it didn't seem likely.

* * * *

PART ONE:
The City of Fine Towers
(Tuesday 17th – Thursday
19th March, 1925)

One

They travelled to Tuscany on a tide of tea.

There were cups drunk quickly in busy, gritty Paris, at the Gare du Nord Station, just off the Golden Arrow train from Dover.

Then more tea was drunk while waiting for the Orient Express connection across town.

Most cups were served with lemon. It seemed milk wasn't on offer.

Or biscuits.

There were further teas served in the Pullman restaurant car, crossing France, down into Venice. Then more during the slow, rhythmic descent to Florence. A journey which took just over twenty-four hours in all. With what seemed like quite possibly hundreds of cups of tea.

It was over one such cup – as the overnight sleeper wagons were turned down for the night – in Venice, that Posie Parker and Richard Lovelace talked about Jacinta Glaysayer properly for the first time, the woman whose wedding they were travelling to.

Richard was acquainted with Jacinta, having first met her on a case he had worked on with Posie, undercover, four years previously.

'Dashed funny woman, though, isn't she?' muttered Richard, placing his Baedeker's *Guide to Tuscany* firmly downwards on the dining-car table, bending the spine. 'I can't see what it is that draws you to her, darling girl. All this bally trekking across countries at seven months' pregnant and she's not even your best bosom pal!'

Posie sighed: 'Oh, Richard. We agreed you wouldn't harp on about the pregnancy. We're on our way now and that's that.'

'I'll say.' He splayed his hands and grinned. 'Point taken.'

Posie fidgeted with the window blind, watching the Orient Express's porters come and go outside in the darkness of Santa Lucia Station: piles of smart monogrammed luggage were being loaded on the train; a few extra passengers embarking. There was no time to get out because this was only a thirty-minute stop. Besides, Posie had been through Santa Lucia before, a couple of years ago.

The sight now of the black-uniformed fascist police bobbing about the place with their many black-shirted supporters in tow didn't quite instil the dreadful fear in her which they once had. Although she still despised all they stood for.

'Dreadful politics,' Posie muttered. 'Dreadful state of affairs here.'

A few things had changed though since her previous visit. Big black banners now cascaded down the grey-stone walls of the station. The image they displayed – the golden axe in among a bundle of wooden rods – was the symbol of the dictatorship now governing the country.

The National Fascist Party run by Benito Mussolini had been in power in Italy for almost three years, but this year – early 1925 – they had upped their controversial governance even more, by banning all other political parties. Mussolini was now running an out-and-out dictatorship, and all the world could do was look on in horror.

Her thoughts were broken into by Richard, who wouldn't leave the topic of Jacinta alone.

'But tell me, darling, *what* it is that draws you to her? I'm curious.'

Posie thought of her friend. Because Jacinta *was* a friend. She thought of the girl who was her own age, with her funny twisted walk and her poor bad back due to scoliosis; of Jacinta's eager, open face, not pretty but pleasant and trusting. Of her courage and determination. Of her acceptance of being all alone in the world, alone apart from one small, beloved dog, Patsy. A Yorkshire Terrier with a feisty character and a colourful bow in her hair.

'She has gumption,' Posie said finally. 'Not many people would have walked away from that mess at Maypole Manor, and turned their lives around.'

'You mean she moved to Italy and bought a Guesthouse?'

'Yes. She'd always loved Tuscany, and San Gimignano in particular, and had dreamt of running a Guesthouse. There wasn't one in the area for English visitors – not like in Florence and Siena – so Jacinta decided to set one up.'

Lovelace looked nonplussed. 'Well, it helped that she had the money though, didn't it? It wasn't that she had to work tooth and nail for every wretched penny, did she?'

'True enough. But she's done it all with heart. It's a beautiful place, right on the nicest square. You'll see, Richard. I spent hours in the city in August – even though it's tiny – in the squares, or shopping, or just looking at the frescoes in the Cathedral. It's a magical place, with the countryside starting right outside the city walls. You can see all the vineyards from the balconies of the rooms at the back of the Guesthouse. But if you have a room at the front you look out on the square with all its drama. *I* like to watch action, and people, so I decided to look at the square last time. But it's hard to choose which is best.'

'Mnnn. You seem to have been captivated.' He smiled at Posie and the dining-carriage lights suddenly flickered into action, their low glow playing over Richard's dark red hair, lighting his eyes, which crinkled now with mischievous laughter.

'But do you remember Jacinta's profession, darling? Or I should be accurate and say "*so-called*" profession?'

'Of course, Richard. Don't be such a wretched Police Inspector about it all, will you?'

'You mean don't be *cynical*?' He laughed.

They were referring to the fact that Jacinta Glaysayer had spent several years working from rooms on Lamb's Conduit Street in central London as a psychic, a clairvoyant. She had had a good business there with large numbers of regular clients. Jacinta had given it all up when she'd moved to Italy three years previously; had decided to give up all her former activities which touched on the supernatural.

'She's a very nice girl but I don't believe all that stuff either, as it happens,' Posie stated defensively, huffily.

She picked at a piece of bread-and-butter, dipping it into a clear broth. 'I was brought up with a Vicar for a father, don't forget, and he wouldn't have entertained any such notions. And neither do I. *He'd* have said it was evil; the devil's work. But I just think it's all stuff and nonsense.'

'I see.' The flash of the green gaze again, a raise of an eyebrow. 'Well, tell me, did Jacinta read all about her forthcoming nuptials in the tealeaves, or whatever? Did she have a vision of this ice-cream God – Lorenzo, isn't it? – becoming her husband?'

Posie gave an exaggerated sigh. 'No idea, darling. As I said, it seems all very sudden. And our correspondence has been very light. Two telegrams since I sent our acceptance, and that's it. Hang about and I'll read them to you.'

She finished off her soup quickly and without much enjoyment.

Posie felt full and squashed and absolutely huge. The seat just wasn't big enough. She dug around in her faithful, now slightly threadbare, carpet bag and retrieved the two telegrams. She placed the first on her mound of a belly and read aloud:

POSIE
   OH HOW TOO TOO MARVELLOUS! I REALLY WASN'T EXPECTING YOU TO ACCEPT, BUT HOW WONDERFUL. I'VE SAVED YOU AND RICHARD THE BEST ROOM IN THE GUESTHOUSE!
   MUCH LOVE
   JACINTA

Richard snorted and poured more tea. He wasn't drinking wine – although he would dearly have loved a glass – out of sympathy with Posie.

'Dash it all! What a complete waste of a good telegram at about two-pence a word! Oh, well,' and here he had the good grace to look slightly ashamed, 'at least we know we have some nice accommodation at the end of all this.'

'Quite. Even *I* felt it was a bit over-the-top and skittish somehow. I suppose Jacinta was feeling lucky and in love and all that jazz.'

Posie picked up the second telegram. 'This is yesterday's. *Slightly* more informative. But similarly, all over the place.'

POSIE
   SHOULD HAVE MENTIONED – WEDDING CEREMONY ON FRIDAY 20TH MARCH AT TEN IN THE MORNING WILL ONLY BE A SMALL AFFAIR. I HAVE NO FAMILY AND NEITHER DOES LORENZO.
   TONY IS ORGANISING THINGS.
   OTHER THAN YOU ONLY SIMON DEVERINE IS

COMING FROM MY SIDE. HE'S MY GODFATHER
AND NEEDS A BREAK, POOR FELLOW. HE'S
BEEN THROUGH THE MILL. DO YOU KNOW HIM
AT ALL?

AND ON LORENZO'S SIDE ONLY ROBERTA
– GIULIA'S COUSIN – WILL ATTEND. YOU
REMEMBER HER? SHE'S STILL WORKING IN
THE GELATERIA. SHE'S A DEAR.

VERY HOT HERE ALREADY – BRING COOL
CLOTHES LIKE LINEN – WEDDING WILL BE
IN THE SANTA FINA SIDE-CHAPEL OF THE
CATHEDRAL. JUST DRINKS AND THE CAKE
AFTERWARDS.

YOU'RE ARRIVING THURSDAY 19TH?
FABULOUS. BECAUSE THE BLACK-TIE WEDDING
DINNER WILL BE THAT NIGHT. SMALL AFFAIR
AT THE GUESTHOUSE. WITH ICE-CREAM!
LORENZO INSISTS.

CAN'T WAIT.

MUCH LOVE

JACINTA

Posie and Richard looked at each other in silence. Richard
munched on an iced French Fancy which turned Posie's
stomach. The scent of the cheap cream filling wafted over
to her, as did the smell of the fondant. Her baby kicked
hard inside, as if enjoying her discomfort.

'Well, well, well. So, not quite the simple little wedding
after all, eh, Posie?'

Richard dusted his hands of cake crumbs, looking
gleeful suddenly, as if an unexpected treat was suddenly on
the cards. 'Simon Deverine, eh? Well, well. *Do* you know
him, darling?'

'Absolutely not. Never met the man. Good job too. I
might punch him.' Posie didn't mention the photographs

26

she had seen of him at The Pink House in Soho. 'He's a prize rat, apparently.'

'Mnnn. So they say, darling girl. Although our reader of the tealeaves seems to feel sorry for him, eh? Family loyalty, I suppose. It will be interesting to meet the man, anyhow.'

He took the telegram from Posie and studied it. 'Who is "Tony"?'

Posie shrugged. 'I don't know. Maybe Jacinta appointed a Manager since I was there in August? When I was out there she had just the one maid, Gloria, and she was a bit of a lazy so-and-so.'

'No cook?'

'No. Gloria buys local pastries for breakfast and serves them with coffee and that's it. For lunch and dinner the restaurants nearby are good and cheap. No English cook could compare. It would be a waste of time and Jacinta's money.'

'I see. And "Roberta"? Who's she?'

Posie felt suddenly overwhelmingly tired. 'You need your policeman's notebook out, darling, don't you? I feel like a real Witness reporting on a crime.'

'Let's hope not.'

'Indeed. What crime can happen at their wedding?'

'Mnnn. So, you were telling me about "Roberta"? The "dear"?'

'Oh, yes.'

Roberta Grimaldi was the unmarried cousin of Giulia, Lorenzo's first wife.

'An odd little story, plenty of history.'

Posie explained that Roberta and Giulia's fathers had been brothers – the Grimaldi twins – and had owned the famous local Gelateria together, named Da Grimaldi, until Roberta's father had fallen in with a bad lot. There had been gambling debts, drink, drugs. In desperation he had sold his half of the business to Giulia's father around the turn of the century.

When Roberta's father died, completely bankrupt, at the start of the Great War, Roberta was approaching twenty years old and was left without a penny. She started to work full-time for her uncle at Da Grimaldi, as a normal paid shop-worker.

Roberta knew no other life, and both she and Giulia had picked up the skills and closely-guarded ice-cream recipes from their fathers. Both girls were the only children of the Grimaldi twins, and their mothers had died young.

Posie sighed: 'It's a sorry little tale. Roberta has carried on working there, on past the death of her uncle a couple of years ago, when the place became Giulia's. And on beyond Giulia's marriage to Lorenzo around the same time. It was then that the Gelateria was modernised and re-named Lorenzo's.'

'Good Grief! How did *that* go down? Surely the Gelateria and its Grimaldi 'heritage' was something of a local institution?'

Posie shrugged. 'I think the townspeople found the re-naming of the place strange, yes. Inexplicable. There is definitely some hostility to Lorenzo. Anyhow, it seems Roberta is *still* working there, even though her cousin Giulia – Roberta's last blood-line connection to the place – died in December. I don't know what will happen to Roberta. She's a bit of an underdog, poor girl. Hard to fathom, hard to *like*.'

'But dash it all!' exclaimed Richard Lovelace, who had paused in the lighting of his Turkish cigarette, looking incensed. 'Didn't Roberta *mind* when the place was re-named? It seems jolly insensitive of Giulia Rosario to go trampling all over her own family history, all for the sake of "honouring" her new husband. And what a cad this fella Lorenzo must be, to have accepted it!'

Posie shook her head. 'But it was Giulia's place to do with as she liked, remember? It was – legally – nothing to do with Roberta. Her father had seen to that, years before.

If Giulia wanted to name it after Lorenzo, that was for her to decide, wasn't it? And, as I understand has happened, if Giulia left the Gelateria to Lorenzo in her Will, that was also for her to decide upon.'

'Still...' The cigarette was lit and puffed at.

Posie peered out of the window. She was watching a huddle of passengers smoking on the platform. Of these, a man's blonde head caught her eye, but his face was obscured by the shadows cast by the low iron beams overhead.

Her thoughts were interrupted again by her husband, curious.

'And Lorenzo? Tell me about him.'

'You can make up your own mind when you meet him at this wedding dinner on Thursday night, can't you? He's a bit of a 'Mr Darcy' type, I think: good-looking but with a brusque exterior, covering up a good heart. Of course, I don't know how he is with Jacinta, or how things stand between them exactly. When I met him I liked him, but then...' she reached forward and stroked Richard's stubbly jawline, 'I suppose you could say I have a weakness for dashingly handsome, commanding men; eager to get on in the world. Ambitious...'

Richard snorted with mirth and kissed her puffy hand.

'How's their English?' he asked, interested.

'Perfect,' said Posie. 'It has to be. San Gimignano is a tourist town, that's how they make their money. Not to speak English, or French, is not to thrive if you have anything to do with tourists. You'll see.'

Richard nodded gratefully, then considered the situation again. 'Well, it all just seems peculiar to me. The first wife's not yet dead three months and he's marrying again. And *Jacinta*, of all people! She's hardly an oil painting, is she? You paint a picture of this fella as being jolly easy on the eye. It all sounds worryingly one-sided to me, love. And we both know Jacinta is rich, isn't she?'

Posie was serious for a moment. To be honest, she'd

29

been slightly unsettled by the invitation; by Jacinta's out-of-the-blue bombshell. Happy for her friend, yes: but there was a slight twinge of worry there too.

It didn't seem right somehow, to marry in such haste after a death not three months before. And this was all added to a layer of some other unease, which Posie had not quite managed to leave behind her in the hot medieval streets of San Gimignano last year.

'She *is* quite wealthy, yes,' she half-whispered. Around them the smart Orient Express waiters were tactfully clearing up, and setting up tables in the Pullman coach for a second set of covers. Posie rose with some difficulty.

'We'd best get along to our cabin, darling, and sleep. We'll need our energy when we arrive in Florence tomorrow. I'm intending pounding the streets, you know. Never sitting down for a second. A full day's programme. We need to do every single gallery and simply every museum in that guidebook of yours.'

'But *darling*...'

'Only joking! We'll go around at a suitably sedate pace. But seriously, I think I need to sleep. Your nervousness and over-active imagination have got me imagining things!'

'Like what?'

She yawned. 'For a second back there I was convinced I saw your favourite police lad of the minute – Sergeant Fox – having a smoke, mingling with all those wretched men in black shirts on the platform. But my eyes must have been playing tricks on me.'

'Definitely, darling. I've left all that police stuff – including Fox – at home. I'm on holiday too, remember? Even if it is just for a few days.'

'Good. Bed then. Florence tomorrow.'

****

Two

Florence was a blaze of heat and white glory as they stepped off the train on Wednesday.

'By Gad, this is roasting!' exclaimed Richard, sweat beading his face as he arranged for their bags to be sent on to the Pensione Bertolini in town. He fanned at his face with a map of the city pulled from his Baedeker's Guide. 'I had no idea it would be this hot in March.'

'It's not, normally. It should be a lovely spring-like day. Balmy.'

'Balmy? I think *we* must be the barmy ones.' Richard was already looking distinctly sticky. He didn't, as a general rule, get along very well with intense heat. 'Will you manage, my darling girl?'

'Of course.'

But their plans changed within a few hours, after having trawled around the Cathedral and after squeezing along the famous Ponte Vecchio with all its medieval warren of gold and silversmith's shops. They had both had enough.

It felt like it was getting hotter and hotter.

'How long does it take to get to San Gimignano from here, darling?' Richard asked, almost desperately, looking at his wristwatch as they stood on the terrace of their hotel after a late lunch, looking across the very dry banks of the River Arno.

'Dash it all,' Richard muttered, tugging at his starched collars. 'I feel like I'm being boiled alive. I know I must look like a deuced lobster and I absolutely feel like one. Fresh from the pot. I know we're not supposed to be heading up to Jacinta's until tomorrow, but I'm not sure I can stand much more of this…'

Posie laughed. She'd been feeling exactly the same.

'It will take us two hours, maximum. We can hire a driver. I'll telephone through to Jacinta's Guesthouse so she knows we are on our way. Hopefully she won't mind our change of plans.'

But Jacinta couldn't be reached by telephone, and Posie arranged a telegram instead, and hired a local driver from the Pensione Bertolini.

And within an hour or so Posie and Richard found themselves – a day earlier than planned – on the road and heading for the cool breezes and open space of the gentle rolling Tuscan hills.

Two hours later the hill town came suddenly into view.

'By Jove!' exclaimed Richard excitedly, craning his neck out of the car window as San Gimignano – with its many grey sky-scraper towers rising up majestically against the silver-blue of the evening sky – appeared like a mirage in the distance.

'It's like New York!'

'Or New York is like *this*,' corrected Posie. 'This was here first, remember? But all of Tuscany's hill-top towns looked like this, you know, six hundred years back. Towers were status symbols for rich families who wanted to show off. They were usually knocked down when a town came under the power of a super-state, like Florence, or Siena. This town was lucky, although originally it would have had many, many more towers. A hundred, perhaps.'

'How was this town lucky?'

Posie reconsidered. 'Actually, I don't know if "lucky" is quite the right word. This town grew rich because it was on the pilgrims' route to Rome. But when plague arrived in the fourteenth century, and the town was desperate, Florence claimed it and ordered the towers of San Gimignano pulled down. But, luckily, somewhere along the way Florence lost interest, allowing a few to remain. So San Gimignano got left in a bubble. A carefully-preserved medieval bubble. Skyscrapers in aspic, if you will.'

'I never saw anything like it in my life.'

Posie covered Richard's hand with her own, and pressed it excitedly. 'I knew you would love it.' She grinned. 'I'm so pleased you left wretched Scotland Yard behind you. We deserve this break.'

Just for a second Posie thought she saw a shadow of guilt cross Richard's already sun-burnt face, but she shrugged it off.

They looped around the city, and then drove up the steep, steep hill, past the fields where later in the summer sunflowers would bloom. A red Fiat charabanc of tourists passed them, driving the other way, leaving the city. There were a couple of local motor-cars and a few horses and carts going in their direction, but otherwise the road was very quiet.

Suddenly a spectacular entrance gate, like something out of a fort, with sconces already lit with burning torches on its top-most level, loomed. The motor came to an abrupt halt in a car park which was full of empty red charabanc tourist buses and the driver informed them he could go no further.

On unloading their few pieces of luggage, and having been duly tipped, the driver and his car promptly disappeared.

Lovelace picked up his and Posie's holdalls.

'Good job you packed lightly, darling. It wouldn't have hurt that fella to have offered to carry our luggage now, would it?'

'It's not far. This is the San Giovanni Gate and we're almost there.'

They walked along the narrow street of Via San Giovanni where the tall, crowded street buildings rose to their jutting tiled rooftops, silhouetted against the darkening sky; torches and lanterns now being lit in brackets on all the walls.

It was as if the town was changing before their eyes, dressing itself in its evening magic of black velvet and candlelight.

At street level, striped shop-blinds were being wound in. Restaurants were opening up instead, with smart waiters placing vases and candles on rickety round tables out in the street. They passed some American tourists, already eating. Richard looked slightly envious as the couple chinked glasses.

And then, opening up before them was a strange, beautiful, three-sided square.

It was a large public place with a shallow-lit beauty, whose houses crowding on every side were tall and gold-dappled, exotic, with long Arabian-style windows. Cafés and parasols were dotted about, and the whole square ran uphill, a crazy-herringbone design leading the eye on.

Two or three of the famous skyscraper-like towers were situated here, but they were dark now, and the focus was the huge, ancient well placed at the centre. Tourists were sitting on the steps of the well, chattering.

'This is the Cisterna Square,' said Posie. 'Named after that well. It was the Cistercian Friars who created it all. And this is our journey's end!'

Posie smiled. In truth she felt exhausted, but she wasn't going to admit that. Not even to herself.

She was looking anxiously at all the awful fascist flags, even present here, and the flocks of pigeons, taking cover up on the jutting rooftops. The fascist black flags were new since she was here last, but an initial glance told her everything else had stayed pretty much the same.

She pointed to a long, tall, thin house of five floors,

covered in a climbing ivy, situated right in the middle of one side of the square.

'Here's Jacinta's place.'

'Good.'

Lovelace put down the two holdalls and snatched off his panama hat. A small, discreet gold plaque declared the 'PENSIONE INGLESE', and underneath this was a small trestle table with a basket atop it, inside which were pamphlets showing the tariff.

The shiny black-painted door to the Guesthouse was firmly closed.

Lovelace went to one of the two windows on either side of the door.

'No-one's at home, darling,' he said, matter-of-factly. 'Although it looks like a lamp is burning in the basement. Is that the servant's quarters? Let's ring the bell anyway.'

He yanked at the shiny gold bell-pull, and they heard a dog barking frantically somewhere below.

'That's Patsy,' explained Posie. 'Sounds like she's been left behind.'

It was at that very minute Posie became aware of a presence behind her, someone very close to them.

She turned sharply in the near-solid darkness and saw a vision of almost comic Englishness abroad – far more so than Richard with his sun-burn and red hair – standing right behind them. A man with a suntanned face, and perfectly round, china-blue eyes. He was probably blonde under his straw boater. He was good-looking, but had a comically cherubic look about him. He was swinging an expensive navy suitcase. He was probably in his late thirties or early forties, in an immaculate cream suit.

His neatness was one thing, but it was his size which struck one forcibly: the man was huge; tall, but solid as a wall. The size of his hands, his fingers, was extraordinary.

A bruiser. A cherub-faced bruiser.

'Oh!' he exclaimed in sudden and real surprise as Posie swung right around to face him.

He narrowed his eyes, looked nervy suddenly. 'Oh! Oh, I say! Aren't you…?'

But then the door was suddenly opened to the Guesthouse, and Posie recognised the grumpy middle-aged maid, Gloria, who stood in a pool of dull amber light. She'd obviously been enjoying some time off, and was clutching at an English penny magazine.

'Yes? Oh. Oh, it's Miss Parker, innit? What d'you want?'

Posie explained about the heat in Florence and their change of plans, and how she had sent a telegram ahead of their arrival, and a deep sigh followed.

'I'll see what I can do, Miss Parker,' said the maid reluctantly, in a put-upon fashion.

'The Mistress didn't know you was a-comin'; you were expected *tomorrow*, along with the other guest. We didn't get no telegram, but Patsy may have chewed it to pieces if it was put through the letter-box. Anyhow, you was lucky to find me in, as Wednesday night is my night off and I'm only jus' back from the pictures. Miss Jacinta's not expected back here until late tonight. Her and that fiancé of hers are tryin' wines at some fancy vineyard, with a big dinner put on for them. I think Miss Jacinta and Mr Lorenzo have a notion to serve the wine here to guests, in the future. Well, I'll let *them* explain all their fancy new plans to you.'

The maid swallowed, as if in disgust. 'They've taken Miss Roberta along wiv'em, and Miss Jacinta's lodger from upstairs. A sort of pre-weddin' treat. Quite a little party.'

Gloria had suddenly caught sight of Posie's vastly increased size for the first time and she became a little more amiable: 'If you both go and have supper in the town and come back in an hour, I'll have everythin' ready and waitin' for you, Miss.'

She darted away into the semi-darkness of the corridor and came back with a key. In the background the yapping of Patsy began again.

'Here. You let yourselves in, won't you? Your room is

up one flight of stairs, on the first floor. Now you give me those bags, sir, and I'll take 'em up fer you.'

Richard smiled his most disarming smile.

'We do appreciate it – Gloria, isn't it? – I'm Richard, Posie's husband. Oh, and there's another fella behind us here. I think he wants a bed for the night too by the look of things. Maybe the dog ate his telegram, too? Hang about.'

But when Posie and Richard turned to usher the huge straw-boater-wearing man forward, they found he'd completely disappeared.

Vanished into the darkness of the evening.

* * * *

Three

A good dinner, a glass or three of the local Vernaccia wine for Richard, a walk in the now mainly shut-up city and then a return to the Guesthouse followed.

Everything seemed much better. It was definitely cooler here than in Florence. A light breeze blew the heat away.

The room they had been allocated was certainly – as Jacinta had promised – the best in the house.

It comprised of the entire first floor, and had, unusually, two balconies, one at each end of the room. The room had been prepared beautifully, with the balcony doors pulled open. One balcony looked over the Cisterna Square, with its groups of people loitering by the well, and the other balcony looked away, out over the countryside, towards the rolling hills. From this side a gentle breeze blew refreshingly into the room.

The style of the place was simple – waxed terracotta floor tiles and white muslin curtains – but it was romantic, too: a large double four-poster bed took centre place in the room. Crafted from unpretentious local ironwork, it fluttered with white muslin drapes and was dressed in plain, rough-hewn cotton.

Posie flung herself on the bed, exhausted.

Gloria had set the table nearest the country-facing

balcony with helpful and thoughtful items: a thermos of coffee with a jug of cream; a carafe of water; a bowl of fruit and – somewhat incongruously – a tin of Eccles cakes.

'Eccles cakes! By Jove, this is more like it!' Richard exclaimed, sinking into a deep armchair, wiping the crumbs of the Eccles cake he had just devoured from his fingertips.

He took out his cigarette case. He looked and felt visibly more relaxed. 'What a day! I can still feel the rhythm of that train this morning! And thank goodness we left that deuced city behind us!'

'*This* is a city,' murmured Posie sleepily. 'There's the Cathedral and everything.' She'd kicked off her shoes already, her feet and legs swollen with the heat.

There was lots to talk to Richard about, for example what they should see in the morning. The towers. The paintings. The sights. All the beauty.

The slight unease underpinning everything.

What was it that had drawn her out here, exactly? Not just this strange little wedding, surely? In her sleepiness Posie fought for and failed to grasp the answer.

'Shall I run you a bath, my darling? You must be bone-tired. Let me help you. Posie, you're still fully dressed!'

But Posie was already fast asleep.

* * * *

Exhausted, they slept deeply.

Posie rose once, near dawn, changing quickly into her crisp tent-like cotton nightdress. She wasn't sure exactly what had woken her, whether it was the baby stretching and jumping around inside her belly, or whether it was something outside, or in the Guesthouse itself.

She unhooked the mosquito nets from the doors and

stood for a moment on the balcony, sleepily looking over the steppes and vineyards behind the Guesthouse, still shadowy and mist-covered in a pinkish light.

She looked towards the cypresses on the hills in the distance, the sleepy far-off villages and white churches. Somewhere below she heard a door bang, and footsteps hard on the cobbles outside. She checked her watch.

Just after five-thirty.

It was cool, almost cold actually, with no sign yet of the heat which had met them on their arrival in Florence. Posie drew her dressing-gown about her. It still fitted. Just.

And then she heard it. Another sound of the front door being pulled open, then closed. Footsteps, soft as anything.

Voices.

Raised voices.

She peeped over the balcony railing into the tiny still-shadowy yard below. A few chairs were set out here for the guests to use. Pots of early red geraniums stood about the place. The doors which led from the dining-room below into the yard were open.

Voices on the threshold. Heeled shoes on stone.

Posie retreated back a little bit.

'How *could* you?'

This was unmistakably Jacinta's voice, raised. So, she had come back from her wine-tasting, then. She was normally calm, gentle. But right now she sounded very angry.

'It's my wedding day tomorrow! It's going to be so dashed awkward! He'll be here by dinnertime tonight!'

Who was going to be here at dinnertime?

A voice followed, low, apologetic. A woman's voice? Posie couldn't hear the words. It was just a murmur.

Jacinta again, sounding resigned. 'Well, we can't very well tell her to go away, can we?' A deep sigh. 'Oh, don't worry about it. It's done now, isn't it? But I can't think why you didn't tell me before, that's all.'

More murmuring.

41

'I see. You only got her telegram last night? Well, if you really didn't know I'd asked him...that's a different story. My apologies. *Of course* we'll make her welcome. I'll see you later.'

And then there was the sound of shuffling below, and when Posie peered over the balcony again she saw the familiar figure of Jacinta Glaysayer.

The girl had come out into the yard, a bottle of something bright yellow in one hand, a cigarette in the other, wearing a dress of some green scaley-looking material. She looked like a beached mermaid, stranded, coming undone. Her hair was mussed up and wild, a matching green ribbon trailing down her back like seaweed. She was quite alone, and barefoot.

Jacinta lapped the yard in a circular fashion in her familiar hunched-up, crooked sort of way, before suddenly sinking down on one of the garden chairs and rocking herself back and forth, weeping.

She's blind drunk, thought Posie certainly. *Gracious.*

Torn as to whether or not to run down to the garden below and help, Posie was relieved to see Gloria, already sporting her black-and-white daytime livery, come plodding out. The maid was carrying Patsy, the dog, under her arm, and a steaming mug of tea.

Gloria rose considerably in Posie's estimations.

'There, there, Miss. Don't take on so. Patsy was locked in my room all night, with me, otherwise she'd have come out and found you of her own accord. Comforted you.'

Gloria pulled away the yellow bottle and the cigarette and disposed of both. She placed the mug of tea in Jacinta's hands.

'Lots of sugar, that's what you need. Three spoons in this, there is. Come in now, Miss: you'll catch your death out here, barefoot in all this mist and dew.'

Posie stepped back, ashamed of having witnessed this small, strange, intimate episode. She heard a light running sound, footsteps hammering up the creaky wooden staircases. Footsteps on the floor above. Doors slamming below.

On an impulse, Posie walked the length of the room and opened up the doors onto the balcony facing the Cisterna Square.

'Oh!' she breathed ecstatically.

Posie stepped out and blinked: realising that on this side of the Guesthouse the sun was coming up quickly now, bathing the yellow stonework of the triangular square in a fresh, glorious beauty.

A flock of pigeons – or were they doves? – were circling the square and a few black-clad monks, huddled together in a group, were moving towards the passageway leading to the main square, to the Cathedral beyond. They were gone quickly and no-one else was about.

The silence was eerie.

But there was a slight smell of coffee in the air, its bitter tang rising and combining with the scent of fresh-bread. So people *were* up, but hidden. Going about their day, living their secrets.

And as if some sixth sense compelled her on, Posie turned to the left on the balcony, as if she was unwittingly following the progress of the monks.

And there, in the corner, hard up against the archway out of the Cisterna Square, under one of the Ardinghelli Towers, was Lorenzo's, the Gelateria. Posie and Richard had walked past it on their stroll right after dinner last night, and it had been disappointingly shuttered, although perhaps understandably if both Lorenzo himself and Roberta – the usual workers there – were out for the evening.

But now, the sunlight dancing over the shutters of the Gelateria, Posie saw movement right outside the shop. Furtive, compromised, awkward movement. A couple silhouetted in front of the silver blinds. Together on the street.

43

Posie gasped.

She saw the top of a man's dark, curly head, a jacket thrown carelessly around his shoulders, a familiar lean silhouette.

Lorenzo.

It looked like he was buried in a woman's neck, her shoulders. Her arms were about him.

The woman was hard to make out in the bright flash of early sunshine and Posie couldn't see her face, shielded as it was by Lorenzo's shoulder, but she wore a shimmering royal-blue gown and some kind of matching blue hat or scarf which covered her hair.

She was slender, tall and upright. Almost as tall as Lorenzo himself.

She was certainly not twisted and hunched over. Not Jacinta, who Lorenzo was going to marry on the morrow.

Posie almost choked, outraged.

Was Lorenzo actually kissing this woman? And in a public place, too?

Posie gripped the rail of the balcony hard, in utter disbelief. Anger flooded through her veins on Jacinta's behalf.

Posie turned back into the lovely room, the unease which had previously been half-imagined now firmly in place; a knot of fear and anger churning inside her along with her unborn, restless child.

* * * *

Four

Breakfast at nine o'clock was a calm affair. There was no sign of Jacinta, or of anyone else for that matter.

Richard looked refreshed, glowing. Posie thought she hadn't seen him looking so relaxed in ages, if ever.

His sun-burn from the previous day had already turned to a tan overnight and he wore a pin-striped white-and-blue holiday blazer. Handsome, a man at ease.

Posie, by contrast, felt tetchy, irritable. She hadn't been able to get back to sleep after the dawn awakening, and she'd lain there, brooding. It was hot already and even her most summery blue seersucker dress felt like stifling winter velvet.

The long, thin dining-room which ran the length of one side of the Guesthouse was stuffy, and the French doors out into the yard – where Jacinta had sat weeping earlier – were wide open, but little air came in. The room was furnished simply, whitewashed walls and the same waxed terracotta floor tiles as upstairs, with white muslin curtains at the windows. A long narrow table ran the length of the side of the room, a snowy-white cloth on it, and this was set with breakfast: a soup tureen which held hot chocolate; flasks of coffee and tea; trays of pastries and slices of the typical Tuscan unsalted bread.

Of the seven or eight small round tables spaced around the room, theirs was the only one occupied.

'You're not eating much, Posie.'

'I think I've lost my appetite.'

'Oh? What's the matter, love? Oh, dash it all! Hello! We have some company!'

The internal glass door to the dining-room had opened, and a man stepped through. He was familiar to them; it was the cherubic Englishman from the night before. He paused in front of their table and almost bowed down low in apology.

'I'm sorry to interrupt your breakfast. No, don't get up, please. We encountered each other last night, didn't we? Outside. I feel to say "met" would be too strong a word. All my fault, of course.'

'Well, you did rather disappear on us, didn't you?' said Posie, a touch more acidly than normally. She clearly remembered the man's look of surprise when she had turned to face him.

'I'm afraid that just as I approached the Guesthouse last night, I realised I had forgotten my passport at the bally old Bus Station. I panicked rather, turned on my heel and ran.'

'All in order now, old chap?' enquired Richard pleasantly.

'Oh yes, thank you. I'm Charlie Seego, by the way.' The man's voice was lovely, authoritatively upper-class English but with a very slight apologetic jokiness underneath it.

Posie motioned to Richard. 'I'm Posie, by the way, and this is my husband, Richard Lovelace.'

'Ah yes, I know who you are. Posie Parker and the famous Police Inspector. You bally well run things at Scotland Yard, what? Well, I'd better watch my step with two Detectives under one roof, eh?'

Charlie Seego seemed intensely irritating to Posie in that moment. She struggled to be *nice*.

'Are you one of Jacinta's wedding guests?'

The man shook his head. Golden curls bounced.

'No, I can't claim that honour. Mine is a last-minute booking. The lady who runs this Guesthouse has kindly let me take a room for a night or so. I only telephoned to book my room two days ago. I'm travelling around Italy at present, hoping to end up in Sicily at the end of it. Then Malta, then on to Africa. My wife died fairly recently; you see. It upset me a good deal, I don't mind admitting, and I find that travelling and time spent alone helps me. But sometimes, I confess, I can still be a little scatter-brained about things. Like the passport…'

'I'm sorry, old chap,' said Lovelace gently, meaning it.

Mr Seego shuffled awkwardly for a second: 'Thank you. I won't detain you. I was just going to grab a couple of pastries and try to find an English newspaper. There's a good kiosk on the main Cathedral Square, apparently. They stock 'em, although usually one day late as a rule. Still, better than nothing! Also, I must warn you, I think there will only be a few more minutes of peace and quiet in here: I saw some distinctly noisy-looking fellas with ladders and measuring tapes outside, waiting to get in.'

'Oh?' Richard stood and looked out of the window facing the Cisterna Square.

'You're right. It looks like a foreman and a team of builders. Maybe Jacinta needs some work doing on the place?'

Richard came back to where Posie was still sitting. 'Would you mind, sweetheart, if I go with Mr Seego here and get a newspaper, too? I'll be an hour or so. I might have a coffee out, too. Stretch the old legs.'

Posie smiled. It suited her, actually, to have some time alone. She needed to find Jacinta. To see if the girl was all right, after the morning's earlier upset. Whatever *that* had all been about.

She also needed time to think about what she had seen Lorenzo doing this morning. How best to go about resolving it.

Or how best to step away.

After all, this was not her business.

'Lovely, darling. I'll have a rest here first. This heat, you know…' She looked at Charlie Seego, now pressing a boater on his head, taking pastries from the table in an expensive-looking white handkerchief, his big pink sausage-like fingers rough and calloused, his knuckles cut and scabbed.

A few minutes later Posie stood at the window watching the retreating backs of the two Englishmen, crossing the square together. Richard was a tall man but he almost looked small beside Charlie Seego.

She was lost in thought, and barely turned as the small team of local builders hurried through the dining-room, on their way to the yard.

She was barely conscious of them as their foreman barked orders in a staccato local dialect. Some men started up measuring the dimensions of the outside space, with others climbing up ladders to get a better view over the ivy-covered walls separating Jacinta's land from the steppes below.

But Posie's thoughts were somehow, unaccountably, still with the man who she had now encountered twice, and neither time comfortably.

Charlie Seego. *Now why did he seem familiar?*

Some things jarred about the man. Seemed fishy. Posie was certain that last night, when Charlie had seen Posie outside the Guesthouse door, he had recognised her. And her presence had been unwelcome to him.

And he had certainly known who she was this morning.

She had simply introduced herself and Richard as being married, with no reference to their jobs. She'd made no reference to herself as being called 'Posie Parker'. She had deliberately not used that surname. She was aware it irked Richard not to use his name, although he never said as much.

Had Jacinta told Charlie Seego who they were?

Two Detectives under one roof.

Posie shuddered now as she thought about Seego's hands.

Charlie Seego might look like some grown-up angel, but his hands betrayed him. His hands were those of a man who lives by his strength and skill as a fighter. Scratched, bruised, worn.

And why couldn't she shake off the unwelcome feeling that Charlie Seego was not here for any kind of carefree travelling? Was there really a dead wife?

Was it his profession that had brought him out here, to the English Guesthouse? And what was that, anyway?

Were those hands ready to fight?

But for *what* exactly?

And why?

****

Five

Setting aside her worries, Posie walked down a narrow, rickety, dim-lit set of steps leading to the basement. Because this was where Jacinta Glaysayer lived.

Downstairs was dark and cool, originally the servant's quarters and service kitchens. When Jacinta had bought the Guesthouse a few years ago, she had taken it over from an Italian couple who had been running it as a local hotel, providing full eating facilities for their guests.

Indeed, a good portion of the basement was still set up in this way, with a long green range of working ovens and a row of three sinks with drying racks placed overhead running the length of the building.

There was a green-painted door down here which Posie knew was Gloria's own small bedsitting room, the former night watchman's personal quarters.

Posie walked the length of the very dark kitchen to the part of the basement which sat right at the back, underneath the yard, and here too was another green-painted door. This was Jacinta's studio, the former cook's personal quarters.

Posie had been here before, of course. Had shared jokes and drinks down here back in August of the previous year.

Posie hesitated before knocking.

Could Lorenzo be down here now, with Jacinta? Was Posie about to interrupt something intimate? After all, plenty of hours had elapsed since Lorenzo was out on the Cisterna Square with the woman in the glitzy, diaphanous royal-blue dress.

In for a penny…

'Jacinta? It's Posie. Can I come in?'

There was a pause, the audible sound of footsteps stamping overhead. The workmen, probably. Then barking, over and over. A scampering sound. Tiny feet scratching on waxed tiles, scrabbling on the other side of the door.

'Patsy?' Posie pressed her ear to the thin wood of the door. There was nothing, or – hang about – *something* hushed. She listened as close as she dared, bending down to the keyhole.

A woman sobbing.

'Jacinta? I'm coming in.'

Giving the door a good hard shove, Posie stepped inside. There was a flurry of movement before Patsy the Yorkshire Terrier retreated into the darkness.

Down here there was no sunlight. Not even a bit, despite the supposed 'light' from the square overhead glass tiles set in the floor of the yard upstairs. There was a suffocating odour of doggyness and old wine, and old coffee gone sour, cigarette smoke left hanging. Nothing fresh.

It took Posie's eyes a moment to get used to the gloom, and then she made out the familiar room, comfortable in an old-fashioned way, with deep wicker basket chairs arranged around a locally-made rag-rug, a coffee table set up between them, laid with a thick red oriental carpet as a cloth. There were cards scattered all over the top of it, their red-and-black chequered backs bright somehow in the darkness.

A simple clothes rail was set up against one wall, hung with Jacinta's several expensive tailored linen dresses, all the same cut to accommodate her hunched back, in a rainbow of light pastel shades.

A mirror was hung about with glittery-threaded scarves and bright beads, mementoes of Jacinta's past life as a clairvoyant back in London.

The bed was over in the corner, a small wrought-iron four-poster with red muslin drapes around it.

Next to the bed on the floor was a dog-basket, its occupant, Patsy, now back in her usual place, but all-aquiver, indignant, alert to something being wrong with her Mistress.

Posie just about made out the form of someone lying in the bed, hunched under the red cotton sheets.

She strode over to the bed, and sat down heavily. She pulled out her handkerchief.

'Jacinta, lovey? I know you're awake.'

At this the small, sheet-covered form untangled itself.

Jacinta, whose normal appearance these days was sharp-tailored, with her straw-colour hair immaculate, looked terrible. Her shingled bob was unrecognisable, a haystack gone awry. Last night's mascara was all over her small, wan face, and tears, both new and old, had made her face puffy and very red.

The girl drew her legs up to her chest. She was still wearing her odd green dress, horribly creased, from the previous night's party.

'I'm all snotty.'

'Yes. That's one way of putting it. Here – have my hanky.' Posie got up and marched to the door. She wrenched it open and almost fell right over Gloria, the maid, who had obviously been listening at the keyhole.

'Oh!' Posie swallowed, wanting badly to chastise the woman but fearing the consequences should she cause Jacinta's only servant to leave her employment as a result of Posie's harsh words.

'Tea, please, Gloria. Quick as you can. Plenty of sugar and some biscuits too, please. And bring Miss Glaysayer a basin of hot water and fresh towels. She needs to get ready for the day. Chop, chop.'

Turning on her heel, Posie flicked on all the electric lights and sat again on the bed, first fluffing up the pillows behind Jacinta's head.

The two women looked at each other, but no words were spoken. Tea came, and Posie helped a tight-lipped Gloria to clear a messy bedside table.

'No need to wait, Gloria. I'll deal with this now.'

After a few sips of strong tea, Jacinta threw herself back on the banks of pillows.

'That's better. And thank you, I needed that tea.' She smiled, a slight light returning to her face.

'And look at you, Posie! You look fabulous. A baby! Oh, you and Richard must be so happy!'

Jacinta grinned coyly for a moment. 'Of course, I *knew*. At your wedding, I mean. Even if you didn't show yet and you didn't tell me. I just knew it! Oh, you naughty girl!'

Posie raised an eyebrow and laughed. 'That pesky old sixth sense of yours, you mean? It's never quite left you, has it? Even if you actively left the professional side of things?'

Jacinta nodded. 'Exactly. It's jolly inconvenient at times, I tell you. When I was in London for your wedding, I kept getting very strong messages about *you*, you know. Odd messages. I'm not sure I understand it all, even now. And now you're here, I swear I'm getting messages again…Still, no matter.'

'Oh, what rot, Jacinta darling!' Posie was dismissive.

'But I see you've got cards set up. Bally tarot cards! You're still doing all that, then? I thought you wanted out?'

'Mnnn. That's what I'd *hoped*. I'd probably be happier without it all.'

For a second a flicker of some dark emotion or shadow spread over Jacinta's face – worry, or fear? – but she seemed to bat it away.

'Thank you, Posie, for coming to find me. And for coming out here to San Gimignano, especially as you're about to…'

'No. I'm not "about to" do anything. And neither is this baby. It's two months off.'

'Really?' Jacinta frowned, creasing up her nose like a puzzled child.

'Are you *sure*? Only, no…no matter. Anyway, I feel wretched I wasn't here to meet you last night after your long journey.'

Posie smiled. 'No matter at all. So tell me, you were at a wine-tasting. With Lorenzo?'

A nod.

'And it went well?' she pushed on, sure the trouble was located there, or had begun there.

Jacinta grinned. 'Oh, it was lovely. Lorenzo was in his element; he adores wine, and everything about wine production. We ate dinner there and tried all their wines. We turned it into a small party. I'd have invited you and Richard if I'd known you were already in San Gimignano. Roberta came too, and Tony.'

'Tony?'

A tinkly laugh, amused. 'Oh, Posie, I forgot you haven't met her. She's become a sort of permanent guest; uses this place as her base. She came out to stay with me in September last year after you left – she took the attic room and she doesn't really pay rent – I don't like to charge anything as she's often away travelling. In autumn she was away almost all the time: first in Collioure, in the French Pyrenees, you know those mountains Matisse painted before the Great War? And then she was in the Bernese Alps, and then here again but only for a little bit, then back to London for Christmas afterwards.'

Jacinta smiled, happily. 'She returned here just a couple of weeks ago. Tony's a nice girl, quite serious, daubs away at small watercolours. She gets a kick out of painting mountains, which is just as well. They're not very good, but then, it gives her something to do, doesn't it? Passes the time. And poor Tony's been downright unlucky in love. Have I *seriously* never spoken of her before to you?'

Posie shook her head.

'She's an old school pal of mine. Tony Harewood. *Antonia*, of course. And she's *Lady* Harewood. Sounds fearfully grand, doesn't it? But the poor thing hasn't got a bean: there's simply loads of girl cousins in her family and not a penny to go around, despite the ancient title. Tony's got practically nothing, poor love. She and her cousin Nella and I were all at school together, in the very same year. Roedean, you know? It was Nella to whom I was closer at the time, as we were in the same dormitory. Nella was such fun: sporty, and a real trickster, and Tony was always much more serious. But the cousins always got on very well together. Like two sides of the same coin.'

Jacinta smiled nostalgically: 'Actually, Nella came out last year, briefly, in the early summer. Before you visited. We had such a laugh. She was on her way to Venice, having been in Rome. She only stayed once, unfortunately.'

Posie frowned. The name 'Harewood' seemed familiar, but for a moment she couldn't quite think why. She turned to practical matters.

'So, Tony's helping you, is she? With your outfits, and things?'

Jacinta pointed to a hook on the wall Posie hadn't noticed until now.

A cream-coloured silk dress, ankle-length and rather plain but nicely made, hung there. There was also a matching cloche hat adorned with a tiny froth of creamy net veil.

'There's not much for Tony to help me with, Posie. I'd bought my dress before she returned from her travels. I bought it off the peg in Siena and I had it altered for me by a woman here. No fuss. How I like it.'

'It's beautiful. Very elegant.'

Jacinta looked at Posie suddenly, as if wedding dresses were really the very last thing on her mind. She started muttering now, and Posie could have sworn she was whispering '*Christopher*' again and again, under her breath.

'What is it, Jacinta? Who on earth is 'Christopher?' Is he here?'

'Sort of.'

The girl on the bed looked at Posie quizzically. As if a sudden odd thought had struck.

'Are *you* going to Siena with Richard on this trip, Posie? To look at churches, maybe?' Jacinta mouthed something silently. 'To the church of *San Cristoforo*, perhaps?'

'The *what* church? Sorry? I'm not following you.'

Jacinta nodded. 'It *must* be the one in Siena. There isn't a San Cristoforo in Florence…'

Posie carried on, briskly. 'Why all this sudden talk of churches? No. We won't be doing any random churches at all. This is a whistle-stop tour. We just about tottered around Florence yesterday, but the heat was too much to bear. Siena would be the same, surely? And never mind *me*, and talking about bally sightseeing! It's *you* I'm worried about. Look, I hope you don't mind me telling you, but I heard you earlier. In the yard. At dawn. Some sort of row? Was it about Lorenzo? Tell me, Jacinta darling: is everything all right between you two? It's not too late you know, to pull out. No shame in it at all…'

A long moment passed. Patsy jumped onto Jacinta's bed and curled onto her lap, staring continuously at Posie.

Jacinta finally spoke in a low voice.

'Everything is fine. Better than fine, actually: I'm the luckiest girl in town to be marrying him, don't you think? I could never have imagined such luck, not in my wildest dreams. Funny, but I never received any forewarning or messages about this marriage. Or about *him*. Of course, the circumstances are far from ideal. Giulia not long dead…' That dark shadow again across the slightly freckled face. A frown.

'But life goes on, doesn't it? Lorenzo and I *found* each other. He says he wants a new future.'

57

'I see.'

Three months was hardly time to grieve an adored spouse though, was it?

Posie coughed a little awkwardly. 'But he *loves* you? You love him?'

'Oh yes. He's told me so, countless times. Look at this, isn't it a sweet ring? It's a promise ring.'

Jacinta shoved her left-hand ring finger with a slim gold band engraved with the towers of San Gimignano towards Posie.

'How beautiful.'

Jacinta looked slightly coy. 'He told me he wants children.'

Oh! Goodness! Was *this* what all the sudden rush with this wedding was about?

Things started to make sense.

'Golly, Jacinta! Are congratulations in order?'

Jacinta flushed, horribly embarrassed. 'Dear me, no. Nothing like *that*.'

'Ah. Well, maybe it's easier.'

'But even if there are no children, Lorenzo's got plans. Big plans for us.'

Posie was instantly on the alert, thinking of Gloria's ominous and disgusted talk of 'fancy new plans', the evening before.

'Oh? What plans?'

Jacinta motioned upwards to where men's feet were criss-crossing the glass floor tiles. 'Lorenzo has a vision: he wants to turn this place into a fine restaurant. The workmen are here measuring up to extend the dining-room, to make a proper terrace at the back for diners to sit out in.'

Posie was caught off-guard. 'But Jacinta, this is *your* Guesthouse. You bought it with the proceeds of money your mother left you, didn't you? The sale of her jewels?'

A nod. Silence.

'So what would happen to your Guesthouse?'

A small shrug. 'I think it would close down. We'd convert it to a house for us to live in. We won't have a honeymoon, instead Lorenzo will move in here tomorrow night, after the wedding. We need a fresh start.'

'And what will *you* do, Jacinta? Work in the restaurant?' Posie could feel a surprising anger in her voice, and she tried not to let it bubble over.

'I suppose I'll be with the children, if we have babies...' *Good grief.*

A horrible thought crossed Posie's mind. Lorenzo had married Giulia and then the ice-cream shop which had been hers had immediately been refashioned as *he* deigned fit, even bearing his name. And here he was again, taking another woman's property for his own devices.

It was as if he was building some sort of business empire here in San Gimignano.

What was it with this man?

What was it which proved so irresistible to women? His good looks? His talk of marriage and babies and promises with golden rings?

The anger she felt building up inside surprised Posie, caught her off guard, as she'd always liked Lorenzo. But now she felt as if the scales were falling from her eyes. She was seeing the man for who he was. Or *what* he was.

And it didn't bode well.

Posie crossed her arms. 'What about the Gelateria? What's happening with that? Is Lorenzo selling it? Or is he doing the right thing and giving it to Roberta at last?'

Jacinta looked confused for a moment. 'I don't think anything is happening, Posie! Roberta will carry on working there and Lorenzo will manage it, together with this restaurant. The flat he lives in, where Roberta has a room, is being rented out immediately, on short-term lets, at ridiculously inflated rates to tourists. An American is already moving in tomorrow.'

'Where is Roberta going to live?'

'She's found a room somewhere else in town.'

'I suppose she had to.'

Poor girl. It sounded as if she had effectively been thrown out.

Another horrible thought crossed Posie's mind. 'This Guesthouse, will you sign it over to Lorenzo? Legally, I mean? Is that what he's expecting?'

Jacinta shook her head stubbornly, her small pointed chin up proudly. 'I'm not as stupid as you think, Posie. Under Italian law, when we marry – tomorrow – this property would go to him absolutely upon my death. But that's *only* if it was completely mine to give away.'

'And it's not?'

Jacinta bit at her lip. She stroked Patsy continuously, and Posie saw the tiny dog had fallen asleep.

'I told you, when I was over for your wedding, in December, I kept getting messages. One of the messages was about this Guesthouse. Remember, this was even before Giulia had died! I wasn't with Lorenzo then, was I? Anyway, I had the very strong conviction – call it what you will – that the Guesthouse needed a clear future. So, I changed my Will. I went to my solicitors in London and I put this Guesthouse into a trust. It therefore belongs to the people I named as the beneficiaries of that trust. It is not mine anymore to give away, or for Lorenzo to receive upon my death. Even if it *is* a restaurant. It belongs to something called the KitKat Trust.'

'Why? After the busy nightclub on the Haymarket?'

Jacinta laughed. 'No. I had my own reasons. Good reasons.'

'I see. And Lorenzo knows about the KitKat Trust?'

Jacinta's face suddenly took on a steely look. 'Not as yet, no. I'll tell him once we are married. I'm sure he will understand. It's a plan I still absolutely believe is the right thing. Besides, there is a little money over, and Lorenzo would get that as a legacy.'

She's scared he's only marrying her for her money, Posie thought with sudden certainty. *She doesn't want to tell him she's signed it away in case he walks away from her.*

Posie blew out her cheeks, exasperated.

What a can of worms. It didn't seem the best basis for starting a marriage.

She thought again of the image which wouldn't leave her. Lorenzo, this morning, with another woman. She was about to ask, but Jacinta cut in. 'By the way, the row you overheard at dawn has nothing to do with Lorenzo. Or the KitKat Trust, or this place. Not at all.'

Jacinta got up suddenly, awkwardly, put the sleeping Patsy in her basket.

She moved to the coffee table, motioning for Posie to join her in the other chair.

Once they were both settled, Jacinta looked directly at Posie. 'What you overheard early this morning was an over-reaction. I'd been out all night, drunk too much wine. Loads of limoncello, too. Stupid of me. Tony told me something this morning and I just lost my senses. I over-reacted. It was about the wedding dinner tonight. A mistake which may make things a little difficult. Not Tony's fault. Not at all.'

'What mistake?'

'Oh, an invitation was made to the wrong person, sent out by Tony. She wasn't to know it would cause me pain and trouble. It's just a misunderstanding which may result in two people coming together who shouldn't ever come together again. It will be fine.'

Posie looked at her friend, seemingly now so calm and collected. Posie was unconvinced. 'Are you *sure*? You sounded pretty overwrought.'

'It's fine, Posie. It will have to be, won't it? Let's talk of something else. The cards want to be read for you. I can feel it…'

Posie hated all this stuff, tarot cards. Said as much.

Jacinta shrugged. 'Suit yourself. Sit with me as a companion then. Anyhow, it's *mine* which are troubling me. I've been laying them again and again for weeks now, hoping for a better result each time. But I'm always pulling out the same three cards.'

Jacinta was cutting the pack of horrible-looking red-and-black tarot cards. 'Imagine! Out of a possible seventy-eight! These same three images just won't leave me alone.'

Posie thought of the image troubling *her*, the girl in the shimmery blue dress.

She had to say something.

'Jacinta, last night…was one of your party at the vineyard dinner wearing a blue evening dress? Royal-blue?'

Jacinta paused and frowned. 'Yes. Why?'

'Oh, no matter.' Posie hated lying but she'd have to wriggle her way out of this one now. 'In the hallway upstairs I found a royal-blue sash. It looked like it belonged to an evening dress.'

Jacinta smiled, lining up the cards in long rows. 'That was Roberta's dress,' she said. 'She looked quite lovely in it. Lots of the men at the vineyard's restaurant couldn't keep their eyes off her.'

Or, later, couldn't keep their hands off her? Posie scowled, thinking angrily of Lorenzo.

But *Roberta*? Really? She'd have known better, surely?

It surprised Posie more than she realised, and she sat, awkward with that information, chewing it over anxiously in her mind.

'Pick three cards.'

Absent-mindedly, Posie picked the cards, her thoughts miles away. She turned them over on the red carpet-tablecloth, three pictures in among so much red-and-black.

Then she gasped, as if she'd been tricked. Which she had.

'I didn't want to do this! That's not fair, Jacinta. I hate this stuff. It's not Christian. It's not *right*.'

Jacinta grinned. 'They're only cards, darling. And yours are happy ones. I knew what they would be, you see. Oh yes, I knew!'

'I don't want to know.'

Jacinta held up the first. A strange white woman with a crown, smiling. 'This is the Empress. The sign of being a mother. That's *you*.'

She picked up the next, a smiling yellow sun, with a small boy riding a horse below it.

'This is the Sun. It's the sign of a very happy child. *Your* child.'

Then the last card, a man in a medieval outfit with a sword. Jacinta smiled. 'This card is the Page of Swords. Your son will be one such as this. Justice and truth will be important to him, and he will seek them out, even at his own cost.'

'A son? *My* son?'

'Yes.'

Jacinta was frowning, muttering again beneath her breath, confused. 'Born in a church…Cristoforo. But I wonder, is that right?'

She shook her head, then moved the three cards into a little pile. 'You want to keep these three for memory's sake, Posie?'

'Absolutely not.' Posie reached across the table and shuffled the other cards together again. Laid them out again in long rows.

'I'll show you this is all a load of rubbish,' Posie said with certainty. 'Close your eyes and keep them closed and then point at three cards.'

Jacinta did as she was bid and Posie picked the chosen cards up, held them close to her face, so Jacinta couldn't see them.

Posie looked at the three images, the first two of which meant nothing to her. Nothing at all. But the third made her shiver. A knight, but with the face of a skull, was riding a white horse in triumph.

'I chose "Death", didn't I?' said Jacinta, matter-of-factly.

Posie said nothing, laying the skull-knight marked 'DEATH' down again. She stared at the other two incomprehensible cards which Jacinta had chosen, nasty images full of swords: one showing a girl inside a ring of seven swords; the other showing a man with ten swords.

'I bet they're the same ones I keep on getting. Nice, eh?' said Jacinta sadly. 'The Seven of Swords? The girl? It means I'm going to be betrayed or let down by someone on the inside. And the man stabbed by the Ten of Swords? That's the very same as death. It's all over for me, apparently.' She sighed, rubbing a hand across her very dry, nude lips.

'I hate these cards. And there's more. I keep getting this message, it started in London, actually, of a woman whose face I can't see. She's handing me a grey-and-green shining card, and when I turn it over it's also "Death". She's angry, I've betrayed her. I can't get this image to go away.'

'You're tired and overwrought, darling Jacinta. Who on earth could this person be? You've never betrayed a person in your whole life, have you? You're one of the kindest people I know! And let's be practical, shall we? Which grey-and-green card can you mean? These are all red-and-black, aren't they? Have you *ever* seen a grey-and-green tarot card?'

'No. Never. They're pretty standardly like this, actually.'

'Well then. As I said, a load of rubbish. See?'

Posie placed the cards Jacinta had chosen atop each other and then with all of her strength ripped them up until they fell like hard confetti from her fingers. Then she picked up *her* cards, which Jacinta had left in a small pile on the side. Posie ripped these up too, almost panting with the effort.

Jacinta shrugged and laughed. 'Doesn't make a blind bit of difference, lovey. Those are your three cards, whether or not you rip them up. They will stay with you, one way or another.'

'No, they won't. Now, no more of this nonsense, Jacinta. If you really want to go ahead with this wedding, you'd better get washed and stop messing around with these nasty cards. For goodness' sake, Jacinta, buck up! It's nearly your wedding day! You should be enjoying yourself. *If* you want a life with Lorenzo. As I said, there's no harm in a girl changing her mind, you know.'

Jacinta touched the small gold ring carved with its eternal towers. 'I *do* want this,' she muttered. 'More than anyone could ever know. I'll tidy myself up and go and meet Lorenzo for a coffee.'

'Jolly good. I'm going for a walk. I think I'll return that blue sash to Roberta and take in some artwork in the Cathedral, too.'

Posie stood. 'Oh, by the way, who's that great hulking fella who looks like a tough-nut Botticelli angel?'

Jacinta looked muddled for a second, then the fog cleared. 'Oh! Charlie Seego? Yes: just a jolly nice fella who's been recently widowed. Called a couple of nights ago wanting a room. He offered very good money; far above my usual rates actually, for an out-of-season stay. I couldn't say no, even with the wedding on!'

'Did you tell him *I* would be staying here, what my profession is? And Richard's?'

Jacinta looked confused. 'No. Not at all.'

'Might Gloria have said something?'

'No. She listens at doorways, I know that. But Gloria's not a snitch, Posie. She's awfully loyal. I swear on my life. She wouldn't have said a word. What's the fascination with Mr Seego for you?'

'Oh, no fascination,' said Posie, stepping into the dark hallway. 'None at all.'

Only some kind of danger, instead.

But she kept that to herself for now.

* * * *

65

Six

Posie stalked across the Cisterna Square.

Lorenzo's Gelateria was right here on the corner.

It was not even half-past ten, much too early for an ice-cream. Besides, Posie saw that Lorenzo's Gelateria was still closed, the chairs and tables folded up, although the industrial metal-slatted shutters were already raised, and the glittering crystal-chandelier inside was brightly lit, its electric fittings all ablaze.

Posie's feet in their tight Mary-Janes were killing her. She saw a solitary chair right outside the glass door of the Gelateria and she sank down into it gratefully. For a couple of seconds she closed her eyes, breathed in the perfume of the place: the incense from the churches wafting on the air; the artificial strawberry scent emanating from the Gelateria behind her.

She tilted her head back, trying to enjoy the warm sunshine on her pale skin.

And then she felt like she was falling back through time to when she was here last in August.

Posie had sat here at a table with Giulia, Lorenzo's wife.

Posie opened her eyes suddenly, remembering it clear as day; almost expecting Giulia to be sitting beside her right now.

She heard Giulia's cackling, infectious laughter in her mind's eye. She saw in her memory Giulia's black curls; wild despite having been shorn into a bob and tamed with hot wax.

She saw again how Giulia played with one of her customary ridiculously-long silk scarves, or with the loops and loops of rainbow-coloured Murano glass beads, like Posie's, but way more expensive, around her neck.

Posie recalled Giulia's expressive way of talking – gesturing constantly with her hands, her fingers covered in their flashes of glittery multi-coloured opal rings – and the way she had tilted her head to one side like an inquisitive robin, and how she had widened her limpid brown eyes in mock horror or sympathy, depending on the conversation.

Giulia had not been Posie's friend – they had known each other for too short a time for that – and Giulia had been an actress to some extent, always searching for the drama in everyone with a greedy curiosity.

But aside from all that, Giulia had been kind, and decent.

And sad.

Yes: that could not be disputed.

Something had been troubling Giulia in August, and Posie had felt at the time that Giulia was often on the verge of telling her what the problem was.

But then Giulia always seemed to pull back. This was unusual: Posie had a knack, and a proven track record, for getting virtual strangers to spill their secrets to her, to take her into their closest confidences.

Posie exhaled. What was it that had been troubling Lorenzo's wife? Did it matter anymore, anyhow? Now that Giulia was dead?

'Oof!'

Her baby was kicking madly, and Posie realised she was hungry. Again.

With an effort she stood, and took one last look through the glass door of the Gelateria, with its etched

'LORENZO'S' in large gold deco script. This time she saw movement. But not from the immaculate parlour itself, with its gleaming chrome display-cabinet, full of the many flavours of ice-cream the shop had become famous for. The movement was far beyond, from an open doorway to the back: the storeroom, usually closed to view.

Posie saw the white-clad form of Roberta Grimaldi, Giulia's cousin, her dark, wild hair hidden under a white cap, scurrying around madly. She reminded Posie in that instant of a wind-up mouse.

Roberta suddenly clattered through into the parlour itself, carrying two or three small metal freezer-tubs. She started placing them into the glass-fronted display-cabinet.

But there seemed to be more at stake here than just the usual setting-up for the day. Roberta looked more strained than Posie had ever seen her, fumbling with her next task of taking fresh wafer-cornets from a box, placing them in their metal-looped holders on the top of the serving counter.

And now here was Lorenzo, similarly white-clad, with a white cap on, darting through into the parlour with yet another metal box in his hands. But instead of coming to the glass-fronted cabinet, he marched up to Roberta and started shaking the box in his hands at her, as if he was threatening the woman.

In the next few seconds, Lorenzo started gesticulating wildly. But Posie couldn't hear a word he was saying through the thick glass door, and besides which, it hardly mattered anyway, as Lorenzo was shouting in Italian, which was incomprehensible to Posie.

Posie was unsure what to do next. Neither Roberta nor Lorenzo had seen her hanging about.

Should she intervene?

Standing there like some dreadful third-rate snoop, she hesitated for a moment, and then realised that Lorenzo had suddenly and improbably burst into an uncontrollable fit of tears, his shoulders shaking in spasms, his white hat ripped off in anguish to mop at his eyes. A fallen, beautiful god: his finely-boned face with its almost equine-like features was barely recognisable in this instant, contorted as it was by waves of desperation.

The metal box Lorenzo had been clutching now lay abandoned on one of the very modern tall tables which served for customers to stand at and drink coffee at or eat their gelato quickly and efficiently.

What was going on?

Roberta had come around from the behind the glass serving counter, and was patting Lorenzo slightly warily on the arm. But her manner was wary, resigned.

Posie stepped back, her thoughts a swirl of incomprehension.

What had she just witnessed? Why were Roberta and Lorenzo so on edge? What was in the box Lorenzo had been holding and shaking?

One thing was certain: it had hardly been the right time to knock on the door and seek out a cheeky coffee.

Instead, she walked on through the arched passage linking both of the town's squares. The archway gave a moment of relief from the heat and the bright, cloudless cerulean blue sky. As she walked, Posie tried to reconcile the unromantic gesture she had seen pass between Lorenzo and Roberta. It was quite at odds with the clinging, passionate embrace she had witnessed out in the square, very early in the morning.

If that had been Roberta.

'Jolly odd,' muttered Posie to herself. '*What* is Lorenzo up to? He seems to be going to pieces…'

She settled herself at the first café she came to in the Cathedral Square, and Posie saw it formed part of one of San Gimignano's smarter hotels, The Dante. Posie sat outside, right up against the wall of the hotel, grateful for the coolness of the stone at her back, and grateful too for the comfort of the cushioned bench.

She ordered a coffee and some pastries, watching the hot-looking tourists fanning themselves at nearby tables and the smart waiters coming and going.

But then her pleasant reverie was broken. She heard a familiar voice, as if it were right next to her.

A beloved voice, but not a relaxed one. Not the voice of a man on holiday.

Richard.

Speaking in low, insistent tones to somebody. Giving instructions, for all the world as if he was still at his desk at New Scotland Yard.

'Check it out, won't you, lad?'

Posie turned about, confounded. She realised her husband's voice was drifting out through the open window. He must be inside the Hotel Dante's Saloon Bar. On the telephone.

'I don't like it, I'm telling you, lad. Who is the fella? I've seen him before. Check it out.'

A pause. Then an even more insistent order: '*All* the records, yes. Dashed silly name. You'll find him, unless he's a fake. He looks too good to be true. Question is: what's he doing here, eh? Well, what am *I* doing here? Getting myself firmly in the soup, that's what.' Lovelace laughed pleasantly.

Posie frowned, and was about to manoeuvre herself out from behind the table, which was no mean feat, and join Richard, but just then her waiter placed a pot of steaming coffee and a delicious plate of ricciarelli almond biscuits in front of her. The soft, sugar-dusted little biscuits looked very tempting and she popped one in her mouth. It was even better than she expected.

She beckoned to her waiter.

'Could you tell the English gentleman whose voice we can hear – he's my husband, actually – to come out and join me? He has very red hair. He's on the telephone inside your Saloon Bar.'

The waiter looked momentarily confused. 'I am afraid we have no telephone inside the Saloon Bar, Madam. We *do* have one, but it is in Reception, on the other side of the hotel, and unfortunately today, it is broken. We are awaiting the engineer.' He bowed low. 'I go in anyway? Wait, I go get your husband for you, Madam.'

And he was gone.

Puzzled to her core, for if Richard wasn't on the telephone, who on earth was he talking to?

The conversation was about a man who looked too good to be true.

Surely the only contender for that particular accolade was Charlie Seego?

So, Richard had noted the wrongness of the fella, too. It was odd that Richard hadn't spoken of it to her. But then, he'd hardly had a chance, marching off with the man himself across the square earlier.

She would ask him about it now.

But the waiter was back, apologetic, wringing his hands. 'No red-headed man, Madam. Not inside. Maybe he go out the front entrance? This 'ere is the back of the hotel. A thousand apologies.'

'No matter. Thank you.'

Posie finished her coffee and the whole plate of ricciarelli, and then, after paying, she decided to see some frescoes.

She needed something beautiful to gaze upon.

She crossed the Cathedral Square, heading for the grey steps which led up to the squat, stone building of the Cathedral. Posie noted the crowds queuing to get inside, a mix of locals wanting to attend a mid-morning Mass, and the inevitable sun-hatted, Baedeker-clutching bunches of tourists.

They were queuing with reason: the place was a treasure box.

Its unassuming exterior hid a riot of jewel-toned paintings inside: fourteenth- and fifteenth-century frescoes colouring the walls of the Cathedral in rising rows as far as you could see. Heaven, Hell, and all those pesky circles in between were represented here, along with gorgeous angels, and prancing devils, and Bible stories picked out in giddying bands of colour.

The crème de la crème of Tuscany's artists had painted here, hired at great cost by the then-rich town; artists whose magnificent and touching paintings were, due to the lack of light within the religious building, almost as fresh and unblemished today – in 1925 – as the day they had been created.

Side-stepping the Cathedral itself, Posie made a beeline for the grey-stone arch on its left, where the Baptistry was located.

Under red-bricked vaulted arches, right in front of her, with not a soul in sight, was, for Posie, the highlight of all the art, perhaps of *everything*, in San Gimignano.

Here was Ghirlandaio's startlingly real *Annunciation*, a large-scale fresco painted on the wall.

Posie sank down on a bench. Rested her hands on her stomach. The seersucker dress was almost fit to bursting.

Here was the angel Gabriel visiting a very penitent-looking Mary, both set within the familiar-seeming interior of a lovely Tuscan house of the fifteenth century.

The angel, fancy in his ochre robes, made a sign of peace. His golden curls tumbled in the heat of that long-ago summer; his cheeks flushed with sweat. The Virgin, painted to resemble an affluent Tuscan woman, wore a fussy little white cap and burgundy silk; she prayed against a background of local hills seen out of the window. A sneaky peek into her red-themed bedroom through an open doorway gave a very human touch to the scene.

The calm of the painting had given Posie a sort of peace when last she had been here.

But something was 'off' today.

The angel.

Today, looking at Gabriel was a different story. It gave her no peace at all.

Posie scowled. *What was it with that angel?*

It annoyed her now.

Of course.

It reminded her of Charlie Seego.

Younger, slighter perhaps, but with that same sort of face and those luscious golden curls. *Why was it that she couldn't forget that dratted man's face, even for a minute?*

Picking up her carpet bag Posie huffed off back the way she had come, back through the looping arch to the Cisterna Square, and then, quite suddenly, she walked right into a small knot of people, huddled outside Lorenzo's Gelateria in the sunshine.

Whatever was happening here, it definitely wasn't good.

Lorenzo and Roberta, both still white-clad, turned and nodded a brief welcome to Posie, but their faces were grim with worry.

Lorenzo's stance was one of aggressive determination, his arms folded across his white-aproned chest in a disbelieving manner. A black-shirted, fascist-medalled policeman, wielding a folder and pen, was looking pompous and talking in knowing undertones to a smart, gold-spectacled man in his mid-forties, holding what looked like a doctor's bag.

Roberta couldn't take her eyes off the gold-spectacled man, desperately trying to overhear the conversation.

Standing a little apart, a tall woman with very golden hair worn in tight plaits pinned on top of her head stood together with Jacinta, who looked her usual self again, thank heavens. As if the earlier melt-down hadn't occurred.

Jacinta was smart in a fresh-violet linen drop-waisted dress, a matching cloche hat with a tiny band of gold pulled down well over her face. She was frowning, also attempting to follow the whispered conversation, occasionally flashing worried looks in the direction of her soon-to-be husband.

There was an uncomfortable, horrible silence which linked the group awkwardly.

And here was Richard too, yesterday's copy of *The Times* stuffed under his arm. He'd obviously had success at the kiosk.

He looked relieved at seeing Posie.

'Ah, darling.' He smiled tightly, looping his arm about Posie's waist, his eyes simultaneously flashing a warning.

'I've just walked into the thick of this, too. It seems to be some sort of official Health Inspection. Seems someone is alleging that the Gelateria here should be closed down. Actually, there's talk of poison.'

* * * *

Seven

'Poison?'

Posie looked at the group again. For some strange reason all she could focus on was the girl with the golden plaits. The girl was about Posie's own age and wore a plain red sundress.

Posie saw now that a livid-looking white scar marked the girl's left cheek, running from mouth to ear in a grim crescent shape.

The girl seemed oddly familiar to Posie, although Posie was certain they had never met.

The girl smiled at Posie suddenly, and then her fairly plain, stern face with rather protruding, staring blue eyes was transformed into a semblance of prettiness. And Posie suddenly knew where she had seen a similar face before. But only in newspapers. Never in the flesh.

Of course!

This woman reminded Posie uncannily of Lady Nella Harewood, the wronged beautiful ex-wife of Simon Deverine. The two women shared the same colouring, and the same old-fashioned, distinctive, alpine-styled plaited hairstyle. *This* must be Lady Tony Harewood, the cousin of Nella.

But the genes which had sought to link the two women

so strikingly had fallen at the last hurdle for Tony. She was like a poor, faded copy of her more famous relative.

Jacinta had told Posie only this morning how she had gone to school with the two cousins. But Posie, preoccupied with Jacinta's sadness, had missed the famous link.

Posie's thoughts were scrambling. Hadn't Jacinta, in her second telegram to Posie a few days ago, informed her that Simon Deverine was coming out to the wedding?

Simon Deverine, the cad who had mistreated Nella Harewood so badly, who also happened to be Jacinta's Godfather?

How was *that* to work out exactly? Perhaps Tony Harewood had remained on good terms with the ex-husband of her cousin? Or perhaps she would just remain coolly aloof and try and avoid the man?

Well, it could be a hundred, thousand times worse, couldn't it? At least it wasn't *Nella* Harewood – that other good friend of Jacinta's schooldays – who was attending the wedding, about to have a run-in with the man she had so publicly and recently divorced.

Because that really *would* have been difficult to manage!

But what if…

'Oh! Gracious!'

Posie suddenly felt an imagined nervous hand of twitchy apprehension clutch at her throat.

'Darling?' Richard muttered. 'Quite all right?'

'Fine. Indigestion.'

But were things really fine? How could they be?

Because if what Posie now suspected was the case, the argument she had overheard at dawn suddenly made sense.

She remembered Jacinta's flimsy explanations: *'An invitation was made to the wrong person, sent out by Tony.'*

What if Nella Harewood – in the South of France, recovering from a broken heart – had been invited out here to San Gimignano by her cousin, Tony? What if Tony hadn't known that Nella's ex-husband, Simon Deverine, had also been invited to this small, sudden wedding?

Or what if Tony had invited her cousin out here weeks back, before this wedding had even been announced? Maybe it had all been some terrible, unfortunate mix-up?

And now there were to be two arrivals: Simon Deverine and Nella Harewood, and all that anger and hurt to be managed under one roof, on the eve of what was supposed to be the happiest day of poor Jacinta's life.

What a dreadful old mess.

Posie tutted.

No wonder Jacinta had been upset. Perhaps it could be 'managed'? Perhaps Nella could be persuaded to stay in another hotel, or not to attend the wedding? To lie low until her ex-husband had left town?

But Posie's train of thought was broken into.

Something had been decided here. Quick Italian, what sounded like staccato commands, were being declared by the policeman. He was reading from a green-coloured sheet of paper, holding it aloft, like some sort of medieval town crier. The theatricality of the man was ridiculous.

But the atmosphere in the group had changed.

Lorenzo punched the air for joy, bounded across to Jacinta and held her in his arms.

Posie realised it was the first time she had seen the couple together, and, to her surprise, she saw how good they looked together: how Lorenzo made sure to hold his fiancée carefully, so as not to hurt her painful back; how his dark stunning looks were amplified a thousand times over by Jacinta's wheat-pale plainness. But in the way he had run to her, it was as if she was genuinely treasured by him.

At least that was something.

'Good news, is it? No poisoning after all?' Richard cast about for an explanation. The black-shirted policeman had turned tail and was marching smartly off.

'No, there's no poisoning here.' The gold-spectacled man was shaking off his white coat, stuffing it inside his big bag. Beneath it he wore dark tweeds.

The man extended a hand to Richard, and then to Posie. 'I'm Doctor Ricardo Mozzato. One of the city's official doctors. Brought in for all manner of things: deaths and pathology reports; Health Inspections in the city's restaurants and cafés. All that sort of thing, most of it pretty routine. But any whiff of food poisoning, I'm on it like a shot. Tourist town, you see. We can't have any bad publicity.'

'Yes, I quite understand,' Richard said. 'I'm a policeman myself.' He made full introductions. 'But why on earth was there a Health Inspection here today? Rotten timing, what? This poor fella's about to get married!'

The Doctor shrugged. 'The town authorities had a report from a hotel very early this morning, an American guest of theirs who had eaten an ice-cream here at Lorenzo's yesterday lunchtime. She tried several flavours apparently, before buying a cornet. Got very sick in the night, although she's fine now. Swears blind it was the ice-cream. The town officials have taken it very seriously – as well they should – and they sent in that policeman as a Health Inspector, together with yours truly. We gave Lorenzo and Roberta here one hour of notice to prepare the place.'

Posie nodded to herself. That made sense. As did the white uniforms, and the stress visible between the pair as they had prepared the Gelateria. She must have witnessed them at work just before the Inspection took place.

Only minutes before, perhaps.

Doctor Mozzato continued: 'We checked it all out: didn't find a thing. Lorenzo's is immaculate and the premises are scrupulously clean. It can carry on trading, thank goodness. San Gimignano – and our tourists, upon whom we rely completely and utterly – would be lost without it. It's a bit of local treasure.'

He smiled at Posie. 'If I can be of any assistance, Mrs Lovelace, while you are staying here, please let me know. I am based at the Torri Gemelle, the Twin Towers, if you need me in a hurry. They are sometimes referred to as the Torri Salvucci, too. Best call me first, though. You're very brave, if you don't mind me saying so, coming all the way to Italy at nine months' pregnant!'

Posie shook her head. 'Oh, golly, no. I wouldn't have come at nine months, that would have been crazy, surely? I'm only seven months along.'

The Doctor raised his hands in something like disbelief. 'Oh? Seven months? Well, my mistake. My apologies… but the offer still stands.'

Out of the corner of her eye Posie saw Richard looking slightly perplexed.

As well he might.

There had only been the one, unplanned occasion between them before their marriage. And this child was the result of that.

And that encounter had been seven months ago.

Not nine.

Nine months ago Richard and Posie were not yet together in any sense of the word. Nine months ago wouldn't have been possible. The child she was carrying wouldn't then have been Richard's.

Posie turned to Richard, as if to reassure him, but he was grinning.

'*I* was a big baby, Doctor Mozzato. So I was always told. And my daughter Phyllis, she's four years old now, she's jolly big for her age, too. Was also big at birth. So, it'll be the same story here, I expect.'

'I'm sure it will all be just fine. I bid you good day, Mr and Mrs Lovelace. And do enjoy your stay.'

The Doctor doffed his hat at everyone and set off through the arch.

'Oh, thank heavens that's all over!' breathed Roberta Grimaldi, and she smiled now, her former tension melting away, excitement bubbling over.

'Posie! How lovely to see you. And how nice you could make it! And *you* are married now, too? How splendid.'

Roberta gestured towards Lorenzo's, where all the inside lights still blazed, and the door stood wide open.

'I don't know about everyone else, but I need a good, strong coffee. Anyone?'

'I'll make some for all of us,' said Lorenzo, firmly, as if thankful for something practical to do. 'God knows, we need a cup. If we were allowed to serve anything stronger, I'd be suggesting a glass of that too. Let me get the place ready for you all.'

Lorenzo started pulling out tables and chairs outside the Gelateria, swiftly placing cloths and ashtrays upon them. He yanked at the handle of the yellow-and-pink striped blinds of the awning and the place looked immediately welcoming.

Actually, Posie didn't fancy a coffee at all: she'd had more than her fill, but to have refused the offer would have been impolite, and besides, it was good to see this little group together for the first time.

She took a chair nearest the door, Richard on her other side, and they watched as Roberta worked alongside Lorenzo inside, heating milk on a separate hob, shaking chocolate powder on top of the steaming cups.

The two worked together seamlessly; a team. Used to each other, day in, day out. No obvious pent-up passion here.

So who was it she had seen earlier in his arms?

Her thoughts were interrupted suddenly by a low, pleasant female voice beside her at the next table.

'Miss Parker, isn't it? I'm Tony. Dash it all: I'm just thrilled to meet you! I've heard so much about you.'

'All of it good, I hope?'

'Of course.'

The girl took out a very old silver cigarette tin. She offered Turkish cigarettes around, then lit up, inhaling deeply. The girl was wearing a heavy red lipstick, and it made a circular mark on her cigarette as she held it aloft. Jacinta was on Tony's other side, and the bride-to-be was playing distractedly with something in her hands, something made of paper, bendy to the touch. Jacinta moved the thing first this way, then that way. And on again. In a world of her own.

Tony smiled. 'You're famous, Miss Parker, and rightly so! I love that you've kept your name, despite marriage. Most wouldn't *dare*...'

'Mnnn.' Posie hoped *this* wasn't about to become the topic of conversation, but fortunately Tony was gushing on.

'And how wonderful to see a strong woman in the newspapers. It's not often we get that really, is it? Plenty of strong newsworthy *men*. Hogging the limelight.'

'Well...er...' Posie saw that Tony was looking at her in a rather meaningful way, but if there *was* a meaning intended it evaded her.

Just then the piping-hot coffee was brought out by Lorenzo and Roberta who threw themselves down with relief into the empty remaining chairs.

'Here's to a successful outcome this morning! What a relief!' Lorenzo smiled, raising his cup as if it were a wine glass, and they all followed suit, and Posie saw again, now he was sitting down and relaxed, how utterly gorgeous he was.

How luscious his suntanned skin was, how luminous his almond-shaped eyes, how seductive his full lips were. How his slightly too-long black hair curled into his eyes. This man – as a new widower – could have had anyone for the taking, for sure.

So, what was he doing with Jacinta?

Posie watched as he put his arm loosely around Jacinta, who sat rather rigidly, her hand lightly on her stomach. 'Darling?' said Lorenzo, a flicker of what looked like worry on his face. '*Amore*, are you all right?'

Jacinta sighed. 'No, Lorenzo. I'm not, actually. I've been

feeling a bit "off" all morning, and now, to make matters worse, I have a stomach-ache. I suppose its nerves: because it's a big day tomorrow...'

Lorenzo was shaking his head. 'Sweetheart, it's *not* a "Big Day"! You don't need to worry. We agreed it would be a small, uncomplicated ceremony tomorrow – just a few friends at the Cathedral and this dinner tonight. What is it you're so afraid of? We're virtually all assembled here already. There's just your Godfather to arrive!'

She hasn't told him about the mix-up, Posie realised with sudden certainty.

She hasn't said that Nella Harewood and Simon Deverine may well arrive at the same time. That fireworks may ensue.

But something else was afoot.

Lorenzo had suddenly torn Jacinta's paper away from her now. And it was as if he was angry.

'No! Jacinta, *amore*! *Mamma Mia*!' Lorenzo ran a hand through his curls. 'Not this again, sweetheart.'

Tony Harewood's cigarette case and her spill of matches were still on the table, and Lorenzo leant over now and picked the matches up, lit one and then set Jacinta's paper alight.

Posie screwed up her eyes in the shady light under the candy-coloured awning and saw that what he was burning was a red-and-black backed tarot card.

A skull-headed Knight riding a horse, to be precise.

Death.

* * * *

Eight

'I thought you were done with all this rubbish? I've had enough of these cards,' said Lorenzo, crushing the smouldering remains into a pink ceramic ashtray. 'This way madness lies.'

Personally, Posie couldn't agree more. But she saw a dark flush of anger spread across Jacinta's face.

'Don't tell *me* when I'm done with anything,' said Jacinta in a frighteningly-calm voice.

Everyone stared, transfixed, as Jacinta stood up. 'You don't give things up, do you, Lorenzo? Or anyone, I should say. Even when you *should*!'

Beside her, Posie was aware of Lady Tony Harewood stubbing out her cigarette hastily, stuffing the tin into her small red clutch bag.

Tony rose and touched Jacinta on her arm gently, speaking in her low, reassuring voice: 'We were going to the florist, Jacqs? At the Porta San Matteo? To check the flowers for your bouquet and for the Santa Fina Chapel tomorrow. Remember?'

Lorenzo crossed his arms, sullen and outmanoeuvred. 'What's that got to do with anything, Lady Harewood?'

Tony looked uncomfortable and Posie saw how she licked at the last remnants of red lipstick on her lips, her white scar showing up even more lividly than before.

'I just thought that everyone's nerves are pretty frayed this morning, what with the late night last night. I thought doing something normal and cheerful would be a good idea.'

Jacinta turned to Lady Harewood. 'You're full of good intentions, as ever, Tony. Doing things will help. But *you* go to the florist for me, please. I'm going back to the Guesthouse. I need to get Patsy her lunch, and I've got to make sure Gloria has made up the new beds.'

Beds.

For the two guests arriving soon.

For the two people coming together who shouldn't ever come together again.

Lady Harewood inclined her head gracefully: 'As you like: I'm happy to do whatever I can, Jacqs. Goodness knows you've helped me often enough these last few months. Especially over this thing with Neville.'

'Don't even mention it.'

Lorenzo had also got to his feet, and he was whispering frantically in his soon-to-be-wife's ear.

He turned to Roberta Grimaldi, who was still drinking her coffee. 'I'll go with Jacinta to the Guesthouse, Roberta. You're fine here, on your own?'

'Of course. I'll open up just as soon as we've finished our coffee. Today's no different to normal, is it?'

Despite an accusation of poisoning, thought Posie in disbelief. *And now these strange arguments on the eve of a probably ill-advised marriage.*

So, no, she thought to herself, sarcastically. *Today was no different to normal.*

Lorenzo mock-bowed in Posie and Lovelace's direction. 'Mr and Mrs Lovelace, I'll see you at our little dinner this evening, at Jacinta's Guesthouse? I look forward to catching up with you both then, properly. It will be seven o'clock for drinks on the terrace at the back, then dinner in the dining-room, cooked and served by the staff of the best restaurant in town. The best of local cuisine, with ice-cream from here as a dessert and some truly wonderful wines. And by then I hope we'll all be feeling more our normal selves. Less "frayed".'

Lady Harewood disappeared off, a slightly dejected figure, and Posie watched as Jacinta and Lorenzo walked – without touching – towards the Guesthouse.

In the quiet left behind, Posie could sense Richard's confusion which matched her own. But still they didn't speak.

She was aware of him shaking out a cigarette from his own fairly battered tin. He lit up, and the air was suddenly blue with smoke.

A notion hung between them, heavy as the smoke itself. *This was a mare's nest.*

Roberta hadn't said a thing as the others had melted away, but now she picked up the smouldering remains of the tarot card in the ashtray.

Posie watched as the slightly weary-looking woman pieced the charred card together on the table-top. She was still wearing her white cloth hat from the Inspection, and now she ripped it off violently and her thick, short bobbed black hair burst free.

'What is it, Roberta?' Posie asked, moving forward on the edge of her chair.

Roberta half-laughed, but bitterly. '*This* card,' she flicked at it dismissively, 'it's trouble.'

'Surely you don't believe in all this nonsense too?'

'I didn't. But I've seen this card before, you know. Well: not this *exact* same one, but the same image of "Death". My cousin, Giulia, she kept getting this card. Several times over, in fact. It makes me afraid.'

'She had her cards read?' Posie was surprised. She'd thought Giulia was pretty sensible. 'She had her fortune told? By Jacinta?'

'Oh, no. Giulia didn't believe in that. Although strangely

enough, she owned a packet of tarot cards herself. Funny, huh? But they were antique; a collector's item from Venice. You know my cousin had always had a fascination with Venice, and in particular with the story of Casanova? It was almost like an obsession really, especially when Giulia was younger. She wanted to move there, you know, to Venice, but my uncle wouldn't allow it: said Giulia's story, and her history, was *here*. In a city of towers, not in a city of water.'

'Goodness,' Posie shook her head. 'I had no idea.' Somehow the drama and exoticism of Venice would have suited Giulia Rosario down to the ground, and this little snippet of information into the dead woman's personality made Posie feel unaccountably sad.

Roberta laughed .

'But the packet of tarot cards Guilia owned should have been in a museum. They were two hundred years old and had belonged to Casanova himself! You know tarot cards originated in Venice? But they were different then: not so many cards in a pack, and they were made using real gold and silver so they shone brightly. They were coloured green on the back, too. My uncle, Giulia's father, he bought them at an auction in Venice for Guilia for her twenty-first birthday. Along with one of her opal rings, also apparently belonging to Casanova. But at least she wore that! The tarot cards were a ridiculous present, because Guilia didn't use them, just looked at them from time to time! And it was a present which cost my uncle about a year's worth of wages!'

'Gracious! What have you done with them?'

'Oh, Guilia sold them off one by one over time, before she met Lorenzo. She needed the money. She only kept a couple, I think, and we couldn't find them when we were clearing out her things. But the cards of "Death" which I am talking about, which Giulia was getting, were modern, and like *this*.'

She indicated to the burnt card on the table. 'They

were red-and-black on the back. They were delivered here, through the letter-box, at the Gelateria, in an envelope with Giulia's name on it. Once or twice a week to start with, then daily. Always this "Death" card. It was horrible. She was scared.'

'*When* was that, exactly?'

Posie had put her thinking cap on. She remembered sitting here with Giulia in August. When the girl had been spooked out of her wits.

'Was it happening already in August?'

'Oh, no. It started much later.'

So, something else had been bothering Giulia in August.

'The cards started coming at Advent. I remember because the town was already getting ready for Christmas. The cards were always in silver or gold envelopes. At first Giulia thought they were simply Christmas cards.'

'I say! Poor girl,' cut in Richard, sympathetically. 'But they were just cards, right? Nothing more sinister happened?'

Roberta shook her head. 'No, I can't say anything more sinister happened, Mr Lovelace. What happened to Giulia was a simple, natural tragedy.'

She took a last swig from her coffee cup. 'I expect Posie has already explained? Giulia got really ill last year in December: aches all over, her mouth and eyes burning. And then she died. Quite suddenly. She was only just thirty-five. Several people in the town died of the flu in December. But all those others were very old.'

Roberta sniffed. 'And all the time Giulia got sicker and sicker the cards kept coming, even on the day she died. It was terrible.'

'By Jove!' Lovelace ground out his cigarette. 'No wonder that poor fella Lorenzo was touchy when he saw that card of Jacinta's just now. I must say I thought his reaction was over-the-top, but now I see it must have put him right on edge.'

Roberta stood up slightly unsteadily. 'I need more coffee. Would you like some? No? Excuse me a minute.'

In her absence Posie and Lovelace looked at each other, eyebrows raised.

'By Gad, Posie. What on earth have we walked into here? I say! I don't think I've ever met a less suitable couple who are on the verge of marriage. What the deuce do they think they are up to?'

Posie bit at her lip. '*Lust*, perhaps, on Jacinta's part? And as for Lorenzo…'

Posie looked over at the Guesthouse, at the small stream of workmen who were trooping out of the door into the bright sun of the square. 'A case of *acquisition*, I think. But there's so much here I don't understand. I think I must warn Jacinta.'

Posie was on the verge of explaining how she had seen Lorenzo with a blue-clad woman earlier, when Roberta returned, carrying a tray with freshly-made coffee. Her amber-brown eyes blazed and glittered and as she poured the drink her hands shook noticeably.

Posie waited until Roberta had finished her next cup. Then she asked casually, in an almost throwaway fashion: 'Do *you* mind, Roberta, about the marriage tomorrow?'

Roberta dabbed at her mouth with a napkin embossed with the gold 'L' of the Gelateria. She shrugged and smiled.

'Why would I mind? I'm happy for Lorenzo. You might not believe me, but Lorenzo *is* happy. He loves this little English girl, more than he dares tell. He wants to make things perfect for her. He wants to make her life easy, so she doesn't have to work. He'd like a family. That was the sadness with Giulia, you know. She couldn't have children. A regret which neither of them could quite shake off. He would love to have a baby, a family.'

'I see. Can I ask you something else, Roberta? Woman to woman?'

'Of course.' Roberta's amber eyes were wide and frank, unafraid. But jittery all the same.

'What did Jacinta mean just now, when she accused Lorenzo of not giving "*anyone*" up? It sounded to me like Lorenzo has a lover. Who is that, Roberta? And was he involved with this same lover when Giulia was alive?'

Posie felt a slight pressure on her hand, at her wrist. Richard was urging her to slow down.

But that blue dress?

Shimmering in the sparkle of the rising sun.

Roberta's eyes opened even wider. It was as if a sudden realisation had hit her.

'Do you know, Posie, I have absolutely no idea how to answer your question.'

'Try.'

That pressure on her arm again from Lovelace.

Was Posie driving too hard?

Well, never mind.

Roberta shrugged. 'I used to live with Lorenzo and Giulia upstairs; for most of their marriage, in fact. It was convenient for the shop and I have no-one else; nowhere else to go. I stayed on with Lorenzo after Giulia died, despite a few wagging tongues in the town. But I can honestly say he's never given me the slightest indication that he has another lover in town. And yet...'

Her voice tailed away. 'And yet...'

'Yet?'

'It's funny you mention this. Because I think Giulia was worried about this same thing last year: that Lorenzo had a lover. I *do* know postcards were arriving late last year, but she wouldn't show me them, or tell me who they were from. When they arrived by post she and Lorenzo had big arguments, and the mood here was terrible. But Guilia never spoke directly of it to me. Not outright. It was as if she couldn't bring herself to speak of it.'

'Why? Did she think *you* and Lorenzo were lovers?'

That blue dress.

A light tinkle of a laugh. '*Mamma Mia*, Posie! You ask

me such a thing? My cousin Giulia was weak in the body but she had a heart and mind as strong as a lion! She would have thrown me out – rightly so – if she thought *I* was having an affair with her husband!'

Lovelace broke in, coughing politely. 'I don't think Posie meant any offence, Miss Grimaldi. I think she's just worried about Miss Glaysayer.'

Roberta laughed. 'I don't take offence, Mr Lovelace. Far from it. But I promise you both I am not romantically interested in Lorenzo Rosario; far from it. I have – how you say? – other "fish to fry". But I *do* understand your concern for your friend: a lone foreign woman, in a strange country. Perhaps he *does* have someone? But if he does, I don't know who or where he's hiding them. There have been a few trips here and there: to Florence, to Venice. When he left for Venice last year Guilia went crazy: begged him to take her with him, because she still had the old fascination for the place. But he refused, and he stayed away at least two weeks. You can imagine the arguments when he returned! It happened a few times last year, in fact. I always presumed they were business trips. I thought Lorenzo might be meeting banks. Always these banks...'

Roberta looked aggrieved. 'I realise the argument today over coffee looked odd, but you must understand Lorenzo was not at his best.'

'The Health Inspection?' asked Lovelace, friendly as possible.

'That's right.'

'I saw you earlier, actually,' confessed Posie. 'I happened to be passing, but you two looked so busy I didn't dare knock! In fact, Lorenzo was holding onto a tin of ice-cream and looking like he might hit you with it. What was all that about?'

Roberta nodded. 'Oh, yes. I'd forgotten about that already. It was very bad timing. This morning Lorenzo came across a tin of Giulia's favourite flavour ice-cream.

He was very upset.' She sighed. 'Giulia adored it. Ate it every day in summer. It was popular with our customers and our restaurant clients too.'

'What flavour was it?' asked Richard, intrigued.

'*Perla D'Etna*. The Pearl of Etna. Equal parts of almonds, lemon and pistachio, with a good soaking of limoncello and almond liqueur. Green in colour, unique in flavour. After Giulia died Lorenzo banned it from the shop: it was off the menu for ever. It upset him too much. He found this one tin of *Perla D'Etna* this morning, in our storeroom. It was old, from before Christmas. It must have been overlooked three months ago. He was angry, as well he might be: it should have been thrown away back then. He's thrown it away now.'

Posie nodded. There wasn't much mystery here, and she felt a bit of a fool now for thinking there might have been.

Roberta had started to stack things up onto the tray.

'Here, let me help you, Miss Grimaldi,' offered Richard, standing. 'Oh! But, wait!'

Atop the rubbish-filled ashtray were Tony Harewood's matches. He swooped upon them. 'If no-one minds, I'll keep these. Always handy.'

But now he was looking at them with real interest.

'Funny! These are from Switzerland. From the Adler Hotel in Grindelwald; where jolly rich people stay when they want to hike near the Eiger Mountain. I wonder what Lady Tony was doing there? Look at that great mountain – the Eiger – taking up all of the photograph! It's a monster.'

Lovelace placed them in his pocket with a deft movement, suddenly very quiet. Posie and Roberta stared at him.

'What is it, love?' asked Posie, surprised.

'Oh, nothing. Just that poor fella, Neville Coleman, who died climbing that monster. It doesn't bear thinking about.'

He tapped his newspaper, still on the table. '*The Times* reports that as he's legally dead, very soon all his legal assets will have been sold off and his monies distributed out to his heirs. Although they never found his body! It seems dashed odd to me.'

Posie scoffed, feeling that Richard was being unnecessarily maudlin. 'What's odd about it, darling? He probably fell into a ravine. He'll never be found. Maybe not for centuries. Who are his heirs, anyway? The usual wife and family sitting cosily in a big house in Kent or Suffolk?'

'Not exactly.'

Richard followed Roberta into the Gelateria, and Posie loitered in the doorway.

She watched Roberta apply orange-scarlet lipstick from a gold tube kept by the till, and the bit of colour made all the difference. The girl suddenly seemed to glow and to appear almost pretty.

Lovelace looked grim as he passed Roberta the overloaded tray, continuing to talk to his wife over his shoulder.

'Neville Coleman was unmarried. He had a nice bachelor flat in Dalmeny Court, St James's, right near Buckingham Palace. He also had a ridiculously healthy portfolio of stocks in the city. He knew how to invest, that lad! But no wife or children. Although there *was* a partner apparently. *She's* to be the heir. Unnamed, as yet.'

'Sensible,' said Posie. 'Imagine the attention she would get.' She yawned. The heat was getting unbearable. It was time to turn tail and have a sleep. Her baby moved heavily inside her, restless.

'You're both talking about Lady Tony?' asked Roberta, with a raised eyebrow.

She had been busy all the while in the Gelateria: flipping over the yellow-and-pink cardboard 'CHIUSO' sign on the glass door so it read 'APERTO'; taking off her white coat and hanging it on a row of wooden pegs; reaching for a yellow-and-pink striped apron, complete with pretty ruffles.

Richard looked perplexed. 'Sorry? Lady Tony? No. Wrong end of the stick, Miss Grimaldi. We're talking about the girlfriend of the dead explorer, Neville Coleman.'

But Posie stared at her husband as a dawning realisation suddenly hit her.

She clutched at his arm. 'Oh! But Roberta hasn't got the wrong end of the stick at all. It makes sense. Tony Harewood must have been Neville Coleman's partner. *She's his heir.*'

Posie mentally ticked off the things which made this idea work: the packet of matches from Grindelwald, where Neville Coleman must have stayed before he had begun his ascent of the Eiger in November; Jacinta speaking of Tony being unlucky in love; the way Tony Harewood had thanked her friend Jacinta just now for seeing her through some rough patches – she had even mentioned 'Neville' by name, hadn't she? – and then of course all the times Tony Harewood had been away, off travelling.

Accompanying her man around mountains.

Posie recalled Jacinta's words: '*She gets a kick out of painting mountains, which is just as well.*'

Yes. That hobby made sense now. But Posie was remembering something else Jacinta had said: '*Tony's got practically nothing, poor love.*'

But that didn't make sense. Why hadn't Neville Coleman set his girl up properly? After all, he was supposedly famous, rich, in the newspapers a good deal.

Newspapers.

There had also been that strange remark from Tony over coffee, hadn't there? About strong, newsworthy men. *Hogging the limelight.* Had Tony been reaching out to Posie in an attempt to find some common ground?

Posie had, after all, been engaged, years before, to Alaric Boynton-Dale, the most famous of all of Britain's explorers.

Posie bit hard at her thumb, remembering.

Well, that hadn't ended well either, had it? Alaric had died in tragic circumstances in a foreign land. The profession carried very low odds for securing a long-term happy ending.

Richard was calling Posie's name repeatedly, interrupting her thoughts.

'Tony Harewood is Coleman's heir? Are you serious, darling?'

Posie turned to Roberta. 'That's right, isn't it, Roberta? That's what you meant just now?'

'Yes.'

The Italian woman shrugged, but her normally placid face looked twisted, unhappy. 'I'm surprised you didn't know already, Mr Lovelace, although today everyone is too busy to discuss the so-called "tragedy" of Lady Tony's life.'

'Hold on a minute!' muttered Lovelace, complete surprise still showing on his face. 'That's a bit strong, what? Neville Coleman's death *is* a tragedy, Miss Grimaldi. A national tragedy back home. No two ways about it.'

Roberta crossed her arms across her thin chest, a little huffily.

'That's as maybe. But it won't be a tragedy when Lady Tony gets all that money sent through, will it? She's told me and Lorenzo about it a few times now. Once was a week or so ago. She sat out here in the square with a letter from the lawyers. She was reading out how much she would be getting and saying how worried she was to handle such a large fortune, like she wasn't worthy of it! Wondered what she should do with it, too. I pretended not to hear and Lorenzo certainly wasn't listening, just cleaning the tables around her, which is just as well, as he'd have been really angry: you know she pays Jacinta nothing for her room here? It's a scandal.'

For the first time Roberta looked angry, and her tired amber eyes glittered with menace. 'But I remember she was already receiving those lawyers' letters back in December, alerting her to what would happen with the money if her fiancé wasn't found. The lawyers seemed very well prepared; I must say! She was reading their letter out to us in here, over coffee, but Lorenzo and I weren't really taking it in, as Guilia was upstairs, very sick, and Lorenzo was out of his mind with worry. Tony *was* upset about her fiancé; I'll give her that, saying again and again that the money could never ever compensate for the loss of her man.'

Roberta huffed again. 'I do feel sorry for Lady Tony. But I still don't like her much, and I'm not the only one. Lorenzo resents her, but more for her freeloading ways. Thinks she's playing Jacinta for a fool! Anyway, I must work now, so I will see you both this evening for dinner.'

They hurriedly said their goodbyes, but then Posie doubled back on herself.

Something had caught her eye behind the counter of the Gelateria.

A flash of blue fabric on the pegs on the wall, beside the white Inspection outfit.

Posie wanted to get closer to the blue thing. *An evening dress.*

'Golly!' she said, innocently, moving nearer, chattering stupidly. 'What a beautiful royal-blue evening dress, Roberta. I adore that colour. It's very hard to find in England, actually. Can you let me know where you purchased it? Will you wear it tonight?'

A small crowd of customers were now gathering outside Lorenzo's, consulting the menu.

Roberta had one eye on the customers, her hand already wielding the ice-cream scoop, but her fingers were shaking and trembling uncontrollably. 'I can't tell you where it's from I'm afraid, because it was Giulia's. I received all of her clothes when she died. And no: I won't be wearing it tonight. I already wore it last night to the San Martin Vineyard. In Italy it would never do to wear the same dress two nights running. Poor though I am, I have the *bella figura* to consider.'

'Of course. Can I feel the fabric?'

'*Certo*. If you wish.'

The colour and the timing fitted, but when she got right up to the dress Posie knew it was all wrong.

This dress was matte, with absolutely no sheen at all. The blue dress Posie had seen from a great distance across the Cisterna Square had shimmered under the morning rays like an unearthly, heavenly thing.

It had been a dangerous dress.

This wasn't a match for it at all.

'How come you've hung the dress up here, Roberta?' asked Posie, feeling like a dog with a bone, refusing to let the matter go.

The tourists were now inside the Gelateria, pointing at the brightly-coloured ices. Roberta frowned, anxious to serve. She bit at her orange-lipstick nervously.

'We were out late, Posie. We all returned together to the Guesthouse in a charabanc about three or four o'clock in the morning; *not* that I remember much of that journey, or of what we did afterwards. I have a recollection that we all drank limoncello in Jacinta's dining-room until people had enough and staggered off. I'm afraid we'd all drunk much too much, and I didn't get in here until about five o'clock. I was very drunk, horribly so. Would you believe I thought I saw lights bobbing about here in the Gelateria as I crossed the square? But of course there was no-one inside. And then I thought there were lights floating about in our flat upstairs, too, as I lay in my bed. But of course, there was nothing! It must have been the limoncello; it's strong stuff. I fell asleep in that blue dress on my bed and then I was woken up by the bell ringing down here at nine o'clock. It was the Health Inspector giving us the one hour's notice. I was still wearing it as I changed hurriedly down here into my work clothes.'

She cast a nervous look over at the tourists, who were now counting out coins in anticipation of ordering.

'I see,' said Posie. 'And Lorenzo? You returned here together this morning, at five?'

'No.'

Roberta was smiling widely at her customers. 'He came back later, just before the front-door bell started ringing at nine. I don't know where he was: with Jacinta, I presumed, in her room. They *are* getting married after all. Now, Posie, *please* let me get on. We've been closed all morning so far, with no sales. I must always justify my existence, and my existence is to sell ice-cream.'

Her amber eyes implored Posie to leave. They were haunted eyes, wary and weary. Nervous and jittery. Dancing with fear. Or was it with something else?

'Of course.'

Posie walked out. Something was very wrong here.

* * * *

Nine

'By Gad, Posie old girl!' muttered Lovelace as they walked to the Guesthouse.

'It was like the Spanish Inquisition in there! I *felt* for that poor woman, and that doesn't happen often! What was it about that bally blue dress, darling? And all those questions? Roberta Grimaldi hasn't committed a crime, has she?'

'No.' Posie sighed. 'At least, I don't think so.'

'Well, then. She's a poor soul. Anyone can see that. You told me that yourself, even before we arrived. She's not valued, not even by herself: I know the sort. It must make her feel sick, watching Lorenzo amassing money out of her family's heritage and talents. I hope whoever this "other fish to fry" fella is, he can sort out her life for her.'

They had reached the Guesthouse, and they saw the front door was propped open. They watched as a lad of about twelve stood holding the reins of a horse in the square, whose cart was laden with wooden boxes of wine. The boy wore a green apron embroidered with 'SAN MARTIN' on its front.

Two men in cambric shirts with identical embroidered green aprons were passing backwards and forwards from the cart, through the open doorway, down into the cellar of the Guesthouse, lugging heavy wine boxes as they went.

'Looks like this will be some dashed party tonight, eh?' Lovelace smiled, a twinkle in his eye. 'There have to be some plus-points to this trip, darling!'

But Posie's face was tight with anger. 'This isn't just for the party, is it? Lorenzo's already stocking up the wine cellar for when this place will become his precious restaurant. I wonder if Jacinta knows the extent of his order of wine? The extent of his ambition?'

She took a deep breath. 'It's a prime location here, you know, on the Cisterna Square! Maybe he has plans to acquire all the houses on the square eventually, one after another! Like some twisted version of that American game, *The Landlord's Game*!'

'Steady the Buffs, and calm down, old thing.'

Lovelace touched her gently on the arm. 'These are not our affairs, darling. As I said, there's no crime here. Jacinta is perfectly old enough to make up her mind to marry this man. She may have years of blissful happiness ahead of her with Lorenzo Rosario, who knows? A big gaggle of babies? Maybe we just encountered them on a bad morning? We should give them the benefit of the doubt.'

'Fair enough. But I can't help thinking there's something wrong here. There's a sort of evil here, at the Guesthouse, even lurking in the square here. It's waiting to trip me up. And I need to catch hold of it before something terrible happens.'

'Darling?' Richard Lovelace bent to kiss Posie on the cheek.

'It's very hot, my love. Lie down and have a rest. I'll join you soon. I saw a lovely little porcelain baby doll for Phyllis in a toyshop window, and a sweet soft rag doll for little Katie. I also have a couple of other presents I'd like to buy before the shops close for the afternoon siesta.'

'*Riposo*, you mean?'

'Ah? Oh, yes. *That*.'

Posie saw the silhouette of Lorenzo in the small dim hallway of the Guesthouse. He was giving orders to a short, tubby man in dark-blue overalls who was wielding a big metal box and holding pliers. A young, gangly spotty lad in his late teenage years, wearing identical blue overalls was lurking behind the tubby man. An apprentice, maybe?

Whatever the case, he was hanging on Lorenzo's every word.

Posie felt a fizz of anger at Lorenzo. Acting so proprietorially! Ordering people about! As if it were *his* place already.

She turned back to her husband, but saw another equally annoying figure wending his way across the square towards her, behind Richard's back.

It was the tall, blonde Charlie Seego, and he was looking worried.

He was carrying a small black boxy case which looked ridiculously doll-proportioned in his big, strong hands.

Posie recognised the black case immediately as an enormously expensive travel-sized Remington typewriter. Prudence had been after one forever, for the office, and Len and Posie had finally agreed, but it was to be a personal gift: a wedding present. It sat in its identical boxy case under Posie's desk in Bloomsbury even now.

Seego was drawing nearer, bound up in some inner conundrum.

'Rum thing, eh? About Tony Harewood being old Coleman's partner,' muttered Lovelace at his wife, softly, still oblivious to Charlie Seego's approach. 'How on earth did you guess? You hadn't spoken to the woman properly yet, had you?'

'No. But Jacinta told me Tony was travelling a lot last year. All were places with mountains. I think Tony must have been at the Eiger when he set off.'

Posie deliberately raised her voice now. 'Yes, the *Eiger*...'

Charlie Seego had drawn level and was now goggling

at Posie and Richard and it was as if he was encountering a ghost.

'Hello, Mr Seego. Having a good morning, are you?' Posie asked fake-cheerily, biting down her rather inexplicable annoyance at the man. The man continued to stare.

'Was it the mention of the Eiger which has caused you to stop in your tracks, sir? Or is it something else?'

At this the man coloured bright red and mentioned something about a bad headache from too much sun, and hurried on past them both, cradling the Remington, not looking back.

He almost collided in the dim hallway with a San Martin Vineyard man coming the other way with several empty boxes in his hands.

Posie saw Lovelace was staring after Seego, perplexed. 'Something you said there rattled that fella, darling. Although you weren't very polite. *Again.*'

'I know. I did it deliberately, Richard. And no, I'm not sorry. There's something odd about that man, and don't pretend you don't think the same.'

'Eh?' It was Lovelace's turn to look surprised.

'Oh, don't treat me like a fool, my love. I wasn't meaning to eavesdrop earlier but I *heard* you. At the Hotel Dante on the Cathedral Square. I was drinking a coffee outside. You were on the telephone to someone in England, weren't you? Was it Charlie Seego you were asking for checks to be made on?'

Lovelace stared hard at his wife, then laughed.

'I say! No good keeping secrets from you, darling, is there? No wonder you're the best in the business. And yes: I was getting someone from New Scotland Yard to check him out.'

'Do you think Seego could be a journalist? A reporter? What's he doing with that typewriter otherwise?'

'I'm going to find out, darling.' Lovelace kissed Posie.

'One of the presents I'm buying is for you, love. Something I saw in a jeweller's window when I passed by earlier. But I expect you knew that already, eh? And if you didn't, you'd follow me around until you *did* know!'

'I'm not tailing you, I promise.'

He laughed good-humouredly. 'See you later, my love.'

No good keeping secrets from me, Posie thought to herself sourly as she watched her husband walk away.

She'd given Richard the chance to explain about the conversation she'd overheard, allowing him to believe she thought he'd been on the telephone. And he hadn't corrected her.

Which he should have.

Because a telephone call at that moment had been an impossibility. Who had Richard been speaking to, in the flesh? What was he playing at?

Posie plodded heavily up the old wooden stairs.

But Richard was right: she should have been gentler towards poor Roberta. And now she felt guilty for it. And maybe she should go a little easier on old Seego, too, now she thought about it.

Sitting wearily down on the newly-made-up bed, Posie thought the last thing she'd be capable of was sleep.

But it was as if her body – and her baby – needed it, and as soon as she lay down she fell deeply asleep, her bitterness and grumpiness and worry packed away in the recesses of her mind.

And so it was that she was totally oblivious to the arrivals of two very separate new guests below, of a perfect but silent storm unfolding around and about her.

Brewing.

* * * *

PART TWO:
The Murders
(Thursday 19th March, 1925)

Ten

Somehow, when she opened her eyes, Posie knew it was already the end of the day. The blues and hazels and that lush olive-green muddiness of the countryside were rolling together into a twilight of Tuscan evening promise.

Posie picked up her folding travel clock from the bedside table.

'*Six-thirty!* How is that even possible? It's almost time for drinks and dinner!'

Posie swung her legs over the side of the bed, rubbed sleep from her eyes. She didn't feel refreshed, despite her long sleep.

She became aware of the slight noises of the Guesthouse around her; the low murmur of two male voices nearby, but not close enough to hear specific words. Perhaps two men out on the terrace?

She heard Jacinta's laugh from somewhere: *that* was something, anyhow. Jacinta was happy.

A man's low, pleasant rumble of conversation and a braying, English laugh came from above.

There was shouting in Italian from the kitchens below, the clanging of metal pots and pans, and a rising scent of cooking – something heavy, a stew perhaps? – and of wine, all shot through with something sweet and artificial as a top note. A smell like ice-cream.

Posie looked over hastily to the row of pegs on the wall, observing that Richard's black dinner jacket and shirt and starched collar were still hanging there. So he wasn't back yet. Or else, he had been and gone while Posie slept, not wanting to disturb her.

Posie cast a brief glance over at her own diaphanous evening gown, a floor-length shimmer of gold-net and spangles, with tiny golden daisies embroidered all over the top as if they had been thrown on haphazardly, in a meadow. There was a peach silk slip the size of a bally great tent underneath.

Posie sighed. *Not long now like this.*

She knew she was supposed to be feeling blooming, but actually she hated it. She was selfish, she knew, but Posie wanted her body back for herself now, and vaguely how it had been before.

She lit the Parma Violet travel candle she had brought with her from home, and headed towards the bathroom, but then Posie stopped in her tracks. There had been an urgent-sounding knock on her door.

She opened it to a blaze of red and gold outside.

Lady Tony Harewood.

'I do hope I'm not disturbing you, Miss Parker?'

'I…oh, er…no. Of course not. Come in. And call me Posie, please. Can I help you?'

'I rather think you can, actually.'

Tony Harewood stepped into the huge room. Her tightly coiled gold plaits had been re-done in honour of the evening ahead, and she wore a washed-silk evening dress, the colour of crushed raspberries. It was hemmed with a tiny border of gold-and-red sequins. She carried a small fancy sequinned bag in the shape of a heart, in matching red-and-gold hues. Her square, serious face was newly-powdered with a colour a little too chalky for her complexion, and she had applied pan stick to her scar, but when she smiled it only served to make the imperfection even more prominent.

Her newly-applied lipstick matched the red dress perfectly. Nothing had been left to chance. The scent of heavy, velvety roses about the girl was strong.

By contrast, Posie felt her own lack of preparation keenly.

'How enchanting you look, Lady Harewood.'

'Call me Tony, please.'

'You suit red, if you don't mind my saying so. Do you always wear that colour?'

'Er, yes actually. It cheers me.'

'Even last night? At the San Martin Vineyard?'

'Yes, there too.' Tony was looking about the unlit room with a keen interest. 'Why do you ask?'

'No matter. Just curious.'

Just ruling you out from being Lorenzo's lover, more like, thought Posie to herself.

Because sometimes an impossibility is not quite that.

There are spaces in the storyline from last night, for example, she felt like saying, reasoning it out.

Everything seems to have been blurry on returning from the San Martin vineyard, in those hours before dawn: people drunk; drinking limoncello here at the Guesthouse; people staggering off to bed at different times, without others noticing; the front door opening and closing.

You could have hurried off to meet Lorenzo after your row with Jacinta? After your bombshell about Nella...

Perhaps the hostility towards you on Lorenzo's part which Roberta described was just a fabrication, an act, hiding something deeper?

More dangerous?

But the girl I saw was wearing blue.

Not red.

Lady Tony smiled. 'It's your job to be curious, isn't it?'

'Oh, yes. My husband would say I was slightly too good at it.'

Posie flicked on one of the electric switches and the

main light buzzed on overhead, illuminating the bed with its mussed covers.

'I say!' exclaimed Tony Harewood. 'What a jolly lovely room. I've never seen it before; it's always booked out. I think Jacqs is wanting to turn this room into their main living area when she and Lorenzo turn it back into a house. I can see why.'

'Quite.'

Tony Harewood only then seemed to take in Posie's crumpled, unprepared state. 'I won't take up more than a couple of minutes. I'll come to the point. I'm here because I'm scared, Posie.'

'Oh?'

Posie indicated to a pair of rattan armchairs over by the balcony to the Cisterna Square. Posie went first, pulling open the curtains, opening the French doors, too. She poured water from a carafe left by Gloria into two glasses, and moved the already-lit candle onto the table.

For all the world it looked as if they were about to have some womanly cosy chat in a glitteringly candle-lit café.

'What's up?'

'*This.*'

Tony had drawn out of her bag a small piece of standard-issue foolscap paper, cut down into the rough size and shape of a postcard.

The top of the paper was pierced with a cut of about an inch long, running diagonally.

Posie took the paper. Read the thing twice over.

It was a short, perfectly evil note, typed.

DEATH IS NOT ONLY ANNOUNCED WITH FANCY TAROT CARDS, YOU KNOW.

CONSIDER THIS A WARNING.

YOUR TIME IS UP.

Posie blew out her cheeks and pointed at the rip. 'What's this mark, Lady Tony?'

'A knife. A bally sharp kitchen knife, actually. From downstairs. The note was speared to my room door this evening, when I went up to dress, about half an hour ago. I pulled the knife out and I returned it to the kitchen just now.'

'I see.'

Posie acted calmly, although she didn't feel calm.

'A warning, eh? Have there been any other "warnings" at all?'

The woman made a moue of distaste as if remembering a very bad meal, best forgotten. 'Yes. This is actually the second note. There was one other. It must have been delivered last night. I got it at dawn, today, when I returned to my room after the vineyard trip.'

'Can I see it?' Posie's thoughts were scrambling, even as she spoke, mentally stringing times and suspects and all the possibilities together.

She was actually picturing Charlie Seego, walking across the Cisterna Square at lunchtime today, with that smart little travel Remington. *He* could have typed this second note, couldn't he? He'd have had plenty of time this afternoon. And he had arrived in odd circumstances the evening before. So, he could have typed and delivered the first note last night, too.

But what, if it *was* him, did he want from Lady Tony? There was no request for money here, just this shivery reference to those wretched cards of Jacinta's. How would Charlie Seego, if he was the perfect stranger he claimed to be, have known about the tarot cards? Either Jacinta's, or, at a stretch, those received by Giulia last year?

Who on earth was the man?

And here was the first note.

Tony placed it on the table now, and the candlelight flickered over the ugly rip, the same knife-stab at the top. Same paper, same typewritten characters.

I KNOW YOUR GAME
AND YOUR TIME IS UP.

No mention of tarot cards here, or death. Less threatening, certainly, but creepy all the same.

'Do you know what this first message refers to, Lady Tony? What might "your game" be?'

'Haven't a clue.' Lady Harewood shook her golden head. She'd taken out her cigarette tin, shaken out a Turkish gasper. She lit it from the travel candle and inhaled deeply, closing her eyes.

'Some crackpot seems to have it in for me, eh?'

Posie swallowed. *Your time is up.* Twice in two notes; over two evenings.

She stared from one note to the other. 'There's no mention of wanting money from you. The main thrust seems to be to frighten you.'

'Well, that's worked perfectly then.'

'Has anything else happened? Anything strange?'

'No.'

Posie watched the closed, immaculate face of Lady Harewood, a woman used to being discreet. Posie would go as far as saying *buttoned-up.* So far Tony Harewood hadn't mentioned Neville Coleman to her once.

Not outright.

She had to ask.

Posie coughed gently. 'I'm sorry to pry, but I must… Do you think someone may have it in for you – maybe they are jealous of you – for your, er, inheritance prospects? I understand you were Neville Coleman's girlfriend, that you are his heiress? That *is* correct, isn't it?'

Tony had stood up abruptly, flung back the doors onto the balcony, and stepped out.

Posie joined her, manoeuvring her bulk onto the tiny balcony. She watched as Tony Harewood gripped the iron railing, the knuckles on her jewellery-free hand completely white.

She's like a china doll, Posie thought to herself suddenly. *The pressure inside her is likely to make her break.*

'Yes,' Tony Harewood said softly. 'I was Neville's partner. We were going to get married this summer.'

'Please accept my condolences.'

'Thank you. I know you must have some idea. That explorer fella of yours… I read about it, years back.'

Posie touched the girl's hand briefly in the twilight by way of answer. A beat of an understanding.

Tony took another drag on her cigarette. 'It's been simply dreadful, Posie. And as for being his heiress…well, that's all been pretty dire. I've been stuck in London since Christmas, near enough: showing his snooty lawyers my papers and signing inventories about Nev's estate, and agreeing to various sales. *So* much form-filling! I've been walking about London these last weeks like a half-dead thing; it's like I'm still waiting to wake up from a terrible dream. I'm still waiting for Neville to come back from that bally mountain.'

Another drag, then a perfect smoke-ring. 'He was so full of life. How can a man like that *die*?'

'It must be hard.'

'It is. You asked me about the money. Yes, I'll have a good deal. But I'd rather have *him*. And who can begrudge me the money? Nev had no other dependants. None! And goodness knows I've had pretty much nothing most of my life. Just a small monthly amount Nev paid me so I could travel to see him, you know? So we could be together.'

'How long had you been engaged?'

'Since last summer.'

Posie frowned. So far, the notes didn't seem to make much sense in the context of Tony's recent history. She changed tack, feeling her way, hoping to goodness she was *right*.

'You invited your cousin to come here tonight, didn't you?'

'Nella?'

The girl sighed heavily. 'Yes. I invited her. It's all my fault. I wrote to Nella from London, actually, asking her to join me out here whenever she could. I was desperate to get back here as quickly as possible; I've come to think of it as a kind of home. And London's bally expensive! Jacinta is so kind to me. The lawyers told me it was fine to leave town; it might take a while to settle Nev's affairs. When I wrote to Nella I thought it would make a nice change for her. We'd spend a fun couple of weeks together out here in the sun. She's been bored out of her brains since this whole divorce fiasco. Besides, the South of France isn't that far from here, is it?'

Tony ground out the cigarette on the balcony rail.

'There's something else, too,' Lady Tony said softly, rather uncomfortably. 'I'll be honest with you. My parents are dead and left me nothing but my name. I've always lived rather hand-to-mouth. It would have changed when Neville and I married. But since he died, my allowance from him has stopped and I'm living on next to nothing, and it could be months until I see a brass farthing. So I...'

She trailed off, embittered, embarrassed.

Posie shifted on her swollen feet. 'You needed Nella to give you some ready money, is that it?'

'Yes, to tide me over. I needed cash. I was sure she'd be happy to help.'

'You didn't intend to invite her to the wedding specifically?'

'Golly, no! When I wrote to Nella from London I had no idea Jacqs was getting married. What a shock. I had no idea Jacinta and Lorenzo had even got engaged!'

'No. It does seem a bit sudden. And odd.'

Tony shrugged. 'When does love ever run predictably?'

'True.' Posie smiled. She was beginning to like Lady Tony.

Tony lit another smoke. 'When I got back here it was all organised: Jacqs told me it would be a small wedding on the 20th March. Just a few guests. I didn't tell her I'd invited Nella to stay, it didn't seem important: I wasn't sure *if* Nella would even come. But then I found out Jacqs had invited her Godfather, Nella's ex-husband, Simon Deverine. I had no idea Jacqs was so close to Simon still! I've been living on a knife-edge ever since, hoping Nella wouldn't want to come, or that she'd arrive much later this month. In fact, I only heard from Nella yesterday, telling me she would arrive today, and I didn't know how to break it to Jacinta. I kept putting it off.'

'My husband would call it a "can of worms".' Posie smiled. 'But I'm hoping "storm in a teacup" might be better. Presumably both Simon Deverine and your cousin Nella have arrived by now? I didn't hear any screams and shouts. So, I take it all is fine?'

Tony Harewood exhaled. 'Amazingly, yes. They saw each other, downstairs, briefly. They acted like grown-ups, tight smiles to hide the surprise. They pretty much hate each other. But they probably realise they owe Jacqs their best behaviour on her special day. You know it was Jacinta who introduced Nella to her Godfather in the first place, a few years ago?'

'Hopefully the peace will endure.' Posie smiled. 'Until after the wedding at least. Is it possible?'

Tony looked hopeful. 'I think I was worrying unnecessarily. They are physically far apart: Nella's up with me, in the attic, and Simon's in a small room upstairs. He'll leave right after the wedding tomorrow. He's heading back to Florence.'

'And you and Nella?'

Tony turned in surprise, raised a blonde eyebrow. The light was beginning to fail. 'What do you mean, Posie?'

'I was under the impression things were moving very quickly here: that Lorenzo has forced Roberta out of their flat above the Gelateria in a hurry to rent it out, and he's moving in here straightaway. So he and Jacinta will live here as their home? The Guesthouse will close.'

No more guests. No continued hangers-on, living indefinitely on Jacinta's generosity.

Posie didn't speak the words aloud, but she let their resonance hang in the air.

'Oh!' Tony ground out her cigarette. She was genuinely surprised. 'Goodness! I hadn't got that far ahead. Well, yes: I see your point. We'll have to clear out, won't we? But I'm sure they'll give us a bit of time. What's the hurry?'

Posie stayed silent, but looked doubtful. It came to her suddenly that those notes might have been typed by Lorenzo, although the English phrases were too perfect. Or perhaps by someone on his instructions, then?

Could it be that the odd Charlie Seego was here on *Lorenzo's* instructions? To scare or frighten Tony away? It was far-fetched, but then Lorenzo seemed the sort of man for whom the presence of two single English women – both in the aftermaths of tragic love affairs gone wrong – in his new marital home would not be a welcome thing.

He seemed the sort of man whose home would most definitely be his castle. A place to be defended.

Tony had turned to look back into the room, where the overhead light was flickering strangely. It went out completely once, then fizzed back on.

'But Posie, you know you've got the wrong end of the stick about Roberta leaving the flat above the Gelateria. She's not being kicked out!'

'No?'

'She's happy to go. Roberta's been looking for an excuse to pant after Doctor Mozzato for ages. *Years*, probably. Well, she's got her chance now. She's taken a small studio in the same tower as him, on the same floor. What luck! She can try and ensnare him now to her heart's content and when she does marry Doctor Mozzato I daresay she can quit being an ice-cream girl. Now *that* will be a loss for Lorenzo. Because it's Roberta Grimaldi who knows everything in that place, back-to-front. Like her cousin, Giulia, did. Those cousins made fantastic concoctions together: lavender ice-cream, coconut, liquorice. They were quite experimental. Roberta knows every essential ingredient to the last drop. I helped her out in the shop when Giulia was sick – well, we all did, everyone was mucking in and lending a hand – and I was astounded. Really impressed. She's a real talent.'

Posie took this all in. Doctor Mozzato must be the other 'fish to fry' Roberta had spoken of. Good for Roberta. Posie hoped it worked out.

Her mind was full with this new information, but she kept circling back to the strange typewritten notes Tony had received. She stared out across the square to the now-closed Lorenzo's.

'Forgive me, Lady Tony, but you just said you were here when Giulia Rosario was sick?'

'That's right.' The aristocrat nodded. 'She died on the 12th December. I'll never forget it. It was my late mother's birthday, so the date is special to me.'

'But *why* were you here at all?' Posie was confused. 'Your fiancé went up that mountain – the Eiger, wasn't it? – in the third week of November, and you were at the hotel there with him. But he went missing pretty quickly, didn't he? By the time Giulia died he must have been missing three weeks. Why didn't you stay out in Switzerland? Await news from the rescue parties? You must have been worried sick.'

The girl looked suddenly distraught. 'I *was*. You can imagine. But it was always our way. I'd be there when Nev started these big climbs, and then I'd leave again. Straightaway. "No point hanging around" he always said. It was the same this time. I wasn't to know it was to go wrong, was I? But yes, as the days passed and no news came, you can imagine my horror. I tried to stay as busy as possible, which was easy, as Jacinta had gone to England for your wedding. So I helped out here at the Guesthouse, tried to do my bit. But it was a dreadful time all round. Poor Giulia. Those wretched tarot cards.'

'Ah.' *So Tony had known about them.* 'You saw them?'

'Oh, yes. A few.' The girl looked grim. 'Giulia was so upset. What kind of madman sends "Death" cards, and in glitzy envelopes too?'

'Quite.'

They walked together back into the room. The light flickered badly. Hearty male laughter could be heard coming from the terrace.

Instinctively they walked to the other balcony. The yard below was transformed. In the early evening light, strings of electric fairy lights illuminated the trailing vines which grew up the walls of the terrace. It was like something out of *A Midsummer Night's Dream.*

Below, Lorenzo, dashing in black tie, was laughing with a slightly-built, tall blonde man, also in black, although his suit was shabby and too short in the arms. The blonde man had his back to the balcony.

He turned suddenly. Looked up at them directly.

And Posie's heart missed a beat.

* * * *

Eleven

There, in an Anglican priest's dog-collar, was Sergeant Fox.

Posie exhaled.

So, she had been right after all!

At Santa Lucia Station in Venice on Tuesday evening it *had* been Fox waiting to board the train, probably travelling third-class. And – it made sense now – it must have been Fox to whom Lovelace was speaking in the Saloon Bar of the Hotel Dante that morning, giving him instructions.

But why had Richard insisted on bringing Fox along on this trip? Why had he denied it was his Sergeant in Venice?

It made Posie feel a stab of anger. Just *when* had Richard been going to tell her he had brought his police Sergeant along?

It was quite ridiculous. As was that pathetic disguise!

Fox looked away, drank from the wine glass in his hand, laughed with Lorenzo again.

And here was Jacinta, darting around frantically, looking bright in a gold lamé drop-waisted evening dress with a matching plaited headdress. Perhaps this was some relic of her days as a professional psychic on Lamb's Conduit Street? A final hurrah to life as a single woman? It was jaunty, if ill-advised. The electric fairy lights illuminated her metallic wrappings like a Christmas tree bauble. Lorenzo had put his arm around her waist and you could hear the fabric crinkling from here.

'I say!' breathed Lady Tony. 'Who's that young priest?'

'I have no idea.'

'What a dish. Shame he's a priest, eh? But an Anglican by the looks of things, so maybe there's hope of romance? Maybe he can keep Nella entertained tonight, although I don't really see *her* in a country rectory supping tea and knitting socks somehow. Nella should be down soon. She was taking an age over what to wear.'

'You said Nella is staying in your room? You don't, by any chance, think those odd notes were for *her*, do you? After all, there's no name for the recipient on them, is there?'

The girl shook her head. 'But I got one late last night, didn't I? And Nella wasn't even here then. Besides, no-one, not even Jacqs, knew until this morning that Nella was coming.'

'True.' So Tony Harewood, and no other, *must* have been the intended recipient.

Tony Harewood made to leave.

'Can I keep the notes for now, Lady Tony?' asked Posie, looking over to the table where the two foolscap notes were laid out.

'Of course. What do you think I should *do*?'

Posie tried to sound reassuring. 'I don't see there is much to do, Lady Tony, just keep our eyes and ears open. For now at least.'

'I see. Well, I shall see you shortly. And thank you. I'm going to jolly myself up now for Jacinta's sake.'

'Good, and do try not to worry.'

After the woman had left, Posie sank down on her bed. Not much of what she'd heard or seen made sense. But did it matter?   •

It was as Richard had said: so far nothing had happened which was criminal.

Hopefully it would stay that way.

Posie checked her watch, which read ten to seven. She'd be late if she didn't get a shuffle on.

She drew herself a bath, throwing in a handful of Fortnum's lavender bath salts, and she climbed in, careful not to muss her shingled, waxed hair, as she wouldn't have time to set it again. She barely had time for this, truth be told. But she gave herself up to the warm, salted, scented water and tried to free her mind of everything. Of her own heavy body, of Richard and his Sergeant, of Jacinta, of Lady Tony Harewood, of those strange Death cards and those typed messages. Of this strange place.

But then Posie sat up suddenly, water splashing all over the floor.

A man's voice could be heard speaking, echoing around the tiled bathroom. It was as if he were right in here.

'I say!' The voice was tinny, but clear. An Englishman's voice, hard and angry.

It must be the old, old water pipes of the building, acting like perfect conduits for eavesdropping, running up through all the bathrooms of the building.

'I say! You come in here now, and darn well listen to me.'

A bang. A door?

That male voice again: 'What's your game? You took it, didn't you? I'm onto you. You know that? And I've told her, by the way.'

Who was it speaking? The tinniness lent an edge to the voice Posie couldn't place. Charlie Seego, probably. Or another man? Simon Deverine?

A faint laugh. A low muttering. The second speaker must be far away from the pipes which were acting as transmitters. The words when they sounded were just hissing noises.

'Pathetic! Who the blazes do you think you are?'

A woman, for sure. Muffled, indistinct. *But who?*

123

A slam of a door. Running of water again. The man cursing. The stamping of feet on wooden floorboards.

Who was that? The famous Nella Harewood?

Posie got out of the bath as quickly as she dared, pulled on her dressing-gown, edged her way over the slippery bathroom floor. She felt a spasm of pain shoot through the centre of her being, which she did her best to ignore.

Still damp, she hurried to the balcony over the terrace. Lady Tony was walking through the garden in her raspberry silk gown, glass in hand, heading for Sergeant Fox and Lorenzo. No sign of Jacinta or Nella Harewood.

Posie ran to the door of her room and threw it open at the exact moment the lights on the landing fizzled out.

She was aware of someone – a woman – coming down the stairs in the darkness from above. The woman rounded the stairs and appeared on Posie's landing.

It was Gloria, the maid, carrying a china pitcher and urn.

'Miss Parker?' she called out. 'Everything fine with you, Miss? Don't worry about the lights. They'll come on in a minute. You'll catch your death there, Miss. Can I help you?'

'No, Gloria. Thank you. I thought I heard an argument. Did *you* hear anything?'

'Can't say I did, Miss. I've been lugging up boiling water to the top for Lady Nella, for her hair.'

'You didn't see anyone upstairs, in one of the bathrooms on the floors above, just now?'

'Bathrooms? No, Miss. But I *did* see that Mr Seego on the landing upstairs, and then that nice Mr Deverine; such a charming man, he is. Lady Tony passed along the corridor a while back, as has the Mistress. Oh, and Lady Nella was up and down to a bathroom too. They don't have one up in the attic, of course.'

'I see.'

The landing above sounded busier than Piccadilly Circus. The conversation Posie had overheard while in the bath could have been between any of the people Gloria had just mentioned, or even with Gloria herself as a participant. But wouldn't it be more likely to have been between the two ex-spouses, brought together again so unexpectedly, after such an acrimonious divorce?

Gloria continued: 'Oh, I nearly forgot! Miss Grimaldi also came up before the lights went out just now, too. Like a wee ghost she was, wearing black silk. *Very* inappropriate, I thought: like widow's weeds. Miss Grimaldi will have to try a darn sight harder if she wants to catch that doctor fella, won't she?'

Roberta's designs on Doctor Mozzato were obviously common knowledge. Poor girl.

Posie was confused. 'What was Roberta doing up here?'

'Mr Rosario sent her up to every room, with storm-lanterns, Miss. He knows there's a problem with the lights and he's fuming. The electric man, Brunelli, has been in all afternoon, and he left not half an hour ago, thinking it was all sorted. Mr Rosario has called him back again, but only Brunelli's useless boy has arrived. It's not the best timing, is it? Still, we'll manage.'

Gloria tutted. 'I think Miss Roberta forgot your room. She's not got her mind on the job, that one.' She sighed heavily. '*I* can go and get you a storm-lantern, Miss?'

But suddenly there was a pop, and the landing lights came on. As did the electric light in Posie's room.

Gloria looked relieved and scuttled off. Posie was just about to withdraw when she heard more footsteps coming around the bend of the stair.

Two sets of footsteps, three if you counted the tiny click-clicking paws of Patsy.

Posie pulled the door to, but kept it a crack open, listening hard.

Jacinta in her gleaming lamé came rustling along the landing, arm in arm with a man Posie recognised immediately from the newspaper; from those terrible photographs Len had shown her at Christmas.

It was Simon Deverine.

He was in his early fifties, and looked his age, but he was tall and well-built, with a grace of movement which belied his heft. He was distinctive too, with a handlebar moustache and thick grey hair.

He was laughing with his Goddaughter now, while smoking a pipe.

Posie overheard snippets of their conversation. Jacinta, happy but worried: 'If you're *sure*, Simon? I'm so, so very sorry. Totally unplanned. If I'd known...'

'I've told you a thousand times, dearest. I wouldn't miss your big day for the world. I'm going to pretend she's not here: that's all. And I'll be gone by lunchtime. Even if *she* ought to be made to set the record straight. I know her game. But what can I do but hope time – that old healer – does its work? People *do* forget these things.'

'I simply had no idea, Simon. Now you've explained it, it all makes sense.'

'Mnnn, well. I'm old-fashioned, and I won't bow down that low, not like she did. But it makes me happy to know she didn't get everything she wanted, eh? The Divorce Settlement didn't work out quite the way she'd anticipated. She just got the cash at Haggerty's and *that* wasn't as much as she'd hoped. Truth is, a good deal of my money is tied up in a copper mine in Africa. And it exists more as a prospect than a reality. No Judge could dish that out to Nella: it would be like handing her hot air, and that's not much use to live on, is it? But secretly I'm thrilled I kept all the mining shares: they're worth a pretty penny, I tell you. There's been a recent change in ownership, but it's still a hefty share I have.'

'Oh, good. I thought Nella might have taken everything from you.'

And then they were gone. The landing was silent, albeit for a strange *tap-tap, tap-tap, tap-tap*, which was coming from upstairs.

Posie closed her door, stood against it in confusion. Simon Deverine's words were still fresh and ringing in her ears: '*I know her game.*'

Posie sighed.

A can of worms.

A mare's nest.

Call it what you will: there was too much going on here.

Too much talk of '*games*' creeping in to all the strange notes and overheard conversations she'd just been privy to.

But she was late.

Posie reached for her gown, tugging at the enormous peach shift, pulling it into place, dragging the zip up the side with difficulty. The silk felt cool against her skin, but tight. In two days' time she wouldn't fit it anymore.

She squirted Parma Violet perfume about herself liberally, then clipped on a pair of rose-pink paste earrings, round like pebbles, and checked her usual pink Murano-glass necklace was still in place.

In the small mirror next to the door Posie hurriedly patted on pink cream blush, and added a quick dash of gold glitter cream on her eyelids. She spat in the eye-black and flicked dark wings outwards at the corner of each eye, then applied lashings of Maybelline mascara. All completed in less than two minutes flat.

She dragged a comb of Richard's through her hair, pulling savagely at the knots. She added a blob of his Brylcreem for good measure and then she was ready.

Ready for what she needed to do next.

She grabbed at Tony Harewood's two notes, stuffing them into her carpet bag.

Posie bounded out of the door and up the winding wooden stairs before she lost her nerve. She was following the sound of the tapping.

Upstairs was smaller and narrower than her own landing, and there were three doors which were closed, with another, a bathroom – where she had overheard that odd conversation? – with its door wide open. A smaller spiral staircase ran on up to the attic.

A light showed under the first room's door, positioned at the front of the house, with a view of the Cisterna Square.

Posie leant right up against the door, and sure enough, the tapping was coming from in here. In fact, she leant in just a little too hard, for the door was not actually closed, and she found herself falling right into the room, stumbling over the door jamb, as surprised as the occupant himself.

The tapping stopped abruptly.

She saw, all in one go, the long narrow room with the standard white muslin curtains blowing; the navy suitcase on the carefully-made bed; the desk set alongside a wall with a big blonde man sat at it in a chair which was much too small for him.

'What the blazes?'

'I'm so sorry!'

Charlie Seego, wearing black tie, turned towards her, surprise flushing his round, fair face.

The smart glossy black Remington travel typewriter was set up on the desk, the carriage return halfway along, paper already half-typed sitting in the machine. All across the desk were typewritten pages strewn about, and several telegrams. There was a big pile of things: a beautiful solid-gold cigarette tin, marked with some fancy crest; blank envelopes; a pad of fresh lined office foolscap paper.

Foolscap paper.

And then Posie saw the maps tacked on the wall above Seego's desk. Orange maps with pins in them. Great maps of swathes of orange land with a border of purple. There were smaller maps showing two unicorns – was it possible? – cavorting above a red shield. An elephant was on the shield itself.

Posie absorbed as much detail as she could in that split-second. There was a newspaper too, on top of a large, addressed envelope. A broadsheet, but not an English one. Not Italian, either. A newspaper which blared out headlines in German.

German?

Posie's heart skipped a beat. She hadn't been able to see what the paper *was* exactly, but she hoped against hope that Charlie Seego wasn't some sort of spy. German, English, Russian: she didn't care. She'd had enough of spies to last her a lifetime.

Seego was standing now, enormous in the small room.

He followed Posie's eagle-eyed gaze and positioned his bulk in front of the messy desk, arms folded. He swallowed down his anger.

'Can I help you, Miss Parker? Only you seem to be very far from the celebrations. You're going in quite the wrong direction, actually.'

Anything she might say would sound ridiculous. *Better bluster it out and hope for the best.* She fixed on the man's black tie.

'I wondered if you might like to accompany me down to the drinks?' She smiled sweetly. 'I have no idea where my husband has got to, you see. And I think I'd like to go in on a man's arm, as it were, in my current state.'

Charlie Seego barked with laughter. 'Your current state? You managed to get up *here* alone, didn't you, Miss Parker? I'm sure you can manage to go down alone.'

And now he spoke in a lower tone of voice, harsh and incredulous. 'And you don't fool me for a second. You're spying on me, Miss Parker. But the question is *why?*'

Actually, Posie had no clue.

But instinct drove her on and she suddenly unclasped her bag and grabbed up the note which had been delivered first to Tony Harewood.

'*This* is why! Look! This horrible little note has been typed on identical paper to that which is on your desk there.'

Charlie Seego's eyes had widened perceptibly and he

lunged for the note, but Posie stepped back smartly. He recognised it, for sure.

'Oh, yes! I think if we examined this note properly, we'd find the foolscap matches exactly with that pad. And the note has been typed on that snazzy little Remington there! Sure as bread is bread *you* typed this ghastly note and the other one, and *you* pinned them both to Lady Harewood's door with a knife. How horrible! What do you have to say for yourself?'

The man stepped back, folded his great chunky arms around his barrel-like body.

'*What* other one? *What* knife? I have no idea what you are talking about, Miss Parker. I think you should rethink your accusations, and take care of *yourself*, not Lady Tony. I have been invited to take dessert later, downstairs, at eight-thirty, so I will see you there. Please go now. I wish you a good meal.'

Posie edged to the door, with no retort at the ready, defeated. Her face was blazing with anger and embarrassment. She stuffed the note in her carpet bag again carelessly.

He hadn't denied the note, had he? But Charlie Seego had seemed genuinely surprised by some of her accusations.

Trudging downstairs again, confused, Posie saw her own door was open.

'Richard?'

'There you are, Posie! We're very unfashionably late, I'm afraid. We'll have to go straight into the dinner. Goodness, you look ravishing, darling.'

'Mnnn.'

Lovelace was pulling off his day-shirt, his muscled body taut in the overhead light. He threw on his dress-shirt, hastily buttoning it and snapping on the starched collar. His presence, one of strength and determination, cheered Posie immensely, as did the smell of him: vetiver and lemon and the sweat underneath, overlaid with that familiar Turkish cigarette scent.

'I did come back earlier, love, but you were asleep.'

'I thought so.' She smiled, handing him his jacket.

'I've had stacks to do, I'm afraid. I've been out organising a few things.'

'I see. And was Sergeant Fox one of those "things"?'

'Ah,' he grimaced slightly, paused for a second before nodding. 'So you know? I'm truly sorry, darling. I couldn't tell you before. I didn't want to "ruin" things for you. But I've had to wheel him out into the open now. He's become necessary, you see.'

'*Necessary*? You brought him all the way out *here*? This is supposed to be a holiday, Richard. Why?'

'I had a suspicion from the start it wasn't a regular trip, old girl. That something wasn't right. Brought him along on the off-chance; one of the perks of my position now. And I was right. Why, just this afternoon, while you were sleeping, Jacinta asked me if I could manage to get some reliable "back-up" for both tonight's dinner and for the ceremony tomorrow. She's worried about something.'

'Maybe these?' Posie brought out Tony Harewood's notes. She tried to give a potted version of everything she had heard or experienced so far that evening.

'Although I got the feeling that Tony hadn't shown them to anyone other than me...'

'I think you're right, Posie. Jacinta never mentioned these. I agree these don't look too jolly. But at least they're concrete, physical things. Jacinta was going on about some bally vision, all about death. Make any sense to you in the context of what you overheard so far?'

'No.'

'All very rum.'

She watched Richard run his hands through his thick red hair, tie his black silk bow-tie – something she always found unaccountably attractive – and turn and grin at her.

His green eyes twinkled mischievously; he was enjoying himself now, a terrier scenting a lead, an opportunity.

'But I've acted on her "vision",' he whispered. 'Thought it best to. I've placed men about the Guesthouse. So, Lady Tony needn't fear anything, nor Jacinta. And we have our secret weapon, too: the Reverend David Harkness. Just stopped off from a trip to Rome, wanting a room for the night. Lovely relaxed fella, very easy company. So jolly in fact that he's been invited last-minute to the pre-wedding dinner. Who can resist such a chap?'

Sergeant Fox.

Posie rolled her eyes and they walked down the stairs together, to the accompaniment of the electric lights fizzing on and off continuously.

****

Twelve

'I say!'

With a grin, Lovelace looked about the room where the dinner was to take place. 'The Italians like to do it in style, eh?'

Lorenzo had really pushed the boat out, that was for sure.

The dining-room of the Guesthouse, stripped of its many little breakfast tables, looked more like a ballroom tonight. Twinkling fairy lights were draped around a long dining-table which had been placed in the centre of the room. It was dressed with white roses and trailing ivy, and tiny tealights in glass holders were dotted about the snowy white cloth. Bottles of a red San Martin wine were placed about liberally. In one corner a small yellow-and-pink cart with a closed glass lid held trays of ice-cream from the Gelateria.

An older man, a lean, little dark man in his fifties with sharp, furtive eyes and a black curled moustache, moved about with all the theatrical concern of the professional waiter, and another much younger man, with a slightly horse-like face, and a fair moustache, carried glasses and silverware.

Posie remembered that Lorenzo had hired the staff and chef of a local restaurant to put this dinner on, but were these two rather feeble-looking waiters part of that arrangement? Or were they something to do with Lovelace, the men he had placed about? And what did *that* mean, exactly? Local police?

Guests were beginning to trickle through into the room from the terrace outside, their mix of laughter and conversation thronging the air along with the cigarette smoke they carried with them, wine glasses chinking in that exciting anticipatory way which signalled a night of pure pleasure ahead.

Here was Jacinta hand-in-hand with Lorenzo, who was more handsome than ever: his eyes ceaselessly scanning the room and everything in it for flaws; for things to set right.

'Posie!' Jacinta called out. 'How beautiful you look! You're such a lucky man, Richard!'

'She's such a good liar,' muttered Posie to Richard, under her breath. 'I look like a whale'. But she was relieved to see that Jacinta looked calm, a perfect host, any trace of the worries she had spoken of with Lovelace seemingly now tucked away.

And here was Roberta Grimaldi, coming in through the French doors. She looked exactly as Gloria had described, smart but awfully sallow in a frothy black silk gown.

A single red rose was tucked into Roberta's short bobbed hair, and it provided the only colour about the girl. She needed that orange lipstick she had worn earlier to counter the dark bags under her eyes and the taut, grim features of her face. Although her eyes were glittering nervously, roving.

Next to her was Doctor Mozzato, smart in what looked like a brand-new black velvet smoking jacket; he was looking slightly bored, playing with his gold glasses, edgy too. Posie was slightly surprised to see him here, but perhaps Roberta had made a special request? Keen on advancing her prospects with the man, maybe? Or simply fed up of always being alone.

Alone like Tony Harewood.

Here she was, stepping into the room in her red silk dress, a solitary figure. *The china doll.* Posie smiled at her but the girl didn't see.

And then came Simon Deverine, pipe still clasped in hand, laughing and joshing with the undercover Sergeant Fox. Both men appeared at ease, as if they couldn't think of a nicer place to be.

'Golly, your Sergeant *does* scrub up well,' murmured Posie, watching the delicate beam from the fairy lights play over Fox's angular cheekbones and his blonde, almost shaven hair. 'Even if he is just a priest.'

'No "just" about Fox, darling. "Tip-top" would be a better description. Come on, time to be introduced and to pretend you've never met him before in your life.'

Posie and Richard moved forward, shaking hands with Deverine and Fox, and then everyone was being seated, and Posie found herself actually quite glad to be sat with Simon Deverine on her immediate right, with Richard on her other side.

Deverine was attentive and charming: pouring water for Posie; passing the unsalted Tuscan bread.

Posie was famished by now and she started to take tiny little bites, hoping no-one would notice.

Opposite Simon Deverine sat Roberta Grimaldi, scowling slightly – as well she might – for she had been placed next to Tony Harewood, who was directly opposite Posie, smoking as if her life depended upon it. Posie saw all too clearly that Tony wouldn't have been Roberta's first choice of neighbour.

Next to Tony and opposite Richard were two empty seats. The Doctor – who Roberta had obviously hoped would sit next to her on her side – was placed well away from her, at the far end of the row on Posie's side, next to Lovelace. Fox was seated at the head of the table at the end, nearest the window towards the Cisterna Square, facing the wedding pair who sat in prime position together at the head of the table at the other end.

There was no sign of Nella Harewood, and Posie felt peculiarly thankful for the girl's tact in staying away.

Posie beamed as Jacinta and Lorenzo stood up, banging their glasses with forks to create a silence among their guests.

Lorenzo was speaking in a quick Italian, signalling towards the small, dark Head Waiter, who started filling glasses with wine, and motioning towards the other young lad, who came in with platters of antipasti; salami and cheese tartlets and very green olives with pâté on crackers.

Lorenzo looked seriously around the room: 'We thank you all for joining us, on the eve of our life together. I think it is fair to say that both my dearest Jacinta and I have each emerged from rather perilous personal circumstances, and have not always been fortunate enough to enjoy long-term happiness.' He cleared his throat huskily, and Jacinta squeezed his hand. 'There have indeed been tragedies and the loss of dear ones…'

To everybody in the room, which was now thick with smoke, it seemed as though the ghost of Giulia Rosario was standing alongside Lorenzo right now, the fairy lights catching the fire of her many opal rings, and that she was breathing down Lorenzo's neck, unhappy too about the lack of long-term happiness.

But how to banish her?

Lorenzo recovered himself quickly: 'Some will no doubt say we have rushed things, but life is short and Jacinta and I have found in each other a rare happiness. I will treasure her. Please raise your glasses to my lovely Jacinta, my English rose, my soon-to-be-wife!'

Glasses clinked and people clapped.

'To the Happy Couple!'

'To Jacinta and Lorenzo!'

Simon Deverine was drinking the good red wine, and smiling just a little too much.

'Rosario managed that well enough, eh, Miss Parker?' he said in a whisper, right up against her ear so she could feel the prickle of his immaculate, curled moustache.

'But he's right, eh? There's plenty of folk who will wonder if they've jumped in too soon, or wonder *why* he's in it at all, eh? Little Jacqs is my Goddaughter, and I love her to bits, but if she had no money and no assets to speak of, a sleek lad like Lorenzo wouldn't have looked at her twice, would he? So it's all to the good that he's delivered this nonsense-filled speech about "a rare happiness". For what *that's* worth.'

Posie turned from her delicious antipasti. 'I say! You *are* cynical, Mr Deverine.'

The older man shrugged. 'I've seen most things by now, my dear. Unfortunately.'

'And you don't think this will end well?'

Deverine attacked his plate of olives. 'I didn't say that,' he said, between mouthfuls. He shrugged slightly: 'But I feel like I have to protect Jacinta. I've had my own fingers burnt before.'

Posie wondered at his sudden silence, thinking of The Pink House in Soho, but not liking to ask more. Instead, she spoke to Deverine about London, and he told her he had a lovely flat very close to London's best auction rooms and galleries.

'Dalmeny Court, you know it? In St James's?'

Dalmeny Court? That rang a bell.

'No, sorry.'

'It's a gorgeous spot. All the busyness of London at its best. Italian restaurants around the corner; tea-shops; barbers; outfitters…' He looked wistful for a second, like he was missing it frightfully. For a brief second Posie missed London too.

'Sounds delightful.'

'I bought the flat when I married my ex-wife, as a home for us. Well, you probably know how that ended. I've kept it, though. Too dashed good a place to sell. I'm there most of the time: it was handy for my work in Parliament; when I *had* work in Parliament. But really it's too bally big for a fella on his own. It's even got a great big shiny kitchen in the newest style. Not that *that* ever got much of a use! Nella had no time or need for a kitchen, not even when she put in an appearance, which was seldom. Always too busy bally travelling about, wasn't she?' He sighed. 'The kitchen *still* doesn't get much use.'

And then as dinner wore on, Simon Deverine was talking more and more to Roberta Grimaldi, directly opposite him, mainly about the food which came, course upon course, each one more delicious than the last.

A pleasant ruby flush started to tinge Roberta's face and she laughed prettily at some of Simon's jokes. With a stab of pity Posie realised she had never heard the girl laugh before, and she felt peculiarly grateful to the old rogue next to her for showing Roberta some attention.

Posie herself was in muddy waters: trying to make stilted conversation with Tony Harewood, opposite, but not with much success. Tony kept looking at the empty chairs beside her, jittery as hell, her nerves all over the place.

'I'm supposed to be saving a seat for Nella,' she hissed at Posie. '*Where* on earth is she? Perhaps I should go up? I'm worried.'

But then, into the smoke, and the wine and the chatter, a sudden cold breeze swept through the room, nothing at all to do with the still-open doors to the terrace, where the now-black night hung velvety as a stage curtain.

Bang.

People turned as one as the door to the Guesthouse's internal hallway swung violently open, and a thin, tall girl appeared: a girl in her early thirties, but who wore her age like a good dress.

It was obvious to anyone at first glance that this girl was very drunk, but she held herself in a completely mesmerising way, arms dramatically outstretched between the door-frame, as if she was making an entrance on a stage.

Nella Harewood.

Posie heard a muffled groan beside her, where Simon Deverine had broken off from his chat with Roberta. 'Nella!' he muttered under his breath. 'You're drunk. Oh, baby.'

And Posie saw how Deverine's handsome face creased in worry; taking on an almost fatherly concern.

He loves her still, she realised with a sudden certainty. *Whatever he did to her, however it ended, he loves her.*

And whatever it was that Nella had done to make him angry, as he had raged about to Jacinta up on the landing earlier, Simon Deverine still had feelings for the girl.

It's complicated for him, Posie thought.

Lady Nella Harewood stepped further into the now-silent room, where the fairy lights lit her as if in a dream, and her scarlet silk gown glowed like the most bewitching of rubies.

Everyone was staring at the staggering beauty of the girl. Even Posie felt her mouth gape open.

No wonder Deverine still loves her.

Photographs hadn't done Nella Harewood justice. Posie could see that now.

How could a black-and-white photograph printed in a grainy newspaper ever capture the ice-blue of those large, doll-like eyes? How could the golden-blonde plaits – so like Tony Harewood's, but neater, finer – sparkle in black-and-white? No picture could convey the intensity of the perfume of the girl: a heavy musk which smelt of black, burnt amber and pine.

And then the silence of the room was broken by Nella laughing outrageously.

She pointed a ruby-red-painted fingertip at Jacinta and wobbled slightly on her high heels: 'Oh, darling!' she roared. 'Who on earth told you to wear *that*? Was it Tony? She likes giving advice on clothes. Only, sweetheart, you shouldn't have listened to her: you look frightful. What a choice to make! What a let-down for yourself! Couldn't you have chosen differently? But it's too late now, isn't it?'

Everyone gasped in horror.

Beside her Posie heard Simon Deverine groan helplessly.

Looking over at the girl, Posie wondered if Nella Harewood was slightly unhinged, but her real concern was for Jacinta, on the receiving end of a horrible public humiliation she had not asked for and did not deserve.

But Posie saw the cruel – if accurate – words had not affected Jacinta at all, and she had shrugged the insults off. She was laughing, in fact.

Not so others.

Tony Harewood's normally serene, square face was now livid with visceral outrage, her blue unmade-up eyes dark with a bleak, useless anger. Her scar was very white now. She was staring at her cousin, her mouth dropped open, apparently lost for words, her fingers gripping at her red bag, almost ripping at it in a kind of tamped-down fury.

Suddenly, as if spurred on by an inner resolve, she pulled her cousin down into the spare seat, where Nella virtually collapsed.

Lorenzo was furious. His dark eyes burned hot, angry. He couldn't stop staring at Nella Harewood and his expression was difficult to read. It was as if he hated her beyond everything. Fury made his lovely face ugly; every angle hard and resigned. Eventually he tore his gaze away, and downed one, then two, then three glasses of wine.

Conversations resumed, artificial and light as air.

The fairy lights flickered for an instant, but buzzed into life again almost straight away.

'I don't like the look of these silly little lights,' muttered Richard Lovelace beside Posie. 'You're not near any of the actual cables, are you, darling?'

'No. They're on the other side of the table, I think, and near that ice-cream trolley, which is all linked up to the electricity too, as well as being packed with big blocks of ice.'

'Just keep well away.'

Nella looked sulky as the black-moustached older waiter swirled around her, ladling hot food onto her plate. She made a show of picking at her dinner, all the while avoiding meeting her ex-husband's gaze. After a few minutes she stared up at Posie quite unashamedly, taking her in with those huge baby-blue eyes which missed nothing.

'You're that woman Private Detective, aren't you?'

Posie smiled. 'That's right. I'm Posie Parker.'

'How utterly divine. Well, Tony here thinks so, anyhow. *She* thinks you're topping.'

Nella took her glass of wine and drank it straight off before continuing: 'Tony couldn't stop raving about you earlier. Bless her. She's quite innocent really. Thought you could help her with a small problem she had.'

'Ah, yes. We've spoken.' Posie was uncomfortably aware of other conversations suddenly going quiet about them. Although Tony Harewood wasn't a client of hers as such, she did owe her the courtesy of *some* confidentiality.

Nella obviously didn't feel the same way and shrugged dramatically.

'Didn't seem much of a problem to *me*. A couple of piffling little notes, eh? Best ignored. Tony's overegged the pudding. Nothing dangerous about them! We can take care of ourselves, Miss Parker. We Harewoods look out for each other, always have. So whatever Tony has told you, forget it. You go back to planning for your baby.'

Nella Harewood cast a withering look in Lovelace's direction. 'And playing happy families with nice old Mr Plod here.'

Posie felt a rise of anger within her, but felt a squeeze on her hand from Richard.

Don't argue; don't try and speak sense with this drunk girl.
'Fine. Suits me.' She smiled.

But Posie hadn't been going to argue. For she now recognised a certain type of bravado on display here, a bravado which covered up fear.

Posie understood that it had taken a good deal for this girl to enter the room tonight. Nella hadn't wanted to come here, after all, had she? It had been Tony's mistake which had led to this unhappy grouping.

Maybe she would have been better off staying away, up in the attic, like she had done for the first part of the dinner? But why should *she* hide like a fugitive?

Nella hadn't done a thing wrong, after all. She'd bolstered herself up with Dutch Courage and come along. And maybe you had to admire that.

Posie looked at the cousins across from her now: at their identical hair colour and style; at the similar red dresses; the very different faces. Overall, it was uncanny how close their resemblance was, from slightly afar. If you blurred your eyes a little, maybe.

Dishes were being cleared, and people were now moving towards the ice-cream trolley in the corner, past Jacinta's seat, past the tangle of electric cables running on the floor. Roberta was laughing and simultaneously plucking at Simon Deverine's sleeve, excited at the novelty of the occasion, at the attention of a man.

'Come on! We serve ourselves the ice-cream, Mr Deverine. Well, actually, *I* will serve you. Yes! *Certo!* It would be an honour to do so!' Roberta was taking up a post right behind the striped pink-and-yellow wagon.

A busman's holiday.

Roberta wielded an ice-cream scoop and picked up a lovely blue-glass bowl and drew back the glass lid of the trolley seductively, almost flirtatiously, the frozen air rising up like a mysterious magic fog into the room. For a strange mad moment Posie wondered, was *this* the reason Roberta had been invited? As some kind of slightly elevated, privileged lackey who would also be able to serve?

But, no.

Lorenzo, still seated, looked embarrassed and reeled off strings of Italian, all protests, from the sounds of it. Instructions to Roberta to sit down, to desist.

'No! No!'

Roberta, flushed with wine, insisted: 'This is my speciality, Mr Deverine! Lorenzo, do not deny me the chance to show off what little I *do* know! Now, what will you have?'

Deverine chuckled and pointed at a couple of pastel-coloured flavours, taking his blue-glass bowl and looping back to his seat. In the door-frame Posie suddenly saw the huge figure of Charlie Seego, down promptly for the dessert course, and Posie realised that the bells of the ancient city churches were ringing for half-past eight.

Jacinta and the two Harewood cousins had formed a group at the trolley, all laughing; Nella's opening gambit to humiliate Jacinta had obviously been forgiven, or forgotten. They were waiting to be served by Roberta, although Nella was obviously only just able to stand.

Tony Harewood had shaken off some of her previous reserve and Posie watched as she broke away to speak to Fox, putting a hand tentatively on his black jacket, looking up into his face with a curious, expectant look, as if testing out a clergyman's capacity for small-talk.

Posie watched her licking at the red of her lipstick, and saw how Fox moved gently towards the girl, placing his hand on her bare arm, bending down to say a word or two in her ear.

Like a blessing.

Golly, he's good, Posie thought with a smile.

Tip-top.

Jacinta was pointing at an ice-cream now, tapping against the glass lid.

'I'll have vanilla please. Oh, no! I've changed my mind! *That* one, please, Roberta darling. *Perla D'Etna!* The Pearl of Etna! Oh, did you bring it here tonight specially for me? What a jolly good idea! I'll have a whole bowl of that, please.'

And then Posie saw that Roberta's face had gone deathly-white, her arms had stopped, mid-action, and she looked like she might scream.

* * * *

Thirteen

'What is it? *Cosa c'è?*'

Lorenzo was bounding up to Roberta. Everyone else was gathering around.

Richard was on his feet, speaking authoritatively: 'What's the problem here, Mr Rosario?'

But Posie saw how Lorenzo was gripping the sides of the ice-cream trolley, shaking his head from side to side.

Roberta had her mouth open, but no words came. Sweat beaded her face, and her eyes glittered like a cat caught in headlights. In her panic she grabbed at the red rose in her hair, started ripping it to pieces.

Lorenzo was almost shouting: '*Come hai potuto?* How *could* you, Roberta? By all the Saints in Heaven!'

'I didn't. I swear!'

'You *must* have!' Lorenzo snarled. For a horrible moment it looked like he might hit Roberta.

'That same box as earlier! It's unbelievable. I threw it out! You're causing me no end of trouble today.'

Richard Lovelace, brows furled, shook the groom's arm. 'What is it, sir? What's the problem here?'

Roberta spoke directly to Lovelace. Quietly, calmly, but looking as if she might cry.

'You remember what I told you earlier today, Inspector,

about the *Perla D'Etna* ice-cream? How – since my cousin Giulia died – Lorenzo instructed it wasn't to be made anymore, nor sold in our – *his* – shop. You remember I told you he found one carton of this flavour when we were preparing for the Health Inspection, and he got upset? He threw it away.'

'Yes, Miss Grimaldi, I remember.'

'Well, we are now in the same position. The ice-cream, it has reappeared!'

She tapped a dark-green ice-cream in an identical metal tub to all the others. 'Here is the *Perla D'Etna* ice-cream. It *must* be the same carton, as we haven't made any since Giulia died, back in December. We haven't featured it in the Gelateria since then; no one has eaten any.'

She splayed her hands dramatically. 'But how did it get here tonight? *I* packed the ice-creams up myself this afternoon. I chose them carefully. There were ten flavours in total. I didn't bring this one. I see now that the tub of *Fiore di Latte* I packed is missing; replaced with this *Perla D'Etna*. But I have no idea how that happened.'

Lovelace looked at Lorenzo with a kind of relief. 'Is this right, sir? So, nothing bad has actually occurred. It's more a sort of superstition thing, eh?'

Lorenzo still looked angry, but allowed himself a small nod of agreement.

Jacinta made a puffing noise, gave an exasperated sigh. '*I'm* the one who believes in superstition,' she said quite reasonably. 'And even *I* think this is all a lot of stuff and nonsense! We're only talking about ice-cream, after all, aren't we?'

She turned to her future husband, grabbed him by both arms imploringly. 'This is silly, Lorenzo darling! It's a mix-up. Giulia would have hated you to have banned this flavour forever. *She* created it, didn't she? Besides, I know there are requests for it fairly often in the Gelateria: it wasn't just Giulia's favourite, you know. People loved it. Restaurants in the town often ask for tubs, don't they, Roberta? Roberta always has to say no, and give some pathetic excuse, don't you?'

Roberta nodded.

Jacinta drew herself up a little in all her golden luminosity. 'Actually, I'm glad it's here. It's *my* favourite, too, Lorenzo.'

Posie watched as Lorenzo stepped away from the trolley, looked at Jacinta with surprise. 'I didn't know that, *amore.*'

Jacinta crossed her arms, fiery, not done. 'Besides, what's all this I hear about not having it in the Gelateria? I'm pretty certain it was there yesterday, when I took over from Roberta at lunchtime.'

Lorenzo frowned. '*You* took over?'

'Only for a short while. Roberta went upstairs for her nap, or maybe she chose a dress for the dinner last night. I don't know. I was passing and she asked me to cover for forty minutes or so. That was fine by me! Any problem with that?' Jacinta looked obstinate, challenging her soon-to-be husband.

Lorenzo shook his head. 'Of course not. But you're imagining things about the carton of *Perla D'Etna* being in the actual Gelateria yesterday. It was in the *storeroom* this morning; I found it there! Besides, it would have tasted bad. That one carton must have been sitting there since Giulia died. More than three months ago.'

Jacinta shrugged complacently. 'What's three months? It's got so much liqueur and sugar in it that I expect it would keep for years!'

Lorenzo groaned. 'No, darling. We are famous for making it fresh each week!'

Jacinta had taken the ice-cream scoop from Roberta's wobbling hand, grabbed at a blue-glass dish.

She pulled back the glass cover of the trolley with relish, the frozen mist escaping again. 'I'll have some of it now, anyhow. It looks perfectly good. And I know it tastes good, too. Because what I didn't tell you was that I tried it yesterday. I don't care what you say: it *was* there yesterday. There were no other complaints, were there?'

'What do you mean?' Lorenzo was staring at Jacinta. 'What happened yesterday?'

'I gave some of it out as "tasters". You know, those tiny wooden spoons you give out when someone isn't certain if they want a flavour?' Jacinta grinned. 'I'm pretty certain it was *Perla D'Etna* I doled out. I took a taster spoon myself.'

'Oh. Tasters…' Lorenzo looked relieved.

He watched silently as Jacinta shovelled several scoops of the dark green-coloured ice-cream onto her dish, Roberta having fled back to her place.

Lovelace rolled his eyes discreetly at Posie. *A fuss about nothing.*

Posie didn't fancy anything more to eat, and neither did Lovelace, but they stood together anyhow, watching those at the ice-cream trolley serve themselves.

Nobody else took any of the *Perla D'Etna* flavour, as if by doing so they might risk another scene. Jacinta ate her ice-cream back at the table, and Lorenzo returned to her side, looking grim and thoughtful.

'I don't understand,' Fox muttered at them both on his way back to his seat, his dish stacked high with strawberry ice-cream. '*Who* put that green ice-cream in tonight's trolley, then? Was it Jacinta herself? Forcing him to move on?'

Posie shrugged. *Maybe.*

Banishing a ghost? Well, it was one way to do it.

'I can't say, Reverend Harkness,' answered Lovelace baldly, still standing against the wall. 'It all seems bally odd.'

But just at that moment all the lights in the room went out, and suddenly there was a strange stabbing, cutting noise.

Something like a swishing of air.

Duh-duh-duh, duh-duh-duh.

Duh.

Seven times.

Richard, quick as a flash, held Posie against the wall near the trolley, covering her entirely with his body.

Fox's voice rang through the strange, buzzing stillness which followed: 'What the blazes, sir? You all right?'

And then the lights came on again, and Jacinta pointed towards the middle of the table.

'Look!'

They all followed her gaze. Most of the plates had been cleared from the table by now, but the ivy and roses had been thrown to the floor, as if in a rage. A few ice-cream bowls remained.

But in the centre of the table was something new.

Silver kitchen knives, sharp as hell, and shining in the light.

Seven of the things.

They were nearest to Nella Harewood, near Posie's empty place, right in the centre of the table. But the odd thing, or the *oddest* thing, was the way they were grouped. They had been stuck down, point-down, into the table, through the white cloth, in a perfect ring. Like a knife-thrower's dream of symmetry.

Jacinta rose, as if in a trance.

'Stay there, Miss Glaysayer, please,' ordered Lovelace calmly, and Posie heard the worry in his voice, even if others didn't recognise it.

'No, Richard. This is meant for *me*. It's a sign.' Jacinta swallowed. 'This is a physical enactment of a card I keep seeing. "The Seven of Swords." I'm going to be betrayed.'

'Don't be crazy!' Lorenzo was pulling Jacinta back into her seat. 'These knives aren't near you, are they? It's nothing to do with you at all!'

But now Nella was standing up, reaching into the circle

of knives. 'Look!' she trilled, as if she were taking part in a treasure hunt at a party.

'There's something in the middle! Oh, this is just way too, too divine! Look!'

Nella Harewood had picked up a card. Posie recognised it at once. On it was the same figure Jacinta had shown her that morning in her studio, which she herself had ripped up, with a good deal of effort. The same image Lorenzo had later burnt outside his Gelateria.

The knight with his skull face on that white triumphant horse.

'It's "Death" of course,' said Jacinta, coolly, coming around to Nella, putting an arm about the beautiful girl's waist and taking the card from her. But then Jacinta gasped, and Posie saw that the back of the card was shining in the light.

A metallic, grey-green gleam.

'Oh!' exclaimed Jacinta softly. '*This* is the card! The card the woman has been trying to give me... So perhaps, after all, it is *I* who will be doing the betraying.'

Lorenzo was up on his feet and for the first time Posie saw real worry in his eyes: 'Not again! Put it down, *amore*! PLEASE! I think this is dangerous. This is something different entirely now. Come here.'

'Fine.' Jacinta returned to her place, but continued to stare at the grey-green card in her hands, as if hypnotised.

Posie saw how Richard and Fox were scanning the room, every professional instinct they possessed at work. Posie saw how Lovelace was exchanging meaningful looks with the oldest and most senior waiter, who had entered the room bearing cafetières of coffee. The small man was looking about himself with a new purpose. *A policeman?*

He must be.

In the not-even-a-minute in which the lights had been down these seven knives had appeared. But from *where* had the person come who had done such a thing? *Who* could have done it? A stranger? But that black-moustached older policeman had been standing outside the room, together with the younger horsey one, hadn't he?

One of them would have seen an intruder, surely?

Roberta stood up dramatically, clutching at her black-silk clad arms.

'It's Giulia,' she said, pointing around. 'She's *here*. Her spirit. And she is angry. *Il suo fantasma e tornato.* Don't you see?'

Lorenzo shook his head. 'This is *crazy*. Of course it's not Giulia. She was lovely: she was never malevolent in life. She wouldn't be in death, either. This is a simple case of the electrics failing us, again, and some crazy person – *Un matto* – taking advantage of that. But who would that be?'

He ran his fingers through his hair. 'This dinner is rapidly turning into chaos. I think we should all finish up. How you English say – "cut our losses"?'

Lovelace took command. He flashed a glance at the senior waiter again, who opened the door to the hallway, and stood with his body against it, ready to shepherd people out.

'I completely agree with you, Mr Rosario. Now, everyone here, please return to your rooms upstairs, or to your homes for the night. I appreciate it is early but we wouldn't want…'

And then two things happened at once.

The first was that the lights went off again. Not just the fairy lights in the dining-room this time but all the lights throughout the house.

'Nobody move!' called out Lovelace. He was still next to the ice-cream trolley, near the French doors, with Posie. Her heart beat faster, fear flooding her body in waves, her senses telling her to breathe as slowly as was possible. Not to panic.

And the second thing that happened was worse.

Far worse.

151

An odd rustle, a pronounced CLICK, and then a thud. A slight moan, a whimper in the night.

'What on earth was that?' yelled Fox, his disguise as the cool, cheery, improbably-attractive Reverend Harkness now abandoned for good.

'I don't know,' said Lovelace, who had grabbed Posie and pushed her with him to the floor.

'But it doesn't sound good. Sergeant Fox, run to the basement and get storm-lanterns. Everyone else – get down on the floor. I think someone has a gun in here.'

* * * *

Fourteen

But the lights came back on again almost as soon as the warning was out of Lovelace's mouth. People stared around, half-stupid, to see what damage might have been done.

At first nothing was obvious, and there was a collective sigh of relief.

But then Tony Harewood, at the table, started yelping, a strange moaning.

'Oh, no! Oh, no! Not Nella!'

The moan was quickly turning to mounting hysteria. 'I say, it should have been *me*! See? Red! We're both wearing red! *I* was the one they wanted. I was warned. It's all a stupid mistake.'

In a flash the damage was revealed.

Posie would never in her life forget the bizarre image before her.

Two women in red, with the same hair. One sitting bolt upright, the other – Nella Harewood – flung across the back of her chair, her arms flailing, her lips moving gently. A dark bloom of blood – almost unnoticed at first because of the scarlet colour of her dress – growing wider, heavier.

Deadlier.

Suddenly people were moving all in one rush: the older

153

waiter-cum-policeman was running for the telephone, for an ambulance; the young waiter with the blonde moustache was barring the door; Doctor Mozzato was at Nella's side, bending over her, listening for her breath, shaking his head despondently.

'*No. Assolutamente no.*'

No. No hope.

Charlie Seego was standing up uselessly, his face aghast, horrified. His angelic eyes were incredulous, his huge hands gripping the table. Lorenzo too was lurching over to be at Nella's side, completely white in the face, almost greenish in fact.

But it was Simon Deverine who struck through the useless group of men, elbowing his way past Mozzato, squatting down next to the chair, cradling his ex-wife in his arms, her blood spreading out all over his dress-shirt, her head lolling on his breast.

'NELLA!' he barked as if he was still in the RAF squadron he had served with. 'Nella? You hear me? Stay with us. By Gad. I'll not let you die here.'

And Posie found she had crept near enough to hear the rasping breath of the girl. She stood right behind the former spouses.

'I'm sorry.' Nella was pulling in air desperately through her shattered lungs. 'In my life, there are secrets too dark to let out. I didn't act alone. I'm sorry, Simon. I truly am.'

'Save your energy, Nella. Be a brick and bally well hold on. I'll get you to safety.'

I'm sorry.

I didn't act alone.

What was Nella talking about?

Suddenly Posie thought she might be sick as she felt a fierce jolt of pain rising up through her whole body, a sickening cramp. Like those times earlier.

She bent over double, holding the baby in her belly. *Not now. Please.*

And then she heard Nella's unmistakable last breaths, and then the sudden silence.

Followed by the sound of keening.

That was Tony Harewood, of course, who had now crumpled up and slipped under the table, hidden from the reality of life and death above her.

'Darling?' Richard was at her side, seeing her strange posture. 'Are you all right?'

But the pain had passed. Again. 'Quite all right.'

Fox was quickly beside Lovelace, pointing urgently. 'Sir? I think you should look there! His right-hand pocket, sir. Nearest Charlie Seego? See it?'

Fox was pointing at Simon Deverine, who was still holding the body of his former wife, fat silent tears running down his cheeks.

Lovelace darted over. And like a magician pulling a rabbit from a black-sateen top-hat, with a handkerchief wrapped expertly around the item, he pulled a sleek gun from the pocket of Simon Deverine's smoking jacket.

'Well, well, well.'

Everyone stared.

Lovelace sighed. 'I know this revolver. Saw it often enough myself in the Great War. An M&P; dashed accurate little blighter, issued in their thousands to army officers like me at the time. And, so it seems, to serving RAF officers, eh?'

There was no triumph on his face as he stared at Deverine, only a sort of sad resignation.

'I'll hazard some likely guesses, Mr Deverine. The first is that if I check out this gun's serial number here, I'll find this was issued to *you*, sometime after 1915, when it was brought in as standard issue. And my second guess is that when this very unfortunate young woman's body is assessed for murder, the bullet in her chest which killed her will be a perfect match for this M&P revolver. My third guess is that your fingerprints are all over this weapon. And a fourth – that the angle of the bullet will match exactly with your having shot your ex-wife from across the table just now. In the darkness.'

Posie looked first at her husband, then at Simon Deverine; at his raw, red face. He didn't seem to care that he was being accused of murder. He didn't look shocked, or surprised, or even remotely bothered, actually. It was as if anything which happened to him now didn't matter a jot.

Lovelace motioned towards the older waiter-cum-policeman who had just come back into the room.

'I'll take this moment to introduce my Italian colleague, Commissario Gianni Maturo, one of the most senior policemen in Florence's constabulary. He was kind enough to drive over here this afternoon, at my request, and get into "character". He's here with his best Sergeant, Lazzio.' He indicated to where the younger man with the blonde moustache was standing, arms crossed, by the door.

'Now Maturo will take over. After all, this is *his* patch, not mine: his jurisdiction, not mine. Although it seems to me that all we've got on our hands here is a sad little case of an English marital tragedy, but transported lock, stock and smoking barrel abroad.'

The diminutive Maturo stepped forward, and Posie saw that he had ripped off his black, curled moustache and his starched apron. But he still had the look of a waiter; eager to please, wondering just where the next summons would be coming from.

Maturo smiled in a friendly fashion, rubbed his hands together as if for warmth. When he spoke, his English was stilted, but excellent.

'Good evening, everybody. An ambulance is waiting outside, and I'll get the stretcher-bearers to come and take the body to the town morgue. Sergeant Lazzio will go with them and first thing tomorrow, the body of Lady Nella Harewood will be sent on to our experts in Florence. And sir,' here he patted Simon Deverine's shoulder, 'if *you* could come with me, I will ensure you have not one ounce of comfort tonight in San Gimignano's single medieval gaol cell. The San Gimignano Police Station forms part of the Town Hall, you see, so the cell is there too. And like your murder victim here, you too will come to Florence first thing tomorrow. But you will be coming for formal prosecution.'

The Commissario turned to Richard Lovelace. 'Thank you for everything, Inspector Lovelace. You were right: harm *did* come. What a pity we could not have prevented it, eh? But what a pleasure to work with you. I never thought the day would come when I would have the honour of working with the Chief Commissioner of the world-famous Scotland Yard!'

He clapped his hands together daintily. 'I appreciate this has been a shock for you all. Now, if there's any more funny business, Inspector Lovelace is in charge. But,' he crossed himself elaborately here, 'God willing, nothing else will happen tonight.'

And then Doctor Mozzato and Lazzio carried Nella's body, still on the chair, out of the room, and there was the sound of voices in the hallway, presumably the stretcher-bearers arriving.

Posie watched, scarcely believing her eyes as Commissario Maturo clipped shining handcuffs onto a now-silent Deverine, leading him out, then slamming the front door of the Guesthouse.

What a mess.

Posie exhaled, was about to bend down and help Tony up from the floor, but then she stopped mid-action, aware of a low but urgent voice.

It was Lorenzo Rosario, on the edge of an all-encompassing panic.

'Jacinta? *Amore?* Get up! GET UP!'

She saw Lorenzo standing at his former place, at the head of the table, bending over his fiancée.

Jacinta had collapsed face-down, her head in her blue-glass ice-cream bowl, her hand still clutching the tarot card with "Death" upon it.

'No!' Posie yelled, running to her friend. Tony Harewood was scrabbling up from under the table, and Lovelace was next to Posie now, as was Fox, both of them almost holding her back.

She found she was screaming: 'Has Jacinta been shot as well? *How on earth?* There was no spray of bullets, surely? Only the one! And Jacinta was in a completely different place! Jacinta?'

He must have heard the scream and doubled back, for here was Doctor Mozzato again.

The Doctor was gently pulling Jacinta Glaysayer up, but her eyes were open and staring, as if she had looked death right in the face and been surprised at what she had seen.

Her freckled wheat-ripe skin was coloured blue as a cornflower, and the blue suffused her lips, and her nose.

Even her hands were coloured bright blue, right to the tips of her fingers, throwing into stark relief the precious gold ring she wore, showing the towers of San Gimignano carved as a symbol of love and promise.

A promise of nothing.

Because Jacinta was as dead as a doornail and had been so for at least five minutes.

And no-one had even noticed.

* * * *

Fifteen

'She's not been shot,' said Doctor Mozzato in a calm, professional voice. 'She's been poisoned, and very recently. My recommendation is that no-one in this room touch anything on the table here. All of you, step away. Now.'

He gently bent Jacinta's body back as she had been lying, head down on the table. She looked as if she were simply resting her head; taking a minute just for herself.

That minute would now last forever.

Posie felt like wailing, a searing fury at her own uselessness threatening to overwhelm her.

Oh, Jacinta. You didn't ask me to help.

But you knew – or sensed – you were in danger, didn't you? I failed you.

Those cards…

Posie found herself staring hard at Lorenzo Rosario. He was standing as if rooted to the spot, mouthing words under his breath, a prayer maybe? Something over and over, at any rate.

His dark, limpid eyes were frighteningly calm, half-closed, and, when Roberta Grimaldi tried to pull something away from his hand, Posie watched him bat her away. But for a few seconds their eyes were locked in a strange shared desperation.

Posie saw then that Lorenzo was holding Jacinta's "Death" card in his hand, the one Nella Harewood had so casually laughed at, plucked from the centre of those knives, before Jacinta had claimed the card as her own, muttering on about her silly premonition.

Up close Posie could now see that the card had an intricate metallic grey-and-green pattern all over the back of it, resembling snake-skin. And the gleam of it was odd. It was creepy, somehow.

Hadn't Jacinta mentioned 'seeing' just such a card?

Posie forced herself to get a grip.

What kind of dreadful thing was happening here? What *had* happened here tonight?

As if he could read her mind, Lovelace muttered in her ear: 'Darling, you were right: there is something very evil in this house. But I will snuff it out. And I promise you this: we are going straight back home as soon as we can.'

She was about to reply that getting back home was the last thing on her mind; that she wasn't worried on her own account. And that if there was any snuffing out to be done, she would get on with it too.

But Lovelace was summoning everyone's attention.

'Listen up, everyone. You all heard Commissario Maturo, didn't you? I'm therefore doing as he commanded. You all know me as Richard, Posie's husband. But I'm now going to take charge formally as Chief Inspector. I'm also going to introduce you formally to my Sergeant.' Lovelace pointed at Fox, who took the opportunity to rip off his dog-collar.

Richard carried on, authoritatively: 'It will be necessary to make a quick body-search of each of you, and then accompany you to your rooms, where you will be locked in overnight. You will be guarded. We'll do this to ensure everyone's safety. As soon as we are able to, in the next couple of hours, we will come to each of you for a full statement regarding both deaths. I will also ask you to relinquish all travel papers such as identity cards or passports to me. Do you all understand?'

Silence met this command, and a heavy, almost suffocating fear hung over the room, but through it all a sniffling, slight crying noise could be heard just outside the door. The sound of heavy breathing.

'It's the maid,' muttered Posie in Richard's ear. She checked her wristwatch. It was ten o'clock. 'Jacinta had given her the night off, but Gloria must have returned fairly recently. Maybe she ran into the ambulance men and heard the news?'

There was a whimpering sound from outside, too, and a slight mournful howl.

Patsy.

'Fox,' snapped Lovelace. 'Get outside and find out how much Gloria knows, will you? Ask her to show you the telephone apparatus and get a call put through to Maturo at the Town Hall and tell him what's happened here: tell him to get as many local town bobbies as they can manage. See that anyone else down in the kitchen – the caterers, or the wine men – remains within the Guesthouse. Keep them in the kitchen if possible.'

'On it, sir.'

When Fox had disappeared, Doctor Mozzato spoke up. He had been examining a wine glass on the table with a great deal of preoccupation. He looked like a fusty owl, a librarian.

'*Ispettore?*'

'Mnnn? Is it important?'

'Yes. Evidence, I think.'

The man was cool, Posie would give him that, but she couldn't see for a moment what a girl like Roberta might see in him.

'Go on.'

'I told you already that Miss Glaysayer has been poisoned. See the blue tinge? It's probably arsenic. Or a poison in that chemical group. Drugs are a kind of speciality of mine, actually. When I'd finished my examination of Miss Glaysayer, I happened to look over at the half-full glass nearest her plate – this red wine here, see? – and it has a sediment within it.'

Lorenzo Rosario appeared to be coming back to his senses, and an angry force came alive in him. He looked incredulously at the Doctor. 'Red wine *always* has a sediment in it, Mozzato! What are you talking about, man?'

The Doctor continued, unflustered. 'Don't be offended, Lorenzo. San Martin wine is excellent, of course, but this *particular* glass has a peculiarly large amount of a mostly-undissolved bright green sediment at the bottom. It has the appearance of a certain type of arsenic to me. The wine will eventually turn green as the poison is slowly dissolved. I think this type is usually used to kill rats. I strongly advise you to keep this glass, *Ispettore*, and perhaps the bottles of wine on the table too…and you should have them all tested.'

Richard Lovelace nodded. 'Absolutely. Now, everyone line up here, by the door. As far from the table as you can manage; yes, that's right. In a row, please. No talking. Quick as you can.'

There was a sudden burst of angry exclamations and curses in Italian.

'How can you be so insensitive, Inspector? You're treating us like suspects,' blurted out Roberta Grimaldi, looking all about her with her wide, amber eyes.

Lovelace harrumphed. 'That's because you *are* indeed all potential suspects, so I will treat you how I bally well wish. Now, Miss Grimaldi, maybe you can go first? I know you live in a flat over the ice-cream shop but you can jolly well spend tonight here under lock and key. In fact, you can stay in Miss Glaysayer's studio-room, downstairs. And *you* will stay here too, Mr Rosario. You can have Deverine's room, once we've thoroughly searched it.'

'As you wish,' muttered Lorenzo softly. 'Although it would not be my preferred place.'

Beggars can't be choosers, Posie thought sourly.

Lorenzo kept looking over at his dead fiancée in complete disbelief. He stuffed the green tarot card in an inside pocket.

Lovelace leaned over: 'I'll be having that, Mr Rosario, please, as evidence.'

Lorenzo surrendered the card without question, almost dumbly.

He hasn't fully accepted her death yet, thought Posie. *It's not real to him.*

But is it real for any of us?

Fox returned to the dining-room, his step firm and authoritative.

'No-one else is here, sir. The caterers left an hour back. Apparently, they had instructions they could leave before the self-service ice-cream course started. None of the San Martin Vineyard men are around, or anyone else, for that matter.'

'We'll need statements anyway. Chase them all in the morning.'

'Of course, sir.'

'Let's get everyone out of here. Search each person, Sergeant Fox.'

Then, at Lovelace's command, Fox moved towards Roberta, but she started squirming, her face flushed red with shame. 'I will not let him touch me! No way. A man! An *English* man! A man I thought until a few minutes ago was an ordained priest!'

'Why is Sergeant Fox so terrible?' asked Lovelace, but a bit uneasily, as he was a gentleman through and through and saw now how it was all in fact very awkward. 'Do you have something to hide?'

'Here,' said Posie, stepping forward, 'let me help. *I'll* search the two women, and *you* can search the men and then me, Sergeant. I've been in this room too all evening and I insist on being treated just the same.'

As Sergeant Fox started to search Charlie Seego, then took him back to his room, Posie systematically worked from the top of Roberta's head to the tips of her toes. She patted all down the silk blackness of the dress, the worn and darned stockings underneath.

In the two deep pockets of the dress Posie found only a few coins. There was also a small, cheap, travel powder-compact. Posie handed the compact back to Roberta, who eyed Posie with a sullen anger.

But why would a girl who hardly ever wore make-up be carrying a face powder?

'Hang about.'

Posie grabbed back the compact. In a flash she pulled it open, and a mist of white powder flew up into the air from inside. A snow-storm in springtime.

'Aha!'

Lovelace came over and took the compact.

'What do we have here then, Miss?' he asked calmly. Roberta had begun to shake, holding herself against the wall. There came a sort of muffled moan from Lorenzo, who covered his face in despair.

So he had known, then.

Lovelace licked his finger and tasted the powder.

Posie grabbed at his arm. 'Darling! *No!* It could be...'

'Don't worry, Posie. This isn't arsenic. As you'd say – sure as bread is bread. It's cocaine. Isn't that right, Miss Grimaldi?'

The girl nodded, and misery etched Roberta's body, her every move.

Posie was aware of Lorenzo behind them all, watching, rocking himself back and forth on his patent-leather heels in misery.

Roberta balled her hands up and rubbed at her eye sockets, tired, desperate, beyond help.

How had Posie not seen before that the girl was an addict? The glittery eyes, the jitteriness, being always on edge. The disappearing for things upstairs. Random naps.

A horrible thought flashed through Posie's mind: was *this* the reason why Roberta worked for next to nothing at the Gelateria? Did Lorenzo pay her in drugs? Had she got herself so addled by the stuff she couldn't see a way to realising her own true worth?

Roberta hung her head: 'What will you do with me, Mr Lovelace?'

Lovelace pocketed the compact. 'Well, you being a drug addict is none of my business, Miss Grimaldi. I'm here to catch a murderer, and, unless you have anything to tell me on that, you're in no trouble. Not *yet*.'

Roberta was casting desperate looks over at Doctor Mozzato as Sergeant Fox returned and led her away. It was interesting, Posie noted, how the Doctor didn't look at Roberta once. He almost turned his back on her.

There go her chances with him, Posie thought to herself.

Posie searched Tony Harewood next, whose whole slim body was trembling violently. There was nothing of any interest in among the pockets of her washed-silk dress, nor in the beaded red bag. The bag was pretty empty, with only a virtually-finished red lipstick inside, together with a tiny, battered tin box of 'Derwent' travel paints and a miniscule watercolour pad. It was an odd choice of item to bring to a wedding party, and while Posie didn't say as much, Tony must have guessed at her incomprehension.

Lady Tony's teeth were chattering wildly, but she tried to speak: 'I take my paint things everywhere. You never know what might prove inspirational, or memorable, do you? I often paint tiny pictures, then re-create them on a bigger scale later. Usually when travelling. Waiting about.'

'I'd love to see your work one of these days, Lady Tony. Mountains, mostly, isn't it?'

'Yes. Mainly.'

Tony accompanied Sergeant Fox up to her attic room, still shaking, and then so did Lorenzo, whose own body-search had revealed absolutely nothing controversial.

Then it was just Lovelace, Posie and the Doctor left.

They all turned instinctively away from the body at the table. Looked away from those seven kitchen knives still stabbed into the table in their immaculate circle.

'You want me to stay here too, *Ispettore*?' asked the Doctor. 'In the Guesthouse, tonight?'

Lovelace shook his head. 'That won't be necessary. Go home. If anything occurs to you, write it down. Ah, that must be Commissario Maturo now!'

A rapping noise, over and over, could suddenly be heard at the front door of the Guesthouse. In the bowels of the building, a small dog barked for her Mistress.

The Doctor walked with them to the front door. Lovelace paused before opening the door.

'One thing, Doctor. Did you know that Roberta Grimaldi is a cocaine addict? Had you any idea?'

The Doctor shook his head. 'Why should I, *Ispettore*? I barely know the girl. *Mamma Mia*! I wasn't entirely sure why she invited me along tonight – I wish in heaven's name she hadn't! – but it seemed polite to accept: we will be neighbours soon, you know. She was one of the applicants for a nice little flat in the tower where I live and I understood her to be a most sensible sort of person. Modest. But now I see I was very wrong. It's a disgrace! A drug-addict! And who knows if she's caught up in these murders?'

'Thank you. That will be all.'

And in the sea-change which occurred, in the sweeping entry of the wave which was Commissario Maturo and Lazzio and at least three local policemen in shiny black-suited uniforms heavy with medals, Posie found she had been washed up, cast asunder, placed in the safety of her own large quiet room.

A supposed oasis of calm and protection.

She lay on the bed and looked at her watch. Almost eleven o'clock.

Time passed.

But Posie was wide, wide awake, waiting for something to happen.

* * * *

Sixteen

In the eerie silence of the Guesthouse, Posie tried to think of nothing.

Outside the weather was turning. A light rain smattered the windows and a sudden breeze blew through the long room, throwing open all the balcony doors, then banging them shut again. The electric lamp on the night-table flickered, as did the candle which stood in a storm-lantern beside it.

A storm was coming.

Nothing like the storm inside here, Posie thought miserably. What a dreadful thing. Two women dead, murdered. On 'her' watch.

One of whom had been a friend, teetering on the brink of an unhoped-for happiness. A good girl.

Clear your mind.

But instead, the opposite was happening.

Images were flashing before Posie's eyes, vivid and disjointed. Things Posie had seen, or maybe imagined? Things connecting the people – the living and the dead – she had been with at dinner.

Death on his horse, of course. Both now and back in December, when he had come wrapped up in glimmery Christmas envelopes for Giulia Rosario. "Death" who had come – surrounded by a ring of seven knives – for Jacinta tonight.

She recalled Jacinta's words: '*The Seven of Swords… I'm going to be betrayed or let down by someone on the inside.*'

Who? Who had betrayed her? *Why?* Why had Jacinta had to die?

Or had it been an accident? Had that arsenic-spiked wine been destined for another? And if so, who?

And now Posie was thinking of other knives. Knives stabbing stupid little notes to Lady Tony's door. Notes which made no sense except as vague threats.

'*I know your game.*'

But *what* game? Did Lady Tony know more than she was letting on? She seemed to be hitting with an extraordinarily straight bat, as far as Posie was concerned, candidly confessing her money troubles and even admitting that she had hoped to touch her rich cousin for money.

Posie sat up, staring into the semi-darkness of the room.

But all she saw now was the face of Lady Nella Harewood in the doorway of the dining-room as she had arrived late for dinner in her red gown; triumphant, angry, drunk. Her cut-you-to-the-quick putting down of Jacinta: '*…you look absolutely frightful.*'

But the words had been loaded, heavy. Nella had carried on, insult after insult: '*What a choice to make! What a let-down for yourself! Couldn't you have chosen differently?*'

What on earth had Jacinta done to Nella to deserve such scorn? For Nella to insult her host – an old school friend, too – in such a public manner was crazy, even allowing for the drunkenness.

And then Posie tried to blot out the image of Nella's dying, beautiful face, her flailing arms. The ex-husband who refused to leave her.

Had Simon Deverine really shot his wife?

It didn't make sense. And Deverine, in cradling the dying Nella, insisting he would get her to safety, hadn't acted like a man who had just shot at her on purpose. Either Simon Deverine was an almightily good actor, or else he had been framed.

Posie was inclined towards believing the latter.

But who had shot Nella if not her ex-husband?

If Simon Deverine was tried in England for this murder, he would hang if found guilty. Public opinion was not on his side anyway. It would be a case of death following death.

Had *that* been the point of all this?

But why then go to the trouble of killing the two women in different ways? It was complicated, not to mention risky.

Were they looking for one killer, or two?

And where did Roberta fit in, with her now-obvious drug habit? And Lorenzo? How must *he* be feeling now? What – if anything – had been his part in tonight's tragedies?

Posie was sure he had had nothing to do with Jacinta's dying. His plans to turn the Guesthouse into a smart restaurant could never proceed now. Legally he owned none of Jacinta's property, and he never would.

And what about Charlie Seego? His maps? His German newspapers? His typewriter? His involvement in the notes on Tony Harewood's door? *What exactly was he doing here?* Was he involved in one of the deaths, or both?

Thoughts reeling, Posie walked towards the desk, where Richard – in what now seemed another lifetime ago – had heaped carefully-wrapped presents from the toyshop for his daughters in a pile.

There was also a small, navy-blue box on the desk, not wrapped.

Posie flipped the lid up and smiled. Inside the lid was stamped the swirling name of the jeweller, Macallè, and nestled within the blue velvet of the box itself was a beautifully-plain, fine silver bracelet; a tiny clasp-button engraved with the towers of San Gimignano being its only adornment. It was lovely, and Posie felt half-guilty at stumbling across the unexpected present, not yet given to her.

She closed the box and placed it back where it had been, on Richard's copy of *The Times*. She noted how he had circled a story, and saw quickly it was the same thing he had been speaking about earlier: about Neville Coleman's estate.

Just then there was a knock at the door. Posie looked at the time. Midnight.

She'd never felt more awake in all her life.

She was still wearing her golden evening gown, and she grabbed at her quilted, comfy dressing-gown to cover it, grateful for its familiarity and warmth. She stood at her locked door, apprehensive, hands instinctively over her belly, protectively.

'Hello?'

'It's me, Miss,' came the cracked tones of Gloria. 'I've got a nice cuppa fer you here, Miss. Your 'usband ordered me to bring you some tea and biscuits. He's jus' arrived back in the building. He sez he'll be along this way soon.'

Posie opened the door and let the maid in. Patsy tripped in, too, looking inquisitively about, from left to right, as if seeking out Jacinta.

Posie saw, with a sudden stab of sadness, that Patsy had a gold lamé bow in her hair at the front, and that Jacinta must have tied it there earlier in the evening, a perfect match for her own odd dress.

Posie cleared a space between the stack of presents and the papers on the desk, and Gloria set down a tea-pot in a knitted orange cosy and a very small tin of McVitie's custard creams.

'Custard creams?' said Posie, eyebrow raised. 'Out here? How did you manage *that*?'

'I have my ways, Miss. You 'elp yourself. Go on. You've 'ad a terrible shock, Miss.'

'Well, so have you. Won't you have a cup yourself?'

'Don't mind if I do, Miss. Oh, *poor* Miss Glaysayer. I'll pour for us both, eh?'

Half a cup of tea later, and several biscuits consumed, Posie realised there was something Gloria had on her mind. And at last, the woman spoke up.

'It wasn't my place to say anythin', Miss, bein' only a servant. But I felt somethin' tragic might happen, all along. I think the Mistress was sort of "dazzled" by Mr Rosario. Irksome man! An' I make no apologies for sayin' it.'

'You don't like Lorenzo Rosario, Gloria?'

'Well, I won't say he isn't easy on the eye, Miss. I'd be lyin'. But looks aren't all they're cracked up to be, are they? Once the initial glow wears off. I'll tell yer this: bad luck follows that man around like a bad smell.'

'Giulia, you mean?'

'Aye. And the way he took over the Grimaldi family business. It's a scandal.'

'I quite agree,' said Posie sadly.

'And it was goin' to be the same story here. Miss Glaysayer's nice little Guesthouse was about to be shut down and I was goin' to be given the heave-ho by that jumped-up Lothario. I wish to goodness this engagement – and tonight's dinner – had never happened.'

Posie was interested in Gloria's turn of phrase. 'A "Lothario"? Do you have any actual proof Mr Rosario was having affairs, Gloria? Someone specific?'

Gloria took another slurp of tea. Posie didn't hurry her, spooned more sugar into her own half-cold tea. Patsy, sitting trembling on the cold floor, suddenly leapt up into Posie's lap, where there wasn't much room, and hunkered down there.

'Well…'

'It could be important, Gloria.' Posie stroked Patsy tentatively. The dog felt nice. Warm, trusting.

'I dunno, Miss. It was a feelin' I had. I'd asked around

– carefully, mind you – several times, among the servants in the town. I almost felt I'd done Mr Rosario a disservice, actually, because no reports came back about him with any local women at all. It's not his fault, after all, that he's so blimmin' handsome, is it? But then, finally, I saw somethin', Miss. With my own two eyes.'

'Oh?'

Posie put down her cup and saucer. Heard the dog start to snore.

'It was just this mornin', Miss. Very early. I was on the doorstep beatin' them rag rugs. I saw Mr Rosario out on the square, Miss.'

'I see.'

'I could hear 'em, Miss, when they all returned from that San Martin Vineyard. All of them drinkin', and then Mr Rosario and Miss Glaysayer spent some time privately together in her studio. I don't know where Miss Roberta and Lady Tony were at this point, but at dawn Mr Rosario left here and went off home. To a *real* homecomin' by the looks of things!'

Gloria coughed tellingly. 'I couldn't see it all, Miss Parker, but he was holding onto a woman, outside that Gelateria. *Passionate*, like.'

'Who was she?' Posie almost whispered.

A shrug. 'Couldn't see much. A nice blue dress.'

'Oh.' Posie tried her best to conceal her disappointment. *Was there really nothing more?* At least the reality of the woman in Lorenzo's arms had now been corroborated by a no-nonsense pair of eyes such as Gloria's. Posie had begun to think it had all been a figment of her imagination.

Gloria rose.

Outside in the corridor there was the hurrying sound of footsteps. Posie recognised them at once as Richard's.

'If you need me, Miss, I'll be in my room. I'll stay on at the Guesthouse as long as I'm needed, and then I'll book my train back home to London.'

'Jolly good. Thank you.'

'That slip of a dog looks happy with you, poor thing. If she's any trouble, just bring her down to me, Miss. Not that I can abide much with dogs; I only put up with this one for the Mistress' sake.'

At the door, Gloria turned, her frown heavy. 'There's somethin' you should know, Miss. I'm not one to put two and two together and make five, but *you* are. And that blue dress I saw…'

'Yes?' Posie's heart beat a little faster.

'There's a dress made of a shimmery, fancy royal-blue material right 'ere in this very Guesthouse. I saw it earlier, when I was carryin' water about the place like some overworked mule.'

She rolled her eyes upwards.

'The attic?'

Gloria tapped her nose. 'As I said, Miss: your job is puttin' things together, an' mine is jus' servin'. And sometimes watchin'. Takin' it all in.'

Just then Richard came crashing through the door.

* * * *

Seventeen

'What's that you're holding, darling? Oh, Jacinta's dog? Good grief! What's that doing here? Oh, well, if you're happy. Look, I've got Fox with me and we need to catch up. It will have to be in here.'

He came swiftly through the bedroom carrying a worn-looking black leather attaché case which Posie had never seen before – but which looked like regulation Scotland Yard issue – presumably something which poor Fox had been tasked with lugging all the way out to Italy.

Richard caught sight of Gloria, and smiled.

'Gloria, thanks for making Posie comfortable. What a bally dreadful night, eh? I couldn't trouble you to bring some more tea, could I, for me and my Sergeant?'

Gloria grinned. ''Course. I'll be right up, Inspector.'

Posie headed to the biggest table in the room, which was nearest the balcony facing the Cisterna Square. Fox dragged the desk chair towards the table and collapsed down into it, momentarily sitting with his head between his hands, exhausted.

'I feel like that myself, lad,' said Lovelace, gently. Lovelace pulled up a chair for Posie and she sat, still holding Patsy. He looked at his wife keenly, as if assessing whether she was really up to helping out, but he obviously decided not to say anything.

Instead, he pulled off his tight bow-tie, unpinned his starched collars and dropped them all on the floor. He got out a police notebook from the black attaché case and threw it on the table in front of him.

Posie had taken up one of her own notebooks and she opened it to a fresh page, with her silver pencil at the ready.

'As I mentioned,' Richard said in a low voice, 'we have no Incident Room at all. *This* will have to do for now. The dining-room downstairs has been locked; everything left on the table as it was, with two of the town's bobbies standing guard at the two exits of the dining-room. Maturo and his Sergeant are dealing with all the practicalities, and will sleep over at the Hotel Dante tonight, like Fox here. I sense the Italians are raring to get back to Florence tomorrow and wrap this all up. Understandably, perhaps.'

He sighed. 'Commissario Maturo tells me there's no Forensic lab in this town, and he's called out his team from Florence. They'll set off at first light.'

Lovelace checked his watch. 'They will be here at eight o'clock, latest. It's not ideal at all, but it's the best we can do in the circumstances.'

Posie raised an eyebrow. 'So, the wine glass with the green poison in it which Jacinta drank from, and the other wine glasses are all just sitting down there? Arsenic, or whatever it is, dissolving. Evidence eroding?'

Lovelace splayed his hands. 'What else can we do?'

'Nothing, I suppose.'

'The Forensics lads will work quickly. On the spot, with a mobile laboratory. We can add their findings to what we've found out tonight about the victims, and the suspects.'

Lovelace reached for his cigarette case. 'You know, I think this is the first case I've worked where I was present at two murders and yet haven't the foggiest idea what actually happened. Or *why*.'

Fox sighed. 'Me too, sir. It's like some sort of nightmare.

Those lights going on and off. Those seven knives. The first girl dying, the second one already dead. It gives me the creeps.'

Richard lit up a Turkish cigarette and inhaled, drawing the nicotine deep into his lungs with pleasure.

'Oh, buck up, Sergeant. It's not as if an invisible, supernatural cause were at work, is it? This is a human tragedy. A first-class shame. We'll solve this one way or another. It's *our* case, even if it happened on Tuscan soil. We'll have to take old Deverine back with us in custody on the train, I expect. He'll hang, poor devil. He's spent his life in the glare of publicity, and he'll die in the glare of it too.'

Posie stared at her husband. 'That's what you think, darling? That Simon Deverine is at the root of all of this? Have you seen him since I came up here to rest?'

'Yes.' Lovelace flicked through some pages in his notebook. 'We dropped in on everyone else first; asked questions and searched their rooms, and then we went to check on Deverine in the cell at the Town Hall. We've come straight from there, actually. He's comfortable, despite what Maturo promised.'

'What's Deverine saying?' asked Posie, curious.

Lovelace stabbed his pencil at something he'd written.

'Deverine says he's innocent. Although he does admit the gun, the M&P, belongs to him; says he famously carries it everywhere he goes, but claims he certainly didn't take it down to dinner with him. Left it in his room, in a black-velvet travel pouch at the back of an unlocked cupboard. He says it was planted on him. Insists he didn't kill his ex-wife. Says he had no motive.'

'I think I agree with him, sir,' cut in Fox. 'Wasn't the divorce all wrapped up? I'd say he appeared like a man wanting to move on. Maybe meet a new woman? Did you see the way he was genuinely enjoying Roberta Grimaldi's company?'

Posie agreed. 'Besides, Simon Deverine and Nella Harewood didn't even know they were going to be meeting here at this dinner tonight! It was all a horrible coincidence.'

Lovelace shrugged. 'Maybe this was an opportunistic crime? Deverine was suddenly in the same place as his ex-wife again and he lost control?'

Posie shook her head. 'But why? *He* was the one who caused a scandal in Soho. It wasn't Nella who shamed him. What had *she* done that meant she had to die? It's all wrong.'

Lovelace took another long drag. 'Maybe he couldn't bear the thought of Nella not being his wife anymore? Thought she'd struck up a new romance? The old green-eyed monster? Jealousy, it's at the root of many murders.'

Posie shrugged. 'I still don't accept that he murdered her.'

Lovelace stubbed out the remains of his smoke, and took up his pencil, suddenly looping swirls on his page, connecting ideas with arrows. 'Or how's this for an idea? Maybe Deverine felt resentful at having paid Nella all that money in a settlement? Maybe the fella needs it back? Perhaps the money comes back to him, on her death?'

'No, Richard. That scenario doesn't hang right.'

And Posie explained the conversation she'd overheard earlier between Deverine and Jacinta Glaysayer out on the corridor. 'I don't think Nella's settlement was as much as we were all led to believe in the press. Deverine hinted at some jiggery-pokery with shares in some mining company, protected so that Nella couldn't touch it. And Deverine seems to have plenty of wealth left for himself.'

Posie stared now at her husband's notes. She could, in truth, make neither head nor tail of them. She scribbled some of her own thoughts down clearly in her own notebook.

No random swirls anywhere.

Posie stabbed at her book, almost angrily: 'And anyhow, how does Simon Deverine killing his ex-wife fit in with

Jacinta being poisoned at the same time, at the same table? It seems madness. Deverine wouldn't kill his own Goddaughter! Not in a million years. He adored Jacinta.'

Lovelace sighed, exasperated. 'I agree, darling. We must be looking at a second killer for Jacinta. Deverine is our first murderer, though. For Lady Nella.'

Posie shook her head.

'No. I think we are looking at a different killer, or *killers*, for both women. Or else, we're not seeing this crime – these crimes – as we should. What on earth was the reason for both of these deaths?'

Lovelace counted on his fingers. 'Who knows? Same old story. It will be one of the usual old reasons: love, or money. Or maybe both. But it's usually money.'

The clatter of a tea-tray made them all turn to the door. Gloria was backing in, the same tray laden up again, the specially-hoarded custard creams this time on a plate with a little lace doily.

'That will be all, Gloria.' Lovelace smiled. 'I like it brewed a bit; we'll pour in a minute. You go and have a sleep now.'

But the woman was reluctant to go. She stood on the terracotta tiles in the low light, almost wringing her hands. The silence enabled them all to hear the sound of rain, hard now, slapping down on the roof.

'Is there something else, Gloria?' asked Posie. 'Something you wish to tell us?'

For a second Gloria looked embarrassed.

'It's jus', as I was comin' in with the tea-tray jus' now, I couldn't help but overhear you talkin' about *money*.'

Lovelace nodded, smiled. 'That's right, Gloria. Did it jog a memory for you? Something to do with Miss Glaysayer's money, was it?'

'Nah, I don't know nuffink about *that*. But…oh well, you might as well hear it. It quite slipped my mind when I was talkin' to Miss Parker in 'ere earlier.'

Gloria explained that in the course of her evening's duties she had lingered on the landing outside the attic room, shared since the early afternoon by the pair of blonde, aristocratic Harewood cousins.

'Not my fault if I've got a light step, is it? I heard a fair bit. And it was money *they* were arguin' about, between themselves. A proper barney! Real angry words bein' said.'

'Oh?' Lovelace frowned. 'Did you hear what the Harewood women were saying *exactly*?'

Gloria drew herself up. 'Near 'nuff, I reckon, sir. It was the beauty, Nella, who was hoppin' mad. She'd been up there drinkin' since she'd arrived. She was almost shoutin'! I 'eard her say: "*I'm completely mad at you! It's my money! It's not right!*"'

Lovelace was puzzled. '"*It's not right!*"? Did you hear any more, Gloria? Bally good work, by the way.'

Gloria flushed and shook her head in disappointment. 'Nah, not much, if I'm honest, sir. She was passionate, I'll give 'er that, Lady Nella. Had a real spark to her. Not like her cousin, Lady Tony: she's a real cool customer. I fink Lady Tony said: "*Who are you to tell me what's right?*" and then I'm pretty certain Lady Tony said somethin' else which didn't make much sense to me. Sounded like: "*You're just jealous of Jacinta. That's all. And good for her, I say.*"'

'Did you hear any more?'

'Nah, I didn't, sir. Sorry.'

'Very well. Thank you.'

But just as Gloria was pulling the door to, Posie called out again, with a note of interest rather than emergency in her voice: 'Gloria? I wonder, did you *like* the Harewood cousins? Lady Nella? Lady Tony?'

Gloria stared in surprise. 'It's not my job to "like" anyone, Miss, is it? I didn't know Lady Nella, only from the newspapers, but like I said, she was a real personality. What a tragedy.'

'And Lady Tony? You saw her here more often, of

course? Do *you* like her, Gloria? I'm interested, that's all. It seems to me several people don't really like Lady Tony, and she's been getting some strange messages. *Threats*, really.'

'I admire Lady Tony, Miss. She's been through a lot, by all accounts, and she's been awful loyal to Miss Glaysayer. Even in that argument I overheard with her cousin, she was happy to defend the Mistress against Lady Nella. That counts for a lot, in my books.'

The maid looked anxious. 'I hope you're not thinkin' *I've* got anythin' to do with any threats, Miss?'

'Of course not. I value your opinion. Thank you, Gloria.'

After she'd left, Lovelace looked questioningly at his wife. 'Something, or nothing, Posie? You seemed to have an idea about that little overheard exchange between the Harewood cousins, or am I wrong?'

'Yes, I think I have some idea.'

She explained about Lady Tony's need for ready money.

'It was one of the main reasons she invited Nella here, actually. I think Gloria overheard the tail end of that conversation. Maybe Tony had asked for cash just one time too many? Maybe Nella's money was being run down too fast?'

Lovelace exhaled in a weary way. Threw his pencil down. 'It seems to me we're wasting precious time on the drunken ramblings of a spoiled, cross woman, denying her cousin a small monetary favour.'

Fox folded his arms, serious. 'But what was that thing about being jealous, sir? Because that's interesting. It gives us a new angle, if Lady Nella – our first murder victim – was jealous of the second murder victim. Doesn't it?'

'Dashed if I know, Fox.'

'Oh! Goodness…'

Posie almost spoke aloud, an idea coming suddenly and clearly into her mind, forming and taking shape there, but she was aware she needed evidence before committing herself to her theory.

She watched as her husband moved on, writing down more notes.

'So,' she said, folding her arms over her belly, careful not to knock Patsy off her knees, 'did Deverine have anything else interesting to say, or to show you tonight?'

Lovelace looked his wife square in the eye. 'There *was* one thing of interest, actually. But Deverine didn't show it to us. We found it. It was a note, up in his room here. We searched Deverine's room before sticking Lorenzo Rosario inside it for the night – with a local bobby guarding the door, of course – a couple of hours back.'

'A note?' asked Posie, curious. 'Handwritten?'

'No. A typed note, pushed under the door. We took it to Deverine and he claimed he'd never seen it before.'

Lovelace dug in the attaché case and shook out a small typed note on foolscap paper, the exact type of which Posie had seen earlier in the evening.

'Here.'

She read:

DEVERINE,
     WE HAVE MUCH IN COMMON. WE NEED TO SPEAK ABOUT SOMETHING WHICH IS VALUABLE TO YOU.
     LATER TONIGHT?
     CHARLIE SEEGO.

Fox explained: 'Deverine claims he's never seen the note, which makes sense, if Mr Seego put it under Deverine's door after Deverine had already gone down for dinner. Seego came down later, remember? About eight-thirty? He was only invited to the dessert.'

'Deverine told us he'd never met Seego before, and had

never even heard the man's name! *As if!'* muttered Lovelace, slightly crossly.

Posie read the note again. 'Why *not* believe Deverine, darling? This note seems like a first introduction by Seego, albeit a mysterious one. "*We need to speak.*"'

Posie stopped, biting at her lip. 'Have you asked Seego about it?'

Lovelace laughed, but without any humour. 'Of course we have! We questioned him up in his room. He admitted it was from him, but said it was a private matter. I wondered for a brief moment there if Seego was some kind of hit-man; hired to kill Nella Harewood on behalf of Deverine. Here to do the act, and pick up the payment. It's a dashed odd sort of note to send, though, if so.'

Posie shook her head. 'This note is written as if between equals, like a business note. And why would a hit-man hang about after having completed his "hit"? It's too dangerous.' She traced the typed name with her gold-painted fingernail. 'Have you had any luck finding out about Seego at Scotland Yard, Sergeant? Is there a criminal past?'

Fox sighed dejectedly. 'I've had nothing back at all, Miss. I think the Yard have drawn a blank. Both the Inspector and I think the man must have an assumed identity. Seego seems familiar, and unsavoury, but we don't know why.'

'So he wasn't cooperative, up in his room?'

Lovelace harrumphed, lighting another smoke. He looked cross, but at himself more than anything. He was reaching into the black bag again, pulling out documents. 'I've messed up, actually, darling. Big time.'

'Oh?'

Lovelace indicated towards a navy-and-gold English passport. 'Seego was hardly communicative, but he handed over his identity documentation and wrote out a Witness Statement with no fuss. Here it all is. But all the rooms have small working fireplaces in them, which I didn't appreciate. So Seego managed – in the time between safe return to his room and when we appeared again more than an hour later – to burn a good deal of his papers. No idea why he felt the need to get rid of it, but when he was questioned, Seego was unapologetic. Laughed when we asked him what he'd been burning. Said it was just a lot of hot air; speculation.'

Posie had picked the passport up and was staring at the cropped studio portrait of the large, blonde man with his angel's gaze.

She sighed and flicked through his passport, which had very few stamps.

There was a British 'DEPARTURE' stamp, dated a few months before, in late September of the previous year, 1924. Another one, an 'ENTER' one for Britain, early this February, 1925. The next 'DEPARTURE' stamp from Britain was a little over a week ago. There was a corresponding French stamp, and then an Italian 'ARRIVO', from a few days before.

But Seego's travel stamp pages contained gaps, for sure, certainly from September 1924 until February this year.

So where had he been? In the countries depicted in the strange maps pasted up in his room? Or in Germany, where the newspaper had come from? But then why were there no German stamps in his passport? Or any others, for that matter?

What had he been up to in those missing months between September 1924 and February 1925?

She looked up. 'Did you see the big maps with the pins on them pasted onto the wall in Seego's room? Several of them? His room looked like some sort of command centre to me.'

Both Lovelace and Fox shook their heads, staring at Posie intently. 'Maps? No, by the time we entered those had gone. You're sure?'

'Yes.'

'Of what? Of here? San Gimignano?'

Posie wracked her brains, but it had been a second's

worth of a stolen, aborted glimpse. 'I don't think so. They were orange, or red. But beyond that I really don't know. Sorry.'

'Never mind.'

Lovelace had put Seego's passport back down on the table. 'He won't be going far, anyhow: not while I keep this. Maps or no maps. What the blazes is the fella up to?'

'Wish I knew, sir,' groaned Fox. 'But I swear a good deal of what was in that grate were burnt telegrams. And I saw him, sir, yesterday, while I was undercover in the town. He was going backwards and forwards to the main San Gimignano Post Office. At least three times. I'm guessing he was mainly sending and receiving telegrams, sir. And that's handy for us. If Commissario Maturo agrees, we can trace the telegrams.'

'Good lad. Get onto it first thing.'

Lovelace raked through his hair, which looked a burning auburn in this strange half-light. He started to take out more documents from the black bag, more Witness Statements, and more personal identity papers. Each handwritten statement was pinned to its respective maker's passport.

He laid them all down neatly, in a row, starting with Charlie Seego's. Here was Roberta Grimaldi's beige-cardboard Italian passport with its blazing legend on the front '*PASSAPORTO per L'estero*'; the inside pages all blank and unstamped, a testimony to a life untravelled. And Lorenzo Rosario's identical Italian passport, but this one with a few scattered coloured stamps inside.

Simon Deverine's navy-and-gold English passport came next, with its small, rather startled-looking studio photograph of the handsome man inside. The Witness Statement he'd supplied here was long, and folded over.

Lovelace then laid down Gloria's English passport, with her Witness Statement. And then came Jacinta Glaysayer's English passport, which Posie didn't touch. A passport was very personal, after all; only surrendered with consent.

And how could Jacinta give that, now?

Lovelace poured tea for himself and Fox from a nearly-cold tea-pot. It was exactly as he liked it: lukewarm, caramel-coloured and strong enough to stand a spoon upright in.

Posie wrinkled her nose in disgust. 'None for me, thank you. Though it looks absolutely delicious.'

She sat and read all the Witness Statements, of which nothing stood out especially. She motioned towards Roberta's and Lorenzo's documents.

'I take it you searched *their* packed-up flat, above the Gelateria? You presumably found these passports there?'

'Yes, but I had their consent to take them.'

'There was nothing else suspicious in the flat itself?'

Lovelace spluttered between his mouthfuls of tea. 'I wouldn't say that exactly, darling.'

Fox put his cup down hurriedly. 'It seems to me, Miss, that simply everyone here is a suspect in these murders, or else, has some crazy agenda all of their own.'

Lovelace took out something else from the attaché case. Threw it down weightily on the table.

Something pretty, gold and silver: glittery with a lacy ribbon edge; expensive-looking. Posie reached out, picked up a small, thick stack of metallic paper, tied up with a smart white ribbon.

Prudence would have been in her element. They looked like something madly suitable for a wedding.

'Gold and silver envelopes!' Posie whispered, eyes wide. 'Like those sent to Giulia last year! Oh, my! Now it's all unravelling! You found these in the flat?'

Lovelace raised an eyebrow. 'Yes. There were only a couple of bags to search through; one suitcase for Roberta and one big suitcase for Lorenzo. They were sitting packed in the hallway, ready to be transported first-thing tomorrow.'

Lovelace shook the pack of envelopes. '*These* beauties

were tucked inside a seam pocket of Roberta's suitcase. Along with a good deal of cocaine.'

He reached down again into his black bag. 'And *these* horrors were all in the same pocket, too. Stuffed in tight. As there are so many of them.'

Richard brought out brand-new packs of cards.

Tarot cards.

Posie gasped in disbelief.

Each pack was fastened with a plain gold band, but the packs of cards had no other protective box or paper surrounding them, so tracing their place of purchase was futile. Lovelace whacked them down onto the table. One after the other.

There were fifteen packs in total. All identical with their red-and-black backs. A slight white powdery residue came off the cards, leaving a sandy, gritty-like trace on the veneer of the table-top.

'I've checked through, Miss,' said Fox quickly. 'Each pack is complete, except for the card showing "Death". Each pack should have seventy-eight cards, but in reality has seventy-seven. Each pack is missing "Death".'

Posie gasped. 'No! I don't believe it. So *Roberta* was sending those awful cards to her own cousin, Giulia, last year? But what about the "Death" card in the centre of the knives tonight? Was that *her* handiwork, too? But why? And how? Besides, that card was different, wasn't it?'

Lovelace was impatient. 'I have no idea if Roberta Grimaldi is behind all of this. Your guess is as good as mine just now, Posie love.'

'Have you confronted Roberta about it?'

'Of course. She denied ever having seen the packs of cards before. Nor the envelopes. But really, Miss Grimaldi was much more worried about my having found her secret stash of drugs. She's down there in Jacinta's studio crying her eyes out. Hopefully this whole sorry affair will make her see the error of her ways. But I'm not convinced. Once an addict…'

This was dreadful. Truly dreadful.

Posie stopped herself saying '*poor Roberta*' just in time.

But she genuinely felt for the girl.

Was it *really* possible she could have conducted a frightening campaign of terror against her own cousin at a time when the woman was sick? And was Posie's sense of judgement really that skewed and 'off', that she could feel sorry for such a woman?

She changed the subject quickly.

'And Lorenzo? Did you find anything in his packed suitcase?'

Please.

Please let him be to blame here. Somehow at the very heart of this tragedy.

'Nothing. Not a dickie bird. Fella's quiet, frighteningly so. He sat in Deverine's room scribbling messages to the priest cancelling tomorrow's wedding ceremony, and then calmly started writing out cheques to pay the caterer for tonight's dinner, and the electrician who came earlier. He told Fox here to get the cheques to the right people, and then get word to the builders that any work on the Guesthouse was now off. Calm as you like. As if he hadn't just sat in a room with a dead, poisoned fiancée. Left her there, in fact! Although mercifully Maturo organised for the ambulance men to come again and collect Jacinta right after everyone had left.'

Fox shrugged. 'I'd say Mr Rosario's behaviour was simply considerate, sir. Maybe his loss hasn't sunk in yet? And people *do* deal differently with grief.'

Posie pointed calmly at the piles of documents. 'You're missing the Doctor's passport and Witness Statement, aren't you? And Lady Tony's. And mine...'

Posie carried the sleeping Patsy over to where her carpet bag was, then shook all its contents on the bed. She picked up her navy passport, where the name underneath the golden lion and the unicorn read, very unfamiliarly, 'MRS

ROSEMARY LOVELACE', and she threw it down on the massed pile.

'We need to be thorough, Richard, don't we? Especially if there's a big trial in England. I'll write my Witness Statement for you myself, before I sleep. *If* I ever can sleep again… Oh! Come to think of it, you're also missing Lady Nella's passport, too. Why? Didn't you search the attic? Won't Commissario Maturo and the morgue officials need that?'

'Absolutely.' Richard Lovelace looked exhausted now, disillusioned. Posie had managed to fold her carpet bag as wide as it would go, and she placed the little dog inside. It was perfect, like a soft, cushioned basket. She sat down heavily next to the dog on the bed, watched her husband frown and check his wristwatch.

It was one in the morning. *And something else was definitely afoot.*

Here it comes, she thought.

'I'm sorry darling, I know it's late, but I need your help. Lady Tony couldn't find her cousin Nella's passport up in the attic. Or her own, for that matter. She turned the place over but to no avail. Seems like someone has been up there, taking things, maybe while the dinner was in full swing? A money-purse has gone too, belonging to Nella Harewood.'

'Oh?'

'Lady Tony's scared half to death at the idea of an intruder, on top of everything which has happened. And there may be some truth in the story of the thefts. Charlie Seego has also reported the theft tonight of a solid gold cigarette tin. And Sergeant Lazzio had reports from a couple of locals who claimed they'd seen someone climbing up on the roof of this building. Could be our thief…'

'The *roof*? Is there access to the attic from the roof?'

'Yes, through a tiny skylight. Lazzio already checked. But of course, there was no-one up there. Would you come up and speak to Lady Tony now, Posie? Woman's touch, and all that. Fresh pair of eyes, too. Maybe it was Nella herself who hid the passport and purse before dinner? She was more than half-cut, after all, and maybe she was actually hiding the money from her cousin, after what we've now heard? Is it too much to ask, my love? I'll come up with you.'

Posie rose again with an effort. But at least there was no repeat of that wrenchingly awful pain from before, at dinner.

'Of course I'll help. I think I'd better go on and speak to Lorenzo, too.' She doubled back and grabbed at Lorenzo's passport, putting it carefully between the pages of her silver notebook, completely ignoring her husband's raised eyebrow.

'Let's go then.'

Because Posie also had another agenda. Other things she wanted to look for in the attic room, besides hidden documents and missing money.

Evidence of a forbidden affair.

* * * *

Eighteen

Tony Harewood was sitting bolt upright in her single bed in sprigged-cotton pyjamas and a matching bed jacket, her plaited hair neat under a towelling bed-turban.

A bright desk-lamp had been placed on Tony's night-table and its beam illuminated what Tony was up to, and it was this which gave a sole clue as to the fact that not everything here was quite tickety-boo.

Tony was painting, but in a manic fashion, her small paint-box set up on her lap.

She'd obviously been at it since Lovelace had visited her a couple of hours back, because the entire coverlet was smothered with tiny, half-postcard-sized watercolour paintings, most of which were still very wet. All were very dark, featuring jagged mountains of impossibly steep sweeping edges.

'Can I sit with you, Lady Tony?' Posie smiled, and without waiting for an answer, she dragged over a rattan chair from a small desk in the corner. She sat close to the head of the bed.

Lovelace had sent the local policeman stationed here down for a break, and Lovelace now loitered on the landing, smoking again, listening through the door which had been left ajar.

Posie didn't interrupt the girl's silence. She sat, feeling the weight of the tragedy hanging palpably in the air.

Tony, biting at her lip, carried on painting regardless of the interruption, her right hand – with which she wielded her little brush – shaking almost uncontrollably.

There was a strong scent of tobacco hanging in the air – a mysteriously masculine smell – as if someone had been rolling cigarettes. And indeed, on the night-table, Posie saw Tony's cigarette case, open but empty. A pouch of cheap tobacco and self-roll French 'Rizla' papers had fallen to the floor. One single Turkish cigarette, half-smoked, had been stubbed out in an overflowing ashtray, maybe saved for later. It was obviously Tony's very last proper cigarette and Posie felt a wrench of pity for the girl. From now on it was roll-your-owns, or nothing.

Posie took it all in.

The attic room was chilly and bare, and Posie saw there was no fireplace up here. No possibility of warmth.

Just four tiny glass skylights for light, and one bigger one, placed directly above the other single bed, which was about five feet away from Tony's. Heavy rain was pounding on the roof, drumming on the skylights as if it wanted to get in.

From near the larger skylight, a steady drip-drip of water was coming in: a small ceramic basin had been set up on the floor to catch the water and the sound of the falling drops rang out horribly. A chill wind was whipping about the roof, whistling in through the cracks in the skylights.

The place felt like a school-dorm, a bad one at that, and Posie saw how it wouldn't be that appealing for guests, and that the 'favour' Jacinta had been extending to Tony hadn't exactly been much of one, after all.

A feeble overhead light made a yellow pool on the linoleum floor and something glimmered there. Red as blood.

Posie got up, bent over with a good deal of exertion and

picked up the glimmery thing. She'd thought it might be a bead or a sequin from Tony's evening bag, but now she saw it was something else entirely.

It was a long, ruby earring.

It looked real, and when Posie looked carefully she saw the small 'C' of 'CARTIER' engraved on the clip. She placed it in the palm of her hand, trying not to look surprised, and sat down again.

She registered Tony's few belongings: her night-table with the tobacco mess and that finished lipstick thrown on it, next to a single, framed photograph which Posie recognised as being one of Neville Coleman, laughingly pulling away from the camera, eyes creased up with mirth in his big, rugby-ugly handsome square face.

Then Posie's keen gaze took in the complete and utter chaos of Nella's bed, the single open suitcase on it. Clothes spilling out, silken French knickers inside-out on the floor, dresses thrown around. It was an impressive feat, considering the girl had only been in residence a few hours by the time she'd come down late for dinner.

'My husband tells me you think someone's been up here, Lady Tony. Taken things?'

At last the girl stopped painting, looked over as if noticing Posie for the very first time. She sank back against her pillow.

The china doll, breaking inside from the pressure.

'That's right. Can't find my passport, or Nella's.' Tony indicated to where a plain brown leather satchel was hanging on a hook near the door. 'I usually keep all my very important things in there. My passport's gone. I suppose Nella's was in her suitcase, but it's not anymore. Neither is her jewellery, nor her money-purse. Your husband looked, as did I. As did that pretend-Vicar of his.'

'Ah yes. Sorry about that.'

A shrug. 'Most things in life are too good to be true.'

Posie held out her palm where the ruby glimmered in

195

an almost savage fashion. 'Is this earring yours, or your cousin's?'

'What?' Lady Tony craned her long neck, and almost gave a start of surprise. 'Why! That's one of Nella's earrings! Where was that?'

Posie explained. 'Maybe the robber dropped this on his or her way out? In their hurry? Here, you take this earring. It may be…useful.'

Maybe you can sell it? For the money? For a life which becomes your title?

Tony looked relieved, placing the earring in the top-drawer of her night-stand. 'Hopefully they got what they came for. Hopefully they won't be back.'

'There are police everywhere at the Guesthouse tonight, Lady Tony. Don't be afraid.'

Posie looked over at the depressing water dripping in steadily.

'I think it's a loose tile,' said the aristocrat, following her gaze. 'It hasn't rained much recently, and when it did I hardly liked to bother Jacinta. Oh, *poor* Jacinta…'

Tony Harewood suddenly hugged at her knees, causing her paintbrushes and sheafs of the miniature paintings to fall to the floor.

'Oh, Posie. I am very, very afraid. I've lost the man I loved, and now I've lost my good friend, and my cousin, too. Nella was a sort of protector to me, and I *know* she was embarrassing at dinner – she'd got herself drunk out of nerves at meeting Simon again – but what she told you was the truth. "*We Harewoods look out for each other.*" It's true. Ever since I was a little girl I was in her shadow, but she made sure I kept up. She looked out for me when no-one else did. I've lost her tonight. I feel like it's my fault. *I* invited her here, after all.'

Tony hung her head.

There was more. Posie let the beat of the silence go on.

'It should have been *me*.'

'Sorry?'

Tears were running down the girl's face. 'Those awful threats from earlier. Delivered to *me*. I was wearing red. And so was Nella. We were next to each other at the meal table, for goodness' sake, weren't we? Maybe that bullet was meant for *me*? In all that dreadful flickering light, maybe the murderer got the wrong Harewood? The wrong girl in the red dress?'

'Oh? You think?'

Tony seemed to be beating herself up a good deal about the threat business, and the red dress. Was she just being fanciful? Posie bit her tongue, just stopped herself from explaining that Lovelace was steaming ahead on the case with the idea that Simon Deverine had killed his ex-wife on purpose. And in that case, there had definitely been no mix-up.

'Who do you think is after you, Lady Tony?'

A sniff. 'There's no-one I'm certain of, Miss Parker. But that strange man – Seego, is it? – he seems menacing. It seems funny I only started getting those horrid messages last night, when he arrived, don't you think?'

Posie didn't say anything, but she thought Tony Harewood's deductions weren't half-bad: after all, when she'd confronted him earlier, Seego hadn't actually denied writing to Lady Tony, had he?

But whatever the case, it didn't help things now. There was no evidence linking the man to either of Nella or Jacinta's murders. So far.

Posie stood, rubbing at the small of her back, pretending to walk up and down the attic in order to get a little relief.

She made sure to observe Tony's dresses hanging carefully on a single rail: a dozen well-made, hard-wearing day outfits in tones of reds and orange-reds. A couple of plain reddish evening dresses, nothing frivolous. Most of the things were English, off-the-peg, from Debenhams or the Army & Navy Store.

The matching hats, three or four, mostly in dull-toned red-and-orange straw, were stacked in a neat pile on a hat-shelf to one side.

There was nothing sparkling here. Nothing blue.

Out on the landing Posie heard her husband's feet shift uncomfortably. Poor dear man, probably longing for his bed, but trying to overhear anything which might prove useful.

Nothing so far, my love.

'Do you mind if I look in Nella's suitcase? You know, this missing passport. It's causing a jolly old ruckus. They really do need it. Just in case it got overlooked?'

'Please go ahead.'

Posie went to Nella's side of the room and flicked on the small bedside light. She moved towards the smart little black Louis Vuitton weekend-sized case, from which clothes tumbled out. She made a show of checking the inside pockets where of course there was nothing at all, save for the torn-off end of an old Haggerty's Bank chequebook. Posie surreptitiously put it up her sleeve, for later.

She was aware that Lady Tony wasn't following her at all, her head was now resting, exhausted, on her knees, as if sleep might, after all, shortly be possible. Posie rushed through the items in the case.

Silk blouses, a pair of daring, beautifully-cut black slacks, everything from 'Galerie Lafayette' in Paris. A shoe-bag with one pair of tan hand-made brogues inside, and one pair of blue-suede heels. A sateen-bag with make-up and a toothbrush inside. A small travel vial of Penhaligon's perfume; that black amber smell of darkness and danger.

Nothing more.

Posie found it jolly odd. There were no pyjamas here, no dressing-gown. No hats, no spare handbags. No hosiery. No other jewellery, unless that had been in the purse the intruder had taken, along with the other ruby earring?

She quickly looked under the pillow of the single bed, felt below the blanket, and then below the mattress. Nothing.

And still nothing when she looked around the walls and night-table – of which all the drawers were empty – nearest Nella's bed. The girl obviously hadn't unpacked properly.

The last place to look was under the bed itself.

Hardly able to move but damned if she'd call in Lovelace and break the fragile trust which held in the room, Posie manoeuvred herself onto the floor like a great beached whale, cursing the tight evening dress with every breath.

From the light of the bedside lamp she felt her way along, lying on her side, the baby kicking inside her in a fury.

There was an upturned glass bottle, a pool of dried-in stickiness on the terracotta floor. Champagne which had been here for hours, drying.

Behind the bottle was a mass of something soft, half-glued into the sticky drink, and Posie, puffing and grunting, pulled at it. There was a slight ripping noise but then she had it in her hands.

A dress or skirt. She felt again to see if there was anything else, but there was nothing.

Half rolling, then sitting upright on the floor again, trying to tamp down her excitement, Posie hardly dared exhale as she shook out the dress in her hands.

The thing was beautiful, luminous: a shining, gossamer-flecked confection of royal-blue taffeta; even in this poor light as tantalising as a mermaid's skin. It smelt of that black amber, and of sweat, and old cigarettes and baked face powder. It needed a wash badly. There was a heavy, sordid scent of desire about the thing, too. It was most definitely the dress of the woman in Lorenzo's embrace earlier that morning.

Posie felt like whistling in amazement: *Nella Harewood and Lorenzo Rosario!*

What terrible story have I stumbled into here?

Although, in truth, this possibility, half-formed, had been in Posie's mind ever since Gloria had said she had seen a blue dress up in the attic.

Pieces of a jigsaw puzzle were slotting into place.

Posie recalled Jacinta telling her that Nella had come out to San Gimignano, only briefly, in the early summertime of the previous year.

That must have been when Nella had met Lorenzo for the first time.

Nella had obviously been discreet: she and Lorenzo were both married, of course, and Nella had never returned here. Until now.

Nella had travelled on to Venice last summer from here. Then on to the South of France.

Had Lorenzo gone with Nella? Or followed her at a discreet distance? It seemed likely. Roberta had spoken of a couple of trips he had made out of town, hadn't she? Including one to Venice.

Posie opened her notebook, pulled out Lorenzo's passport, felt a stab of nervous excitement. Of course, any trips to other Italian cities wouldn't be registered, so there would be no incriminating evidence of a trip to Venice. *But there might be something…*

And yes, here was a border stamp for France.

'ARRIVEE – REPUBLIQUE DE FRANCE – June 30th, 1924.' And then there were town stamps for Cannes, and for St Tropez. Likely proof that Lorenzo had gone on to join Nella last summer, to continue the affair.

Posie tried to imagine it: a tantalising affair between two completely unsuitable, beautiful, mismatched people.

What was meant to be a secret affair.

But Posie was certain that it hadn't remained a secret.

Posie remembered Giulia Rosario's sadness in August. The woman had known her husband was cheating, Posie was sure of it.

But what about Jacinta?

It seemed likely, bearing in mind the strange confrontation with Lorenzo at the Gelateria earlier that morning, that Jacinta also knew about the affair; had found out about it somehow.

Posie remembered the ringing accusation: *'You don't give things up, do you, Lorenzo? Or anyone, I should say. Even when you should!'*

Lorenzo had probably lied and told Jacinta it was over, if he'd admitted it at all. But it had rankled with Jacinta, understandably.

Was that why Jacinta hadn't invited Nella – her old school friend – to the wedding in the first place, quite aside from the awkwardness with Simon Deverine?

Was that why Jacinta was so wretchedly upset at learning that the girl was, after all, attending?

But Posie was certain she still didn't have the complete picture. There had been that strange snatch of overheard conversation between Tony and Nella: *'You're just jealous of Jacinta. That's all. And good for her, I say.'*

What was the meaning of that?

Why had Nella been jealous? Presumably Nella could have married Lorenzo a thousand times over, and the man would have come running? Both lovers were now free of their former spouses, after all. So what had happened? Why was Lorenzo marrying Jacinta, anyway?

And what implications did this new knowledge about the affair have for the murders which had taken place? If anything?

Sighing, knowing she must make one last visit before sleeping, Posie hoisted herself with difficulty to her feet, grabbing at the royal-blue dress.

'Did you find anything?' came a sleepy voice, and Posie turned, smiling, to Lady Tony, who had obviously nodded off sitting up.

'No passports, I'm afraid, Lady Tony, and no money-purse either. The intruder must have taken it all. But there *was* this dress. It's Nella's, I take it?'

'Huh?' Tony Harewood was squinting in the dim light, shielding her eyes to see better. 'Oh! *That* one.'

She looked suddenly stricken with grief. 'It was Nella's favourite. She argued with me just before dinner, actually. She wanted to wear it, and I told her "no". She hadn't had it laundered since wearing it in France a couple of days ago. I told her to wear her lovely red one; it was just as nice.'

Tony had put her head down on the pillow now properly, looked as if she might fall asleep at any moment, but she yawned and carried on speaking sleepily.

'Poor Nella. She wasn't at her best. Nella was so drunk that she was talking nonsense all afternoon: talking about someone following her all the way around Nice, who was now hanging about here, chasing her! A ghost, she kept saying. I told her she was talking like a crazy woman! She was drinking champagne straight from the bottle and she ended up in a bit of a rage with me, actually. She kept pawing at that blue dress and saying "It was his favourite". Over and over.'

'"*His favourite*"?' Posie felt a tug of interest. *Lorenzo?*

'Whose favourite would that have been?'

'Well, Simon's of course.' Tony Harewood had a sleepy frown on her face. 'Who else's? He'd wronged Nella badly but there was still some pride left. Nella wanted to show him she still had "it", you know. Brazen the thing out.'

'Really? There was no-one else here she would have wanted to impress?'

'Gracious, no! Who else could you mean?'

'I just thought…Ah, it's nothing.'

So Tony didn't know about Nella's affair with Lorenzo then.

Unless she was lying for some reason.

Posie looked sympathetic. 'Try and sleep now, Lady Tony. I'll need to take this dress with me, by the way, for the Forensics team. Samples, you know?' The lie rung hollowly as she said it. 'I hope that's all right with you?'

'Of course. Take anything you like.'

Posie walked out to Richard, still on the musty-smelling landing. She closed the attic-room door softly behind her.

She waved the dress. 'This is evidence. Where do you want me to store it?'

'Oh, shove it into this black leather case.'

Crumpling the skirts down tightly into Richard's bag, Posie suddenly felt something hard from within the softness. Something quite heavy and unwieldy, about the size of a pin-cushion.

'Hang about. What's this?'

She pulled a small metal tin from a pocket of the dress.

It was green enamelled, with the name 'Benger's PARIS GREEN' on it. There was a flip lid, closed over but not properly sealed.

For a moment what she was holding didn't register at all, and Posie frowned at the clear sign of the skull and crossbones and the words in English – 'DANGER' and 'POISON' – which were printed boldly on the tin in a blazing red.

'Oh. Dear Lord, Posie, no! Don't touch it! Don't open it. It's Paris Green for heaven's sake!'

And Lovelace, handkerchief in hands, had grabbed at the thing.

'Darling! You didn't get any on your hands, did you? It's a tin of pure arsenic, the Paris Green variety! Usually used for killing rodents. But I'd say in this case it was used to get rid of a certain Miss Glaysayer. Oh, my days!'

And Posie sank down on the top step, thinking she might be sick.

* * * *

Nineteen

They sat together in a kind of mutual horror. The tin of arsenic was far apart from them.

'By Jove, this is something,' muttered Lovelace. 'This place truly is a hell on earth. So Nella Harewood was carrying arsenic with her, eh?'

'There's no proof she used it, though, is there? It'll be hard to prove it was *this* exact tin of arsenic, won't it? And we only have Doctor Mozzato's word that it *was* arsenic.' But these words sounded unconvincing, even to Posie's own ears.

'I dunno, darling, but if we give this tin to the Forensics laddies maybe they can try for a match, eh? The real question is *why*, of course. Why did Nella want to poison her old school chum?'

'I think I may have half the answer,' said Posie, hauling herself to her feet, the dress still in her arms. 'I need to see Lorenzo. Now. You'd better sit in.'

And so it was that at almost two in the morning, they knocked on Simon Deverine's guestroom door, a room currently occupied by Lorenzo Rosario.

He was sitting in complete darkness, wide-awake, cross-legged, on the floor under the window.

The single bed in the plain room showed no signs of

having been slept in, and the window was open to the blackness of the night, the mosquito nets and the white muslin curtains blowing in the fierce wind: rain was sweeping in, down the walls and over Lorenzo, soaking his dark curly hair and the shoulders of his dinner jacket and shirt beneath.

He didn't seem to mind when Richard Lovelace snapped on the overhead electric light and marched across the room, pulling the window smartly shut, closing the nets and the curtains. Lovelace grabbed at a fresh towel from beside the china water pitcher and passed it to Lorenzo.

'Dry yourself, Mr Rosario. I don't need a third death on my hands tonight. Not from pneumonia. Please get up from the floor and take a shirt from Deverine's bag and put it on. I'm sure he won't mind.'

The man did as he was instructed, and Posie turned away, slightly embarrassed.

She noticed the extreme neatness of Deverine's room.

The desk however bore the recent traces of someone who had been busy writing, and Posie saw an expensive brown leather writing case, and several blue Basildon Bond envelopes stacked in a pile, a bottle of blue ink and a very expensive Mondaine fountain pen placed neatly together.

Posie remembered Fox saying Lorenzo had been writing. It looked as if he had borrowed Deverine's things. Settling business affairs, being organised. Or believing he was himself going to be incarcerated, and put away for a long time?

She heard the bed creak and turned to see Lorenzo sitting on it, wearing an unbuttoned white, dry, much-too-large shirt, without a collar.

Lovelace grunted, 'That's better, lad,' and took out his cigarette tin, offering it to Lorenzo, who shook his head and stared at the floor.

'Suit yourself.' Lovelace lit a cigarette, then fetched the only chair from the desk, helping Posie sit.

'My wife has some questions, Mr Rosario. But we won't be keeping you long. I'll just place *this* here, on the desk, for now. Where you can see it.'

He put the Paris Green tin next to the envelopes, but out of anyone's immediate reach.

Lorenzo stared at the tin, his eyes suddenly wide in fright. 'What is that?' he demanded. 'Where you find it? It is not mine!'

Posie stared at Lorenzo, who matched her gaze. In the harsh light of the small, undiluted bleakness of the place, the man's complete beauty suddenly hit her.

He was, half-damp, like some tortured saint in a Renaissance painting. He looked as his father and grandfather and all his great-grandfathers before him must have looked; he carried the history of San Gimignano in his face and in his blood.

In fact, he would have fitted in beautifully in any of the frescoes circling the walls of the Cathedral; looking down, hauntingly beautiful – imposing an unbalanced mixture of guilt and desire upon the viewer.

Oh, get a grip, Posie told herself crossly. *He's just another good-looking man. Ten a penny.*

Posie fluffed up the royal-blue taffeta dress, gave it a shake and let it unfurl.

The stench of the black amber perfume, the unwashed nature of the thing, was suddenly very much in the room.

Suffocatingly so.

'Nella Harewood was your lover, wasn't she?' Posie said calmly, but accusingly. 'I saw you together, and I wasn't the only one. So don't bother denying it. Yesterday morning, dawn, the day before your planned marriage, you and Nella were together, outside your Gelateria. She was wearing this very dress. And there's a couple of hours unaccounted for, aren't there? Because Roberta Grimaldi told me you returned home just before the Health Inspectors rang the bell, at nine. So where were you between dawn and nine o'clock? With Nella, right? But I wonder *where…*'

Richard Lovelace turned in barely-concealed amazement from his wife back to Lorenzo, who remained silent.

But Lovelace clamped his cigarette between his lips and reached for his police notebook from inside his jacket.

Posie crossed her arms over her bulk. 'You'll have to help me here, Mr Rosario, because I've just been in Nella's room upstairs, looking for identity documents, and that's where I found this dress. Your favourite, I think? But what I can't understand – and why I need your help – is *why* Nella felt the need to carry a tin of arsenic with her. It was in the pocket of this dress.'

At this, Lorenzo sat up, ramrod-straight, and looked from Posie to Lovelace, as if they might be spinning him an elaborate lie.

'This is impossible!'

'Why?'

The man crossed his arms, shaking his head over and over. 'No. You are joking with me!'

'I'm not. So tell me about it. Were you were *both* in on it? You and Nella? Nella came here again yesterday, newly single – by a strange, third-party invitation – and you realised you couldn't go through with the marriage to Jacinta. Is that how it went? Did you promise Nella you'd leave Jacinta? But if that was the case, why couldn't you both have cleared out? Just vanished? Why *kill* Jacinta? She was simply lovely.'

Posie choked back a raft of tears. 'And you treated her appallingly! Both you and Nella. Those awful words Nella spat at Jacinta last night! And besides, Jacinta *knew*, didn't she? About your affair with Nella? As did your wife, last year. You're really a dreadful man, you know that?'

Posie heard the cry in her throat, the jagged hoarseness.

I won't cry in front of this man, she told herself sternly. *I will not.*

I'm too close to the heart of all of this, she suddenly realised.

This should be an interview for Sergeant Fox to conduct, or Commissario Maturo.

She was almost rising to leave when she heard Lorenzo speak, softly this time: 'You're absolutely right, Miss Parker. Jacinta was lovely, and better than all of us. And I suppose I *am* a dreadful man. But I didn't treat your friend appallingly. Forgive me, but you don't understand what was happening here.'

Posie raised her chin in challenge, looked at him straight on.

'Go on. Tell me then.'

Lorenzo swallowed, tried to ignore Richard Lovelace, expectant with his open notebook.

'I admit, I had an affair with Nella Harewood. There!'

Lorenzo looked at his hands in his lap, sighed and carried on. 'It was last year. It was wrong. We both knew it was going nowhere; we were both married, for heaven's sake! I was smitten: like a love-sick puppy, you say? I followed Nella where I could, burned through money to meet her in exotic places. But this bubble burst. She was a beautiful woman, but she was dangerous too. Sometimes I thought that Nella was almost mad, like a devil.'

Lorenzo paused, shaking his head in disbelief before starting up again.

'I realised this for certain when Nella telegrammed to Giulia, telling her all about our affair. Giving details. There was no reason for it! Just to cause trouble. It was the start of August. Giulia was devastated. I was apologising every second of every day to Giulia, feeling dreadful; promising I would be a better husband, but I think it was too late: Giulia didn't believe me anymore. I wrote to Nella asking her how she could be so cruel, and I ended the affair. Nella wrote back telling me she didn't care anyhow: she was seeing someone else, had already moved on! She was going to leave her old husband for this new man. *That* was her plan.'

Posie pretended all of this made sense. She heard Lovelace's scratchy writing next to her.

'Who was this new man?' she asked quickly.

'I have no idea. I cut all contact. But Nella continued sending Giulia postcards, taunting her. On and off over the next few months. See what I mean about being cruel? There was no reason for it.'

Lovelace pointed at the tin of arsenic. 'How do you account for, or explain *this*, then? Because it's looking pretty rotten for you, my lad. I'll have to hand you over to Commissario Maturo unless you can provide an explanation.'

Lorenzo shook his head desperately. 'I *can't* explain it. All I can do is be honest with you and tell you that Nella started writing to *me* again, directly. Many times, sometimes every week. The letters started coming in large numbers from the South of France after her divorce, properly from the end of January onwards. Nella wanted me to invite her *here*. She'd heard Giulia was dead. Nella said she wanted to pick up where we had left off.'

'And what did you say?' Posie asked carefully, anxious not to rock the boat.

'Nothing. I never answered her letters,' Lorenzo said with a shrug. He flicked a stray curl of hair from his eyes.

'I thought by this stage she really was crazy. Best avoided. Besides, Jacinta and I had got together. I know you will find this difficult to believe, but I truly loved Jacinta. I'd known her when Giulia was still alive, but I came to know her – and love her – for her own sake these last few months. She was so sweet, and lovely, and accepting. She wanted to believe the best of everyone. Always determined to do the right thing, even if those dreadful cards told her the opposite. *That* was our only ground for disagreement. Jacinta tried to downplay being a medium, had tried not doing it, but it was always a current flowing underneath everything. It frightened me a little, I suppose. Sometimes she came out with things which turned out later to be chillingly accurate. Things she couldn't have known all by herself. We argued about it.'

'It wasn't your only topic for arguments, though, was it?' snapped Posie. 'Jacinta knew about Nella, about the affair, didn't she?'

'Yes, she did,' Lorenzo said bitterly, flicking his hair back.

'I explained it all; swore it was all over. But the letters to me from Nella kept coming. I made Jacinta read them. Told her Nella was a bad girl; not to be trusted. I think Jacinta believed me, but she was angry and upset yesterday morning that Nella was arriving for our wedding, as if it was all my fault! As if I had engineered or encouraged it! But, to be honest, I felt slightly guilty, because I *had* received a warning.'

He paused, as if wondering whether to continue, then rushed on anyway. 'You see, there was one letter I didn't show Jacinta, and that was one Nella wrote to me a couple of weeks ago, telling me she would be coming through here, this week, at her cousin Tony's invitation. That stupid Tony! Making an invitation as if she owned the place! Nella wrote that she would take the best room at the Hotel Dante, wanting me to join her there. She would simply pretend to stay here at the Guesthouse. Of course, Nella had no idea I was engaged to Jacinta, or that our wedding was going ahead.'

'How awkward. Did you reply?'

'No. I hoped she simply wouldn't come if I gave her no encouragement. I told Jacinta all of this yesterday, after that awful Health Inspection, when I finally got her alone. I was honest about it all, and Jacinta accepted it, finally. I told her *everything*. I explained to Jacinta that when I went home yesterday morning at five-thirty, there was Nella outside the Gelateria, waiting, all dressed up. I told Jacinta that Nella pretty much jumped into my arms, threatened to scream the place down if I pushed her away. I managed to take her back to the Dante, to her suite. Then we argued, big-time. Nella had heard the news about my engagement in the town when she'd arrived: told me she would break me and Jacinta up; that she would never stand by and watch us marry. She was screaming the place down. At one point the Manager of the Dante knocked on the door and I answered. Go on, you can ask him! I swear on my life Nella Harewood was a bad, bad woman.'

Posie bit at her lip, tried to blot out the theatricality of the tale. 'I see. So, you're telling us that you were *rejecting* Nella Harewood? That what I saw in the square was an ambush, not a mutual embrace?'

'That is correct, Miss Parker.'

Well, it made a mad sort of sense, if you turned the story around as Lorenzo suggested.

'So Nella was angry with you?'

'Oh, yes. Angry with me and mad at Jacinta. And those words at dinner, they were really for me. They were nothing to do with what Jacinta was wearing! You remember? Nella shouted: "*What a let-down for yourself! Couldn't you have chosen differently?*" For *me*, you see? But I chose right. And Jacinta knew it, too. We just had to get through last night.'

Posie understood now the spurned girl's vitriol, and Jacinta's calmness in the face of the words.

'Did Lady Tony know about your affair last year with Nella? Know that Nella wanted you back, now?'

Lorenzo laughed mirthlessly: 'Old stony-face? No. She didn't know any of it. She's only interested in those awful little paintings of hers.'

Richard Lovelace cut in quickly: 'And are you surprised – if it turns out that Nella *did* use this arsenic on Jacinta – that she murdered your fiancée, Mr Rosario?'

'Well, I *am* surprised, Inspector. Yes. As I say, Nella was bad, and dangerous, but this seems a step too far.'

Posie exhaled wearily. There was so much, and yet so very little to this case. She stood.

'Look, I need to tell you something,' said Lorenzo. He looked nervous, almost desperate. He was talking directly to Posie, not Lovelace.

'I know you don't like me. That's okay. I have a – how you say? – a thick skin? But I want to clear something up. I know you and many people think I treated my wife badly and that I pay Roberta nothing; that I took the Grimaldi business and stole it from them.'

Posie couldn't deny it. So she said nothing.

'There are two sides to every story,' Lorenzo said quietly, rubbing at his eyes, as if coming to a difficult decision. 'I need to tell you mine.'

He took a deep breath. 'My parents died when I was young, but I've always been good at making the best of things. I learnt English so I could work as a tour guide at the Cathedral here, and in the town itself. That's what I was doing when I got engaged to Giulia. People thought I was lucky, landing on my feet, you say? But what most people didn't know about both the Grimaldi brothers – not *just* Roberta's father – was that they were both drunks; that they frittered away everything they owned. They spent money ridiculously, on crazy things! It ran in the family.'

He sighed: 'When I first married Giulia I knew – she told me – that Roberta was heavily into drugs, and that we needed to protect her from herself. Giulia and I arranged at that time to pay virtually all of Roberta's proper salary into the Banca della Toscana in town, for Roberta to receive at age thirty-five, or on marriage. We let her live with us for free, gave her a tiny wage, but even *that* she frittered away on drugs. I've managed to chase most of the suppliers of drugs out of town, but Roberta seems to have a dealer still. When I find him I will beat him to pieces.' He caught Lovelace's stern eye. 'Oh, well, not literally.'

Lorenzo shifted his seating position. 'But it turned out that Giulia was an addict too. She'd kept herself clean all the while we were courting. I hate drugs. But it all

213

started up again a few months into our marriage. Cocaine, mostly. Opium when she could. There were headaches, ill periods with Doctor Mozzato coming every day. There was nothing natural about her 'sickliness'. I was hiding money away from my own wife to force her to stop; to cut off her supply, but she too always found a way. She and Roberta were in it together...'

'Oh, goodness,' Posie exclaimed, feeling like the whole back-history she had known was tilting on its axis. 'How dreadful for you.'

'I can't prove those things to you. But I *can* prove this: when I married Giulia, Grimaldi's Gelateria was bankrupt. Completely. Her father, and then Giulia herself, had run it into the ground. I had no idea! I was very naïve. It was never revealed to me before the wedding, but because I married Giulia the Bankruptcy Order immediately applied to me, too. So I took out loans from the bank here to start the Gelateria all over again. But one of the conditions of the Bankruptcy Order being lifted was that a new name was given to the Gelateria.'

He shrugged. 'I gave it my own name; there was no other obvious choice. But I faced hatred from people in the town because of it, because they don't know the true story. Of course, the tourists don't care, and that's our main income. You can check this all out. Go to the Banca della Toscana: ask about the loans I took. Ask the Town Hall who made the Bankruptcy Order in the first place.'

Lovelace was hurriedly noting all of this down.

'And Jacinta's Guesthouse?' asked Posie stubbornly. 'Why did you want to change this? Was there some issue of Bankruptcy here?'

'No. It wasn't that bad, but the Guesthouse wasn't even making a few liras of income. Jacinta was paying the maid and the cleaner out of her own personal income. Buying the breakfast pastries with her own savings. I hated to see the place losing money, and with dreadful hangers-on leeching off her good heart. Most tourists come to this city for just one day; you see them heading in and out on those red buses, don't you? And for those that *do* stay, they want a luxury hotel. Like Nella Harewood. I convinced Jacinta the Guesthouse should become our home, with a restaurant below which would finally make some money. We could shake those leeches off.'

Posie rose and walked to the door. *Tony Harewood*, she thought to herself. *He really doesn't like her one bit. Probably because of the close connection to Nella.*

Lorenzo called out. 'You asked about identity papers for Nella, Miss Parker. But I expect they were never here! I'd search at the Dante. She'd paid for a huge room over there: I expect all her things are still there, passport included. Coming here this afternoon was a show to keep her cousin happy. Lady Tony, she has no clue about anything.'

'Thank you.'

'Can I ask you one favour, Miss Parker?'

'Of course.'

'I will never live here now, I know that. I have no claim on the place now Jacinta is dead. So I need to go back to my flat above the shop. It was supposed to be rented out from tomorrow to an American. It's too bad, but I have to pick up the pieces of my life and keep going. Death will not come for me anytime soon; not on a tarot card, and not even the real deal.'

He picked up the first letter from the pack on the desk. 'Could you see your way to delivering this to the Agent – a Mr Trussardi? I've explained what's happened and I have asked for my spare key back, and I've enclosed a promise of money as compensation for the American gentleman. I trust you, Miss Parker, as did Jacinta. You seem reliable, in every way. You'll find Trussardi in his office under the Torri dei Salvucci, or the Twin Towers, as they are known locally.'

'Isn't that where Doctor Mozzato is based?'

'Yes. He has his flat and his consulting rooms there. On the same floor is a small empty flat he's helped prepare for Roberta. I haven't seen it, but she was excited about it.'

'She'll still move in?'

Lorenzo shrugged. 'She's thirty-five next week. She'll have access to her money, and maybe the time has come for me to let her go? Besides, she's got Mozzato nearby. He can keep an eye on her. You know she's crazy about that man?'

Posie smiled wanly. 'I did know. And yes, I'll deliver this first-thing. I promise. Oh, one last thing, Mr Rosario.'

'Yes?'

'Did you recognise that greenish tarot card you were holding tonight, sir? The one which was in between all those seven knives? Which Jacinta was so interested in?'

The man shrugged uneasily. 'They all look the same to me. I hate them.'

'So, that's a "no"?'

A dark shadow crossed the man's face momentarily. 'It seemed familiar, somehow. But no: I don't know where it came from.'

'Thank you.'

Outside on the landing Lovelace took Posie's arm.

'Do you believe him, darling?'

'Actually, against all my initial gut feelings about the man since I returned here, I *do* believe him. Yes.'

'Hmnn. Me too.' Lovelace sighed. 'A strange chap, but honourable, in his way. But I'll check with the bank and the Town Hall tomorrow. Check he isn't talking baloney.'

'Better check with the Hotel Manager at the Dante, too, darling. Check Lorenzo was there with Nella; that they were having an argument.'

'That they were fully *clothed* and having an argument, you mean, darling?' said Lovelace with almost a twinkle in his eye.

But now, at almost three in the morning, with the wind

still blowing a gale and the rain still slapping hard against the medieval walls and roof of the Guesthouse, it was high time for bed.

* * * *

PART THREE:
The Day of the Wedding
(Friday 20th March, 1925)

Twenty

Posie woke as the church bells were ringing for nine o'clock. She sat up in bed, clear-headed and alert, aware Richard was not at her side. Today should have been Jacinta's wedding day.

Posie felt her heart lurch with pity, a sudden rush of sadness and anger flooding through her veins.

The doors to the balcony facing the Cisterna Square had been left slightly open, and Posie sensed that the storm of the night had blown itself out, although the smell of rain drifted in, heavy in the air like salt-spray.

Not a good day for a wedding, anyway.

For a second Posie thought she might cry; sudden, painful tears. But then she was distracted by a bark and a jumping dog landing on her feet, settling there contentedly. Posie smiled.

'Good morning, Patsy.'

Then she saw a note on the pillow next to her in Richard's dear, familiar writing and she snatched it up:

Darling,

Maturo's Forensics lads arrived pronto, at 8 o'clock sharp. I'll be down with them most of the morning in the dining-room. There's lots to get through. Fox is at your disposal, but for goodness' sake take it easy. Remember Dr Mozzato is nearby, if you need him.

That tiny excuse for a dog has been fed and walked, but wanted to return to you. She seems to like you, eh? Make sure she doesn't eat your notebooks though.

We'll be having an update at 11.15 in here, our room. I'm afraid it's the only suitable space. I'll ask Gloria to nip in and make it presentable, with coffee etc.

She's been an absolute brick: providing trays of breakfast for everyone locked in their rooms, and for the bobbies standing guard. I'll be buying her the biggest tin of custard creams I can organise when we're safely back in London.

Love,

R

P.S. Dashed awful time we're having out here, but there's a present on the side for you, from me. I hope you like it.

Posie heaved herself off the bed. Even now, her husband wasn't to know her nosy ways; the fact she had already 'discovered' the Macallè bracelet. She clipped on the beautiful cuff.

Just as she was about to move to the bathroom, she looked down at *The Times* Richard had bought yesterday.

The story about Neville Coleman's estate again caught her eye. A London firm of solicitors, Pratchard's, in Gray's Inn, leapt out at her, or rather, the words 'Dalmeny Court' did. Where Neville Coleman had owned a flat. The announcement recorded it had been sold and the monies gathered in.

'Dalmeny Court' was a familiar name, but why? Posie was sure she had never visited that address herself.

And then the confusion cleared.

Oh, of course.

Hadn't Simon Deverine, at dinner the night before, mentioned how lovely and well-positioned his own flat in Dalmeny Court was?

So conceivably Neville Coleman and Deverine had been neighbours at Dalmeny Court, or had at least known each other?

But how did that help, or hinder things here?

Probably it was an irrelevant detail. A small coincidence.

Posie wrinkled her nose: she didn't normally like coincidences one bit. And neither did Lovelace. But this was a small, intertwined group of people, a cobweb all radiating out from the spider at the centre of it, Jacinta Glaysayer.

It looked as if Jacinta had introduced her old school chum Nella to Simon Deverine, her Godfather. When the two had married, and Deverine bought Dalmeny Court as their marital base, didn't it seem likely that Lady Tony had met Neville Coleman, the neighbour, on a visit to see her cousin there?

Posie filed this information away for now in a dark, unimportant, dusty little shelf in the back of her mind, and began to make herself as presentable as she could in the shortest amount of time.

She grabbed at a blush-pink jersey day-suit, piped in a white grosgrain ribbon, which was the most comfortable thing she had packed, and she added a good amount of coral blush to her very pale face and a couple of white grosgrain hairclips to the side of her parting.

Sergeant Fox was obviously very much at her disposal – or very bored – for when she came out of the bathroom a note had been pushed under the door to the effect that a tray of coffee and pastries were outside, as was Fox himself.

'Hello, Sergeant,' Posie called through the door. 'Are you able to bend down for those breakfast things? If I reach down, I don't think I'll ever get up again.'

'Absolutely, Miss.'

Posie let him in with a smile. 'Place the tray over on the table near the Cisterna balcony. And share my coffee, won't you?'

'I won't say no, Miss. I feel like I've done a full morning's work already!' Fox was wearing an off-duty frog-green suit in a thick Harris Tweed, a look which didn't altogether suit him, and Posie could only suppose it was from his reserves of 'Vicar costumes' he had been instructed to bring along on this trip.

'What news is there, Sergeant?'

Fox explained he'd been dispatched on official police business by Lovelace to the Hotel Dante, where he himself was staying – but in a very small room, suitable for a single vicar – to search the suite which Lady Nella had booked. Fox had been shocked by the amount of dresses and luggage in the room, but had found Lady Nella's passport easily, with no problems.

He patted the breast pocket of his jacket, as if indicating safety.

'It's in here. I'll give it to the Boss when I see him next. I also spoke to the Manager of the Dante, and he confirmed that Lady Nella and Lorenzo Rosario *were* having a blazing row yesterday morning. The Manager went up to Nella's suite about seven o'clock, as he was getting complaints from other guests about the noise. The couple were screaming at each other,' he coloured suddenly, blushing a fiery red, 'and he confirmed they were fully clothed. Evening dress, both of them.'

Fox had also been to the Town Hall, to request a copy of the Bankruptcy Order for the Gelateria, and to the Banca della Toscana, requesting Lorenzo's loan documentation.

'We should have something back later this morning,' he said, slurping his coffee gratefully, before telling Posie he had also been to the Post Office to request the exact details of the telegrams sent and received by Charlie Seego since his arrival in San Gimignano on Wednesday evening.

'They should be able to let us have something by lunchtime today.'

'Golly, you *have* been busy,' said Posie, feeling slightly guilty, but determined to make haste now. She grabbed up her cream cloche hat and a small leather clutch usually reserved for evening events.

'Shall we go, Sergeant? I've got to deliver a letter. You're to come with me, apparently. By the way, that's really a terrible colour on you, Fox. You should give that jacket up. It's a rotter.'

'Mnnn. I know. Fancy dress, Miss. That's all.'

Posie was scooping up Patsy now, ensconced in the carpet bag. The dog's hair was not pinned back today and was all over her eyes, and Posie, without thinking, snatched off one of her own white ribbon hairclips and fastened Patsy's hair back with it.

'That's better, Patsy love. You can actually see now, can't you? Now, I'm going to drop you off with Gloria, as I've got too much to do in town, and I can't look after you properly while I'm doing it. Forgive me…'

But Posie turned at the door as Fox had just hit his own forehead in mock despair, as if he were an idiot of the first degree, which he most definitely was not. 'Oh, *rats*! I didn't tell you!'

'What?'

'I quite forgot, Miss! The Forensics team seem to have made a breakthrough downstairs. It's all sewn up! Well, *apparently…*'

'*What?*' She gripped the door-frame, the new bracelet cutting into the flesh of her wrist.

'They've been at the morgue and viewed the body of Nella Harewood. The Forensics team say that from the way the bullet ripped through her body it was never – never in a million years apparently – fired from a gun where old Deverine was sitting. Even if the general angle is sort-of correct. No, they say it was close range. And her fingerprints were all over it. So they think Lady Nella did it herself. Killed herself. Suicide.'

Posie sighed heavily, leaning against the wall.

'*Oh!*'

The word was nothing and everything; disappointment and yet total acceptance of an inevitability which made a sort of sense.

Fox sounded agitated: 'The Boss – your husband, I mean – is cock-a-hoop, and so is Commissario Maturo. Two birds, two stones, but same reason. Means they can say it's all solved.'

Posie looked incredulous. 'You mean Lady Nella poisons Jacinta in a fit of jealousy, and then kills herself for the same reason; as she'll never get her man? All over an affair with *Lorenzo*?'

Fox shrugged. 'Apparently.'

'A woman like Nella Harewood! Beautiful like that, she'd have no problem catching another man in a trice! No. It doesn't ring true.'

'She was a looker, Miss: I'll admit that. A first-class stunner. It seems odd to me that she would kill herself like this. No, it's not all sewn up for me. Not at all.'

'No?'

Fox shrugged. 'I think we're still not seeing the entire picture here, Miss. Something's going on with that Seego fella, and the solution the Boss and Maturo have put together doesn't even factor him in, does it? Nah, something's off. It stinks.'

'I wholeheartedly agree.'

* * * *

Outside, the night's rain had washed the terracotta brickwork of the Cisterna Square quite clean, and the sky was now interspersed with patchy bits of blue. Fox, wearing a khaki-green felt homburg and a similar parson-like overcoat which reeked of moth-balls, hovered protectively at Posie's elbow.

Bells were ringing out for half-past nine. Posie swallowed hard. In half an hour, if Jacinta had lived, she'd have been standing outside the door of the Cathedral in her tissue-thin dress and snazzy little hat, about to get married. Posie should have, about now, been walking this very route, to take her place as a guest in the small Santa Fina Chapel inside.

A sudden, dreadful pain grabbed at Posie's insides and tore at her.

Not again, surely?

'Oh!' She stopped suddenly, breathless, bent double, pulling in air hard and fast. She stared in front of her, tried desperately to concentrate on anything other than the pain: on the white marble-like tower rising up behind the old well on the northern part of the square.

The Devil's Tower.

The prosperous man who had built the original tower had left San Gimignano on a business trip in the fourteenth century, only to return to find his home mysteriously taller, another floor having been added; despite his having issued no instructions to builders and never having paid anyone to do the work. It had been the devil's doing, the local people said. And the name had stuck.

Was that what was afoot here, now? Devil's work of some kind? Had that devil *really* been Lady Nella Harewood?

'Miss?' There was a slight panic in Fox's voice. He touched her elbow, something he'd never done before.

'It's fine, Sergeant.'

Posie stood up, and just as suddenly as it had come, the terrible pain went away.

227

'If you're sure…'

'Sure as bread is bread.'

They slipped under the arch next to the Ardinghelli Towers, in the bottom of which Lorenzo's Gelateria sat dark and boarded-up. The Cathedral Square beyond was busy with morning shoppers, a few priests and nuns, crossing and re-crossing the red cobbles.

'Where we heading, Miss?'

'Over there. The Salvucci Towers, otherwise known as the "Twin Towers".'

She pointed straight ahead, where the Cathedral Square led onto a big, busy street.

'You know the story, Sergeant?' And at his shake of the head Posie explained.

'Back in medieval times, the Salvucci family decided to build a tower on the busiest road nearest the Cathedral. It was law that no-one was allowed to build bigger or higher than the tower of the Town Hall, the Torre Grossa. So, the Salvuccis thought they would be clever and build *two* towers side-by-side, both high, and that the combined height would "beat" the Torre Grossa. But it backfired: they were ordered to lop them down. What you see today is only about two-thirds of the original height of those twin towers.'

'Served them bally well right,' said Fox, pleased, ever the law-enforcer.

'Yes.' Posie smiled. 'Now, I think we need to cut through to this tiny square behind. The Erbe Square. That's where the entrance is…'

'I've been here before, Miss. This is where Seego's Post Office is located.'

The Erbe Square was completely empty, with a few straggly leaves blowing about the place. Even though the rain had cleared, and now a tentative sun was trying to shine, the place felt like it was wrapped in the shadows of the past.

The grey, fortress-like plainness of the two 'twin' towers, joined together at the bottom floors by one house, were oppressive. There was nothing like the Arabic grace of the white 'Devil's Tower' here. In fact, there was scarcely one window to be seen in among all the grey brickwork rising ever upwards.

'Not very cheery, are they?' muttered Fox. Then he pointed at what looked like a small glass-fronted shop set in the bottom floor of the towers. A small gold plaque at the side bore the name 'TRUSSARDI'.

'Yes, this is the place.'

Up close, Posie saw the 'shop' was in fact more like a cave, going back a long way, and as she pushed open the glass door, and heard the customer bell jingle to announce her, a small, bearded man in his late forties emerged from the back of the shop. Posie stood with Fox at her side, Lorenzo Rosario's letter clutched in her hand.

'Signor Trussardi?'

'*Si*. You English?'

'Yes.' Posie explained who she was, where she had come from. 'I have a letter here from Mr Rosario. It's about the key to the flat above the Gelateria. It's rather urgent.'

The man looked anxious. 'Oh! I see. Another one! *You* need the key now? It's fortunate that the American hasn't turned up yet.'

Posie was confused. 'What other one? This is the only letter as far as I know, and I don't need the key. Read the letter, please. It's all explained there.'

'Is everything well with Mr Rosario, Miss? Why *he* no come?' A slight panic lit Trussardi's tawny eyes, which grew wide behind the spectacles. 'And Miss Roberta? Tell me. She stay fine?'

Posie blew out her cheeks, thought it best to stick with optimism. '*They* are both fine, yes. But you need to read that letter.'

For a second her natural curiosity got the better of

her. 'You're a land agent, Mr Trussardi? You look after properties in this city? Is that correct?'

Mr Trussardi, still holding the unopened letter, smiled suddenly, slightly wolfishly. 'Oh, no! I am not a land agent, my dear! I am an *agent*. A fixer, a man of affairs. I look after many things, properties included. I hold the papers for most of the families and buildings in this town, actually! There is not much I do not know.'

'Gosh, how useful you must be.' Posie would have liked to have asked more, but was gripped by that now-familiar piercing pain again, albeit fleetingly. Fox noticed and bit at his lip.

'Doctor Mozzato? He's in this building too?' she asked, breathless, through slightly gritted teeth.

The little man paused for a couple of seconds, frowning, but then beckoned to near the front door they had entered by. Tucked inside, to the far-left of the glass door, was a heavy green baize curtain hung on hoops. Trussardi flung it aside like a magician to reveal an ancient door. He pushed at it and it opened.

'This is his entrance, goes up to the right-hand tower. He's one floor up.'

Trussardi checked a gold fob-watch he'd dragged from a pocket. 'It's Friday, no? Almost ten o'clock? He normally doesn't work on a Friday. I don't know if he'll be ready for visitors. I know he's been very busy clearing out that place on the landing upstairs, for Miss Roberta. It used to be his medical supply storeroom, but, well, the Doctor *does* own the whole tower, his family have done for centuries, so I suppose it is his to do with as he likes.'

Trussardi looked momentarily upset, then wary, as if he'd said too much. The man recovered himself quickly.

'And I think the Doctor was out late last night. What I am saying is that you may find him not quite *ready*, shall I say. Usually people telephone, in advance.'

'We'll find out if he's up and about. Thank you, sir,' said

Fox authoritatively. And he and Posie started to tramp up the tiny, dark, winding staircase.

'Good job Roberta's not got much luggage, isn't it?' puffed Posie. 'If this is how she'll have to drag it up?'

'Mnnn. Shall I wait with you, Miss? Or shall I run and get the Boss?'

Fox sounded uncomfortable. But the place was so small and narrow it made you feel uncomfortable anyhow, claustrophobic.

'Let's see, shall we?' In truth the sudden pain had gone again, as suddenly as it had come.

They had reached a tiny landing, very dark, lit by two dim electric lamps placed in medieval cast-iron sconces.

In front of them in the gloom was an arched old oak door with a small metallic plaque stating Mozzato's name and occupation. On the opposite side of the landing was another door, less grand, with a piece of paper taped up with the words 'ROBERTA GRIMALDI' on it. The door was open.

Posie, curious as ever, patted it with her Mary-Jane.

'Oh, look! How clumsy of me! Or was it that sudden breeze? I'll close the door…'

She saw inside, and almost gasped. The place was tiny, probably the smallest flat she'd ever seen. A small room, of perhaps eight-foot square, with no natural light at all, was furnished with a single bed which took up nearly all the space, and one chair. It had been newly whitewashed and smelt of paint. To one side of the room was a tiny hob, and a miniscule sink, obviously just installed. To the other side of the room was a flimsy-looking door which must house a bathroom.

Through that open door you could see one tiny high-up window. The facilities were new, but the tower room was truly the last retreat of the desperate. It was cold, and a scent of damp permeated the place.

'Good heavens!' said Fox, who had followed Posie inside.

'This is not right at all. Our cells at the Yard are better than this! This is a cupboard, not a flat! No wonder old Trussardi downstairs looked unhappy about it all. Shame on the Doctor for allowing it! Even if Miss Grimaldi did agree. *She'd* agree to anything, poor woman.'

Posie, angry, but not quite sure who or where to direct her anger at, turned her attention now to Mozzato's door.

Fox instinctively stepped back. But then Posie saw that this door, too, was open.

'Doctor Mozzato?' she called.

'Hello? Anyone at home? It's Posie Parker here. You know, the Police Inspector's wife? You said if I needed you, I should drop by. Well, funnily enough, I'm sure it's nothing, but a couple of times now I've felt this pain and …'

She had pushed the door open, and inside, in a room with no natural light, but much bigger than the size of the ridiculous flat opposite, was an empty waiting room. She walked through it, noticing the same electric lights in sconces, and then she entered a consulting room, this one thankfully lit by the sunshine coming through a small tower window.

Fox was behind her.

No-one was about. A white coat was placed over the back of the desk chair, and a stethoscope was draped over it. The desk was completely bare, and the place, though spartan, was very clean.

'Doctor Mozzato?'

'Maybe he's been called out to some emergency, Miss.'

'Maybe.'

Posie saw another door, also open, leading off the consulting room. A room for storing medicines? A private flat? Surely there could be no more room in this very narrow tower?

She walked through, Fox at her side.

'Oh!'

The room they had entered was tiny, not much bigger than the one Roberta was to take up residence in. One small night-lamp was on, and it reflected in the glass of the well-stocked medicine cabinets running right around the walls. It looked as if this tiny windowless place had become both Doctor Mozzato's living quarters *and* his medical supply room, combined. In contrast to the neatness of his public rooms, here there was mess everywhere.

Last night's black dinner jacket lay discarded on the floor, white powder dusted like snow all over it.

There were empty packets of medical supplies lying about the place, bags ripped open, and neat lines of white powder laid out on mirror-tiles on the floor, unused.

And on the single bed pushed up against the far wall, next to a bowl containing a few used syringes, was Mozzato, one arm with a tourniquet around it.

He was dead to the world.

'I think he *is* the emergency, Miss.'

'Would you believe it, Sergeant Fox?'

Posie drew a frightened breath. 'I say! Is he…is he dead?'

But they both realised in that second that Mozzato was fine.

He was snoring.

* * * *

Twenty-One

Anger drove her on, clattering down the tower steps, followed closely by Fox.

'*Not quite ready!*' Posie fumed, getting to Trussardi's office at the bottom, now deserted. She pushed open the glass door and emerged onto the gloomy Erbe Square.

'Calm down, Miss,' instructed Fox, behind her. 'Shall we find another doctor for you?'

'No. It's absolutely fine. It was just that we happened to be there. I have no need of medical attention, I assure you.'

'Good. The Boss will have my guts for garters otherwise.'

She stood for a minute, trying to breathe.

'He *knew*, didn't he? Trussardi? He knew what we would find up there? That Mozzato is clearly an addict. And one of the most unscrupulous men I think I have ever come across. No wonder Roberta is in thrall to him: it's not about love at all, is it? Lorenzo wondered where Roberta and Giulia got their supply of drugs from, and now we know. Mozzato must be the dealer; easy as anything. Who questions a doctor? A highly-esteemed doctor, too, who serves on the town council and is obviously very well-regarded…'

She almost gasped for air: 'The man's been laughing at us all along. Do you remember Mozzato even had the audacity to tell my husband last night while we were standing next to Jacinta's poor dead body that drugs were a 'speciality' of his? The sheer nerve of the man frightens me! Perhaps *he's* behind the murders?'

'Calm down, Miss. From what we've seen we have no evidence of him supplying anyone, other than using drugs for his own personal use, which probably isn't a crime. I agree, it doesn't look good, and I promise we'll report it. But as for the murders, what's his motive? Forgive me, Miss, but I think you're being too hot-headed. Do calm down.'

'Fine.'

Posie clutched at her pink jacket as a sudden shrill breeze rustled through the tiny square.

'You're right, Sergeant Fox. Of course. But I think Trussardi *wanted* us to find Mozzato, didn't he? I think he knows exactly what's going on and he's horrified. Maybe Trussardi carries a torch for Roberta? I didn't see a wedding ring on his finger, did you? And Trussardi knows Roberta will move in there and have drugs available to her night and day, all the while living in that dreadful place, and – if Lorenzo is correct – we know that Roberta is about to be handed a big sum of money which she'll whizz through. In no time she'll get "sick", just like Giulia did, and die, and who will ever think of questioning Mozzato? Every which way, that man's a winner.'

Fox was buttoning up his coat. 'We'll look into it. I promise.'

'I think Richard should view Mozzato as one of the suspects too. He's been taken in by that fella, just because he's a doctor.'

'I agree, for what it's worth.' Fox checked his watch. 'It's quarter-past ten. We have an hour before the big briefing. Is there anything else you want to do?'

'Goodness, loads.'

They walked on to the Cathedral Square, which was

sunlit and bustling, a complete contrast to the Erbe Square. The café outside the Hotel Dante was already jam-packed with locals and tourists alike, and a photographer had positioned himself by the Cathedral steps, next to a street artist who was chalking iconic images of the town onto the floor, a rag cap out for money.

'This is my first time in Italy, Miss,' said Fox suddenly. 'I like it, and this town especially. It's very special. Even if the case is peculiar.'

Posie smiled. 'I like it here too, and so did Jacinta, and she was normally a good judge of things. I think, on the whole, she even judged Lorenzo right.'

Posie nodded: 'She'd have been married by now. I'd have been about to throw rice and the rosebud confetti I'd brought especially from Fortnum's all over them.'

They heard the chimes for the quarter-hour ringing out from the Cathedral, and also from the biggest of all the towers, the famous Torre Grossa, which had outfoxed the crafty Salvucci family all those hundreds of years ago. The tower was right next to the Town Hall, almost a part of it; the whole institution set at right angles to the squat Cathedral.

Posie indicated towards the Town Hall. 'Is Deverine still in that police cell in there?'

'Yes. He hasn't been moved yet. Won't be, now, will he? He'll be released most likely, later. Now they don't think he killed Lady Nella. What do you want with Deverine, Miss?'

'Truth is I'm not quite sure.'

They walked slowly up the steep steps to the Town Hall, Posie watching the red flags of the town council far, far above them, fluttering in the breeze. She saw Fox looking with interest at the faded painted coats of arms on the white marble level of the building, symbols of long-dead families, six hundred years past their glory days.

'I've been inside before, and it's lovely, Sergeant,' she

said, half out-of-breath. 'You should have a look around if you have time. Dante came here, you know. There's a beautiful room named after him upstairs, with gorgeous frescoes all in glittering red and gold, as fresh as if it had been painted yesterday.'

Fox looked rather unimpressed, and led the way carefully along a corridor inside the Town Hall and told Posie to wait for him. She watched as Fox got out his police identity papers and then disappeared inside a glass door, complete with gold-emblazoned bold declarations: 'CARABINIERI, COMANDO STAZIONE, SAN GIMIGNANO'.

When he came out Fox was wielding a very large, ancient-looking key on a ribbon of red moth-eaten velvet.

'Next door along, Miss.'

The cell was considerably bigger than the whole flat Roberta Grimaldi was moving to, cheerier too. It faced out over the square, and its large arched open window was barred with thick rods of iron. From outside came a steady burble of noise: tourists calling out to each other with their American and English accents; the photographer plying his trade. A reminder of life going on like usual.

A jug of water and some untouched biscuits sat on a tray on the floor.

Simon Deverine was still wearing last night's dinner clothes, somehow not at all crumpled, considering he had spent all night here, but the dreadful rust-red stain all over his shirt-front was a horrible reminder of the tragedy.

Deverine sat with his arms crossed on a small truckle bed, which was immaculately made-up. That military bearing, that military training couldn't be taken away by a night in an Italian prison cell, with the threat of death as a punishment hanging over his head. He viewed Fox and Posie now with not an ounce of surprise or malice.

He's very calm for a man accused of murdering his wife, thought Posie to herself.

Fox had gone for more chairs, and in the silence of his absence, Deverine smiled. 'Thank you for coming to see me, Miss Parker. I enjoyed our chat last night.'

'Me, too. In fact, that's why I'm here.' She grabbed her notebook and a pencil from the clutch bag. 'I wanted to follow up on two things you said.'

'Oh? Of course. Anything to help.'

But Fox was back, dragging two chairs behind him.

'Why haven't they moved me yet, Sergeant?' cut in Deverine quickly, for the first time a glimmer of unease sounding through that hearty, ringing voice.

'They took away my watch when I was placed here but from the trajectory of the sun outside, I'd say it was after ten o'clock now; half-past, more like. I understood I'd be on my way to Florence first-thing?'

Fox took off his hat, folded his arms, still standing. 'Congratulations are in order, sir. Looks like you'll walk out of here a free man, Mr Deverine. Sometime later today.'

'Oh?' Deverine was unshaken. 'How so?'

Fox explained the theory which had been arrived at, about the Paris Green arsenic which had been found.

Deverine looked from Fox to Posie, his bushy eyebrows knitted together, his arms still crossed.

'So you're telling me that Nella poisoned Jacinta with rat poison, then shot herself with the gun she had stolen from my bedroom?'

'Apparently, sir. You don't seem surprised.'

Deverine barked with laughter. 'I'm old, laddie. Nothing surprises me anymore. This whole affair is a bally shame though. Those two women shouldn't be dead. No, not at all. A terrible waste of life. What were your questions, Miss Parker?'

'I'd like to ask you about your wife, sir.'

'My *ex*-wife.' Deverine rolled his eyes in mock despair. 'And don't I know it. Yes. What about her?'

'What was it like being married to her, sir?'

Fox coughed behind Posie at this personal question, but Posie stood her ground, stared right back into Deverine's bright blue eyes. Eyes which had loved and lost, had betrayed and now knew a sort of betrayal. He smoothed the ends of his handlebar moustache.

'It's a fair question, Miss Parker, and I don't mind answering it. It was all right at first, even though I was warned there was madness in the Harewood family, and that Nella didn't have a penny to her name. Well, I didn't believe the first thing and I didn't care about the second! We were only married two years, and for the last year she was barely around.'

'She travelled about, you said?'

Lorenzo, of course.

'That's right. I let her do as she wished, indulged her. I'm a busy man myself, as it happens. I was off in Africa a good part of last summer and autumn. I own half a mining interest over there. We were like ships passing in the night, Nella and I, certainly by the end.'

'Does it surprise you, about the Paris Green arsenic, sir?'

Deverine shrugged. 'As I said to the good Sergeant here, nothing surprises me. I thought she might poison *me* one day. Heaven knows, she tried to poison my name.'

'What do you mean by that, sir?'

Deverine looked quickly away, down at his hands with their long fingers. No wedding ring. 'I can't go into it. I'm sorry.'

He looked up again, frowning. 'I must say, it all seems well-planned-out, though. Mostly everything Nella did was in a chaotic frenzy. She loved drama, but not the boring day-to-day details. She loved spending money, but she was terrible with it. I tried to cure her of that by only giving her a one-off settlement on the divorce, so she'd *have* to be careful with it. Gracious me! It's only just sinking in. Arsenic, eh? You're sure?'

'Yes, sir. I saw it.'

'And all of this was over that dashing ice-cream laddie, eh?'

'You *knew*?' Posie was caught on the hop.

Deverine laughed. 'I may be older, but I'm not stupid. I knew there was *someone*. I realised Nella was getting on and off boats and trains and planes for someone last year. And then last night I knew for sure, as soon as Nella walked into the dining-room, her eyes blazing. I knew it was *him*. What a horrible, damnable, sticky old mess. Wretched Nella.'

'But I watched as you held her, sir, as she was dying. You loved her still, didn't you?'

Deverine looked briefly away, out of the window with its view of terracotta roof tiles and blue patches of sky, pigeons, here as anywhere.

He turned back: 'You're dashed astute, Miss Parker. Suppose you have to be in your job, eh? Well, love came late for me, and I was crazy about Antonella Harewood. I swear I didn't see that flash of madness below the surface. It remained hidden, at least for a few months. I was taken in. But you don't forget your first love.'

'Can I ask you about Neville Coleman?'

Deverine looked surprised, but happy to be changing subject, and Fox shifted in his chair, pointedly checking his watch.

This won't take long.

'What about him, Miss Parker?'

'You knew him?'

'Of course I knew him! I met Neville before the Great War; he was a lunatic even then, with all his outdoor pursuits. I convinced him into joining the Royal Air Force for the Great War and mercifully we both survived! We were in the same squadron for a couple of years actually. I was getting old, and at the point of taking a desk-job, but Neville, so much younger, convinced me to keep flying.' Deverine passed a hand across his eyes.

241

'There was one occasion, over the Somme, 1918, when we were both in aerial contact with the Red Baron and his Flying Circus. But we all survived, by the grace of God alone…' Deverine trailed off, lost to his memories.

He sighed heavily after a few seconds: 'The trouble with Coleman was that he, like the Red Baron, thought he was invincible. And no-one is invincible.'

'And you lived in the same building? Dalmeny Court?'

'That's right. Although "lived in" is a bit strong to describe Coleman's arrangements. After the Great War we lost touch. Met again in about 1922, or early 1923. I'd met Nella, was thinking of marrying. Coleman told me about this fancy set of apartments he was buying into, convinced me it would be a good thing to do the same. Best decision I ever made. Lovely flat, worth much more now than what I paid for it. But Coleman was barely there: he was always off doing something for the Royal Geographical Society. They sponsored him climbing, you see. I ran into him again properly last year. It was in the lift, late one night, and he was with some mindless, gorgeous, pretty little thing, one of many. But he was very rude to me, as it happens.'

Deverine laughed sadly. 'I was with Nella, coming back from the theatre. He asked why I hadn't ever told him I had a daughter! Nella almost slapped old Coleman round the chops, despite this other girl being there! It was quite heated. But we smoothed things over. We had a party in our flat the next evening, the theme was "Venice" or some such rot. Everyone in masks, that kind of thing. Coleman came alone, and that's where he met Tony.'

Deverine beamed. 'Tony was looking pretty sparkling, actually; must have borrowed something of Nella's. I think Coleman fell for her there and then. She wasn't his usual bit of fluffy-headed stuff, and he had had many girls by this point, believe me! But he adored Tony. I think it was her calm; the opposite of himself, really.'

'I see.'

Deverine sighed heavily. 'But we had other dealings, Coleman and I.'

'Oh?'

'Yes. We owned this mine together, in Africa. He told me about it last year. Said it was a prospect. Not like the diamond mines and all the problems those mine-owners and the poor workers were facing. This was speculation, but probably a runner. A copper mine. A Copperbelt up in Nkana, North Rhodesia. Those devils at the British South Africa Company weren't biting, wouldn't go near it. Well, the fact *they* weren't interested made me want to pursue it, and I told Coleman I was ready to pump most of my savings into the project. He said he'd do the same. We would own it outright, together, in equal shares. We set off last summer to see Nkana, and I stayed on to oversee the setting-up of the thing.'

'Is the Nkana Mine prospering, sir?'

'Not yet!' Deverine laughed. 'But it *will* work. It will be a long-term thing. Probably won't get rich on it for at least another five or six years, but there seems to be a big seam of copper up there, and it's starting to come up now. It's a very exciting mine. The irony is that the British South Africa Company suddenly realised they were missing out on a good thing. They came in on it. Stamped their wretched red crest with those silly goats on it all over the bally place. Now everything I sign has that abominable shield on top of it.'

'Oh?' Posie was confused. 'But how could they, if you and Neville owned the shares equally?'

'Because unbeknownst to me, while I was back in London and Neville was off on his ill-fated climb in Switzerland, he sold his shares to them, without telling me. The swine! Good job he fell off that ruddy great mountain otherwise I would bally well have pushed him off!'

Deverine looked shaken, almost wiping tears away from his eyes. 'I'm only joking, of course. Maybe the fella needed the money? I don't know. He'd have done jolly well out of the sale, though.'

'One last thing, sir.' Posie looked at her notes. 'I know you got a note from Charlie Seego last night. He said you had "a great deal in common". You told my husband you didn't know the man. Is that really the case?'

'Absolutely. Never heard of the fella. Maybe he confused me with someone else? Although, I must say he looks a little familiar.'

Posie was clawing at ideas.

'Did Nella know Seego? Or does Tony know him?'

Why was he sending Tony notes, then? If he didn't know her?

What was the connection?

'Haven't the foggiest, but I don't think so.'

'Thank you.'

'By the way, Miss Parker, that's a very lovely little bracelet you've got on there. Is that the one your husband bought you? I was chatting to him about it last night at dinner, before things turned sour. He was very proud he'd found you something he thought you would like. Said something about you only ever wearing the same wretched string of pink beads; how he thought you might take them off, but you never did!'

'Mnnn. Well…'

Posie blushed, shy, wrong-footed: instinctively feeling her collarbone, where her string of pink Murano glass beads nestled there cosily, always warm. The gift, years before, of another man. Another man whose memory, like his gift, would never be discarded. No matter how much Lovelace wanted that to happen.

Deverine smiled sadly. 'I always thought that would be a perk of having a beautiful wife. I had visions of us going along the Burlington Arcade, or Bond Street, shopping for jewels. But it was not to be with Nella. She hated jewellery. Hated the feel of it. Refused it! Wouldn't even wear a bally watch! She liked swimming, you see, and hockey. Actually, anything sporty. She said jewellery got in the way: had hated it since school. Asked me for the cash instead to go off travelling, or to buy clothes from Paris. Well, that suited me fine. She never had a regular allowance from me, but I'd give her chunks of money, just as much as she wanted.'

Deverine pulled at his magnificent moustache again.

'Puh! I only ever gave her one pair of ruby earrings as an engagement present. And her engagement ring, of course. *That* was a ruby too, great beautiful thing it was: cost a fortune. But she threw it down a drain in front of Dalmeny Court on the night of…on the night of…'

The Pink House, Soho? On the night of the grounds for the divorce?

Well, Posie had to hand it to Nella Harewood, she had certainly had flair. And courage.

Promising to call for him later, they left the cell, and left the Town Hall.

'Got everything you needed, Miss?'

'No idea.' That, at least, was true.

'I have a few things to do, Miss. It's quarter to eleven. See you back at the Guesthouse for the meeting? Maybe you should go and have a quick lie down?'

'Absolutely not. See you shortly.'

Posie wasn't about to lie down. She had puzzles to solve, and answers to find.

'Oh, Sergeant? That passport of Nella Harewood's. Can I have it, please? Just for the next half hour?'

Fox narrowed his eyes, not happy, but he dug in his smelly old Vicar's green coat and handed it over just the same.

* * * *

Twenty-Two

Posie watched Fox walk away.

Instinctively she walked up the steps to the Cathedral, not going straight in, but rather through the Baptistry Loggia, past the stunning *Annunciation* where the angel Gabriel was still giving his piece of earth-shattering news to a fifteenth-century Madonna.

That unexpected communication.

Wretched Charlie Seego with his strange typed communications!

Where did he come into all of this?

And what was it which Simon Deverine had told her just now which had felt – for a couple of seconds at least – important? Something about Seego?

A thought which had broken to the surface and then disappeared again, like a deadly ice-berg slipping from view...

But the thought continued to escape her.

Posie walked on. A stone-cold breeze was whistling along the corridor here, and she was quite alone. She ducked through a small archway and was immediately inside the beautiful Santa Fina Chapel.

'Oh!'

The place was deserted, lit by burning candles. A Mass

was taking place in the main part of the Cathedral next door, and Posie sunk down onto one of the pews in the small space.

White roses, Jacinta's bridal flower of choice, covered everything: the pew ends, the small altar, the lectern. The florist at the Porta San Matteo obviously hadn't been informed of the fact the wedding could no longer go ahead, for want of a bride.

One thing which Lorenzo had let fall through the net.

Posie picked the nearest white rose from its little green wire holder and pressed its fleshy petals between her hands. She smelt the sweet, clear scent, rising up stronger now as the petals were crushed. She offered up a small prayer for Jacinta.

Hands on her stomach, eyes tearing up, Posie looked at beautiful fresco of the teenage Santa Fina, laid out in her tragic pink robes beneath the impossible blue summer sky which Ghirlandaio had painted so skilfully five hundred years before in this chapel. She saw the towers of San Gimignano painted so realistically you wanted to reach out and touch them. The one incongruous note was that a real-life angel with blue wings was fluttering in the air near one of the towers, ringing out a peal of bells.

A blessed town.

A visual trick, obviously. But believable, nonetheless. Angels in the sky of San Gimignano. Well, why not?

Tricks worked, as long as people were willing to believe in what they saw.

As long as what they saw was convincing.

Posie sighed and pulled out her notebook. She read in the dim light the notes she had taken at Deverine's interview.

Not much, to be honest, that she hadn't known, or guessed at. The only new pieces of information were Coleman's back-story, his training as a fighter pilot, and the story about Deverine and Coleman going in on the copper mine together.

Mines.

What was it Deverine had said? He'd talked of a '*wretched red crest with those silly goats on it.*'

'*Oh!* What a fool I've been!'

Posie was rising, blindly, white rose petals dropping to the floor all around her. She picked up her clutch bag, missing the weight of her normal carpet bag.

What if the connection between Simon Deverine and Charlie Seego was simply the copper mine?

Hadn't Posie seen a map, all red-orange, dotted about with pins, on Seego's wall? And hadn't there been a red crest with two goats above it?

They were goats. Not unicorns!

Was Seego something to do with the British South Africa Company? And with that particular mine – Nkana?

Had *he* been in charge of buying out Coleman's half-share? Was it a stretch of the imagination to think he was some sort of representative, maybe here to smooth things over with Deverine?

Hadn't Deverine said the mine was little more than speculation at the moment; that it wasn't yet producing anything?

And hadn't Seego, when questioned by Richard about the materials he had been burning in the grate claimed it was '*just a lot of hot air; speculation*'. He must have thought he was being oh, so clever.

But why was Seego being so cloak-and-dagger about the whole thing? Owning a mine or a half-share in one wasn't illegal. Unless he wanted to now buy out Deverine's half-share too? That could be something to be tight-lipped about, surely? A cautious, secret approach? Which even Simon Deverine was unaware of.

But even if that *were* the case, what had that to do with the murders here, if anything?

I need a telephone, Posie thought desperately. *I need to speak to someone who will listen to my jumbled thoughts.*

Not Dolly, her best friend.

Dolly Cardigeon was in the South of France still, keeping warm and dry in Nice, following doctor's orders, trying to tamp down the wretched illness and hacking cough which overcame her every single winter in England. Besides, Dolly was usually out of the Hotel Negroni when Posie called, and generally difficult to track down.

It had to be Len.

Len Irving. Posie's partner at the Detective Agency.

Rushing down the steep steps to the Cathedral Square, Posie tore across the cobbles as fast as her swollen feet could carry her. She wove through the crowds outside the Hotel Dante, and went inside, hoping the telephone for public use had now been repaired.

She was in luck.

Dashing to the booth, Posie hoiked herself up with great difficulty onto the high stool as she waited for the International Operator to connect her to London. She heard the fuzzy bleakness of the line, and she thought of her flat, and her work, far, far away.

'Wotcha, Po!'

It was Len. Bright and cheery as a row of bunting. 'Thought you'd be at Miss Glaysayer's weddin', Posie. Anythin' up?'

'I'll say.'

Having explained about Jacinta's murder, but omitting anything about Lady Nella Harewood, and having received suitably outraged and horrified responses from Len, Posie came to the point.

'I thought you might be able to help me, Len. I'm hitting a brick-wall. There's a man out here, and I feel like I should know who he is. And *you* know most people – by sight or name anyhow – in London, don't you? Can I run a name past you? This man might be a criminal; he might not.'

'Give us a go then.'

In the background Posie could hear the excitable murmur of Sidney the office boy.

'Ready, Len? It's C-H-A-R-L-I-E, first name. Then S-E-E-G-O, surname. Yep, that's it.'

Posie could hear him repeating the name to himself, muttering slightly. She could visualise Len now, in the Grape Street office, leaning against the main reception desk, his handsome face contorted with concentration, hating to fail at a task with which he had been entrusted.

'Hmnn. Nah, sorry, Po. It doesn't sound familiar to me. What about asking old Sam Stubbs at the *Associated Press*? He's Editor there now, isn't he? He'll have a rustle around the archives for you, for sure.'

'Perhaps.' Posie blew out her breath in frustration.

'Hang about, Po.'

There was a sudden clattering noise, like the sound of the telephone receiver being dropped. A lot of background noise.

'Miss, Miss?'

'Sidney?' Posie asked, slightly panicked. 'Is Len all right?'

She could hear Len in the background whooping and shouting: 'He's only gone and bally done it! Atta-boy, Sidney! You tell her, lad!'

'What? Tell me *what*?'

The teenage Sidney's voice was calm-sounding, but he was obviously very proud of himself.

'Mr Irving wrote that name you gave 'im down, Miss, and I was lookin' at it, and I played one of my usual scramblin' games, Miss. So I scrambled this name "CHARLIE SEEGO", and guess what you get? *Who* you get! It's an anagram, Miss! And yes, he's famous!'

Posie tried to keep up. Anagrams and word games had never been her strong suit.

'Tell me.'

'It's only Leigh O'Crease! "Charlie Seego" is an anagram

of "Leigh O'Crease". You remember? The posh chappie they called the "Diamond King" who killed his best pal in a duel, and probably then his own wife, too!'

'Oh, golly.'

Posie closed her eyes for a few seconds, hearing the excitable chirruping of the men in her office, hundreds of miles away.

Oh, yes. Now she realised where she had seen that angelic face before; staring out from every news-stand in London last year, as the summer days had cooled into autumn.

She recalled the story of Leigh O'Crease, the second son of Lord McMahon, who had been out in Africa for several years together with his best friend, Padraig Kennedy, the son of the Duke of McGarry. They'd been busy setting up diamond and gold mines, until it had all gone spectacularly wrong when Padraig had started an affair with Leigh's wife, Áine.

Posie recalled the reports from the papers about what had followed: a duel between the two old friends on an autumn morning on British soil; Padraig killed; the dead man's father, the Duke, declaring Leigh a murderer, offering a reward for Leigh's capture.

Regardless of whatever the Duke was offering, under British law Leigh O'Crease was a murderer, and all the ports and airports had closed to him. But Leigh O'Crease had simply disappeared. As if by magic.

And then just before Christmas the story had re-emerged, but this time with an extra sting in its tail; Áine O'Crease had also vanished.

Posie remembered laughing about the story with Len on Christmas Eve, but there seemed nothing funny about it now.

Nothing at all.

Len was back on the line.

'Well, well, well. Nice little hot-spot you've got yourself into there, Po. You think O'Crease may have killed Miss

Glaysayer? Is he insane? He's wanted for two counts of murder over here now, you know? The authorities want him for the murder of Padraig Kennedy, *and* for the murder of the lovely Áine.'

'Although there's no body?'

'You don't need a body, do you, these days, to register someone as being dead? Look at the Neville Coleman case.'

Posie didn't go into how *that* particular case was impacting things out here, too.

'You need to keep this a secret, Len. You and Sidney.'

'Oh, okay.' Len sounded sorely disappointed.

'Anything else, Po? We're quiet just now. What a thing! Leigh O'Crease! Are you going to bring him in to English justice? Claim the bounty money on his head set by the Duke of McGarry?'

'I doubt it. I say, Len. Can you find out some background for me on Leigh O'Crease? Is there a connection with the British South Africa Company?'

"Course. I'll go round the corner to the *Associated Press* offices now.'

'Call me back at the Guesthouse, soon as you can, Len. And thanks awfully. Sid, too.'

Replacing the receiver in its cradle, she checked her small red wristwatch for the time: almost eleven o'clock.

She flipped to her notebook, reading her transcript of Deverine's interview yet again. She read about money. How Nella was bad with money.

'Oh, yes.'

This might be worth investigating.

And then Posie pulled out the tiny, much-folded butt of the Haggerty's chequebook she had taken from Nella Harewood's suitcase in the attic room, and she lined it up together with Nella's passport, and picked up the receiver again.

Just enough time.

She asked the International Operator for a connection to the Manager of Haggerty's Bank in London. While she waited, she flicked through all the stubs of the chequebook, but they were too worn to read.

Posie turned to the passport itself, saw the photograph inside of an unsmiling Nella, with her signature plaited hairdo. She was wearing those same ruby drop earrings, one of which Posie had found on the attic floor; Deverine's engagement present.

It seemed that this passport had been obtained on the occasion of her marriage, and Nella's new married name of 'LADY ANTONELLA DEVERINE' had since been blacked out by some official stamp, and re-written underneath as 'LADY ANTONELLA HAREWOOD'. A stamp stating 'DIVORCED WOMAN' had been printed right over the bottom of the photograph. As if it was some terrible stigma.

Which to some, *most*, even, Posie supposed, it still was.

Posie felt suddenly angry on Nella's behalf, to have been forced to carry around such a demeaning document, when it had been her husband who was all to blame for the divorce.

'Putting you through now, Madam. The Strand, 8934. London. Connecting…'

Posie's eyes ranged quickly over the other pink pages of Nella's passport, at the stamps and handwritten entry dates to various countries listed inside.

A deep, friendly voice came clearly down the line: 'Good morning, Lady Harewood, is it?'

For the first time in her career as a detective, Posie lied. She took a big gulp, spoke as normal, but added Nella's aristocratic drawl.

'Yes, this is Lady Harewood.'

'Soames here. We met after Christmas? Before you left for the South of France.'

'Oh, yes. As the Operator told you, I'm calling from Italy.'

'How lovely. I'm sure you'll understand, Lady Harewood, but can I have some form of *proof* as to your identity? Just to be on the safe side.' The man coughed delicately: 'We have had some unfortunate cases of...'

'Oh,' Posie sighed theatrically, as if it was all too, too much. 'Yes, of course. How frightfully boring. You want my account number?' She reeled it off from the stub of the chequebook where it was just visible. 'And my passport number, too, perhaps?'

She read it aloud.

'That will do nicely, Lady Harewood.' Mr Soames sounded apologetic.

'Now, how can I help you today?'

'I wanted to check my balance, Mr Soames. I'm worried I'm running out of money. Nearly through that lump-sum settlement from my ex-husband...'

'Oh? Let me have a look in the ledger.'

There was a slight sound of pages turning. A scramble for the receiver. 'Well... Here we are.'

Posie held her pencil in taut excitement.

'Your husband's settlement – six thousand pounds – is almost gone. Spent, from what I can see here, in cheques cashed in the South of France, mainly in Nice. You will recall that I *did* advise buying something with that money. A small house in the Home Counties, perhaps? But you told me you had no need. You were planning on re-marrying.'

'Quite.'

Posie's heart hammered so loudly in her chest she thought it had upset her unborn child, who started to thrash around energetically.

What re-marriage? To Lorenzo?

A spurt of pain.

Ignore it for now. Breathe through it.

'And of course, those large regular monthly payments which were coming in have all stopped.'

'Regular payments? Oh, yes…'

'But you've curbed your expenditure a bit, haven't you? You've stopped bailing your cousin Tony out all the time. Every month.'

'That's right. Couldn't continue.'

'Well, I should think there was no need, now.'

It sounded as if Nella Harewood had really sat down and opened her heart to this man, Mr Soames, right after the divorce. And he had listened, and wanted to help her. But then, what man wouldn't? Posie remembered the eyes of every man in the room riveted upon Nella Harewood; upon her fatal beauty.

'So how much do I have left?'

'Er, let me see. A thousand. More or less.' Posie could hear Soames snapping his ledger shut.

Soames spoke in an undertone now: 'But don't forget, Lady Harewood, you *do* have that reserve. As agreed, I placed it in our safe and it's there still. You give me the word, and I will arrange a sale. I'm sure we could get at least another three thousand for it, *minus* sale costs of course.'

What on earth was he talking about?

'That sounds a good idea. Hold tight for now. I'll make contact again soon.'

Posie felt dreadful saying this, because of course Nella would never make contact with anyone ever again.

She rang off, trying to make sense of what she had heard.

Oh, for some clarity.

Her watch told her it was five-past eleven. Richard's catch-up meeting back at the Guesthouse was in ten minutes.

She hated being late. But she'd *have* to be on this occasion.

She needed to urgently understand how it was possible for one woman to get through almost five thousand pounds in less than three months in Nice.

And she knew just who to ask.

Posie plucked up the telephone again, and asked the International Operator for a connection to the Hotel Negroni, in Nice. And she twined her fingers for good luck.

The man at the Negroni reception desk answered in what felt like record time.

'The Countess of Cardigeon?' asked the Frenchman, pleasantly. 'Ah, but she 'appens to be passin' me right now! On 'er way to the beach! Can I get her to speak to you on *this* apparatus, Madam, at the desk 'ere? Or is it a matter *très privé?*'

Urging the man to grab Dolly right this minute, Posie waited a couple of seconds and was rewarded by hearing Dolly's dulcet, reassuring cockney tones; her deep smokers' cough which preceded any words.

'Posie, darlin'? You all right? Nothin' awful to tell me, I 'ope? The baby? All fine?'

'Absolutely. Everything is simply tickety-boo. I'm in Tuscany, you know, in an awful mad rush. I need your opinion.'

'Oh? 'Course, darlin'. What is it?'

'Nice is expensive, Dolly, isn't it?'

'Gawd, yes! Makes me eyes water, but Rufus is payin' for everythin'. Why? You thinkin' of stoppin' by on yer way back? Bad timin' if so. I'm on me way back to London tomorrow!'

'No. I'm not coming through. Listen, there was a girl out there, an aristocrat. Her name was Nella Harewood.'

'Oh, yes of course! Nella! Everyone knew her here. I saw 'er a good deal, you know. But she was stayin' at The Ritz, not 'ere at the Negroni. She was livin' like she was on some crazy trip: handsome private driver; trips to the finest boutiques on the Promenade des Anglais every single day; a whole suite to herself, with a private swimmin' pool; tennis classes at all hours; champagne drunk like it was water. She was in and out of the sea about a hundred times a day, too. Gave parties which were completely wild. I've never seen anythin' like it!'

Dolly paused for a second, and Posie imagined her lighting up a smoke.

'Maybe Nella was celebratin' gettin' shot of that awful cheat of an old husband, eh? Anyway, she's gone. She left a few days ago. I saw her about a week ago in her suite at the Ritz for a farewell champagne tea. She seemed a bit different then, come to think of it. A bit sad. A bit unsure. I thought she might have drunk herself off her rocker.'

'How so?'

'She was blitherin' on to me about regrets. About lost chances. I thought she was talkin' about her ex-husband at first – we do all read the newspapers out here! But no: turns out she thought she had a stalker. She was convinced someone was followin' her about the town! I told her that with a face like she'ad, it was a wonder she didn't get people followin' her about town every day of her life!'

Dolly sighed. 'Place sure feels quieter without 'er right now, though, I can tell yer!'

'Was there a man with her, out in Nice?'

'Not in the way you mean, lovey. I had the feelin' she was just here to enjoy herself. Or she was waitin' for somethin', or for better times to come. Why? Somethin' happened to her?'

Posie lied and said no. It wasn't her job to report on Nella's life, or death.

She rang off and gathered her things together, thinking hard.

What a change it must have been for Nella Harewood to swap the highest glamour possible in Nice, The Ritz, no less, to come *here*, to an out-of-season San Gimignano, to the quiet tranquillity of the Tuscan hills, where the bells rang a quiet peace over a town where saints slept and medieval angels flew among the towers.

All for Lorenzo?

From what Dolly had said, it sounded as if Nella was spending her way through her settlement as if she hadn't a care in the world. Had she been biding her time, waiting for the right moment to come here? Hoping Lorenzo would answer one of her many letters? Saving up her cousin Tony's invite until the moment when it seemed certain Lorenzo's wouldn't be forthcoming?

And who, or what, had Nella Harewood imagined was stalking her?

Because that was just downright odd.

As she made to leave the booth and pay for her calls Posie suddenly had a final, throwaway thought. It was madness, utter madness. Ridiculous! But still...

Angels flying next to towers.

Tricks.

A trick.

A half-baked suspicion had occurred to her, but the idea wasn't fully-formed as yet.

Posie stepped back into the booth. She put a call through to her Detective Agency once again and Sidney answered.

'Oh! Hullo, Miss! I'm afraid Mr Irving went out, on your orders. It's just me here.'

Posie smiled. 'It's you I need, Sidney, especially after that sterling effort earlier.'

'What, Miss? Anything!'

'I need two things. The first is to get a birth certificate for me, along at Somerset House on the Strand. I need you to then call me with the details you find on it. And here's the second thing: it sounds bally odd, but *find* me someone, will you? Probably an old, retired person, actually. By the sea. Have you got a pencil ready?'

She gave him the details.

'And I need you to ask this old person if they'll speak to me by telephone. Here's the Guesthouse number. Tell them it's a National Security issue, and Scotland Yard are involved. But they need to speak direct to *me*, and it has to be today.'

* * * *

Twenty-Three

Lovelace was pacing the cobbles outside the Guesthouse. When he saw Posie waddling towards him he almost broke into a run.

'Where were you, darling? I was going crazy here! Especially as Fox told me you had a pain. Have you had it again?'

'Oh, it was nothing, Richard. Sorry about making you late for the meeting.'

'Oh, hang *that*.'

'Let's push on, I know everyone is waiting.'

But as she started to follow Richard into the Guesthouse and up the stairs, past a policeman who was still standing guard outside the dining-room, a telephone started ringing and Gloria came rushing out into the hallway.

'It's fer you, Miss. Mr Irvin', is it? From Grape Street, he said. Ooh! A real charmer, that one, isn't he?'

A short and elucidating conversation with the charming Len followed, under Richard's somewhat impatient eye.

'There's something else, Len. It's nagging away at me.'

'Tell me, Po. Let me help. I told you, we're quiet.'

'Could you step around the corner to Soho for me? Be as charming as only you can be. You might need money. Take whatever is in the change tin. If necessary, promise more. I'll pay it myself next week, when I'm back. But don't for goodness' sake mention any police connection, or *me*.'

When she'd finished explaining what it was she wanted, and Len had promised to telephone back, they headed upstairs.

Their bedroom had been transformed: the lovely double bed pushed back against a wall, covered with a heavy black sateen overlay; the small tables moved to the sides of the walls and anything personal tidied away. Two normal-sized dining tables had been placed together in the centre of the room, with room for at least twelve people to sit. A carafe of water, together with a pot of steaming coffee was placed in the centre. With biscuits. Italian this time.

Posie found herself looking almost automatically for Patsy. And Lovelace rolled his eyes: 'The maid still has the dog, darling. Don't worry.'

'Oh, fine.'

The usual lingering perfume of Posie's Parma Violet perfume had been overlaid with a scent which was familiar to her from all the times she had been in any police headquarters or Incident Room: sweat and fear and determination.

Fox was busying himself with the coffee, whilst Commissario Maturo was already sat at the big table, with the horse-faced Lazzio next to him. Copious notes were piled up in front of them. Richard sat down opposite Maturo, and beckoned Posie to sit next to him, Fox on his other side.

Lovelace, by some unexplained but general acceptance, took charge.

'Anything new, Commissario?' Lovelace asked briskly.

Maturo shook his head. 'Not really, Chief Inspector.' He crossed his arms over his black-uniformed chest and smiled his tragic smile. The medals he wore twinkled and tinkled as he flipped through his papers: 'A sad, sad case, ah? Let's deal with Lady Harewood first. The mobile

Forensics team have concluded, as they first thought, that this bullet was self-administered. Suicide.'

Lazzio patted his own pile of papers, cutting in. 'The body of Miss Jacinta Glaysayer has also been examined, and the death was certainly poison. Arsenic. The Forensics team are still down in the dining-room running a few last tests, but I doubt they will have anything new to add. That glass with the green arsenic crystals in it was pretty strong evidence, huh? So, at present we are saying that Lady Harewood poisons her friend, the owner of the Guesthouse, and then kills herself. It's all been planned ahead, and hence the tin of green arsenic. Quite neat, huh?'

Lazzio smoothed down his small blonde moustache, looking pleased with himself. 'However, there are some other small matters I have personally checked out. I have gone through all the statements from everyone in the house at the time of the dinner, including the catering people who cooked the meal. I have also checked and re-checked the movements of the electrician, Mr Brunelli, who Mr Rosario hired yesterday afternoon to repair the faulty cables here at the Guesthouse. They'd been on the blink awhile, apparently, but it was getting worse.'

'But the electrician wasn't at the Guesthouse at the time of the dinner, was he?' asked Posie, confused.

'No.' Lazzio smiled smugly.

'Mr Brunelli left here at about six-thirty. He'd been busy all afternoon here, with his young assistant, Carlo Belloni. The assistant was even climbing up on the roof, fixing cables, just before they left! *That* was the person who was reported to me by two separate locals as being on the roof, as being a possible thief. So at least we can eliminate that! Rosario telephoned Brunelli to come back here at about seven o'clock when the lights started to fail again but Brunelli didn't get the message. Only the assistant, Carlo Belloni, returned, and there was precious little he could do on his own, so he left. Carlo is not very experienced; I spoke with him. But I wondered if the story stacked up, or if Brunelli *had* somehow been responsible for those lights going off and on during the dinner, huh? If he had been paid handsomely, maybe, to create a convenient darkness? If he was hiding somewhere here, or had arranged it before he left at six-thirty?'

'Good thinking,' said Lovelace approvingly. 'Very thorough of you, Sergeant Lazzio.'

Lazzio shrugged. 'Thank you, sir, but it's a dead end. Brunelli, the electrician, has a very good reputation in this town and he has an alibi. He was eating in one of the town's taverns and was seen by many people there. When I questioned him Brunelli was adamant that he'd fixed the electrical problem before he left. He couldn't understand it. So, we must conclude it was just bad luck, the lights failing. Or poor work by Brunelli. But nothing sinister, or planned.'

Commissario Maturo folded his arms across his chest, slightly defensively. 'We checked about those knives, too – the seven sharp knives which were thrown into the table during the darkness? – and we can't find an answer to that. Not at all.'

Posie was miles away, recalling again Jacinta's words: *'The Seven of Swords, the girl, means I'm going to be betrayed or let down by someone on the inside.'*

She dragged her thoughts back with an effort to listen to Maturo. His voice was not commanding, rather the reverse in fact.

Maturo was jabbing at his papers. 'The knives were definitely from here in the Guesthouse; they're kitchen knives, normally stored together in a big professional chef's block of about fifteen knives. No fingerprints were found on any of the seven knives nor on the block they were from; not a single print. And too many people had touched that tarot card at the centre of the ring of knives for the Forensics team to make any sense of it. But interestingly, the tarot card didn't match to any of the packs you had found at Miss Grimaldi's flat. It wasn't from a brand-new pack, either. It seems to be very, very old: made out of a special waxed, gold-plated card. The Forensics team say they've never seen a tarot card as old before. At least two hundred years old, they think. It's most peculiar.'

'*Two hundred* years old?' repeated Posie, flabbergasted. But what could the age of the card signify? If anything? It didn't seem to help at all.

Lovelace smiled. 'Well, it sounds as if you've been most thorough, gentlemen.'

Maturo shrugged. 'Hopefully, all being well and with sufficient preparation, the bodies will be back in England within twenty-four hours. If you want complicated autopsies doing, you can arrange it in London.'

You could almost hear the man's relief in his words, in the way he was happy to wash his hands of this horrible and complicated case.

His patch, but not his legal problem. Not at all.

'Well, yes. Maybe.' Richard Lovelace rubbed at the bristles on his chin, unconvinced. 'Now, Fox. What have you to add for us, Sergeant?'

Fox smiled. 'I've been checking out some anomalies concerning other people who were at the dinner last night. The first, as you instructed me, was to check out Lorenzo Rosario's entire back-history.'

Fox reported that both the Town Hall and the Banca della Toscana had confirmed Lorenzo Rosario's story about the Gelateria being bankrupt.

'The fella took over a sinking ship when he married his wife. No, a *shipwreck*, in fact. And Mr Rosario has built it all up again himself over the last couple of years, with a great big 'BANKRUPCY' sign around his neck, to boot. You have to admire him, really. And Mr Rosario is quite right about this Guesthouse, too. The bank confirmed Jacinta was making absolutely no profit on it. Rosario is, above all things, a good businessman.'

Lovelace scribbled this all down, but Maturo and Lazzio didn't touch their own notepads once. Their folded arms and polite nods were indicative of the fact that they wondered exactly why Fox was bothering with these loose ends. But Fox carried on:

'I also checked on our pal, Charlie Seego. I wanted to know where he'd been sending things. What was so sensitive that it had to be burnt before we searched his room?'

He drew his notebook towards him. 'And now I know *where* he was writing to, if not what about.'

'Go on,' urged Posie, who had her own knowledge about Seego which she hadn't yet shared. Her *pièce de résistance*.

Fox jabbed his finger triumphantly down at a list he'd made. 'He was sending telegrams to Africa. To a place in North Rhodesia, and to another place in Southern Rhodesia. Lots were sent yesterday. He also received telegrams from both those countries yesterday.'

'Africa, eh?' said Lovelace, an eyebrow raised in surprise. 'Bally odd, what?'

'Gets odder, sir. He sent a telegram to a tiny village just outside of Dublin, Ireland. And he also sent a telegram to London yesterday evening. To a firm of solicitors.'

Posie's ears pricked up. 'Which firm?'

'Pratchard's, Miss. Gray's Inn. And Charlie Seego sent a big parcel to Pratchard's, too. He sent it at the same time as the telegram, about seven-thirty. He must have popped out before dinner. He hasn't received anything from them though. And sadly the Post Office couldn't give me the text of each telegram, only the place it was being delivered to, or from.'

Fox took a cigarette from his tin, shook out a match to light it, offered one to Lovelace and the Italians too. 'So, we know Seego was up to funny stuff, but we don't know why. And we still don't know why he burnt papers in his room.'

'*I* know,' cut in Posie, although her mind was still playing catch-up, scurrying to make sense of the Pratchard's connection, failing to grasp it.

Lovelace held his gasper mid-air, hid his surprise well. 'Go on, my love.'

Posie took a deep breath. 'Are you ready? This is quite a bombshell.'

Everyone stared at Posie, concentration and nerves heavy about them, prickling the air almost.

She spoke quickly, all in a rush: 'Charlie Seego does not exist. His name is an anagram formed from his real name – Leigh O'Crease – he is, in fact, the famous "Diamond King". The man who is currently a British outlaw, with a price on his head for killing his best friend in a duel!'

'Oh, my giddy aunt.' Lovelace looked horrified and almost dropped the gasper.

Posie added what Len had confirmed for her a few minutes before on the telephone. That there was more than a slight connection with the British South Africa Company.

Leigh's father, like Padraig's, were both Chairmen of the Board at the company. That Leigh and Padraig had been out in Africa since before the Great War, not prospecting for themselves, but deeply involved in the company's business.

They'd been active in setting up the Bushtick Mine, a gold mine in Southern Rhodesia, on behalf of the British South Africa Company, which was now starting to turn a huge, huge profit.

'I'll continue to call our man "Seego" because it's easier,' said Posie, looking about at the flabbergasted policemen.

'Seego, despite what happened with Padraig, is obviously still active with the immensely successful Bushtick Mine, and is, I think, still working for the British South Africa Company. And I think he recently organised a buyout of half the shares in another mine, Nkana, in North Rhodesia. Copper, this time. He arranged this in November, a purchase from a private owner. All on behalf of the British South Africa Company. He's a businessman who likes to know what's happening wherever he has an interest, and hence the orange maps of Africa in his room, some with the crest of the British South Africa Company on them. Hence the telegrams, and the typewriter and papers, too.'

Fox was almost frothing at the mouth in astonishment. 'But how could he travel about, Miss? He's a wanted man!'

Posie shrugged. 'Where there's a will, there's a way. Especially when one has an enormously wealthy father who can probably help out with a very convincing "fake" second passport, and send money wherever it's needed. I suppose Seego and his father are in regular touch, and hence the Irish telegrams. Seego has been very clever: travelling in and out of Britain as "Seego", but for the most part on the Continent – and certainly when transacting business – travelling under his real name. After all, as "Leigh O'Crease" he's not a wanted man on the Continent at all, is he? The story about the duel would hardly matter anywhere else, would it?'

Lovelace looked grim and then ground out his cigarette with a heavy hand. 'I don't like the sound of this, Posie. Not one bit. Fella's a rotten egg. And actually, we can't do a dashed thing as he's right off our territory. As you say, he's not a wanted man *here*.'

Richard tore his hands through his hair. 'But what's he doing here, Posie? What has he to do with all this mess?'

Posie was not one hundred per cent sure of the answer to this herself, but she'd be dashed if she'd admit it, especially as Maturo and Lazzio were now staring at her as if she were about to produce a particularly sparkly rabbit from a hat.

'There *are* some connections…'

She explained about Deverine owning half the Nkana Mine along with Neville Coleman, the dead explorer, Tony Harewood's fiancé.

She explained how she thought Seego, on behalf of the British South Africa Company, had personally met with Neville Coleman and bought out his half-share. This had been after the duel of September 1924, when Seego had got out of Britain, but before Coleman had begun his ill-fated climb of the Eiger in November.

'I don't know where this meeting between Seego and Coleman took place. But I *do* know from the second passport in the name of "Charlie Seego" that he was back in England in February this year. Perhaps he was secretly visiting his father, or trying to track down his errant wife, if he hasn't killed her? But perhaps he was also delivering the papers which Neville Coleman had signed – selling his half of Nkana – to Neville's solicitors, Pratchard's. Maybe he'd promised Neville that he would do so? And perhaps that's why he's still in contact with Pratchard's? Otherwise, I have no idea.'

Lovelace raised an eyebrow. 'Likely as not. Maybe that's what the parcel was, going out to them last night? More deeds? Maybe co-signed by Deverine? Didn't you say *he's* the other owner?'

'Yes, darling. But I don't think Deverine has signed anything. The odd thing is that Deverine has no idea who Seego is. He knew Coleman had sold up, and that the British South Africa Company are the new owners, but he genuinely has no idea of Seego's real identity or interest in Nkana. I think that the typed message to Deverine from Seego you found yesterday, stating they "had much in common" was what it seems to be on the face of the thing: an introduction.'

Lovelace sighed loudly. 'This is complicated, but is it possible that Seego is simply here on unrelated business, then? That he wanted to engineer a meeting with Deverine, you think? Got wind of the fact Deverine would be staying here for a wedding and hoodwinked his way in? Nothing to do with the murders, then? That his furtive, suspicious manner is purely his own fear at his real identity being uncovered? Hence his unease at encountering *us* staying here, darling. His worries about "Detectives"?'

'I don't know any more than you do now, Richard.'

'Hmnn.'

Maturo looked as if he wanted to get things finalised. 'So, Chief Inspector, I think our mutual findings regarding the two deaths – cause and motivation – remains unchanged.'

Lazzio cut in: 'Yes, we will arrange for the bodies to be sent on tonight, huh? For loading onto the train leaving Florence in the morning?'

He looked from Fox to Lovelace and then briefly at Posie. 'You want to travel on the same train? I can arrange the passage back for you to England, huh? You come back with us to Florence this afternoon, in the police motor-car, huh?'

But just then a very important-looking Gloria popped her head around the door. She searched out Posie, but put up a hand, as if stopping traffic, to indicate Posie shouldn't bother getting up.

'Telephone message, Miss. Oh, nothing *confidential*-like. That wee slip of a boy at your work, it was. Got some cheek, h'ant he? Said to tell yer that a bird from Brighton was going to call you here, prompt, at two o'clock. And that he hadn't got the birth certificate yet. He was going to telephone you later, Miss, as soon as it was available.'

'Thank you, Gloria.'

Lovelace turned to Posie. 'Are you *sure* I know everything, Posie? Who or what is the "bird from Brighton"?'

'I don't know. Probably one of Sid's little jokes, that's all.'

Feeling peculiarly disheartened at the wait for her information, Posie watched as the four men stood, shaking hands as if they had just sealed a deal. Which, in a way they had.

She was reaching to pick up the pot of lukewarm coffee

to pour herself a cup, and wishing for a custard cream, when a heavy, urgent pounding was heard at the door.

The four policemen turned as one. '*Avanti*,' summoned Maturo.

A man in his sixties, bald, bespectacled, clad in black overalls and holding a big leather box of a briefcase in one hand and a piece of paper – which looked like a report with big official stamps all over it – in the other, stood in the doorway. Posie saw that the gold glitter and glimmer of the Italian fascist police extended even to their overalls, to the embroidery which read 'FIRENZE POLIZIA – ESPERTO DI MEDICINA LEGALE' on a breast pocket.

The man started wagging his index finger, talking in a fast Italian. He was obviously the head of the Forensics team, and Maturo seemed to hold him in high regard.

Maturo indicated the man should calm down and come into the room, which he did, in a hurry. He opened up his big briefcase on the floor, and Posie, rising from her seat, saw immediately the pink and blue litmus papers within, coloured with use. She saw the Paris Green tin of arsenic secured inside the briefcase and wrapped in some clear cover.

Posie saw how Lovelace and Fox were frowning, trying to make sense of what was going on. How they watched the bald man from the Forensics team point again and again at the tin of poison, then back at his litmus papers, shaking his head. He was picking up another smaller metal sample box, shaking it angrily.

'What is it?' cut in Lovelace at last.

'There's been a mistake, huh?' said Lazzio, groaning.

'A bad one.'

* * * *

Twenty-Four

They all sat down again. Carried on listening to the Forensics man, who, just as quickly as he had arrived, blustered out again, leaving his report slap-bang in the middle of the table.

A mare's nest, Posie thought, sharing a raised eyebrow with her husband, but not daring to voice the thought aloud.

Commissario Maturo sat, looking suddenly exhausted, reading the report, while it fell to Lazzio to give them the gist.

'Jacinta Glaysayer *did* die of arsenic poisoning,' he said, almost irreverently. 'But we were too quick with that wine-glass idea. We jumped to the wrong conclusion, huh? It wasn't that at all. Our fault.'

Fox narrowed his eyes. 'No arsenic in the wine glass? But there were crystals in it, and they looked green, didn't they? Like that jar of poison.'

'Mnnn. It's strange, huh? The Forensics team are saying Jacinta Glaysayer died of arsenic poisoning, and there *was* definitely arsenic in that glass of wine. But it was ineffective. It wouldn't have killed her.'

'I'm sorry?' exclaimed Lovelace in sheer disbelief. 'How's that possible?'

Lazzio continued to read out from the report, over the Commissario's shoulder, translating as he went.

'Apparently, arsenic of this type – Paris Green – needs to be absorbed by a food or drink substance over some time to be effective, and then you'd need a really big dose. Unless it is mixed into a porous, flammable material, and then it works very quickly. The arsenic crystals in the glass hadn't been in the wine long enough to be absorbed properly, and also, the dose wasn't big enough. But the Forensics team are certain that the Paris Green crystals *were* placed directly and deliberately into Miss Glaysayer's glass at the dinner itself, as the other glasses at the table and the wine bottles themselves didn't have a single trace.'

Posie was confused: 'But Sergeant Lazzio, you just said Jacinta was killed by arsenic? So how did *that* happen? Where was the arsenic which killed her? Was it another type of arsenic? This Paris Green poison in the wine, was that just for show? Or was it a miscalculation?'

Maturo met Posie's anguished gaze. 'It seems, Miss Parker, your friend died from eating ice-cream. That green ice-cream.'

'The *Perla D'Etna*!' Posie breathed, her heart thumping wildly. 'It was Jacinta's favourite!'

The Commissario made a regretful face. 'Well, it killed her. It was her undoing.'

He quickly translated the relevant page.

'The Forensics team tested everything in the dining-room and in the kitchen, but this particular tub of ice-cream, it was laden with arsenic. Absolutely full, but very well distributed. They think it was sprinkled in when it was being made. Arsenic tastes sweet, a bit metallic, but it would be entirely concealed in a strong-flavoured, sugary ice-cream. A scoop would have been enough to kill her. I think it is lucky no one else took the same flavour, correct?'

Posie nodded quickly. 'That's right. It's a very unique, strong taste. Most people don't like it, but some adore it.'

Maturo sighed. 'So we have a very dangerous, reckless killer on our hands. Someone who didn't care if another dinner-guest took some of the poisoned ice-cream and died. Someone who knew that Miss Glaysayer liked that particular flavour.'

Posie was remembering the conversation last night at dinner, by the ice-cream trolley, when the *Perla D'Etna* tub of ice-cream had re-surfaced, again, much to Lorenzo's horror and consternation. She remembered Jacinta saying, in front of everybody, how much she loved it, and how she had seen it out on display in the Gelateria on Wednesday, even handing it out as tasters to some tourists. Jacinta had also taken a spoon of it herself.

'*Oh!*' Posie clapped her hands to her mouth, thoughts tumbling together into some sort of order.

'Darling?' Lovelace looked grim.

'Jacinta had a stomach-ache, didn't she? Yesterday morning? It was put down to nerves. But she'd eaten a tiny amount of the ice-cream the day before. And that tourist who complained of feeling sick, well, she had probably eaten a spoonful of the *Perla D'Etna*, too, on the Wednesday, hadn't she? As a taster? Like Jacinta did. I'm supposing one spoonful would have had that effect? It was just this one rogue tin which had turned up, by chance. Because Lorenzo had outright banned that flavour.'

'Good thinking, Posie,' said Lovelace. 'But it sounds like it didn't turn up by chance, though, did it? Sounds like this rogue tin of ours turned up exactly how and when it was supposed to. And when Jacinta didn't eat enough of it on Wednesday, it conveniently turns up again, as a dessert at her own wedding dinner last night. How ghastly. Whose idea was it, anyway, to serve ice-cream last night?'

Posie shook her head, but reluctantly. 'I think it was Lorenzo's.'

Richard took out his tin of cigarettes, and in his consternation didn't offer them around. Just lit up, started smoking in an almost urgent fashion.

'Seems we misjudged Lorenzo Rosario by accepting his jolly-good-fellow sob story, eh?'

Posie shrugged. 'It could very well have been Roberta, couldn't it? She was tasked with choosing and bringing all the ice-cream flavours to the dinner. She could easily have hidden it after the "rediscovery" yesterday morning, and packed it in the trolley for the dinner. Perhaps she even *made* it in the first place?'

Maturo tapped at his report again. 'There is something you don't know as yet, Chief Inspector. It's pretty odd.'

Lovelace gave a bark of laughter, tapped off the ash from his smoke almost violently on a saucer. 'What isn't odd here?'

Maturo shrugged. 'That tin of Paris Green arsenic poison you gave us, which you found among Lady Nella's clothes?'

'Yes?'

'It's a make which is quite widely available in Italy, and lots of other countries too. Although you wouldn't be able to buy it here in San Gimignano. Nearest place would be Siena, or Florence. But this tin itself is a good couple of years old, and the Forensics team could match it exactly, because the arsenic has degraded slightly. Almost a whole tin of crystals was used in that tub of ice-cream, they think, and about one spoonful was placed in the wine glass. But it was the *exact* same tin of poison, used in both the ice-cream and in the wine.'

Lovelace looked uncomprehending. 'So?'

Posie turned to him, trying to reason it all out. 'The Commissario means that it's odd, because the Paris Green arsenic was added to the ice-cream when it was being made, and that must have been at least a few days ago, if not more. So how could Nella Harewood have done *that*, when she wasn't even in San Gimignano a few days ago? She only arrived late on Wednesday night, like us, and stayed at the Dante. So while she *could* have used this poison in Jacinta's glass, she certainly couldn't have been poisoning the ice-cream. It doesn't make sense.'

'It doesn't, Miss,' interjected Lazzio, smugly. 'Especially as the Forensics team were keen to tell the Commissario and myself that this particular tub of ice-cream was very old. Edible, of course. But not fresh, huh? So this particular tin of poison was used last night, *and* to make that ice-cream. And that was at least three, most probably four months ago.'

Lovelace groaned. 'What tomfool trickery are we dealing with here? What sort of crazy person premeditates a murder that far in advance? And *why*? What was it that Jacinta had which our killer wanted, three or four months ago? She wasn't even engaged to be married to Rosario back then, was she? If we are claiming jealousy over *that* fella is the motive. And why wait until last night, in that case?'

Fox interjected. 'It doesn't mean Lady Nella's off the hook for Miss Glaysayer's murder, though, does it, sir? She could have got that tin of poison yesterday from someone, couldn't she? From someone who had previously used it to make the ice-cream? Or...' His eyebrows knitted together in concentration. 'Maybe she paid someone – from afar – to make the ice-cream with the poison, in advance, and thought she'd really go for a full belt-and-braces approach last night by topping up the wine glass? Maybe she didn't realise that the arsenic needed to dissolve more...'

'The 'someone' you are talking about is Roberta Grimaldi, I suppose?' asked Lovelace, taking a final drag of his smoke. 'You mean that Nella – who was, I suppose, in London four months ago – paid Roberta to do all of this with the ice-cream? And then asked for the tin of poison back again last night?'

'Perhaps, sir. Miss Grimaldi is a drug addict, sir. Maybe she's more desperate than we realise? Mr Rosario kept her on a tight leash and maybe the good doctor wasn't playing nicey-nicey with the medicine cabinet. Maybe Nella Harewood gave Roberta lots of money? Maybe she'd have been happy to do anything for money?'

'That's a lot of "maybes". It seems bally far-fetched to me.'

Posie got up and walked to the balcony facing the terrace, towards the Tuscan countryside. The bed had been shoved hard against the French doors, but she squeezed her bulk past and got outside.

It was as if she had been stuck in a burning, smoke-filled building; her lungs hungry for air.

She stood now as the chimes of bells from churches all over the city were ringing the day in and out as they had done for centuries. As they had when artists had painted angels flying near the bell towers.

Posie gripped at the iron hand-rail, looking determinedly ahead, past the steppes with the growing vines, towards the olive-coloured hills and their bluish woods and at the lines of cypress trees in silhouette against the sun.

Nearer at hand, on the golden-brickwork of the medieval city wall which ran right around most of San Gimignano, a builder was scrabbling to the top of the very high wall, tools strapped to a leather work-belt. He had thick straps attached to him, in case he fell, and Posie saw that a couple of his workmates were standing beneath him on the ground, getting ready to climb up too. They were laughing and joking, impervious to any danger.

The sort who had probably been daredevils as boys.

Somehow, incongruously, she thought of Neville Coleman climbing. Tackling an impossible mountain. The missing, heavy shadow of a man whose legend threw itself continually over this strange little party out here.

She shivered and drew the collar of her pink jacket up.

So far it felt as if answers had eluded her. There were so many loose threads here.

There had been flashes of insight, yes, and moments

of bright clarity. Like earlier, when she had had that lightning-bolt moment, asking Sid for that information. But Posie doubted herself now.

It was probably wrong, or a hopeless shot in the dark.

She'd look a fool later, at two o'clock, on the telephone. But actually, she didn't care.

I failed you, Jacinta, and I'm still failing you.

Inside she heard the weary policemen talking, murmuring about the ice-cream.

The ice-cream. That wretched green ice-cream.

Three, probably four months ago.

Posie grabbed at her clutch bag. She pulled out the passport of Nella Harewood, flipped past the slightly-accusing eyes, flicked on through the pink travel pages. Pages she'd cast her eye over very briefly, earlier, before speaking to the Bank Manager.

'*NICE.*' Here it was. The stamp in Nella Harewood's passport.

Now Posie made sure to read over the pink pages carefully, in detail, matching what she read with other details and dates, timelines she was assembling from memory.

Pieces of a puzzle she had barely understood were now clicking into place.

'Oh, I've been an utter fool! *Of course.*'

She patted her belly, felt the pressure of a small active foot within.

'I've not lost my touch,' she announced resolutely, proudly, to her unborn child. 'That *must* be it. The solution. Oh, how dreadful! Although of course I have no real evidence.'

Posie looked across at a tiny white road bending and twisting somewhere far-off, leading to places she would never, ever go. A shaft of midday sunlight fell upon a vehicle moving on the road: a shining red-and-gold Fiat tourist omnibus, such as she had seen parked up outside the San Giovanni gate on their arrival on Wednesday evening. Buses in a line at a touristy little Bus Station.

Of course.

'But I think I know someone who does have evidence of some kind. That's it! If it's anywhere, it's *there.*'

She walked back into the room snappily. The two Italian policemen were on the verge of leaving. She tapped her husband on the sleeve. 'I've got to go out, darling.'

'Where?'

'The Bus Station.'

'Like the blazes you will! You're going to rest up here, my love. I'll send Fox. Or go myself.' He looked at her closely, curiosity lighting up his eyes. 'Darling? You're onto something, aren't you?'

'Yes.'

She felt suddenly, overwhelmingly tired. The idea of staying here in one place, just quietly, for a little while, rather than stamping off through a lot of hot squares and busy streets and bus stations was suddenly very appealing.

'I need a couple of hours before I can tell you if my idea is correct, Richard. I'll have clarification at two o'clock. But I have a hunch there is something at the Bus Station which will be useful. Might be a sort of back-up.'

'Good-o. What is it exactly that you're after?'

She told him, and Richard nodded. 'Fox and I will go now.'

Commissario Maturo looked at Posie and Richard, sensing the urgency and excitement. 'What can *we* do, Miss Parker? Is there anything at all?'

Posie nodded. 'Yes. There is something you can do, Commissario. Can you assemble *everyone* who was at the dinner last night in *here*, at quarter-past two? Get Gloria to sit in on the meeting and make sure you bring Mozzato, too. Wake him up if necessary. And while you're about it you might want to investigate the legality of the drugs in that tower surgery of his; investigate the people he is supplying as well. Because sure as bread is bread, Doctor Mozzato is acting as this town's main dealer, and the sooner he's put away, the better.'

Maturo looked from Posie to Lovelace wide-eyed, as if wondering if she had lost the plot.

But Lovelace, surprised yet resolute, shrugged impatiently: 'I'm right behind what my wife thinks is best, Maturo. She's not been wrong about anything yet. Other than bringing me here in the first place, that is! And telling me it would be a nice little holiday!'

'Fine.'

Just as Maturo prepared to depart, putting his black hat back on, Lazzio opening the door for him, Posie spoke again, louder than before, surer of herself with every passing minute.

'Oh! And Sergeant Lazzio, can you track down someone you've already questioned? But really take them to task this time. Find out if they are going around town having come into some sudden money. Threaten them with imprisonment if they don't talk.'

She took out her notepad and wrote down a name and thrust it at the surprised-looking Lazzio.

'Oh, I've just thought of another thing, on the same topic. Question this same person about what they've *hidden*, won't you? And then you're going to need a ladder.'

She wrote down her idea, thrust the new sheet again at the now put-upon-looking Lazzio.

'And, Sergeant Lazzio? Something else. Can you go to all of the locksmiths in town? Find out if they've been asked to make a copy of a key.'

She wrote down the type of key she wanted him to ask about.

Posie turned to Sergeant Fox. 'And, oh! I say! Sergeant Fox, can you go and see that Agent, Trussardi? He knows somebody who might be able to shine a certain kind of light on all of this.' Again, she scrawled on a piece of paper and thrust it in Fox's direction. 'There!'

Fox read the note and looked confused. 'Bit vague, isn't it, Miss Parker?'

'Oh, Trussardi will know exactly who you mean.'

'Very good, Miss.'

Posie started to unbutton her Mary-Janes. She threw them aside and she grabbed at the funereal black coverlet, pulling it off, desperate to lie on her own sheets again.

The men were already out of the door as she climbed into bed.

She closed her eyes, muttering to herself as she fell into a doze:

'And it's *three* murders you are investigating here, gentlemen. Not one. Or two. But *three*.'

* * * *

Twenty-Five

Lovelace had seen and understood Posie's tiredness. He recognised the need for her to sleep.

He remembered his first wife Molly, those last days of her pregnancy before Phyllis was born. How she'd been exhausted, barely able to keep her head up. He saw it again now in Posie and it worried him.

She still had two months to go, after all.

And so he left her alone, and walked with Fox to the Porta San Giovanni, to the small Bus Station there, and watched as the local bobby located the locker in question – one red locker in about a hundred – and then forced it open. A couple of Bus Station employees hovered around nervously, wondering what was so important – or so dangerous – that it needed three policemen to recover it.

'Dunno how Posie thought of this,' muttered Lovelace somewhat testily, as he watched the unwieldy metal bar being rammed again and again against the sturdy lock. It took some minutes for the locker to yield.

'Makes sense though,' said Lovelace to his Sergeant.

'When we first met Seego, he ran away from us and explained later that he had left his passport at the Bus Station. I never gave it a second thought, of course. But what if – in his panic – he spoke aloud the truth? He suddenly had a need to hide his *true* identity as Leigh O'Crease, because a real-life Scotland Yard Inspector with his famous Detective wife were suddenly staying at the Guesthouse where he needed to be? It was dashed inconvenient for the fella, not to mention dangerous!'

Lovelace laughed, almost in disbelief. 'So Seego turned tail in the dark and came and hired a locker and hid his *real* passport here. Hid other important things too. Makes bally sense, doesn't it? That's why we found precious little of importance in his room last night. He could afford to burn what he had with him as his real and important documents were elsewhere.'

'Very clever, isn't it, sir?'

'Reckless, more like, Fox. Dashed convinced of his own cunning, that one. Never be surprised if he *has* done away with his wife. He seems the type. All that clever initial bluster he gave us about being a widower! More double-bluffing, eh?'

'Mnnn. I reckon I have some sympathy for him, sir,' Sergeant Fox said, slightly longingly. 'Áine O'Crease! *I* would have fought for her too in a duel, I reckon, sir. That face…like Louise Brooks, but better. Never seen a more beautiful woman in my life.'

'*I* have.' Lovelace grinned. 'I married her. Lucky me.'

And now they were back, bearing what had been stored inside the red locker in the name of Leigh O'Crease.

It was an expensive navy canvas holdall. Heavy. Packed out. But with what?

Lovelace had decided it would have to be opened up in Posie's presence. Or by her, alone. As she wished.

When he got back to the Guesthouse it was almost one-thirty.

He listened to Posie's steady, shallow breathing, wanting her to rest for as long as possible.

It had got hotter and hotter outside again, and he felt sweaty and filthy. He crept past Posie and quickly bathed and dressed again, this time in the light oatmeal linen suit he would have worn to Jacinta's wedding. He shaved and splashed his face liberally with his best cologne, Penhaligon's 'Blenheim Bouquet'.

Some instinct told him to pack up, urgently, and he quickly placed his own clothes and the presents for his children into his bag.

He'd never chosen Posie's clothes for her before, would have thought it presumptuous, and odd, but time was now of the essence.

Richard knew she'd want to look her best today, in front of everyone, and he was aware that the plain linen-and-silk dress in cornflower blue, the exact colour of her eyes, which was hanging in the bathroom, had been Posie's chosen dress for Jacinta's wedding. Most likely Posie would want to wear it now.

He left it hanging there and quickly packed all her other things away, leaving only her make-up and her hairbrush by the basin. They were ready for a quick getaway.

He'd have liked to let Posie sleep more, but there was the small matter of Gloria needing to 'make up' the room again for the hastily-called meeting of the dinner-party guests at two-fifteen. He could already hear Gloria knocking at the door, as he'd requested her to do.

'Darling? Posie, old girl? You were bally well right! I've got Seego's bag here. Thought you'd like first dibs at looking inside it?'

He watched his wife now, sitting up, stretching. Sleepy, a crease from her pillow running down her right cheek.

He saw the flash of the new silver bracelet he had given her, slightly too tight on her wrist. He saw the glint of her pink glass beads. Still there, then.

'You'll want to get ready, darling. And you had telephone calls to take, didn't you, before the meeting? Let's sit outside on the balcony so Gloria can work her magic in here, eh? We'll look at the bag out there.'

After Posie had dressed hurriedly and eaten some cheese and crackers, they sat together on the small balcony over the terrace, mercifully shady in the heat.

Lovelace watched as Posie drew Seego's navy bag to herself. Watched her unbuckle the front, flip it up, look in.

'What is it you're after, love?'

'I'll know it when I see it.'

She started pulling documents out, placing them carefully on the small wrought-iron table: a British passport, as expected; what looked like share certificates; several documents in folders with a red crest showing dancing horned animals above an elephant.

Three identical manila files. Each one stamped on the outside with 'ZEITUNGSARCHIV – FÜR INTERNEN GEBRAUCH'.

Inside each was an identical German newspaper. They looked to be the same thing Posie had seen on Seego's desk the evening before.

Richard spoke German and so he translated: '"Newspaper Office's Own Copy for the Archive." What's all this about, Posie? Seego is also a spy of some sort?'

But Posie stayed silent, flicking through the newspapers instead.

She stopped, grinned: '*This* is what I'm looking for. Such good evidence that Seego has three copies of it. It's better than I could have imagined.'

She got up, nerves and excitement making her feel jittery. 'I'll head downstairs now and wait for those incoming calls.'

Lovelace sat on for a few moments alone.

He could hear Maturo and Lazzio downstairs now, chattering together excitedly, co-ordinating the local bobbies who had previously been standing guarding doors.

A few dinner-party guests from last night were beginning to arrive now too, with their local police escorts. Lovelace heard Deverine's brisk, commanding voice down in the hallway, the braying, confident laughter.

And was that Doctor Mozzato's slightly bored tones ringing out? Probably as yet unaware of the unravelling of his career to come. *If* the evidence stacked up, of course.

Lovelace vacated the room, and as he went downstairs, he heard Posie on her call.

'Thank you so much,' she finished her conversation abruptly. 'Yes: history can mean *so* much, I quite agree.'

The bells of the Cathedral were ringing out for two-fifteen. And then Fox was rushing over to Posie, flushed, not in any sort of Vicar get-up this time, just his usual off-duty blue flannels. He was holding a telegram:

'It's from Sid at your office,' he said, breathlessly, passing it to Posie. 'Seems like he's sent this in a panic from Somerset House on the Strand: it says you were on the telephone here for ages and he couldn't get through.'

Posie read the telegram and bit at her lip.

'Makes sense.'

Lovelace read it too, over her shoulder, eyes narrowing. He read a name. But in truth, it made no sense to him. And it certainly wasn't controversial.

Fox spoke again in a mad hurry. 'I called in on Trussardi, by the way. He understood what you wanted.'

'Perfect. Thank you. I'll need you, Sergeant, to listen out for Trussardi. He'll come up here, no doubt about it. He might wait outside the room, on the landing. Listen for him and go and greet him, won't you? Bring him in?'

'Of course, Miss.'

And then the telephone was ringing again.

It was Len this time, and while Posie took the call Richard Lovelace saw a blotchy-faced Roberta Grimaldi in a fresh navy dress being led by Sergeant Lazzio up from the basement, and there was a pounding of feet on stairs and along landings as everyone entered the bedroom.

Lovelace leant on the wall next to the telephone as Posie chatted to her business partner. He unhurriedly lit a Turkish cigarette. His favoured brand, a Murad.

The Chief Commissioner of New Scotland Yard was quite happy to admit that in all of this, he had, quite simply, as yet, no idea what was going on.

* * * *

Twenty-Six

'This is a strange case for sure,' said Posie by way of introduction, standing plumb centre of the big table, with Richard at one side, and Fox on her other. At her foot, almost *on* her foot, sat Patsy, and the small dog's presence gave her comfort.

'There are wronged men, and wronged women here. Devils dressed as angels, and angels who behave like devils. But, like in most murder cases, *love* – simple, crazy love – was behind these murders. And, to a lesser extent, money.'

Everyone was assembled, and Posie took them all in. Sergeant Lazzio on guard at the door, fingering his little moustache and Gloria – in her slightly incongruous Sunday best – sitting on the edge of the group, on the bed.

Directly opposite Posie was Lorenzo, in a white open-necked linen shirt, his hair still wet from a hurried wash, his scent of clean soap tangy in the hot air.

Next to Lorenzo, to Posie's right on the other side of the table, was Simon Deverine, immaculate in a dark-navy three-piece suit. He was smoking his pipe with the kind of relaxed stance you might encounter him in at his London Club.

And next to him was Tony Harewood, hair smartly pinned in place, but puffy-eyed, as if sleep had evaded her, after all. In her ashy-skinned state, the white scar by her mouth stuck out more than ever. There was no lipstick today, and her red beaded bag was placed at her feet. In her hands she held onto the single dangly, ruby earring of Nella's. Deverine had obviously noticed this gem too, and watched in some surprise as Tony's long white fingers played continuously with the glittering jewel.

Next to Tony, further along to Posie's right, sat Charlie Seego.

Seego was in his habitual pristine cream linen, his skin like summer strawberries. His round angel's eyes glanced up and down the table, as if wondering what Posie's words might mean for him, or for anyone. Under one hand was a gleaming gold cigarette tin, which Posie recognised as having been in his room when she had burst in on him. *Was this the one he had reported as having gone missing?*

Seego had packed, that much was obvious. A small navy suitcase – a match to the navy holdall from the Bus Station – and his black typewriter case were over near the door, ready to go.

On Lorenzo's other side sat Roberta Grimaldi, and she was the least composed of all. Shaking, with sheeny spots of moisture covering her face, her too-thick navy dress looked too tight for comfort, with sweaty rings showing under the arms. Her black bobbed hair kept swinging into her eyes, sticking to her forehead. She was gripping the table, as if to steady herself – a boat in a storm – and Fox had been instructed to pour her water.

She needs a fix, badly, thought Posie. *Or some medical intervention?*

Posie looked instinctively towards Doctor Mozzato, next to Roberta, but he paid the girl almost no attention, looked away.

Mozzato was almost unrecognisable from the man Fox and Posie had peered in on, earlier that morning. Clean in a jaunty off-duty brown cord suit, he sat with his arms folded across his somewhat protruding stomach, seemingly surprised at having been called here.

At the head of the table to the very far left of Posie sat Commissario Maturo, the Forensics report placed under one hand, and a fresh pad of paper with a pen laid atop it under the other, like a Judge.

The known and the unknown.

He stared now at Posie, his teeth gritted. *Hurry up.*

Well, Maturo was right. What had she been thinking of with that introduction, going on about angels and devils? *San Gimignano must be getting to me,* she thought suddenly.

Posie thought fleetingly of the friezes in the Cathedral, the rising frescoes of heaven and hell.

It's getting under my skin.

That, and the increasing heat.

Posie started over.

'Two girls were cut off in the prime of their lives last night. It was a first-class tragedy.'

'Hear, hear,' boomed Deverine, between puffs of his pipe.

Posie went on. 'A tragedy which is being explained neatly as a suicide on the part of Nella Harewood, and Nella's murdering of Jacinta Glaysayer, at the table, with arsenic. But is that *really* the case?'

Charlie Seego was looking carefully at Posie, eyes narrowed, and she smiled at him, before going on: 'Because on the surface of it, this explanation is an odd thing to me. You see, Nella Harewood and Jacinta knew each other of old. They were schoolgirls together, and their friendship had survived on into adulthood. But maybe this theory makes sense if we understand that something *had* happened between the two of them, fairly recently. Let's not forget that Jacinta hadn't invited Nella Harewood to her wedding, had she? Nella was only here by a strange coincidence,' and   Posie turned towards Tony Harewood, 'which was that *you* had invited her out here yourself, Lady Tony.'

Lady Tony was still playing with the ruby. She nodded unhappily. 'That's right. The whole thing was a mess.'

Posie smiled. 'Yes. A mess. But Jacinta carried on as if it was all fine; calmly, methodically, despite feeling an unease which came from her heart, and her mind, and, perhaps...' and here she drew from Richard's black case at her side the green-backed metallic tarot card of "Death", and she showed it around, '...perhaps from some other-worldly kind of warning?'

She looked at Roberta for a couple of seconds, but the girl turned away, her face burning, desperate somehow, troubled.

Posie placed the card down on the table and Roberta looked away from it nervously.

'*This* was one of three images Jacinta kept getting, when she read her own cards. The general message seemed to be about death, or betrayal. It pains me to say it, but Jacinta's cards were absolutely right in what they foretold. You see, Jacinta suddenly became a focus for jealousy.'

Posie suddenly flipped the card over so that its ghastly image was hidden from view.

'Jacinta was the sort of girl who had been passed over many times in her life. And yet she had – quite suddenly and unexpectedly – found that she had *everything* on a plate. She had Lorenzo Rosario.'

Everyone turned to stare at the Gelateria owner, and he blushed.

Posie carried on. 'But the fact that Jacinta "had" him caused some other people immeasurable problems. Indeed, there was one person who viewed him as her own.'

Posie looked at Simon Deverine apologetically. She realised she was almost seeking his permission to continue. He inclined his head, but just perceptibly.

And so Posie explained about the affair between Nella and Lorenzo, amid a few gasps and mutterings all round.

Lorenzo thumped his fist on the table angrily, wretchedly: 'But it was all over! Finished!'

Lorenzo sat with his arms crossed, his face still burning scarlet. '*I* ended it, Miss Parker! As I told you! And Nella had moved on. She told me that herself.'

Roberta Grimaldi, eyes blazing, now started up a stream of rapid, hysterical Italian; what sounded like awful insults. She was grabbing at Lorenzo wildly.

'*Come hai potuto farlo*? How could you *do* that? To your wife?'

Posie watched as Doctor Mozzato moved his chair as far away from Roberta as was possible, a look of disgust on his usually placid face.

'Miss Grimaldi, do calm down,' Lovelace instructed. '*Now.*'

'Are you just cross that you didn't realise, Roberta?' asked Posie. 'Well, don't be. Because Lorenzo and Nella managed to keep their affair secret from most people. Even from you, Lady Tony. Isn't that right?'

Everyone looked at Lady Tony, who nodded briefly, sadly.

Posie looked sympathetic. 'Although I think you found out yesterday, Lady Tony, didn't you? Even though you pretended to me last night that Nella wasn't trying to impress anybody here, other than her ex-husband. But you *knew* Nella was jealous of Jacinta marrying Lorenzo, didn't you? You were overheard saying as much…'

'That's right,' said Tony, her chin up. 'Nella only admitted the affair yesterday afternoon, after she'd got herself in a complete state with the drink. And you're right: I was glad that for once Nella wasn't getting her own way. I didn't tell you, Posie, because I wanted to save Nella's reputation. It would have been in tatters otherwise…'

Roberta cut in now. First in Italian, then switching to English. 'But my cousin, Giulia, *she* knew about the affair! All the time, and it drove her crazy. Made her sick!'

Posie shook her head.

'No, you're wrong, Roberta. By the time Giulia found

out, it was all over. Nella *did* send your cousin postcards last autumn and winter, but those were just cruel, strange taunts. The affair with Lorenzo was long over.'

Roberta was hysterical. 'I'm sure you are wrong, Posie! Maybe Nella was behind those tarot cards in December, too? Or maybe Nella and Lorenzo were organising those *together*? Hounding Giulia to death? I must tell you, Miss Parker: when everything happened here last night, my first thought was that Lorenzo had caused another tragedy! People *have* been talking, Miss Parker. All over town. Ever since he got engaged to Jacinta. *"Why is he with that English hunchback cripple? Just for her money, I suppose? Like he went after Giulia and her profitable little business…"'*

Posie looked briefly at Lorenzo, his eyes focusing on a point far off, out the window somewhere, his sullen beauty terrible to look at. *Fight back*, she wanted to hiss at him, but his stubborn silence endured. She gritted her teeth and carried on.

'That's as maybe, Roberta. But let's focus on facts. Besides, I am learning that in San Gimignano not everything is clear-cut.'

She took the bundle of glittery metallic silver-and-gold envelopes which had been found in Roberta's suitcase and slapped them down in front of the girl.

Posie took out a packet of red-backed tarot cards, too, and threw them angrily on the table. Everyone stared as Roberta winced, as if she'd been touched by a burning fire.

'Just like finding these in among your belongings doesn't mean *you* actually sent those "Death" cards to your own cousin in a campaign of terror before Christmas, does it, Roberta? And talking of Giulia, I'll come back to her in a minute, so don't you worry.'

Posie addressed the table again. She felt a prickle of anger rising in her and tried to stay calm.

'This is what I meant about it being a strange case. Nothing here is as it seems. Half this town doesn't trust

Lorenzo, but he is one of those people I would describe as an angel disguised as a devil.'

And she explained briefly about the history of the Gelateria, the bankruptcy, the addictions which had plagued the Grimaldi family. How Lorenzo had saved it all, without ever telling a soul.

Posie turned to Roberta now, who was open-mouthed, red as a beetroot, almost stammering.

'Oh yes! He kept *your* secret, too, Roberta Grimaldi. So, don't try and shame Lorenzo Rosario with false accusations here, please. He tried to rescue *you*, Roberta. And Giulia. But now it's *your* choice if you move into that horrid little cell in the Torri Gemelle and die there, completely addicted, with drugs to hand, but unloved, and stony broke.'

Posie flashed a look of sheer hatred at Doctor Mozzato, whose eyes behind the gold glasses widened for one telling second, and then he looked suddenly away.

Cornered, trapped, forced to sit and simmer in the unsaid accusations which blew about him, he avoided the sudden piercing gaze of Commissario Maturo, who was writing things down hurriedly in his big, thick notebook.

Richard Lovelace, brow furrowed, cut in. 'But Mr Rosario told us that Lady Nella had moved on. She was with another fella, wasn't she? So, Mr Rosario wasn't Lady Nella's love interest anymore. So why the jealousy?'

Posie smiled at Lady Tony. 'Well, it was a bit of a moveable feast, Nella's love for Lorenzo. Lady Tony was quite right about her cousin always getting her own way. Nella Harewood had been used to picking things up and discarding them again her whole life. She'd moved on from Lorenzo: yes. But then things had gone badly awry, and she wanted Lorenzo back. And when she got here she couldn't believe he didn't want her anymore, that he would want to marry Jacinta. The words we all heard last night – those cutting words at dinner – were the lashings out of a frustrated, scared woman who has been horribly rejected.

But they were much more than that. They were the words of a woman whose possibilities were closing rapidly. Whose dangerous long-term plans had failed.'

Charlie Seego spoke for the first time. He picked up his gold cigarette case, played with it, but didn't open it.

'Then surely, Miss Parker, what you are describing would fit with what the Italian Detectives here are proposing? A suicide following the murder of the woman Nella Harewood was jealous of?'

'Hmnn. I wonder...'

Posie started to pull items from the black case again. She slapped down two passports. Identical but for the names.

She opened them up and the same studio photograph of Charlie Seego stared out of both.

When Seego caught sight of them his eyes widened and he stared from Posie to Lovelace, to Maturo.

He gripped the table and sweat broke out on his forehead.

Posie smiled winningly. 'I think you are playing devil's advocate here, Mr Seego. You cannot believe what the Italian Detectives are proposing for one second. And that is because *you* know exactly what's happened here, don't you? How deadly this game of love really got, and what was behind it all. But now you've done your part and you're keen to get away from all these policemen, and no wonder. You're desperate to leave! And that's because you are one of the most wanted men in Britain.'

Posie spoke aloud the man's real name, amid general gasps.

Deverine was turning, staring at Seego, and Lady Tony, right next to the man in question, quivered slightly. She spoke up bravely: 'What is he wanted for, exactly?'

'Double Murder. Just for a start.'

* * * *

Twenty-Seven

Lovelace stood up quickly, hands outstretched apologetically. 'I must state officially that I, and my colleagues here have no powers of arrest over this individual. Unless of course, he was implicated in what happened here last night.'

He sat again, frowning.

'You spoke about how Lady Nella's long-term plans had failed, Posie?'

'Yes. She wanted to escape from her marriage to Deverine. And she did this spectacularly well. She prepared well. Didn't she, Mr Deverine?'

Deverine gave a bark of bitter, pent-up laughter.

'You're right, Miss Parker. It was all planned out. Do you remember those images of her which became famous last year, her standing with a bloody nose at some party? As if I'd hit her? It was all fabricated! I'd never touch a fly, let alone my own wife. She laughed about it at home: told me she'd mussed up her hair and stuck tomato sauce up her own nose for the special effect. That's when I started to think she was truly mad. Nella loved the attention she was getting in all the newspapers, and it suited her to have me cast as a villain. She could be downright nasty at times.'

'"Nasty"!' said Posie scornfully. 'That's an understatement!

Do you want to tell everyone here about The Pink House in Soho? Or shall I?'

At Deverine's silence, she shrugged and continued.

'The Pink House was your public fall from grace, Mr Deverine. Visiting such a place, committing adultery, was enough to lose you everything. And yet you were too honourable to tell the world how Nella had set you up!'

Gasps echoed around the table; eyes widened.

'Good grief!' muttered Lovelace, reaching for another smoke.

Posie looked at Simon Deverine sympathetically. 'I had my partner in London investigate for me. He tracked down the very beautiful girl concerned – the one with the feline eyes – and got her to admit she'd been paid handsomely to seduce you. How long was that encounter on the steps? In the room she pulled you into? Five seconds? Ten? But the camera *does* lie. That encounter goes on forever in people's minds.'

'Don't tell me about it!' Deverine groaned. 'I *knew* Nella was behind it all. Hated her for it, but admired her too. She got herself out of our marriage quite neatly with that little scenario, didn't she? With the Courts already believing me to be a terrible sort of wife-beating husband?'

Posie nodded. 'So, we can see that Lady Nella Harewood was playing a dangerous, slanderous long game. But it was unravelling, fast. In fact, it had failed. And unfortunately for her, Nella's card was already marked. She *had* to die.'

'How so, Posie?' asked Lovelace, inhaling the smoke from his Murad.

Posie bit at her lip. The whole thing seemed too, too much. As the truth, when it came, often did.

'Because of the identity of the man this was all *for*. The man she wanted to leave her husband for.'

A man she adored. Would wait in the South of France for, at first patiently. Then hopelessly, frantically.

A man who would ultimately fail her.

'Another man? *Not* Lorenzo?' asked Lovelace, confused, flicking off some ash.

'Not Lorenzo,' agreed Posie.

She turned now to look at Charlie Seego, as did everyone else, as if in unison.

The huge man flushed.

The atmosphere in the room was fit to bursting, like a string pulled taut, about to snap.

'Would you like to explain who the man was, Mr Seego?' she asked, politely.

Seego, who had been pulling out an Abdullah, about to light it, said snappishly: 'You know, I don't know that I do.'

Posie laughed. 'What do you have to lose? You've come all this way! At considerable risk. It must have been strange, I suppose, to come here for some completely different business, and then to find Deverine sitting right here! The man you have so much in common with! The man who half-owns the copper mine at Nkana together with the company you represent; the British South Africa Company.'

Deverine looked quickly, suspiciously, at Seego, his eyebrows raised, pipe held mid-air as if frozen.

But the silence beat on.

Posie heard a sudden burst of men's laughter outside, from beyond the terrace. She thought of the men climbing the walls there.

Daredevils.

Yes, of course this all made sense now.

How could any other explanation have ever been right?

She sighed heavily. '*I* will have to tell you about Nella's man, then. But his identity is hidden behind another small story, so bear with me. You see, yesterday, Lady Tony told me she'd received threatening typewritten notes…'

She avoided meeting Seego's eye and hurried on.

'Lady Tony was upset, but not as much as her cousin Nella was, when she realised Tony had been chatting to *me*, a Private Detective! Nella warned me off. She said: "*We Harewoods look out for each other, always have.*" And at the time, I didn't think too much about this. But today, I've thought about it a good deal.'

Lady Tony shook her head sorrowfully. 'I told you, Nella was blind drunk! I apologised.'

'Oh, there was no need! I thought about how it must have been for you: two girls of very noble birth but with no certainty of anything in the world. It was like that at school for you, wasn't it? At Roedean on the South Coast, near Brighton? You promised to stand by each other.'

'We were good chums, yes.'

'That's what Jacinta told me, when I first got here. She spoke of you, Antonia, as being the serious one. And Antonella, being sporty, and fun and a trickster. Jacinta knew Antonella more, as she had shared her dormitory. She said you two cousins always got on well together. But things can get remembered wrong, can't they?'

'How so?' Tony's face was a study of consternation.

'Jacinta didn't know the half of it, Lady Tony. But the three headmistresses – sisters, Penelope, Millicent and Dorothy Lawrence who shared the job – *did*. Today, at two o'clock, I managed to speak to Penelope Lawrence. She was the headmistress in charge of your year group. She confirmed *you* were serious, calm and clever. But that Lady Nella wasn't just a trickster: she was mad. A daredevil. Went swimming off the famous chalky cliffs below the school every single morning, come what may. Thrived on danger. Loved knives, fencing, guns. Once she attacked you, and you were cut, very badly. On the mouth. Miss Lawrence said Nella was a cruel girl.'

Tony touched her face suddenly, self-consciously. 'Oh, not at all. It was long ago. The cut was nothing. I wasn't the beauty of the family, so it didn't matter.'

Posie laughed. 'Is that how it was? You were the brains, and Nella was the beauty? That's how Jacinta described you: two halves of the same coin. But Jacinta was wrong about the most fundamental thing in all of this. Something which the headmistress told me, and my assistant Sid confirmed for me when I sent him to dig about for your birth certificate. *Your name. Both* your names.'

Everyone had turned, riveted, to watch Tony Harewood. Lovelace had an eyebrow raised, but didn't speak. Ground out his smoke.

Posie read from her notebook.

'*Antonella Mary Harewood.* That was both your real name, *and* Nella's real name. It's a Harewood family name, isn't it? A tradition. Given to all the females in your family. Although Jacinta had always mistakenly thought you were "Antonia".'

Tony nodded vigorously. 'Yes, that's right. When Nella and I were sent away to Roedean, to avoid confusion, Nella called herself "Nella" and I became "Tony". No one at school ever called us by that silly, long, antiquated name!'

The aristocrat shrugged. 'Hence Jacinta's not knowing my real name, I suppose. "Tony" is, after all, more like "Antonia", isn't it?'

'I suppose.' Posie smiled. 'The two of you worked well together, though, didn't you? Like last year, last summer, when Nella Harewood met and started an affair with the man who would become her *raison d'être*. And you, Lady Tony, helped her. And in return, you got paid a monthly salary from Nella's bank. Haggerty's, on the Strand, wasn't it?'

Tony Harewood looked thrown for a second. 'Yes, Nella did pay me a small amount. She could afford it: she received a big allowance from Simon. Every month.'

Posie consulted her notes. 'But Nella *wasn't* receiving a monthly allowance from you, was she, Mr Deverine?'

'No.' The older man shook his head. 'Never.'

'Posie,' cut in Lovelace, eyeing Maturo nervously. 'Who was this lover?'

'Good question,' said Posie. 'He was rich, massively so; capable of paying out big monthly allowances to the woman he adored. A woman who could not appear with him in public, *ever*, as his lover.'

Posie laid out British passports in a row. One, two, three, four. She opened them all on their pink inside pages, revealing rows of travel stamps.

'Right now I have my hands on the passports of Nella Harewood, Tony Harewood and the two passports of Charlie Seego – or, as he really is, Leigh O'Crease.'

Tony was standing, hands clasped to the cut on her face. 'Oh, I say! Jolly good show! That's *my* passport! Where was it? You found it! How wonderful.'

'Yes. It was found. Thankfully!' Posie smiled around at everyone, the picture of professionalism. 'What I notice from these passports is that all three of the people I just mentioned spent a good part of the end of last year in the same places.'

'Posie?' muttered Lovelace darkly, impatiently.

She rushed on, gathering speed as she went. 'But there is one passport missing here, one which would complete the picture. Bearing the same travel stamps. One I will not find by looking in hidden places. It is likely frozen in ice to the body of a man on the Eiger, in Switzerland.'

Deverine stood, quite involuntarily. 'Neville!' he breathed.

'*Neville Coleman?*'

Posie hated being the one to break this news, and it tore at her.

'I'm afraid that's right, sir.'

* * * *

Twenty-Eight

Posie explained how the famous explorer and Lady Nella had met in the summer of the previous year, and fallen deeply in love.

Two "daredevils".

She spoke gently to Deverine. 'Didn't you tell me that when Coleman first met your wife he was rude to you, and she almost hit him? Theirs was an instinctive, animal passion. You mentioned a party in masks, the next night? How convenient for Nella and Neville to get to know each other. And for the deception to start.'

Tricks.

'Are you sure of this, darling?' growled Lovelace, beside her.

'Yes.'

Deverine spoke out, and his voice was breaking: 'You mean Tony was *never* Coleman's girlfriend?'

'No, sir. That masked party was an ideal moment for Nella to bring Tony in on the scene. Tony became the cover: the "fake" girlfriend. From that moment on, both women started wearing their hair the same way. They were the same height and had the same colouring, and from afar, if it ever happened, Tony could be taken for Nella. And the other way around. A trick. But an easy one to pull off. And people *are* easily taken in. They *were* taken in.'

Posie sat down at last, wearily. 'Of course, if people had questioned it, they would have found the whole relationship between Tony Harewood and Neville Coleman odd. Coleman was reckless, an attention-seeker. A man who fought the Red Baron and lived, for goodness' sake! And sure as bread is bread, he met his match in Nella Harewood, with all her crazy love of danger. She'd have climbed that mountain herself, if she'd been allowed.'

Deverine had sat suddenly, head in his hands. It was the first time Posie had seen him ever lose his composure.

Everyone was looking at Tony Harewood, and the girl shook her head, pleading. 'This is a mistake. A bad one. Yes, Neville and I were different, but opposites attract! We loved each other.'

Posie carried on as if Tony hadn't spoken, virtually ignoring her: 'It was a dangerous game. What Nella and Coleman were doing was illegal. *Adultery*. Tony was quite correct when she was overheard berating Nella up in the attic yesterday when she said: "*Who are you to tell me what's right?*"'

'You're wrong!' cried Tony Harewood, incredulous. 'You don't have a scrap of evidence for any of this!'

Posie looked at her now. 'Oh, you're quite right, Lady Tony. I didn't have any evidence. But then I saw *this*.'

Posie pulled out one of Charlie Seego's manila folders, opened it to the newspaper with its German headings. She looked at Seego. 'Can I explain, Mr Seego?'

'I suppose so.' He had picked his gold tin up again, was playing with it, nervously. 'But you had no right to go through my private things, you know. No right at all.'

Posie sat, her hand quivering on the newspaper's front page, and everyone stared at the document as if it might combust at any given second.

'When I entered Mr Seego's bedroom last night, I saw a newspaper identical to this one on his desk. I didn't understand that this wasn't actually a German newspaper, but a *Swiss* one, written in the Swiss local language of German. A paper from Bern.'

Lorenzo Rosario was looking unimpressed. 'Why is *this* important, Miss Parker?'

Posie addressed everyone. 'This newspaper solved the puzzle for me. Having seen it, I realised that Mr Seego here and Mr Coleman met the night before the climb, in Grindelwald. Coleman wanted out of the Nkana copper mine business, and the money being offered by Seego was very, very good.'

She looked at Seego now and spoke to him directly. 'You signed the paperwork together, didn't you, Mr Seego? And Coleman entrusted you to take the completed paperwork back to London, where it could all be registered. But that wasn't the only thing Neville Coleman wanted of you, was it, Mr Seego? There was a little extra? Something which appears here in this newspaper. Something sparkling?'

Charlie Seego looked at Posie with his head on one side. 'You're good, Miss Parker.'

He nodded. 'And you're absolutely right. Coleman had asked me to bring him a diamond, best I could get my hands on at short notice. Get it set in a ring. I had something with me from Pretoria, just the ticket. A beauty, a pink diamond. Near flawless.'

Posie remembered her strange, illicit conversation with Soames, the Bank Manager to whom Nella had obviously confided. '...*don't forget...you do have that reserve. I placed it in our safe ...I'm sure we could get at least another three thousand for it.*'

'An engagement ring,' explained Posie to the room.

Tony Harewood was white and quiet, and her own ringless fingers calm and still as she gripped the edge of the table, the ruby earring forgotten now.

'This is all wrong, Miss Parker. *Please.* Your error here is personally insulting to me.'

Posie ignored her and turned to Seego again. '*You* saw Neville with Nella, didn't you?'

Seego laughed. 'I'll say! She was there in the room when Coleman was signing the mine papers, at the Adler Hotel. Very drunk. She was still there when I showed Coleman the Pretoria diamond. I watched him give it to her; saw her reaction. It was funny, she obviously adored the man, but she didn't give two hoots about the ring! But she wore it all right, that night. Coleman and I sealed the deal with a belt of whiskies. It was hardly ideal, the night before his climb, but I'm afraid we all got very, very drunk.'

'Which was when *this* happened,' said Posie, quietly. She opened the manila folder at last. She flicked to pages two and three of the newspaper.

'The title says: "FAMOUS EXPLORER CELEBRATES WITH HIS LOVE THE NIGHT BEFORE HISTORIC CLIMB!"'

Posie shook the thing out.

And there was a clear-as-day photograph of Nella Harewood, large eyes bleary, her pinned plaits askew, a fur coat falling from her shoulders, in the arms of Neville Coleman, who was raising one hand to shield himself and Nella from the cameraman, who nevertheless had captured in his flash-light the crazily large diamond upon Nella's finger.

Deverine took a long hard look, then rose abruptly and marched out, out onto the balcony, grabbing at his pipe as he went. Lazzio made to follow him, but Lovelace shook his head.

Leave the man.

Seego ignored Lady Tony at his side, talked straight at Posie now, as if he was relieved the truth was out at last.

'That photo was snapped as we were just leaving their hotel room where we'd done the deal. I left early the next morning for Africa, stayed out there. I was lying low, especially with lurid stories about Áine, my wife, circulating at Christmas. But later, in February, I dared to travel back to Britain. I registered the purchase of the shares in the

Nkana Mine. Of course, by then everyone knew Coleman was dead. But I suddenly realised things were badly wrong in even more ways than that.'

'Tell us.'

'I was at Pratchard's, Coleman's solicitor's office last month – handing over Coleman's signed papers for the Nkana share sales – when I saw Lady Tony leaving. I asked who she was and the secretary there – who shouldn't have told me – said it was poor Mr Neville Coleman's fiancée, and that she was soon going to be a very rich lady. Well: I knew *that* was plain wrong.'

It was obvious that Seego was burning up with a tight, barely-contained anger.

Posie checked her notes. 'But the secretary wasn't wrong, though, Mr Seego, was she? On the face of things. Neville Coleman's Will was clear, leaving everything to *Antonella Mary Harewood*. That was Tony's name! And no-one was contradicting Lady Tony, after all. Nella, the real heiress, in the aftermath of her divorce, was in Nice, far away. Her plans having failed.'

Seego laughed bitterly. 'I had to do something. "*Another woman about to make a fool of a man*", I thought to myself – just like my wife Áine has done to me – although poor old Coleman was dead by this point. But I thought I'd avenge him anyhow. I spoke to the Senior Partner at Pratchard's who was organising Neville Coleman's Probate, but he just laughed in my face! Said he'd seen Lady Tony's birth certificate and her passport and that was enough for him.'

Seego shrugged.

'I got it in mind to get proof that Lady Nella was old Coleman's fiancée, not Tony. I reckoned they'd been jolly discreet, but then I remembered *that* snap. I started calling all the newspaper offices I could in Bern, asking if any of their journalists had taken it. And I got lucky. The *BERNER ZEITUNG* had used it! I ordered all of their archive copies, determined I'd stop Tony Harewood claiming a fortune which wasn't hers to claim.'

In all of this, Posie noticed, Charlie Seego didn't once turn to address the woman at his side; it was as if hatred forced him on.

Deverine came back into the room and sat down, slowly. It was as if he had aged years in the last few minutes.

'What happened next, Mr Seego?' she asked.

'I was going to stay in Britain for a while longer; go to Ireland, as my father is ill. But then I saw a report in a newspaper saying that Pratchard's were getting close to finalising Coleman's estate. I realised I had to act, pronto. I left the country immediately.'

Another angel, again with the reputation of a devil.

Seego explained that he had tracked Tony down to the Guesthouse here; that he had left one single typewritten sheet for her on his arrival, by way of warning, to show he meant business. He'd hoped to sit down with Tony properly, and get her to relinquish her wrongful claim.

But in the end Seego hadn't needed to.

Seego had been both astonished and relieved to come across Lady Nella Harewood herself in the thick of things at the Guesthouse yesterday.

He'd invited her to his room, made her re-acquaintance and told her bluntly what her cousin was up to.

'Nella Harewood was furious, and flabbergasted. After we spoke she went back to that attic room all ready for a big row with her cousin yesterday afternoon. I thought I had done what I needed to, so didn't seek Tony out anymore. But yesterday evening I ran into Tony as I was coming out of the bathroom, and we argued. I told her it had been *me* who had informed Nella what she was up to, and that I knew her game. What I *didn't* tell her was that I was about to send off one of those Swiss newspapers to that fool of a partner at Pratchard's, so he could see for himself that I was speaking the truth.'

Seego laughed, satisfied.

Lady Tony was shaking her head. 'This is all nonsense,'

she said calmly. 'I'm not a cover-story! I would like to be excused from these proceedings.'

'How *do* you explain the newspaper photograph, Lady Tony?' asked Lovelace quickly. 'And the fact that Nella was with you in Grindelwald?'

Lady Tony crossed her arms over her chest. 'She just liked parties, and attention, and action. The climb in Grindelwald was all of those things, and Nella wanted in on it.'

Lovelace spoke guardedly. 'That makes sense, Lady Tony. But the diamond ring? The embrace in this photograph? Seego's story of seeing them together?'

Lady Tony shrugged, slightly embarrassed. 'My cousin had carnal desires. Lusts. See what happened with Mr Rosario here? Her disgusting conduct? Maybe I was having a bath that evening. Maybe she lunged at Neville and he was flattered? He was, after all, just a man, and my cousin was a well-known beauty. Besides, Mr Seego here only met Neville the once. And frankly, given his own criminal leanings, I'm surprised you set such store by his words!' Then she pointed at Simon Deverine. 'Besides, we've already heard tonight how the camera can lie, distort the truth. Haven't we?'

Lovelace put his pen down decisively. His mind made up. 'Thank you, Lady Tony. On what I have heard so far, I believe this is a civil matter for Pratchard's to take forward. *Not* a criminal matter for us.'

Lovelace muttered in an undertone to Posie: 'Darling, is the heat getting to you? What has this imposter story to do with the murders?'

But before she could reply, Posie saw a shadow on the floorboards outside the door to the room.

She reached behind her husband and tugged at Fox's arm.

Go. Go now.

Fox jumped up, crossed the room, past Lazzio on guard there and went out.

Oh, thank heavens, she breathed.
I was right.

* * * *

Twenty-Nine

Patsy stirred at Posie's feet, settled down again.

Posie addressed the room again, confidence flooding back. 'Let me tell you all that this is most *definitely* a criminal matter. Do you remember I said that *love*, and to a lesser extent, *money*, was at the root of these murders?'

A few nods.

'However, there was also a terrible, basic misunderstanding at the heart of this whole wretched case, which makes me want to weep. And our killer murdered three times because of it...'

'*Twice*, darling,' muttered Lovelace, just under his breath.

'No.' Posie spoke even louder now. '*Three* times.'

The silence in the room was absolute.

There was barely a gasp, just a horrified sort of waiting. Even Commissario Maturo stared hard, gripped his paper so his knuckles were white.

Posie nodded.

'Because, you see, there were rumours in this town about bad-boy Lorenzo, and how he had only married Giulia Grimaldi for her money, for the Gelateria. Rumours about how Lorenzo was the sort of man who was on the lookout for money. *Big* money.'

Lorenzo shook his head. 'Ridiculous! *Mamma Mia!* Anyone who knows me properly knows this is not true! Giulia knew it, of course. Jacinta knew it! Even Nella knew it!'

Posie smiled sadly. 'Ah, but Lady Tony Harewood, newly-arrived in San Gimignano last September, and suddenly, inconveniently, fallen madly in love with you, head-over-heels in love with you, didn't know it, did she? It was a first love. A fatal love.'

Everyone turned to Tony Harewood. Posie included.

'Yes. *You*, Lady Tony. You fell in love with Lorenzo a mere few months after your cousin's affair with Lorenzo had started.'

Posie watched the white scar grow tighter, the girl in front of her shaking her head to-and-fro.

'But this was a silent, adoring love. Lorenzo, did you have any idea?'

'What? *Naturalmente no!* Of course not!'

Posie shrugged.

'Well, why would you? Lady Tony probably barely registered with you, did she? She was supposedly engaged, and she was just the poor friend of Jacinta Glaysayer, who was also not of much interest to you at that stage. But Lady Tony noticed *you*. You became her passion. And later, her love for you became the reason she decided to pursue Coleman's money as if it were her own. Her only aim being to get the money to you, Lorenzo. Hoping you would take it – as you had with Giulia – and therefore fall in love with her. She'd been dropping hints about the forthcoming riches, but casually, pretending to read out from letters, hoping you were taking it all in. Which of course, you weren't. You never even listened to her!'

Tony Harewood laughed. Posie realised it was the first time she had ever heard her do so.

Roberta, jittery with nerves and withdrawal symptoms, stared past Lorenzo: 'But this is ridiculous! Lorenzo was married when Tony came out here in September. He had a wife!'

Posie raised an eyebrow. 'Roberta, your innocence is very touching. I told you I would return to the subject of Giulia, didn't I? Well, as soon as it became clear that Neville Coleman had breathed his last on that mountain, Giulia Grimaldi's days were numbered.'

Richard Lovelace was looking thunderstruck. Horrified.

'Oh, my days! *Three murders…*'

Lorenzo was lagging slightly behind, but then he heard Lovelace's exclamation.

'*WHAT?*' he roared. '*GIULIA?*'

Posie felt weary. This story was truly dreadful in the telling.

'That's right. It was very easily done, I'm afraid. Tony had seen, first-hand, how Giulia was sickly, probably as a result of her long-term drug-taking. Tony decided on a course of action which proved easy to implement. A tin of poison – arsenic, Paris Green – was purchased on her way back here from Switzerland, then maybe surreptitiously stirred into drinks which Giulia consumed in that last week of November and the first week of December. Tiny quantities, not properly dissolved. Not more than to make Giulia sick. The *real* poisoning came when Lady Tony mixed nearly the whole tin of Paris Green into a freshly-made tub of *Perla D'Etna* ice-cream, in the second week of December.'

'How?' demanded Lorenzo, almost shouting at the woman along from him.

'How did *you* get into the Gelateria? How was that even possible?'

Everyone was mucking in and lending a hand…

Roberta made a pathetic noise, like a whimper, before she spoke up:

'There *was* one morning, Lorenzo. You were at one of your meetings with the bank, I think, and I was upstairs with Giulia in the flat, looking after her. She was very sick. Jacinta was away in England for Posie's wedding. Tony offered to help out, to cover for me for half an hour or so. She'd been back a couple of weeks, and had helped out before, alongside Jacinta. Well, I was happy to accept, as I was exhausted myself. I'd spent the morning making tubs of ice-creams in our most popular flavours, including *Perla D'Etna*, of course. They had been placed in the storeroom at the back, to freeze. I'm so, so sorry.'

Roberta started to cry now, but silently. 'Tony wasn't at the Gelateria very long at all. But she must have got into the storeroom, mixed in that horrid poison…'

'It was time enough,' stated Posie, sadly. 'I expect it was Tony's idea later to bring a bowl of ice-cream up to Giulia, a favourite flavour, conveniently coloured green, to cheer her up? But it finished Giulia off. It was saturated with the Paris Green.'

She looked at Lady Tony without flinching. 'You really were a devil masquerading as an angel, weren't you? And then, I suppose, you went down into the Gelateria again and hid the tub well away, somewhere it wouldn't be found.'

Roberta had now covered her face, with Deverine suddenly going to her, surprisingly, putting an arm about her, consolingly.

Lorenzo was angrily dashing tears away with the back of his hand. 'My poor wife! So she didn't really have the flu, at the end, then, at all? And everything she had suffered before! All those horrid cards arriving?'

Posie grimaced.

'They were Tony's doing too. I expect she thought it would add another dimension to Giulia's death, throw the spotlight well away from herself. Perhaps throw some blame in Jacinta's direction, *if* that ever proved necessary; if arsenic was found? But, as it turned out, no-one deemed the death suspicious, did they? There probably wasn't even an autopsy?'

Lorenzo shook his head. 'Doctor Mozzato said it wasn't necessary.'

'He may have had his own reasons for that decision, eh?' countered Lovelace, staring directly and unrelentingly towards Doctor Mozzato, who sat, stony-faced, saying nothing.

Richard Lovelace wrenched his gaze away, called out to Lazzio regretfully: 'There had better be an exhumation order arranged, Sergeant. Right away, lad. Can you start the process?'

'*Certo.*'

Posie spoke to Tony directly now, but the girl suddenly refused to look at her, stared down at the table instead, as if planning for something big which was much more important than anything going on *here*.

'I expect you saw tarot cards here at Jacinta's, didn't you, when you first arrived? Jacinta, for all her trying, could never give them up. And packs of the things – *many* packs, in fact – would have been fairly easy to obtain in the big cities you would have passed through on your way back from Grindelwald: Bern, Zurich, Venice, Florence. It would have been as easy as anything to buy some distinctive glittery envelopes and start sending the worst card – *Death* – in the pack to Giulia, again and again and again. Convince her she was going mad. Poor woman.'

Posie went on, explaining how after Giulia Rosario had died, Lady Tony returned to England in time for Christmas. She'd met up with Nella there, who'd hatched her own devious plan to ensure a divorce from Deverine.

'You were involved in that, too, weren't you, Lady Tony? Because when Len Irving, my business partner, tracked down the woman at The Pink House, she confirmed she had been paid by a woman with blonde hair worn in tight plaits, with an ugly-looking white scar right across her face.'

All eyes swivelled to Deverine, still standing with Roberta.

He stared over at Tony, whose focus on the table in front of her continued, intensified, and Deverine's bright blue eyes were dark with disgust.

'So *that's* what Nella was going on about, when she lay dying – she said she didn't act alone. By Gad! I think you were both touched by the Harewood madness.'

Posie shrugged. 'It was a calculating sort of madness. Because from this point onwards, getting rid of Nella was the only thing in Tony's mind. Nella was the only obstacle to Tony's claim on Neville Coleman's estate, and Nella therefore had to go. Before she spoke the truth about being Coleman's 'real' fiancée. So while Lady Tony was still in London she wrote to Nella and invited her here to San Gimignano. It was an invitation to death.'

'I'll be blowed,' said Lovelace, flabbergasted. Maturo, who was smoking in measured, calculated puffs, his eyes narrowed, spoke now:

'But where is the evidence, Miss Parker?'

'I'll come to it in a minute.'

She had precious little, actually. She was just blustering. In fact, when it came down to it, everything she had rested on precious little.

A jewel.

A tread on the landing.

Posie drew a deep breath.

'I've nearly got to the end of this sad tale. Because when Tony got back here, she was already too late. Lorenzo had already found a shoulder to cry on. *Jacinta*! And so Jacinta had to die, too, like Nella, but Jacinta had to die *before* she married Lorenzo. Tony didn't want Lorenzo banged up for Jacinta's death: two wives with money suddenly dying on him might look a little odd. Tony fastened again on the same method as before. The ice-cream.'

'But *how*?' whispered Lorenzo. 'I understand now how she got in once, in December. But not *now*. We're strict. We only have one key each. She couldn't take either of ours!'

Lazzio laughed from the doorway. 'You might be strict, Rosario, but don't forget those weren't your only keys, huh?'

Lorenzo scowled, uncomprehending. Then realisation dawned. 'The agent? Trussardi? The key he held for letting the flat!'

'Exactly,' confirmed Posie. 'When I went there earlier today, he thought I needed the key and I'm sure he would have given it to me. He said *Another one! You need the key?* But what he meant was, he thought I was *another person* who needed the key. The other person who had borrowed it before was Lady Tony.'

'That's right,' said Lazzio, satisfied. 'Trussardi confirmed she borrowed the key on Tuesday this week, and I tracked down a locksmith in town who told me – under threat of prosecution, mind – that Lady Tony had got him to copy it the same day. Paid him a good amount of money, too.'

Posie blew out her cheeks in exasperation, watching those neat golden plaits bowed low, the face hidden.

'You became like a ghost, Lady Tony, didn't you? Slipping in and out of the Gelateria this week with a torch, under cover of darkness: finding that old tub of deadly ice-cream and putting it out on display on Tuesday night; then hiding it again in the dark, murky, hours before dawn on Thursday morning just after you'd returned from the party at the vineyard, while the others were drinking limoncello, and before your row with Jacinta. You were almost spotted, you know? Roberta saw lights moving about in the Gelateria as she returned home, but put it down to her own drunkenness. You were dashed lucky! And last of all, you re-located the ice-cream yesterday and set it up on the trolley for the wedding dinner, probably when Roberta was upstairs in her flat for a few minutes, taking drugs in the afternoon; while Lorenzo was still here at the Guesthouse sorting out preparations for last night's dinner.'

Posie laughed in disbelief. 'You were good at *placing* evidence too, Lady Tony, weren't you?'

Posie ticked off on her fingers: 'With the copied key to the Gelateria you could, of course, also enter the flat above it, and you took the chance yesterday morning, before dawn, to hide the many packs of tarot cards you had bought, plus the distinctive envelopes, in Roberta's suitcase. As damning evidence.'

Lady Tony suddenly held her head up high. The white mark stood out, luminous. 'No proof! This is just embarrassing, Miss Parker.'

'Proof! I'll give you proof! Proof must be somewhere on the gun – your fingerprints surely? – which you stole from Simon Deverine. *What a gift*! You knew of old that he always travelled with a gun, and the animosity between the ex-spouses was such that Nella's death could easily be explained at Deverine's hands. Nothing simpler than sneaking into his room when he was already down for dinner and taking that gun, hiding it in your little red painting bag, and then ensuring you sat next to Nella at dinner. You just needed to angle the gun so close to her that it looked like suicide. Then, in the darkness, after you'd shot her, you placed Nella's fingers all around the gun, before snatching it away, and, in all the confusion afterwards, you slipped it into Simon Deverine's pocket. *Suicide or Deverine*, take your lucky pick! Whatever the outcome, the focus would never be on you, Lady Tony!'

Posie shook her head in disbelief. 'And you were sure that Jacinta would take a big bowl of her favourite ice-cream to eat, but to be *extra* sure you laced her wine with arsenic, too, didn't you? You probably carried some Paris Green in that empty lipstick case I saw. How handy! It would have been easy as anything to slip it into Jacinta's wine as you moved past in the crush around the ice-cream trolley. Although you weren't to know that the poison couldn't ever have been effective like that.'

Posie tried to keep calm, although she felt like screaming now. 'You make me sick: Jacinta was right, she *was* betrayed, and by someone on the inside. Someone she had treated with kindness. And to end up like that! Well…'

'But she's right. Where is the *proof*, darling?' came her husband's small, worried voice in her ear.

Lazzio came forward suddenly, relishing the attention. He produced something from his pocket with a flourish. It sparkled, ruby-red.

A match to the other red ruby Cartier earring lying on the table.

'Here is the proof, Inspector Lovelace! The lights, you remember, they kept going off at the wedding dinner last night, huh? We thought it odd, because the good, reputable electrician had fixed everything?'

'Go on,' encouraged Lovelace.

'Turns out his assistant, young Carlo Belloni, was less reputable,' said Lazzio conclusively. 'He was poor and willing, especially when it was explained to him that the sale of *this*,' he waved the earring, 'would keep him and his family going for a long time.'

'He was here during the dinner, wasn't he?' asked Posie, sure of the reply. 'Carlo Belloni went up on the roof for a second time. And that was because he was cutting and then re-connecting the electric cables there at a very specific time. Probably at the time he heard the caterers leaving the Guesthouse; the moment when the ice-cream course would start. There was nothing supernatural about the lights going out at all. It had all been arranged beforehand between Carlo Belloni and Lady Tony. I bet that Tony told this lad Belloni to use the broken tile up on the attic roof too, in which to hide her passport, in a weather-proof bag, of course. So, we wouldn't learn her exact name. *That pesky identical name she shared with her cousin.* Which is at the heart of all this mess. This greed. This destruction.'

Lazzio looked slightly defeated.

'Absolutely right, Miss Parker. I have the boy in custody at the Town Hall. Carlo Belloni is willing to testify. He's a broken boy, crying. He's even talking about stealing something here in the Guesthouse, but what it is, or *was*, he wouldn't say.'

'This is dreadful!' said Seego.

He turned to Lady Tony. 'How did you hope to get away with it? I suppose Nella realised you had her backed into a corner when she confronted you about the inheritance, did she? That her claim was going to be difficult, poor to establish? Even if she told the truth as to her relationship with Coleman, and even if the money was truly *hers*. I say! Dash it all, you're resourceful as hell. I almost have to admire you! That stealing of my typewriter...'

Posie was distracted, watching the shadows moving out on the landing.

'Typewriter? Ah, yes. I overheard a snippet of your argument in that bathroom yesterday evening. That's what makes Lady Tony so truly frightening. She killed two women in cold blood last night and in the lead-up to these murders she was already putting on a show! Trying to confuse things; add different layers. She used Mr Seego's warning note to her as a foundation for inventing other threats. She stole Mr Seego's typewriter to bash out another, similar missive. And then she stabbed knives through the notes, fixing them to her door to make the whole thing look more threatening.'

Charlie Seego inclined his head. 'She *did* take my typewriter, but I know nothing about knives. Apart from those horrible creepy knives at dinner, around that green card.'

Posie didn't like to admit she knew nothing about those. Not the knives nor the very old green card. There was no explanation for them at all. Not yet. Maybe not ever.

Only an uncomfortable sort of feeling which wouldn't go away.

So she ignored it.

Posie concluded now. 'Tony Harewood showed the

notes to me, and she was at pains to point out last night that the killer had intended to kill *her*. That the mistake had happened because she and Nella were both wearing red dresses! And all the while she was busy 'placing' yet more evidence: Nella's blue dress; the tin of Paris Green. So that late last night she just had to "stage" a convenient theft so her passport wouldn't be found, adding to the authenticity of the thing by purposefully leaving one earring on the floor for me to find, and she was done.'

'It seems you thought of everything, Lady Harewood,' said Lovelace quietly, but Posie could tell he was worried.

'You know what I find strange,' muttered Seego. 'Is that I knew about Lady Tony's fake claim. And she knew I knew! Yet she let me live! Why?'

'I really don't know,' said Posie, worried, looking over at Lady Tony. This had occurred to her as well.

'You cannot hold me,' Lady Tony said briskly, starting to stand up.

'Miss Parker, hand me my passport back. You have no legal right to keep it. There is not one of you here who can tell me without doubt that I have done anything wrong.'

Posie saw Sergeant Fox put his head around the door. She gave him a nod.

Now.

* * * *

Thirty

The door swung open, and everyone swivelled in their chairs, with Tony Harewood still standing; her poise of someone in flight.

A man filled the doorway, a black silhouette, and for a brief moment it was as if he was taking up all of the light; his huge frame certainly blocked the very bright light on the landing.

Lovelace was muttering in a low growl: 'Darling? Who's this big fella?'

The Italian policemen also looked confused, but Fox was grinning broadly, in what was certainly one of the strangest, yet highest points of his career so far. He winked at Posie and then made a slight bow.

'Ladies and gentlemen, I give you...Mr Neville Coleman, the already registered-dead climber who apparently disappeared on the Eiger. The fiancé of Lady Tony Harewood.'

The man stepped right into the room and everyone gasped.

He was more handsome than in the photos, but only just. His ginger hair was shorn short and turning grey at the temples. He had a thick, florid red skin, and big cauliflower ears, like the rugby-playing boys Posie had known from her brother at school. He wasn't attractive, not at all, but his eyes were beautiful: grey-green-hazel, they glittered like icy Christmas lights in a face ravaged by harsh weather; by extreme temperatures.

He took up all the energy in the room, drew it to him. Posie could quite see what had attracted Nella Harewood to this huge ugly man.

He crossed his arms and he turned those glittering eyes first on Deverine: 'I'm so sorry, old chap,' he said quickly, in a raspy, gravelly cut-glass voice. 'I'm sorry for everything. All of this.'

Deverine was still next to Roberta, standing, but he was shaking now.

'Coleman? By Gad! This is too much! What the blazes? Where *were* you? Do you know about Nella? She's dead. *Dead.*' Deverine was a husk of a man; he looked impossibly old, like he might pass out.

Fox rushed to get him a chair but Coleman was quicker, and he stood next to his former war-companion, as if guarding him.

Coleman stared around the table, keeping one big hand on Deverine's shoulder. He smiled at Charlie Seego, but then his gaze came to rest on Tony, and under it, like a snake in a charmer's basket, she recoiled.

She faced Neville Coleman, and Posie thought in all of her life she had never seen an expression like it.

The calm, composed mouth was now a gaping black hole, the lips drawn back; the white scar was livid, and an energy which had never been present before in her dull blue eyes was terrible to behold. She had grabbed at the ruby earring – possibly her only wealth at this very moment – and she was clutching wildly at her small red bag, which she'd picked up off the floor, holding it in front of her like some amulet. Her whole being was a dark flame of hatred whose fire burned without words.

If Posie Parker had ever had any doubt what madness

looked like, or evil, she could stop now, for here were both, personified. At last, a devil who looked like a devil.

Fox edged nearer to Tony Harewood, and Lazzio blocked her escape.

'What happened, Neville?' croaked Deverine, feeling for his pipe, and trembling, failed to light it. Coleman reached for his inside jacket pocket, brought out a lighter, lit the pipe for him.

'It happened exactly as Miss Parker here explained,' rasped Coleman, looking over at Posie. 'All of it. I was listening.'

He hung his head. 'I'm ashamed of myself now. I feel like I was bewitched. Under a spell.'

'You mean by Nella herself?' asked Deverine, slightly more himself now. 'She was like that. Had that effect.'

'Well, I'm sorry anyhow. And Miss Parker was right: it all started with Nella at that wretched masked party you hosted at Dalmeny Place, and before I knew it I was involved in a complicated and clandestine love affair, with Tony here travelling across countries as a stand-in. I was always having to co-ordinate my diary with Nella's, and also with Tony. It was crazily difficult.'

Coleman stared at Tony now, as if he had never seen her before. He looked sickened.

'Nella and I always called Tony "the wooden dummy". Sometimes we called her "the ventriloquist's dummy": God knows she never had any conversation of her own and I had her on my arm enough. Nella and I were cruel, I suppose. Tony heard us once, actually, laughing about her, but she never mentioned it, nothing ever ruffled her. Calm as calm could be. But we never imagined in our wildest dreams the things she was capable of. I never imagined in a million years she was capable of *love*; still less of being able to kill for love. By Gad!'

Posie looked briefly at Lady Tony but it was as if she had been turned to ice, or stone, frozen in time, listening to Coleman.

It was Lovelace who asked the question on everyone's lips. 'What happened on the Eiger, Mr Coleman? How come you are here, *now*?'

Coleman exhaled wearily. 'The climb had been in the diary a long time. I knew it was risky, but I couldn't back out. The ice conditions were perfect, the weather still very mild, and the Royal Society had paid for my stay at the fancy Adler Hotel, along with the costs of the expedition. All the newspapers were chomping at the bit. Nella was pretty crazy with worry about me, actually, and we hatched a plan.'

'Oh?' Lovelace was guarded, watchful.

'I expect you know what I'm going to say…'

'It was all a set-up?' said Lovelace, calmly.

Coleman sighed. 'Nella and I wanted out. Out of all the shame, the secrecy, away from the charade of being with Tony. We planned a new life together; far, far away. Nella wanted to divorce Deverine, get that over with, so we could marry for real and settle in the Argentine; buy a nice big ranch. I needed a good deal of ready money for that, though; hence my selling of the Nkana Mine shares in a bit of a hurry to O'Crease here.'

Coleman took out a tin of cigarettes and lit up, still never taking his eyes off Tony. Posie saw how the girl was now shaking, violently. But Coleman didn't seem to notice as he continued:

'The logistics of the set-up were easy. Tony here – my pretend girlfriend – was in tow, just in case there were any official photographs before the climb, and Nella was there too, backstage, keeping – we thought – well out of the limelight. I planned to start the ascent as if it was a normal climb, with all the newspapers following me for the Royal Geographical Society, and with two local Swiss mountaineering guides for company. And then, after maybe two full days, I'd insist on the guides turning around; say I wanted to go on alone.'

The man laughed ironically: 'The plan was that I'd ditch my gear a few hours later, and, under cover of darkness, I'd descend; travel incognito by third-class rail with fake papers and pick up a kit which was already waiting for me at the Railway Station in Bern. I'd wait a few weeks for Nella's divorce, which she said she could secure quickly, and then we would meet up in the South of France to embark on our new life together.'

Posie kept on watching Tony Harewood, at her snake-like face, the hurt, outraged eyes. There was something like disbelief, just detectable, under the mask. And it was raw, *real*.

Posie called out: 'Lady Tony, you had no idea about this plan at all, did you? Although you must have wondered at your cousin's behaviour? The way she left Grindelwald so quickly, despite the fact Neville had probably died. And then her high spirits when you met her in London at Christmas?'

Tony shrugged, just perceptibly, not taking her eyes off Coleman.

Posie addressed Coleman again: 'So what happened, Mr Coleman? Why didn't you get to the Argentine? Because Nella was waiting for you, as planned, that much I know. Why was she waiting so long in Nice for you, sir? Getting through all her money? Because you were *there*, weren't you? Although Nella never knew it. She never saw you again face-to-face, did she? She believed you really had died, falling off the Eiger. That it had been for nothing; the carefully-hatched plans laid to waste. And she started going crazy, looping herself into wild anguishes, looking for ways out, and other options. Old loves, like Lorenzo, if necessary. And never mind if old loves had found new love, eh?'

Lorenzo rubbed at his eyes with the back of his hands. If there were tears there, they remained hidden.

Coleman met Posie's gaze, eyebrow raised. He blew out smoke wearily.

'By Gad, you're pretty on the ball, aren't you, Miss? How the devil did you know I was in Nice?'

Posie smiled, recalling her conversation with Dolly earlier. 'Because Nella started imagining she was seeing ghosts. She told a few people someone was following her. I think it was *you* following her. Maybe she caught sight of your face as a reflection in a shop window or a mirror or something? She thought it was a ghost; *your* ghost. And of course, there are no such things. So, what happened?'

Coleman blew a smoke ring ceiling-ward, and then another.

'What happened was that I had had time to be away from Nella Harewood, and all the crazy circus we had got ourselves into. I watched from abroad as all the horror of what she did to my old friend here was played out across the front pages of the British newspapers.'

He patted Deverine on the shoulder.

'I knew at once the girl at The Pink House was a set-up, and poor old Simon here had blundered right into it, shedding years of respectability overnight. I was livid with Nella! She'd talked of getting a divorce, but not like that! And I suppose that's when the rot set in. The spell was broken. I felt this kind of relief. *I had escaped!* But I didn't find the courage to tell Nella. I delayed meeting her. We were supposed to meet in Nice, and eventually I decided to go there. See how I felt about her still, in the flesh, as it were.'

'And?' Lovelace raised an eyebrow.

Coleman's ruddy face darkened. 'It was worse than I had thought. I followed her about surreptitiously, and saw how she was ripping through old Simon's money like the world was about to end. Probably in expectation of *my* money coming, I thought. It made me utterly sick. I kept thinking of that pink diamond I had bought from O'Crease, and I regretted giving it to her. It was all over.'

'Did you know they were going to wind up your estate?' asked Lovelace, frowning.

'Pratchard's are very efficient, I'll give them that,' muttered Coleman darkly, leaning over the table to stub out his smoke.

'I stopped buying the English newspapers after the divorce news had settled down. But I *did* see the story two days ago: how Pratchard's were ready to dole out my estate to my fiancée; had sold my flat on her instructions. I thought it would be Nella claiming the money, and I wanted to speak to her face to face. I'd decided to admit to her it was all over between us; that we'd been kidding ourselves that we had a future together. I'd steeled myself for a big scene, a show-down. But I never imagined in a million years it would have been *Tony* who would be claiming my monies for herself! Like Seego here, I almost have to admire her. Her audacity! I came here because I asked at The Ritz in Nice for Nella's forwarding address, and this is the place they gave. I arranged to take a flat here in town…'

Lorenzo turned. '*You* were the American who was going to move into my place?'

'Sounds about right.'

Lovelace was slowly gathering his papers. He reached across and took hold of two passports. He pushed them across the table to Charlie Seego.

'Take these, sir. I think your work here, and it is work which is much appreciated, is done.'

Seego looked surprised. 'Thank you.'

'I'll have a word with the Home Secretary,' went on Lovelace. 'See if he can do something about removing this murder charge hanging about your head, although I doubt you'll ever be allowed home. And do you actually bally well know what happened to your wife, sir? Are you really a widower, as you told us that first morning?'

Seego shook his head. 'No, I'm not. Áine absconded with our Estate Manager at the Bushtick Mine, brash sort of fella called Chris Salter, all brawn and no brains. Once she knew Padraig was out of the picture, she sure as blazes didn't want to be with *me*, and so she was biding her time in London for a suitable period before going off with the next best thing. I'm guessing old Salter couldn't believe his luck.'

'But have you proof, sir?'

'Yes. A letter she wrote me, on letter-headed paper, from a hotel in the same area, Matabeleland, Southern Rhodesia. Telling me she was going to live with Salter as his common-law wife; head off to another prospecting area. She adores Africa, maybe even more than me; the thrill of the wild. But, you know, we are still legally married, and I don't want her name made mud. *I* have some honour, too. Maybe it's better she's thought of as missing?'

Posie almost rolled her eyes.

'That's naïve, lad,' said Lovelace. 'People believe, and will continue to believe, that she was murdered, and by you. Better a cuckold, sir, than a murderer, eh?'

What is it with these men? Posie thought to herself. She looked from Lorenzo Rosario to Simon Deverine to Charlie Seego.

Too dashed honourable for their own good.

'Give me that letter and I'll get this sorted,' Lovelace was saying, and Seego was ferreting about in his navy holdall, and all the while Posie was still watching Tony Harewood.

The woman was backing towards the door, very slowly, very stealthily, holding her red clutch in her hands. Fox had seen, and was barring her way, one eyebrow raised as if her departure might actually be funny.

Under the table Patsy growled.

Commissario Maturo was standing too, arms crossed, small but menacing. 'Lady Tony. Wait. You cannot simply leave. You will *not* leave. That is my order.'

Neville Coleman stared at Tony in revulsion. Then started to laugh: 'What are you up to, wooden dummy? Still not speaking?'

The effect on the girl was instant. The bared lips and hellish rage were back and Tony pulled something from her small red bag. Something glittering and shiny, a kitchen knife. She ran at Coleman now, brandishing the knife. Her voice was raised, high, and shrieking:

'Never, ever speak to me like that again! *You will not*! You deserve to die. You should have died on that ice, like you tricked us into believing happened. Nella died believing you were dead! You monster! But she deserved to die, too! And I'm not sorry about a bit of it. She was a self-important, destructive viper! Ruining every life she ever came into contact with. I'm glad I did that to her! And Jacinta too, with her new-found smugness. I hope she died in a lot of pain, choking on that ice-cream. And as for Giulia, with all her talk of Venice! Well, I wish she'd gone off and drowned there in the filthy lagoon; wish she'd left Lorenzo alone. She didn't deserve him, not at all…'

Tony drew back her arm to get the force necessary to strike Coleman, but she had underestimated the sheer brute strength of the man, and he simply grabbed at her forearm, pinioned it in place behind her back, and watched as Fox prised the knife out of her fingers.

'Take her away,' ordered Maturo, watching as his Sergeant snapped handcuffs onto the girl's thin wrists.

But Tony turned suddenly, and she stared at Charlie Seego. He was sitting, having handed his letter from Áine over to Lovelace, and he was now, finally, pulling a cigarette from his solid gold tin.

'You asked why I didn't kill you too,' Tony called mockingly. 'Well, the answer is *I did*. You're a dead man walking.'

'What the blazes?' Seego had clamped an unlit cigarette between his lips, looking in puzzlement into the now empty doorway.

Posie frowned, not quite understanding.

But suddenly she saw.

Oh, how clever.

The tobacco smell in the attic room. The roll-up cigarettes. The stolen cigarette tin. That dreadful tin of Paris Green, so well used.

The Forensics team who had explained to Lazzio that Paris Green arsenic didn't absorb well. Unless it was mixed with something porous, flammable.

Something like tobacco.

'Is that the tin which was stolen from you, Mr Seego?' Posie asked quickly. 'When was it returned to you?'

Seego looked completely bemused. 'It was outside my door this afternoon as I was coming on down here. I thought one of your police lot must have recovered it. I did report it last night as missing.'

Lovelace shook his head. 'Nothing to do with me.'

'Or me.' The Commissario was shaking his head.

Posie shouted: 'Get it out of your mouth! Now! *And don't light it!*'

It works very quickly…

'It's been tampered with! I think Lady Tony arranged for this poor electrician boy, Carlo Belloni, to take it from your room last night and deliver it to her room right after he had finished with the lights. She couldn't steal it, because she was down here for the meal. I expect she stuffed the cigarettes full of Paris Green arsenic last night, in between police visits to her room. It would have been very easy. As would returning it to you now, on her way down from the attic. A small bob down, or a stumble in front of your door, and the return of the tin was complete.'

Seego placed the cigarette carefully back in the tin.

Closed the lid and wiped his lips slowly.

'And I thought Africa was bally dangerous.'

****

Thirty-One

It was evening of the same day, the blues and greys and pinks like summer, although it was barely spring.

Florence.

It felt more refreshing than it had done two days previously. Calmer, although not quieter.

Posie and Lovelace had accepted a lift in the police motor-car with Commissario Maturo, who had left Lazzio in San Gimignano to sort out all the paperwork so that autopsies could be carried out, and an exhumation order made regarding Giulia Rosario, and repatriation papers set in motion.

It had not been a simple case after all – as Maturo might have liked – of packing up bodies and murderers onto waiting trains and decanting them off Italian soil as fast as the wheels of the locomotives would carry them.

Fox had stayed on at the Hotel Dante, with Lady Tony being held in the cell at the Town Hall which Deverine had occupied the night before. She would be moved on the next day to Florence, with a full police escort, and returned to Britain as soon as possible with a team of Italian policemen headed up by Sergeant Fox.

But Lovelace wanted to get home. He felt it like an urgency. As did Posie, although she wouldn't admit as much to him.

They were staying overnight at the Pensione Bertolini, and were booked on the first train next day which would take them to Paris, and then they would change for the Golden Arrow to Dover.

Right now they were walking slowly through the city. They'd eaten at a small, cheap restaurant by the Duomo, and now they were eating ice-cream cones. Vanilla for both. Nothing green. Possibly ever again.

Posie carried two bags, although she was on the lookout for another. She had her clutch bag looped about her shoulder, and her carpet bag in her arms, in which Patsy rode, looking all about her with curiosity. Patsy had a blue ribbon in her hair now which Posie had bought at a small market they had strolled by, to match her own outfit, and the dog would be accompanying them back on the train to London to live with them.

'Dashed odd case, darling,' muttered Lovelace. 'And it's going to follow us for months, eh? Tony Harewood will be tried very publicly, unless she gets a brief who can declare she's insane. And who knows, perhaps she is?'

'Funny lot of people who will have to be called to give evidence, too,' said Posie, giving the ice-cream cone her full attention. 'Seego – as I'll always think of him – has invited Neville Coleman out to Africa to work for the British South Africa Company. I heard them chatting. Do you think Coleman will take up the offer?'

Lovelace shrugged. 'Why not? Fella's shot his reputation to smithereens back in England, all by himself. He's an adventurous type; I expect he'll love Africa. They would both be advised to stay away from dangerous women for a while, though.'

Posie smiled. 'That's a piece of advice you should have given to Simon Deverine. He looked like he was getting pretty cosy with Roberta Grimaldi when we left. He told me he has a big, modern kitchen at his place in Dalmeny Court which has never been used. Not once. And Roberta apparently loves to cook. Do you think there might be a love story in the making there?'

Lovelace shrugged. Ever the realist. '*If* she can kick the drug habit. It's dashed hard, but at least Maturo has set in train the proceedings to get that terrible Mozzato disqualified as a doctor, and hounded out of San Gimignano.'

'True. And what about Lorenzo?'

Posie would never forget leaving San Gimignano earlier that afternoon. The yellow stones, the scent of incense from the Cathedral. The promise of the vines and the ripe harvest after summer. The tourists. The history and art. Twined together perfectly.

She'd never forget the look of haunted abandon on the face of Lorenzo Rosario as he closed the door to Jacinta's Guesthouse for the last time, after everyone was out.

It had been a place Jacinta had loved. Had found happiness in.

'Lorenzo told me he's going to sell the Gelateria,' said Richard. 'He's more interested in vineyards. He might work at San Martin, to learn the ropes first, then set up his own place in a couple of years' time. I think he'll do well.'

Posie nodded. 'I hope he finds happiness. Third-time lucky. He deserves it.'

'Agreed. But what happens to Jacinta's Guesthouse?' asked Lovelace, wiping his mouth with a clean handkerchief.

'Here, give me that dashed dog, darling, so you can finish your ice-cream in peace!'

He took Patsy rather gingerly under one arm, like a parcel. 'So does Lorenzo get the Guesthouse, even though they didn't marry? Don't tell me Jacinta left it to Tony Harewood in an act of compassion! Because that really *will* be a can of worms.'

Posie shook her head. 'I didn't understand it really. But Jacinta told me she'd left it in a trust. Something odd back home called the KitKat Trust.'

'Sounds bizarre. Probably a dog's home or something of that ilk.'

'Poor Jacinta. I'm so glad she was happy, right at the end.'

Lovelace's thoughts had drifted, and they were now entirely focused on Posie.

'Are you feeling fine, darling? Walking along like this? All these crowds? We have a long journey tomorrow…'

'Oh, yes.'

The pains of the morning had not returned. Thank goodness.

But now, perhaps having tempted fate, and quite without warning, the same pain ripped its way up through her body again. And then again, and again.

Mercilessly.

'Oh! My days!'

Posie crouched down instinctively. She looked down and saw her cornflower-blue silk dress was soaking wet.

They were on a busy thoroughfare, filled with people enjoying their early evening *passeggiata*. Above them, a set of stone steps ran up steeply to an empty space, like a small deserted square. It was the only empty spot for what seemed like miles.

'Darling?' Lovelace half-dragged Posie up the steps to the empty little square. Got her to a bench, but she crouched on the floor.

'I'm going to get a doctor,' he said calmly. 'It's started.'

He looked at Posie, smiled encouragingly. 'The baby – our baby – is coming now. It's so exciting. Don't be afraid, love.'

A small crowd had formed at the bottom of the steps, goggling. Lovelace called down to them, and a couple of people ran off, looking for a doctor.

Through the pain, Posie concentrated on Lovelace, on his unwavering calm, on his sunny smile. 'It's all right, darling, we can do this together.'

Patsy was on the floor, still in the carpet bag, quivering, worried. The Yorkshire Terrier started licking at Posie's face.

Curled on one side in her soaked dress, Posie stroked the dog gently, and then, completely inexplicably, she heard Jacinta's voice, as if from very far away.

'Born in a church... Cristoforo. But I wonder, is that right? How can that be?'

Lovelace was speaking again. 'It will be fine, Posie. Look, doctors are coming.'

Posie saw men running in white coats, a stretcher party at the bottom of the steps with a motor-ambulance, crowds clearing.

She tried to sit up.

She caught sight of several family crests dotted about the walls around the small place Lovelace had dragged her to. There was a sign for tourists here, written in Italian and English. It read:

'THIS IS THE HISTORIC SITE
OF THE CHURCH OF ST CHRISTOPHER
– IT WAS DECONSECRATED IN 1786.'

She turned to Lovelace.

'*This* is the place. Jacinta told me we should go to a church called St Christopher's. Well, she said it in the Italian, *San Cristoforo*. She thought it would be in Siena, because there is no church of St Christopher in Florence. But it turns out there *was*...'

'I know. Save your strength. You'll need it.'

'She said it would be a boy.'

'I know.'

Posie knew it was too late to move, even just down the

337

steps. The men running wouldn't move her, wouldn't have time to.

She heard Lovelace yelling at the medics to put up some sort of screen, to give her some privacy, but all she could concentrate on now was hunching down, crouching the pain up into herself.

She knew it wouldn't last long now.

'Christopher,' she breathed.

'I can't wait to meet you.'

* * * *

Sunday 14th June, 1925
(Central London)

EPILOGUE

A sunny, dry day in June. Boiling hot.

A christening.

A grand affair at the Swiss Church in Holborn, where their parents had been married. Two babies christened, in matching ivory gowns, both with the surname Lovelace.

Although one, a big bouncing boy of three months – but weighing more like nine – with his vivid flame-red hair and green eyes, was obviously very much a genetic Lovelace; big, despite being born prematurely. And the second baby, already almost a year old, but tiny, blonde, delicate-looking, and very, very beautiful, was adopted; brought home at last to Museum Chambers after nearly a year spent being looked after at Great Ormond Street Hospital.

A not-quite brother and sister.

The boy, when placed in the same cradle as his adopted sibling, already seeking her out, making sure of her presence, of her beating heart. His calm placidity was the opposite of her panicky cries; his gurgles of contentment a foil for her colicky screams.

Christopher and Katie.

Phyllis Lovelace, four years old and proud as a big sister should be, had had a brand-new yellow summer frock made especially for the day and had spent the christening service and the hotel reception afterwards wheeling the babies around in their huge double perambulator, 'helping' Masha, the Housekeeper.

A Norland Nanny, an extremely capable girl called Peggy, had been hired to help out with the babies on a daily basis. Peggy had been with them all for three months and had fitted in superbly.

That evening, as Posie Parker, the proud mother, fetched a bottle of wine from the refrigerator in the tiny but very modern chrome kitchen of the flat at Museum Chambers, she reflected that it seemed as if she had spent the day in a dream-like whirl of shaking hands and passing babies around. And smiling incessantly.

In fact, her arms ached from the weight of carrying around her hefty baby son. He weighed so much.

To be honest, she was unused to it.

Unused to *him*.

It wasn't to say that Posie didn't love Christopher. She loved every inch of him ridiculously. His podgy, gorgeous little body which moulded to her own so naturally when she held him against her. His milky-sweet breath which she missed when she passed him across to Masha or Peggy for feeds or naps or whatever else babies were supposed to need.

But Posie had been so determined to continue working after Christopher's birth, to trail-blaze her way through the flurry of publicity which had resulted from the murders of Jacinta Glaysayer and Lady Nella Harewood in San Gimignano, that baby Christopher had been palmed off on Masha straight away, immediately upon their return to London.

Posie usually clapped eyes on her baby son only a couple of times a day. And those times were jauntily brief. On her way to and from the office on Grape Street.

Now, this evening, Phyllis and the babies were all sound asleep, and Masha had retreated to her room.

Posie and Richard were alone at last, in the living-room of the flat, the summer evening breeze lifting the curtains at the open window; the dry London air, scented with tar and grit and market flowers was seeping lightly into the room. Outside it was still quite light, and a purple twilight danced on the red-and-white mansion blocks.

It was still very hot even though it was past ten o'clock. People were talking about it being the hottest month since records began, and there were fears of droughts in the countryside.

They sat companionably on two armchairs by the unlit fireplace, facing each other, a glass of white wine from San Gimignano, from the San Martin Vineyard, held aloft in each of their hands. Patsy, the Yorkshire Terrier, had taken to life at Museum Chambers as if she'd always been there, and she ruled the roost. She scurried in now, jumping up into Posie's lap.

Richard Lovelace ran his hand through his hair and exhaled. He looked tired out. There were dark lines under his lovely green eyes. He was working too hard.

There was a massive case on at Scotland Yard, and the beginnings of the trial against Tony Harewood were starting up at the Old Bailey. The fact he'd taken the complete day off for the christening had been little short of a miracle.

'Cheers, Posie. It was a beautiful day. Here's to *us*, my love. To our lovely, unconventional little family.'

'Cheers, my darling.'

Posie kicked off one of her cream satin house-slippers and took a deep sip of wine. She was wearing nothing but a white silk slip and matching housecoat but she still felt too warm, especially with the roasting little dog on her lap. She threw off the Housecoat carelessly, letting it pool on the floor.

She watched as her husband drained his glass. Poured another. She watched him unknot his tie and pull it off, throwing it on the floor, tugging at his starched collar. He looked up, caught her gaze directly, and grinned: 'Penny for your thoughts, *Miss* Parker?'

It still rankled with him, then. The fact she hadn't – *wouldn't* – change her name for his. But he only mentioned it now and then.

She smiled, breezing on: 'I'm thinking about *you*, Richard. What a wonderful father you are. I've seen you, late at night, when you've come home from work, exhausted; when you've thought I'm already in bed. You go straight to the nursery, peep at them all sleeping. You cover them when they've kicked off the blankets. And I've seen the moonlight on your face through the blinds when you've held Christopher in your arms, giving him his bottle when Masha hasn't woken at his cries. I've seen you rocking little Katie in the dead of night, walking with her, trying to calm her down, and you manage. It's very often. You're more in their room than in ours just now. I feel terrible! You're a wonderful parent. You love them so much. I simply stand there looking, and I'm ashamed. I don't know what to do. I *literally* don't know what to do.'

Richard Lovelace laughed easily, lines creasing around his eyes. 'I've had more practice.' He slugged down the rest of his wine and leant forward, taking Posie's free hand.

'Is there something you want to tell me, Posie? It's making me feel nervous, actually.' He raised an eyebrow, and his gaze fell for a second on Posie's white skin, her exposed shoulder.

He grinned again wolfishly. 'Are you wanting to *add* to this happy little family we've just toasted?'

'*What?* Oh! Oh gracious, no. *No.*'

'Shame.'

Posie put down her wine glass. The sun and stones and angels and devils and murders in San Gimignano felt a long way away right now.

'No. One baby for me is more than enough. One baby

born *from* me; I mean. Katie is a blessing, our beautiful darling child, and I adore her more than anything. But Christopher...well, to be honest I feel I've missed out. I've never got to know him. He feels alien to me, even though I'm his birth mother. Even his name I was never that happy with. It felt like a good idea to call him after that church on the steps in Florence, but it doesn't really seem to suit him. Oh, dear!'

'It's only been three months, old girl. You're speaking as if he's a grown man and you've made years of mistakes!'

'That's what I *don't* want. Years of mistakes. I want to put things right now.'

Posie was firm now in her conviction. 'I've made a decision. We'll keep Masha on, of course. But the whole thing is too much for her. She's just too old. We'll get Peggy to stay on, but only for the nights. *You* need to sleep sometimes, darling. And Peggy can sleep inside the nursery itself, so she'll hear them if they wake.'

'Fine by me. But by day?'

'*I* will help Masha. We'll divide up the weekdays and I'll take the children on my own. For whole blocks of time; days if possible. I want to get to know them all. Christopher, Katie, and Phyllis too. I want to be waiting for Phyllis when she comes out of school. With that double perambulator, of course.'

Lovelace looked incredulous for a moment and he cracked at his knuckles, a singularly unappealing habit, but Posie refrained from commenting.

'And the Detective Agency?'

'That will carry on, of course. Did you think I'd give it up? Even if I have to work my cases at night. At least for the next couple of years. Then I'll work at full capacity again.'

Her husband shrugged. 'Fine by me, sweetheart. I just want you to be happy. To live your dreams as you wish.'

'I *am* happy. I promise.'

'Mnnn.' Richard put on his fairly new reading glasses and they spent the next half an hour slowly and steadily opening christening cards and presents, making a careful list of who had sent and given what, ready for the battalion of Fortnum's printed 'Thank you' cards to be completed. Both of them were sleepy.

'I think we're done here, love,' yawned Richard. 'Bed?'

But just as he made to get up from his chair, he cursed under his breath.

'Dash it all, I quite forgot in all the excitement.'

'Forgot what?'

He fumbled behind him, on his small reading table, among the mess of his Sunday newspapers, and among some Scotland Yard files he shouldn't really have brought home.

Eventually he found a long, thin envelope, in a good-quality heavy cream paper. There was no stamp, only a handwritten name and address.

'Ah, here we are. This came for you on Friday night, darling. Ted the Porter signed for it, and only gave it to me yesterday. And then I confess I forgot all about it. I hope it's not urgent?'

Posie shook her head while opening it. 'I'm sure it's fine.'

Posie shook out a sheet of expensive cream paper, with the fancy navy heading of a solicitor's office in Lincoln's Inn Fields swirling across the top of it.

She read the typewritten letter once, and then twice.

Then a third time.

She looked up, her face grey in the lavender light. She put Patsy quickly down on the floor.

'I say! Everything okay, Posie?'

'Mnnn.'

She was shaking out a small sealed Basildon Bond blue envelope now, an enclosure which was so unassuming she had overlooked it initially. She opened it and inside there was one flimsy piece of paper. Pale blue with spidery inky writing on it. And something else, tied with ribbon. Posie pulled the ribbon-tied package and three cards fell out.

She recognised them immediately, and she gasped.

The Empress, the Sun, the Page of Swords.

These were the cards Jacinta had turned over for Posie, in San Gimignano, what seemed like a lifetime ago now.

Posie had refused to take the cards from Jacinta, had ripped them up angrily, and Jacinta had said that it made no difference, because Posie's cards would stay with her. One way or another.

It made no sense.

Posie now read the enclosure, the flimsy blue letter, then read it all over again.

She looked at Richard, whispered: 'I think I need another glass of wine. Now.'

Wordlessly, unquestioningly, Lovelace poured the wine, following Posie with his eyes as she snatched up the glass and walked to the window. She sat on the window-seat there, a black silhouette etched against the gathering Bloomsbury gloom. Posie stared down into the street, which was silent other than for a couple of young lads hurrying on home, carrying a huge and beautiful sailing boat between them.

Richard watched his wife but didn't break her silence. All the while she was stroking the tissue-like blue paper between her fingers, sipping at her wine. She'd dropped the three cards from the same envelope onto the floor, as if they might burn her. As if she never wanted to see them again. It was most odd.

At last Posie turned.

'The cream letter is from Jacinta's solicitors here in London. They've read her Will. She had no family – well, we knew that, didn't we? – so they had no obligation to read the Will out to anyone.'

'Mnnn?' Richard fidgeted on the edge of his chair.

'She made the Will in December, just gone. When she was over for our wedding. The day before it, actually. Some monies are going to charities, and there is a legacy of five hundred pounds to 'Mrs and Mrs Rosario, of Lorenzo's Gelateria in San Gimignano'. So, of course that goes to Lorenzo alone.'

'Jolly good. Why do *you* need to know all this? You're not her Executor, are you?'

Posie shook her head. 'No fear. The solicitors are doing all of that. But Jacinta left a peculiar legacy of pretty much all of her wealth: the Guesthouse in San Gimignano. It's been sold already by the London solicitors for eight thousand pounds. They have the money here now. That's why they are writing to me.'

Richard was on his feet. He whistled. '*What?* Is the money for you, darling? That's a life-changing amount!'

Posie shook her head.

'No, that's what's so odd. I am to be a caretaker of it, a trustee, because the legacy is for two infants. That is all the solicitors know. They call it a "Secret Trust". Jacinta had called it the KitKat Trust. The details of the two infants are in the sealed, private blue letter which Jacinta wrote herself, in their office, back in December. She did not tell the solicitors the contents, but sealed it up in front of them, asking them to look after it alongside her Will. *This* is the blue letter which she wrote back then, back in December, which the solicitors have now sent me.'

Richard Lovelace came bounding over.

He snapped down the sash window suddenly, drew the curtain with one hurried movement and flicked on the nearest reading lamp.

He read over Posie's shoulder:

5th December, 1924

Posie,

I have this feeling I can't shake off. I was never anyone's Godmother, but, from afar, I'd like to do my 'bit' for your unofficial twins.

I mean of course your daughter, Katie, and her 'brother' Kit.

Kit is Christopher, born by or inside a church called San Cristoforo, in Tuscany. I can't give you more details of where exactly, it's cloudy to me. But his name is apt, because according to legend St Christopher has always carried the weak to safety. And your son will do the same, especially for Katie.

But the actual name 'Christopher' doesn't suit your boy and you will come to call him 'Kit'.

I feel sure of it.

I'm leaving my Guesthouse to them equally. Look after it – or the money from it? – for them. One day Kit will need it to carry Katie to safety.

With much love, your friend,
Jacinta Glaysayer
X X X X

P.S. Thank you for looking after Patsy. I have the feeling you will have fun together.

P.P.S I've been getting an odd message lately about a woman delivering a grey-green card at a party. I think you are connected to this, somehow.

Something beyond my understanding is at work here. Perhaps this is a woman whose memory is in danger of being washed away? Who feels she has been betrayed? Who was always, somehow, in the wrong place?

Does this make any sense to you? I confess, it doesn't to me!

P.P.P.S I enclose some cards which belong to you.

Lovelace whistled beneath his breath.

'By Jove! It doesn't make sense. Although...' he scratched his head, confounded, desperate to impose order on things.

'Jacinta *did* know we had adopted Katie, didn't she? When she was at our wedding? But *our* baby? Had you told her you were expecting in December?'

'No.' Posie shook her head. 'It wasn't obvious, either. The cut of my dress hid it awfully well. Besides, this was written the day before our wedding. I hadn't seen Jacinta yet for her to guess anything at all! But the extensive details here. They precede everything...'

Posie sat, numb.

Forcing her mind to think rationally, along clear lines, she picked up the solicitor's cream letter, waved it in the air almost cheerily:

'The letter from the lawyers asks us to come to the office and present them with this handwritten letter from Jacinta. So they can note all the details down. Heaven knows what they'll make of it!'

Lovelace was chewing at his lip. He looked nervous and on edge.

'Any chance we can just rip this letter up and be done with the thing? We could pretend there was nothing in the envelope. We could simply say the legacy fails. Give the eight thousand to those named charities, eh?'

Anger suddenly clouded his handsome face. 'Dash it all. We don't need to live our lives with false prophesies, do we? And we don't – our children don't – need that money. I'd rather they make their own way in the world.'

Posie exhaled slowly. She replaced the letter carefully. 'No, darling. Tomorrow I will go to that office and set this thing up. It's what was *wanted*.'

Richard took her hands. 'I don't like the content, darling. How could she *know*? And all this talk of Kit, carrying Katie? A KitKat trust! That's a load of stuff and nonsense if ever I heard it!'

Posie grinned. 'Spooked you, though, hasn't it? Good and proper, I'd say.'

She chuckled. 'What was all that you used to say about Jacinta being some kind of imposter?'

'Point taken, darling. It does seem a sort of madness to deny them it. After all, who knows what the future holds for them? Plagues? Wars? We can't tell...'

Posie frowned, lingering at the window. 'But what about the mention of the grey-green card, and the circle of seven knives? Those were the only details we could find no evidence for in the murder cases, weren't they, Richard? Those knives on the table making a ring? Jacinta kept telling me that seven knives were a sign of someone betraying her, didn't she? And that's what happened, isn't it? Tony betrayed her...'

Richard Lovelace shrugged, uncomfortable.

'But I suppose Giulia Rosario could have said the same thing herself, couldn't she, if she'd been present? That Jacinta had betrayed *her*, by marrying Lorenzo? That her memory was being washed away?'

Posie was eager to banish this idea right away from the cheerfulness of the day. '*If* Guilia was present...'

Lovelace looked slightly guilty for a second or two. 'Oh, I forgot to tell you, love. The card, that shiny green one, which turned up so oddly at the dinner?'

'Yes?'

'I heard from Mozzato. The Forensics team had it tested properly and they were absolutely right. It was two hundred years old, from Venice. You know, it apparently belonged to the personal pack of that old rascal, Casanova? It has found a new home in America, with a collector who has assembled Casanova's whole tarot pack over the years. He's delighted, as it was thought "Death" was lost for good. Paid a fortune for it. Goodness knows where it's been, all this time.' Richard seemed uneasy. 'Or *why* it re-surfaced like it did, at that dinner, eh? And because the police didn't know who it really belonged to, the money from the sale has gone to the state. To the fascist party, I suppose.'

'Oh! Well...'

Should she say something, interfere?

Claim the card had been Giulia's, and that the money should rightfully go to Lorenzo?

But what possible good could that do? Besides, these were murky areas Posie had no knowledge of; areas best skimmed over.

And perhaps Lorenzo, and Roberta, had recognised that grey-green shiny card all along. But felt the same way, and had stayed silent.

Wanted to move on, away.

'Enough oddness, love,' said Richard. 'Let's go to bed.'

Richard was turning the light off quickly, moving Posie towards the door. Patsy followed, trotting along.

Richard stopped in the hallway: 'I think I'll just look in on the little ones before bed.'

'Let's *both* look in, darling. At Phyllis, and darling Katie, and little Kit...'

Richard turned in the almost-darkness and smiled. 'Jacinta got that bit right, though, didn't she? *Kit.* It suits him much better.'

'Absolutely.'

And as they turned the handle into the nursery, hoping not to wake the three children sleeping there, Posie smiled to herself.

Life had a way of sorting itself out most of the time. Righting wrongs, crossing out mistakes. Explaining the past, even weirdly, sometimes.

Old friends, from far away, telling you things would work out just fine. Throwing hope into the future for things you could never, ever control.

And here was Kit Lovelace, sleeping in his cradle.

Safe and sound.

Riding impossible dreams.

* * * *

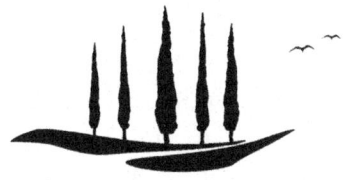

Historical Note

All of the characters in this book are fictional, unless specifically mentioned below. However, weather, timings, general political events, and places (and descriptions of places) are historically accurate to the best of my knowledge, save for the exceptions listed below.

As in the other Posie Parker books, I refer to the First World War of 1914–1918 as the 'Great War' throughout, which is simpler for the modern reader, although it would not have been referred to in this way in 1924 and 1925.

This novel is set (in the main) within San Gimignano, a jewel of a hillside city in the Val d'Elsa hills, Tuscany, Italy.

Please note I refer to it as a 'city' in line with the Italian 'città', with which description it was officially designated in the 1940s.

It is known for its medieval stone towers (see the photograph section, next) and is known as the 'City of Fine Towers' and by some as the 'Medieval Manhattan'. In the twelfth, thirteenth and fourteenth centuries when San Gimignano was an extremely rich and self-sufficient city, it had seventy-two towers, all built by competing rich families who wanted to show off their wealth and power. Today only thirteen survive, of which a few can be visited, climbed, and even rented out as apartments. Each tower has its own name and specific story. (See the Photograph Section, Image 1 for a picture of today's skyline.)

For consistency and for ease of reference, I have anglicised the Italian names for places and locations, so 'Piazza della Cisterna' is 'Cisterna Square', 'Piazza del Duomo' is the 'Cathedral Square' and the Duomo in San Gimignano is referred to simply as the Cathedral etc. Please note that in real-life the Duomo also goes by the name of '*The Collegiata di San Gimignano*'. I have, however, tried to stay faithful to the names of the famous San Gimignano towers. For more of which see Note 15, below.

As ever, Posie's work address in London (Grape Street, Bloomsbury, WC1) and her home address around the corner (Museum Chambers, WC1) are both very real, although you might have to do a bit of imagining to find her there.

1. (Prologue and throughout) The Pink House in Soho (which Simon Deverine visits) is fictional.

2. (Throughout) The character and story of the British climber Neville Coleman is fictional. As is the association and sponsorship of his endeavours by the Royal Geographical Society. In November 1924 (when the ill-fated climb in this novel is set) the perilous North Face of the Eiger was yet to be 'conquered'. The Eiger had been climbed in 1911 by the Englishman, P. H. Thorp, but the summit had not been reached. It was finally conquered in August 1932 by the Swiss climbers, Hans Lauper and Alfred Zurcher with a team of local guides.

3. For Jacinta Glaysayer and her history at Maypole Manor, see the third book in the Posie Parker Series, *Murder at Maypole Manor*.

4. (Chapter Two) The Pensione Bertolini in Florence is

fictional, but here I have borrowed from fiction itself. It appears in E. M. Forster's *A Room with a View*.

The Pensione Bertolini as depicted in the Merchant Ivory film of *A Room with a View*, is actually the newly-renovated Hotel degli Orafi. (See: https://www. hoteldegliorafi.it/come-raggiungere-hotel-degli-orafi-situato-nel-centro-storico-di-firenze/)

5. (Throughout) The English Guesthouse in San Gimignano which Jacinta Glaysayer owns is fictional, but such English Guesthouses famously existed in big Italian towns at this time. The location of Jacinta's Guesthouse is based on the wonderful Hotel Cisterna. (Also see the Photograph Section, Image 2.) Likewise, the Gelateria in this novel (Lorenzo's) is entirely fictional, as is the Hotel Dante (Chapter Six and then throughout). Other places I refer to in San Gimignano are real.

6. (Chapter Five) The KitKat Club, which Posie and Jacinta discuss, was in reality the Kit-Cat Club on the Haymarket, Piccadilly, S.W.1. This was, in 1925, a roaringly successful lunch, dinner and dance venue, owned and run by the same group of managers as the nearby Café de Paris, whose fame went on to eclipse that of the Kit-Cat Club.

7. (Chapter Six) Ricciarelli biscuits, such as Posie eats at the Hotel Dante, are originally a delicacy of Siena made especially for Christmas, but they are now available all over Tuscany, all year long.

8. (Chapter Six and later Chapter Twenty-Two) The fresco of *The Annunciation* which Posie loves can be found in the cloister next to the Duomo. It dates from 1482 and has been variously attributed at different times

to both Domenico Ghirlandaio (who also painted the Santa Fina Chapel) and Sebastiano Mainardi. These two artists were brothers-in-law and there are stylistic similarities between their work. At the time Posie was visiting, it would have been believed to have been by Ghirlandaio. (See also Photograph Section, Image 4.)

9. (Chapter Eight) The florist at the Porta San Matteo is fictional.

10. (Throughout) The San Martin Vineyard and the wine I have described is fictional.

11. (Chapter Fourteen) The M&P revolver (full name – Smith & Wesson Model Ten Military & Police Revolver 4th Change) was introduced in 1915 and was known for its accuracy and reliability. It was issued in huge numbers during the Great War and remained a popular weapon throughout the twentieth century.

12. (Chapter Sixteen and Chapter Twenty) The fictional bracelet Richard gives to Posie is from Macallè. This lovely jewellery store exists and is on the Via San Matteo, 20, San Gimignano 53037. (See: https://www.matteomacalle.com)

13. (Chapter Eighteen and throughout) Benger's Paris Green arsenic poison (so-called because of its emerald-green, crystalline properties) was very real, and was used in the 1920s for a variety of reasons, including as a pigment in paints (used by many famous artists, including the Impressionists), and as an actual poison for killing both insects and rodents. It was used to kill rats in Parisian sewers, which is how it acquired its common 'street' name.

14. (Throughout) San Gimignano Police Station can be found (in reality) on the Piazzale Mantiri di Montemaggio. In my story I moved it for ease of plot device to be housed within the Town Hall, together with its prison cell. I would take pains to point out that this is a fictional device of my own, and does not reflect historical reality.

15. (Throughout and also Photograph Section, Image 2) For more information on the Torri dei Salvucci (or the Torri Gemelle as they are locally known, the Twin Towers), the Devil's Tower and the other towers of San Gimignano, a good resource is: www.italyguides.it/en/tuscany/san-gimignano

16. (Chapter Twenty-One) The 'Red Baron' (1892–1918) as referred to by Simon Deverine is the famous German pilot of the Great War, whose real name was Manfred Von Richthofen. He is deemed (even today) as being the ultimate fighter pilot of all time, the ace of aces, and he died, shot down, right at the end of the Great War, over the Somme in France.

17. (Chapter Twenty-One and onwards) The Copperbelt Mine which is mentioned as being at Nkana in Northern Rhodesia (now Zambia) was and is very real. Today it is part of the town of Kitwe. Part of a rich copper seam, the mine started up in 1926, showing real promise of wealth, but didn't start being mined properly for copper until 1931. This mine was, unlike in this story, owned by the Anglo-American Corporation.

18. (Chapter Twenty-One and onwards) In this story some of my characters have an association with the British South Africa Company. This is a thorny and unpalatable period of history to write about, but any historical fiction referencing British men mining out

in Africa at this time cannot fail, in one way or another, to include a reference to this mammoth company. I include a reference to the company's logo, or crest, which is accurate. And to a gold mine called Bushtick, which was really established by the British South Africa Company in Southern Rhodesia, becoming incredibly profitable after 1924.

19. (Prologue and Chapter Twenty-Two) The story of Leigh O'Crease and the duel he entered into with his best friend Padraig Kennedy is completely fictional, as are those characters themselves.

20. (Throughout) Haggerty's Bank on the Strand is fictional, as is the solicitor's firm of Pratchard's in Gray's Inn, London.

21. Richard Lovelace's signature scent, 'Blenheim Bouquet', by Penhaligon's, is very real and is the longest surviving of their perfumes still being produced, first created in 1903 for the Duke of Marlborough. (See: https://www.penhaligons.com/us/en)

22. (Throughout) The Adler Hotel in Grindelwald (where Neville Coleman stayed) was real and was indeed the best accommodation there in 1924.

23. (Throughout) Roedean School, set in 118 acres of land on the cliffs at Brighton, on the South Coast of England, has always been a leading school for girls. Established in 1885 by the three Lawrence sisters, as detailed in this story, they ran the school together until 1924. It thrives today. (See: http://www.Roedean. co.uk)

24. (Chapter Thirty-One) The stone steps leading up to the tiny, central and deconsecrated church of St

Christopher in Florence are very real. Known as the 'Antica Chiesa di San Cristoforo degli Adimari', the church was part of the Cathedral Chapter House in the fourteenth century, restored in 1545 and later restored again in 1732. It has an association with the Adimari family, whose tombs are there. It was deconsecrated in 1786, becoming a private house. The church is a mere garage today for the ambulances of the Archconfraternity of Mercy, and all that remains of the church itself to the public view are a few family crests on the plasterwork of the walls.

* * * *

Thank you for joining Posie Parker and her friends.

Enjoyed *Murder in Tuscany* (A Posie Parker Mystery #11)? Here's what you can do next.

If you loved this book and have a tiny moment to spare, I would really appreciate a short review on the page where you bought the book. Your help in spreading the word about the series is invaluable and really appreciated, and reviews make a big difference to helping new readers find the series.

Posie's other cases are available in e-book and paperback formats from Amazon, as well as in selected bookstores and at Audible and other main audiobook retailers. You can find all of the other books, available for purchase, listed here in chronological order:

http://www.amazon.com/L.B.-Hathaway/e/
B00LDXGKE8

and

http://www.amazon.co.uk/L.B.-Hathaway/e/
B00LDXGKE8

You can sign up to be notified of new releases, pre-release specials, free short stories and the chance to win Amazon gift-vouchers here:

http://www.lbhathaway.com/contact/newsletter/

Photographs

1. San Gimignano

View from the approach from Florence.

2. View over the Cisterna Square

View of the triangular-shaped Cisterna Square, with its central well, and where Jacinta's Guesthouse is fictionally situated. (See Note 5.)

3. View of the Cathedral Square

View from the steps of the Cathedral, with the Town Hall on the far right, and the Torri Gemelle on the far left. The tower in the middle of the picture is the so-called Devil's Tower. (See Note 15.)

4. *Annunciation* *

(See Note 8.)

5. Detail of Santa Fina Chapel*

Painted in the fifteenth century, this is
the fresco Posie notes has angels flying among
the towers on the left-hand side.

* Both Images 4 and 5 are by Domenico Ghirlandaio

(Copyright for all of the above images remains the
property of Shutterstock, from whom these images were
purchased specifically for insertion in this novel for
reference only purposes.)

Acknowledgements

I have been meaning to write a Posie Parker story set in San Gimignano ever since the start of the series. I'd like to thank my parents for first introducing me to this wonderful place, and for all the subsequent visits. It truly is a town which captures the imagination.

Thank you to Marco for his help with the Italian and German, and for all his support during the writing process. Thank you also to my wonderful girls for their encouragement and understanding.

A big thank you too to Wendy, Jane, Ruth and Clare Wille, who help make Posie Parker step out of these pages and zing afresh, every time.

* * * *

About the Author

Cambridge-educated, British-born L.B. Hathaway writes historical fiction. She worked as a lawyer at Lincoln's Inn in London for almost a decade before becoming a full-time writer. She is a lifelong fan of detective novels set in the Golden Age of Crime, and is an ardent Agatha Christie devotee.

Her other interests, in no particular order, are: very fast downhill skiing, theatre-going, drinking strong tea, Tudor history, exploring castles and generally trying to cram as much into life as possible. She lives in Switzerland with her husband and young family.

The Posie Parker series of cosy crime novels span the 1920s. They each combine a core central mystery, an exploration of the reckless glamour of the age and a feisty protagonist who you would love to have as your best friend.

To find out more and for news of new releases and giveaways, go to:
http://www.lbhathaway.com

Connect with L.B. Hathaway online:
(e) author@lbhathaway.com
(t) @LbHathaway
(f) https://www.facebook.com/
pages/L-B-Hathaway-books/1423516601228019
(Goodreads) http://www.goodreads.com/author/
show/8339051.L_B_Hathaway

Made in the USA
Coppell, TX
14 June 2023

18054885R00218